THE STORM OF SHADOWS

NINIAN CARTER

This is a work of fiction. Names, characters, organisations, places, events, and incidents are either products of the author's imagination or are used fictitiously. Any resemblance to actual persons, living or dead, or actual events is purely coincidental

No part of this work may be reproduced, or stored in a retrieval system, or transmitted in any form or by any means, electronic, mechanical, photocopying, recording, or otherwise, without written permission of the publisher

ISBN 978-1-9996373-0-9

For Finlay and Ned, may
you have many grand adventures.

With thanks to Gemma, for putting up with my
endless ramblings about writing a book one day.
I'll shut up now . . . ooh, how about a sequel?

And to Mum and Dad—Morag and Ian—for
encouraging me to write from an early age.
Sorry it took so long.

Special thanks to copy editor Lesley Jones,
the Kindle Press editorial team, and
Jane Lander for their keen eyes.

— CONTENTS —

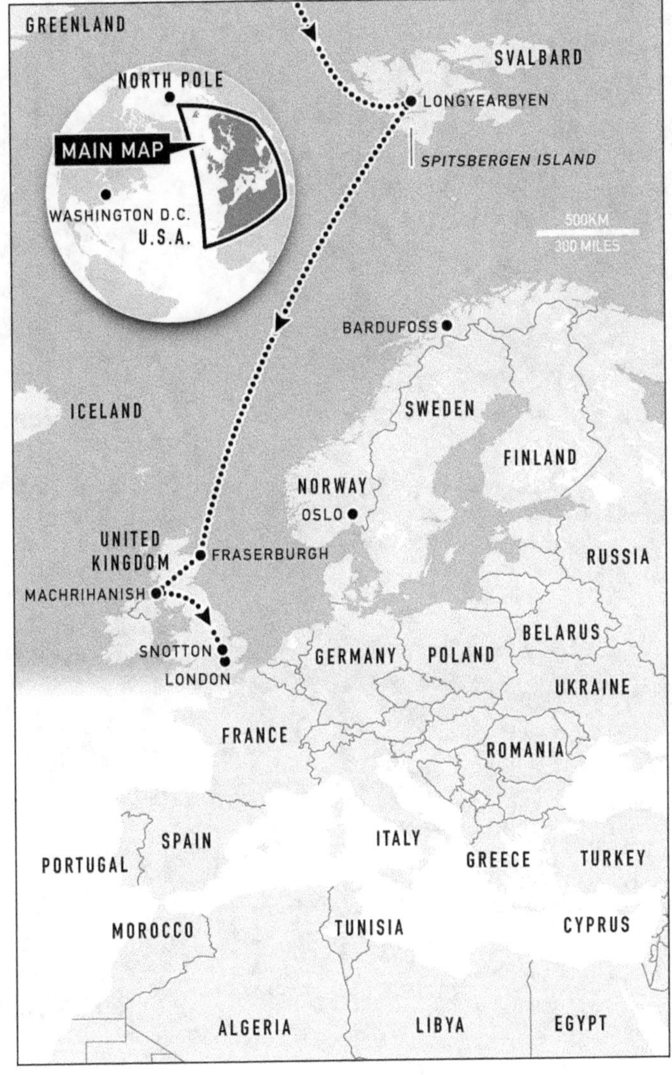
GREENLAND
SVALBARD
NORTH POLE
LONGYEARBYEN
MAIN MAP
SPITSBERGEN ISLAND
WASHINGTON D.C.
U.S.A.
500KM
300 MILES
BARDUFOSS
ICELAND
SWEDEN
FINLAND
NORWAY
OSLO
RUSSIA
UNITED
KINGDOM
FRASERBURGH
MACHRIHANISH
BELARUS
SNOTTON
GERMANY
POLAND
LONDON
UKRAINE
FRANCE
ROMANIA
SPAIN
ITALY
PORTUGAL
GREECE
TURKEY
MOROCCO
TUNISIA
CYPRUS
ALGERIA
LIBYA
EGYPT

— PROLOGUE —
A Rude Awakening

He was going to die.

Now.

Of that, he was pretty much certain.

He was, not to put too fine a point on it, completely stuffed. Knackered. Washed out. Had it.

That, and the small matter of a homicidal alien nutcase that was stalking him, pretty much meant it was game over for Mr William Aldgate Twigg.

Another lightning bolt cracked open the sky like a window shattering. A bright sheet of light flashed and rebounded off the surrounding grandiose marble buildings, followed a second later by an almighty bang that echoed around the square. Undulating sheets of heavy rain pounded the paving slabs and bounced back up into the electrified night air, creating a fine haze.

There was an uncanny glow to the abandoned landmark, caused in the main by flickering, unreliable streetlights and numerous fires that had escaped the rain so far.

Billy was lying on his back amid the rubble of a smashed fountain, squinting through half-closed eyes at the hammering downpour. Thunder rumbled through the enclosed city space, and thick black clouds swirled in an unnatural manner, their edges occasionally sharpened by bloodred crackles of light from deep within.

His organic metal-armoured suit was now torn, burnt, and pretty much useless. Even his helmet had been smashed and no longer offered any protection—the only vestiges being a few jagged fragments of glass poking out of the collar where the dome had once been attached. Broken electronics hung from wires around his face, occasional sparks and flickers of light from the mangled apparatus illuminating his tired, yet resolute, countenance.

On a normal day, Billy Twigg was a handsome thirteen-year-old boy with a kind, narrow face framed by unruly blond hair and set with hazelnut eyes. But today was not a normal day. Not by any stretch of the imagination. Today Billy looked haunted and gaunt. His eyes were grey, and his hair was matted down with congealed blood. He looked like someone who'd seen and done things he wished he could forget all about but knew would haunt him until his dying day. Still, if there was a plus side to any of this, that dying day was here. Now.

Billy called out a girl's name—Laura—but it was lost in the cacophony of the storm. He yelled it out a few more times in a wavering voice that betrayed his declining health. It was useless. Nobody could hear him. Nobody was coming to his aid. He could taste blood in his mouth too, which, in an oddly poetic moment, he concluded was what defeat must taste like.

He tried to stand up and yelped in pain. He was trapped across his shins by a heavy, larger-than-life bronze sculpture of a mermaid clutching two dolphins. *How had it got there? How had he got there?*

The best he could manage was to sit up, which in itself was surprisingly hard work because of the large amount of rainwater that had poured into his suit through the exposed neck ring, making it several kilograms heavier.

When he finally sat upright, his heightened posture offered him an improved view of his surroundings. It was complete carnage.

Overturned vehicles, including black cabs and red double-decker buses, lay strewn amongst scattered rubble and broken masonry in every direction he looked. Some vehicles had fires blazing inside, where rainwater hadn't managed to seep in and extinguish them, making them glimmer like surreal lanterns.

There were no people anywhere. Not even bodies. Everybody had vanished into thin air. Everybody except Billy, that is.

The boy was tired and in considerable pain. He slumped back down, and a couple of litres of water sloshed out of the suit's neck hole and over his face. He was breathing hard, and despite the acute pain in his legs, he tried to wriggle free of the obstruction. But try as he might, he was stuck fast.

He gazed up at one of the enormous bronze lion sculptures around the base of the decapitated commemorative column and wished it would come to life and rescue him. It ignored his mental pleas and gazed stoically into the distance from its lofty stone plinth.

Another lightning crack split the sky in half and accentuated the masterful curves of the lion's imposing muscular form.

"I'll give you one last chance, Twigg," rasped a slow and sinister male voice from behind him, only just audible above the noise of the continuing storm. "Tell me where it is. I'll end your suffering quickly." Deep, hacking laughter then followed.

Billy sat back up instantly and twisted his body painfully around to look behind himself. An impossibly tall, spindly man was hovering off the ground nearby, his feet together and arms outstretched. His body was twisted and malformed, as if he'd been walloped with hammers—one shoulder poking up too high and a knee at an awkward, broken angle.

But the eyes. It was his eyes that mesmerised. They were ablaze like twin suns, searing a hellish memory into Billy's mind. The devilish creature's entire body was wrapped in a dense, black, bandagelike material that made him look like a silhouette. Behind him, several lengths of jet-black cloth formed a tattered-looking cape, but one that seemed alive—the strips bobbing in the air like charmed snakes.

"Go to hell. I'm not scared of you," shouted Billy, spitting a gob of blood at the aberration before collapsing painfully onto his back again, exhausted.

He lay there panting for a moment or two and then leaned his head as far back as he could, until the world appeared upended. The abomination came back into view, looking like a charred, inverted crucifix.

"I almost feel sorry for you, actually," said Billy. "You're wretched and pathetic." He laughed back at him in defiance.

"So be it," growled the ancient traveller. "We'll do it the long way and kill your entire planet. You can die knowing you murdered them all."

He motioned his hands toward the boy, an action that was immediately mimicked by his threadbare, writhing cape. Nine bands of fabric extended from his shoulders and quickly slithered through the air toward Billy, transforming into snakes of dense black smoke as they gathered pace.

The boy could see bloodred veins glowing inside their undulating forms as they grew ever nearer. Then when they were close, they stopped, recoiled back slightly, and sprang their attack.

Billy closed his eyes, resigned to his fate, only for recent incidents in his messed-up life to flash before them like a hyper fast-forwarding video. Three moments leapt out at him in particular: a comet smashing into the moon, telling a girl his big secret, and the day he met Sal . . .

— ONE —
Sal

Billy awoke with a jolt, one of his arms flicking out and knocking over a saltcellar. He blinked his eyes a few times to try and focus, but all he could make out was a blurry condiment rolling across the tabletop. He stopped it just before it fell over the side and placed it back upright next to what appeared to be pepper and sugar dispensers. He rubbed his eyes hard for several seconds and then looked around.

He could see he was occupying a dimly lit café booth, and was slumped over the table. It was set for one, with a knife and fork wrapped in a paper napkin lying to his right. Strangely, the handle ends were levitating about a centimetre off the surface and swinging left and right like a slow-motion metronome. Music was playing in the background, an old rock 'n' roll track vaguely familiar to him. A Bill Haley song, he thought.

He sat up slowly, rubbing the back of his neck. It was stiff, as if he'd been lying at an uncomfortable angle for a while. His booth was the middle one in a row of nine running flush against a wall on his left. There were large windows above every table, each with rounded corners, framed by riveted chrome. It was dark outside apart from blinking, gaudy colours that suggested neon lights might be flashing somewhere out there.

To his right was a narrow strip of linoleum flooring and then a long, thin counter that ran the full length of the room. In front of it were at least twenty chrome stools bolted to the floor and topped with round, burgundy, cushioned seats that matched the upholstery in the booths.

Overall the decor was a mixture of aluminium and stainless steel. It looked very much as though he was inside a vintage railway carriage refitted as a diner—like the ones you sometimes see in old American movies.

At the end of the room nearest him was a very sturdy looking double-glass door with a large red illuminated box above it. A white icon of a hand, palm outward in a stop gesture, was printed onto it. It didn't fit in with the rest of the 1950s period surroundings at all. It looked peculiar—as though it belonged in a modern airport. But, then again, peculiar things had become something of the norm for Billy lately.

During the last few months he'd become quite the international traveller. To begin with, he'd been all over Britain. Then to Paris, Sydney, Toronto, and New York. All for free and without needing to pack a passport or even catch a plane.

More remarkable still was that this feat had been achieved while asleep—for his journeys had all been in dreams. Incredibly vivid, lifelike dreams. Dreams that at first happened in a conventional manner during the night, when normal people slept.

Lately though, things had taken a slightly awkward turn. Now his dreams were capable of sneaking up on him in the daytime. One minute he might be playing football in the park. The next he could be lying flat on his back, completely out cold, while his mind took a short vacation up the CN Tower, or went for a walk along the Champs-Élysées, or decided to wander over the Sydney Harbour Bridge.

As romantic or fun as these little excursions sounded, the reality of suddenly collapsing asleep in front of your mates was not fun. Collapsing asleep in front of people you didn't like was even less fun. And collapsing asleep in Mr Hagnaby's double maths lesson was just plain and simple asking for trouble.

Unfortunately, the last thing Billy could remember was double maths. Now he wasn't in double maths. Now he was in an American diner, probably in America too, given his recent track record. Since, as far as he was aware, teleportation was the stuff of science fiction TV shows and didn't actually exist, it could lead to only one inevitable conclusion: he had fallen asleep in maths and was dreaming yet again. And not just that, but in the classroom of a teacher renowned for his grumpiness and penchant for underhand violence.

A pained expression found its way to Billy's face, and he let out a long, exasperated sigh. If such a thing as a sigh-reading machine existed, it would have translated this one as, "Oh no, I'm going to get detention again for this." He then inhaled deeply to fill up his depleted lungs and in the process got an unexpected whiff of a wonderful, greasy, fast-food smell coming from somewhere behind him.

He then noticed his stomach was rumbling and realised that he was absolutely starving. He turned to see what was cooking, the burgundy plastic-cushioned bench he was sitting on squeaking as he twisted around.

At the back of the long, narrow room was a stainless-steel kitchen area and serving counter. Working the grill was a chef who made Billy's jaw slacken and droop open.

The short-order cook looked up. It was a flabby green creature, wearing a baggy old *Star Wars* movie T-shirt covered with food stains and stretched over a full bosom. It was mostly bald except for a sprout of purple hair that rose vertically from the centre of its overly large head, tied at the top with a red ribbon. The creature's skin was lumpy and blotchy and wet looking. It was wiping down the counter with one hand, turning down a gas hob with another, and selecting music tracks on an old Wurlitzer jukebox with the third one.

"Well, I'll be darned, you made it," it said, in an unlikely American cowgirl drawl. "I have no idea how you did that, but I expect you're hungry, right? What can I get you?"

The strange green creature stared at Billy. After an uncomfortable few seconds it nodded its head slightly, in a gesture that clearly meant, "Come on, your turn to speak."

Billy stared at it in silence.

"Darn, this is a little awkward. Ahem. You okay, sonny?" enquired the cook.

Billy's eyes remained frozen wide open, unblinking. He was quite literally dumbstruck at the sight before him. A three-armed alien was talking to him as if this was a normal, everyday situation. And it apparently wanted to cook him a meal.

"Come on, sunshine. What'll it be?"

After a pause that felt like an age but was in reality just a few seconds, Billy whispered, "A cheeseburger would be nice."

"Coming right up. Want fries with that?"

"Uh, yes please," croaked Billy, feeling rather ridiculous.

"Soda?"

"No, thank you."

"I got Coke, 7-Up, Dr Pepper, Hires, or Squirt. Or you can have one of my pretty darn amazing milkshakes. What'll it be?"

"What kind of milkshakes do you have?"

"Pretty darn amazing ones. You ain't listening too good. I got raspberry or raspberry. Oh, or I could do you a raspberry one . . . if you ask real nice."

"I'll try one of those then, please," said a bemused Billy.

"Which one?"

"Uh, the raspberry one . . . please."

"Right you are." The strange cook turned away and began collecting ingredients—a bun, two slices of cheese, a meat patty, two lettuce leaves, a dill pickle, half an onion, and mustard and ketchup bottles. She got the patty sizzling immediately on the hot plate with what looked like a large lump of lard and then glided over to a big fridge-freezer and pulled out some milk, ice-cream, and a big tub of fresh raspberries.

"So what brings you to these parts," said the slippery-looking cook, a small puff of green smoke wafting out of a dribbling nostril.

"I have no idea," replied Billy, feeling extremely awkward and out of sorts.

"Just passing through, then?"

"I guess that might be the best way to describe it," said Billy, suddenly having a thought. He felt around his waist. He didn't have any money on him. In fact, he didn't even think he had pockets. His clothes felt weird too, but it was difficult to see what he had on in the dingy booth. "I'm sorry, you'd better stop," he said hesitantly. "I don't have my wallet with me."

"No worries, kid," said the cook before switching on a very loud blender. She then glided over to a fryer and pulled out a mesh container full of fries; she stood them on a drainer with one arm while expertly chopping an onion and tossing the rings onto the hot plate next to the burger with the other two. "I've started now. We can come to an arrangement over payment later."

Billy sat and watched the cook in silence. She was zooming about the kitchen almost in a blur, arms flying all over the place grabbing, chopping, and pouring things. He'd had some pretty remarkable dreams over the last few months, but this one was unlike anything he'd ever had before.

"Shoot, where are my manners?" said the alien. "My name is Sally Magmajude. Folks around here call me Sleepy Sal, on account of my place rocking to and fro." She paused a tick and gestured an arm to her surroundings. "Folks have a tendency to nod off up here, you see? I don't mind it. I owns this joint, so let me welcome you to Sleepy Sal's Star-Plucked Café."

She glided out from behind the counter and across the chequered floor, carrying a round tray laden with food. Her podgy legs were stuffed into roller skates, allowing her to make unsteady pirouettes as she went. She drew to a stop beside Billy, slid the tray onto his table, curtsied, and pulled a grimace that he assumed was meant to be a smile. Instead, she looked as though she'd strained something.

Billy studied her up close. She had a wide, froglike mouth with only a few square teeth in it. Her nose was a small, pudgy, upturned thing, and she wore very vivid, blue eye-shadow around her bulbous eyes. Angular glasses completed her ensemble, along with a small apron tied around her flabby waist that was far too small for her build.

"Eat it while it's hot, sonny," said Sal, making an unintentional whistling sound on the "s" of "sonny."

Billy was staring again.

"Try the milkshake. They're amazing, even if I do say so myself." Sal then grabbed one of the two she'd brought over and slurped half of it up a stripy straw. "Hmmm, that is so good." She then burped loudly and apologised with a little giggle.

Billy slowly picked up his drink and took a cautious slurp. It was absolutely delicious. Quite possibly the best milkshake he'd ever had. He took another, bigger slurp. Yup, it was definitely the best milkshake he'd ever had. He smiled.

Sal smiled back. "Best milkshake you've ever had?"

Billy was starting to feel less alarmed. It was, after all, just a dream, albeit a really, really weird one. He might as well enjoy it before waking up in his maths lesson and getting into a heap of trouble from Hagnaby, and being made to feel a complete idiot by the rest of the class. "It is fabulous, Sal. Absolutely delicious."

Sally beamed. "I knew it would be. So, what's your name, son?"

Billy had just taken a big bite out of his cheeseburger and so had to wait a moment while he chewed. Once he'd swallowed it, he said, "I'm Billy Twigg."

"Pleased to meet you, Billy Twigg," said Sal, warmly. "Where you from?"

"Snotton," said Billy. "It's a small town near Cambridge, in Britain."

"Wow," said Sal. "You've come a ways."

"Where are you from, Sal?" asked Billy. "I don't think you're American, even with that accent."

Sal frowned briefly and said, "Oh, I ain't American, Billy, no matter how I sound. I've lived there, though—at the, uh, well, uh, shoot, let's just say I was a guest of the marshal for a few years."

Billy snorted a little laugh. Sal had a really strange way of speaking, like an old-fashioned cartoon character or someone in an old cowboy movie.

Sal went on. "Originally, I came from a town called . . . well, there ain't a way of saying it for human ears. I came from a planet orbiting a star you guys call Vega, in what you guys call the Lyra constellation."

Billy choked on a French fry and had to take a swig of his drink to recover. "You . . . you really are an alien?"

"Hey, that's rude, Billy," said Sal, sounding a bit peeved. "You're an alien too, you know? Out here in the wilds, we're both aliens."

Billy looked down. "I'm sorry, Sal. I didn't mean anything by that." He looked up again and met her eyes. "I'm just confused by this nightmare I'm having, that's all."

"Oh, shush your mouth, Billy," tutted Sal. "This ain't a

nightmare, honey."

"Okay, if you say so," he replied. He paused a moment and added, "Where are we, then? And why is that fork floating?" He jabbed a finger at the odd cutlery on the table that was still swinging left and right, as if almost weightless.

"Your cutlery is floating on account of us having a little gravity problem up here. The darn stuff used to slide all over the place, especially in summer when the sun-pull is at its worst, so I had it all magnetised. Shoot, if I can't be a real smartass sometimes, heh, heh! You see?"

Billy didn't see.

Sal expanded. "The ends of the cutlery are magnetised so they stick to the metal tables. Now they don't slide about. I thought it was pretty smart, myself."

Billy raised an eyebrow but remained quiet. Contemplative. He was enjoying his meal.

Sal added, "And where we are is about halfway between Vega and your Earth—about twelve light years away from Earth. My humble little rock, called Balta. Been here forty-odd years running this here eatery. It ain't a big earner or nothing, but it keeps me going." She smiled at Billy and took another drink of her milkshake. "How's your burger?"

Billy smiled and made a thumbs-up gesture, which seemed to please her. They didn't speak for a couple of minutes. Sal let Billy eat most of his food before saying, "So, you ain't got no money to pay for this here dinner you're having, right?"

Billy gulped and blushed. "No, I don't. Sorry about that."

"Yup, well that's okay, I guess. But on account of me getting no coin from this transaction, maybe we can play a little game instead, you and I? I ask you some questions. You give me some answers. After that, we're evens."

"Oh, I don't know about that," said Billy warily. "That sounds a bit dodgy."

"You don't have to do anything unpleasant . . . or stupid . . . or painful. In fact, you don't even have to leave your seat. How about it? Shake on it?" Sal extended a hand comprised of three fingers and a thumb.

Billy thought about it for a moment. Why was he even being cautious? It was a dream. It didn't matter. "Okay, Sal," he said, and shook her hand. Her skin might have looked wet, but it felt dry, like a snake's.

"Excellent," said Sal, making an unfortunate squelchy-squeaking sound as she forced her considerable body mass into the small booth seat opposite his. "I want you to try this: close your eyes and tell me if you can remember anything unusual. Any memories that maybe don't feel quite like they belong to you."

"I dunno," said Billy apprehensively. "That's a weird question. What are you trying to do?"

"Just humour me," said Sal, in a soothing tone. "Close your eyes and imagine you're opening a door into your own memories. See if there's anything unusual in there that you haven't noticed before."

Billy's heart was starting to beat a little faster. He felt a bit sweaty. Reluctantly he closed his eyes and quickly tried to remember something unusual. But how do you do that? You can't just say to your brain, "Find something unusual that I didn't know was there." It was a silly question. It couldn't work. He tried anyway but drew a blank.

Sal seemed to be able to tell he wasn't finding anything but must have known that he wasn't really trying. She said, "Remember and imagine the big door opening."

Billy did as he was asked and imagined a big door. He made it a very tall, old, heavy oak door with a large, iron ring for a handle, right in the middle. He imagined pulling on it hard and heaving it open, its old hinges creaking in protest. Inside, it was dark and empty. The creaking noise echoed away into a vast void. Billy stared into the abyss, and the abyss stared right back at him. Nothing. No miraculous flood of memories. Just a sickly, empty, lifeless feeling.

Billy gulped on a dry throat, then suddenly he saw something. A faint glimmer of recognition far away in the distance, like a muted sparkle. It was accompanied by the echoing voice of a girl saying, "Come on, Billy. I'll chum you home." It sounded like his neighbour Ellie's voice. She had a fairly distinctive Canadian accent.

"Nope, I can't remember anything unusual, Sal," he said, opening his eyes. "I just heard my neighbour's voice speaking, that was all." He didn't know why, but this was making him feel very uncomfortable. "I know I'm dreaming, Sal. Can't we just move this bit along? I know that in reality, I'm probably asleep at my desk at schoo—"

Suddenly a batch of fragmented, abstract images flashed into Billy's head: laughing school children; trying to protect Ellie on a narrow bridge; hiding from a monster in a tiny cave; flying through Saturn's rings; a car exploding; warplanes crashing in flames; burning buildings and a flaming red sky; something tearing painfully into his chest; the silhouette of a willowy man with a dozen limbs; a strange dark pit hiding in space; a brilliant white explosion.

Billy gasped out loud and opened his eyes, shaking his head. "I was in school," he panted. "I saw my friend Ellie. We were in danger. I saw planets. Fire. A weird, slender man with lots of arms. Creatures falling into a terrible dark hole." Billy felt sick, and took a sip of drink to try and calm himself.

Sal regarded him, a concerned but unsurprised look on her face. It was as if she knew unpleasant memories were buried inside him and needed to come out. She said, "It's okay. Take your time."

Billy was about to say something when he heard the sound of knocking on wood in his head. He closed his eyes again and saw the great oak door. It was closed but something was knocking on it from the other side. He again imagined himself heaving it open.

This time, standing directly behind it, was Ellie Roundtree, the same cute Canadian girl he liked from next door. Behind her, the vast deep abyss remained a black nothingness. She looked alarmed and was mouthing something, but no sound was forthcoming. Billy tried to force the memory into sharper clarity.

A shape was starting to materialise from the inky black background. It was hazy and impossible to make out at first. Ellie looked behind her and then back to Billy, a look of fright on her face. She tried to run toward him but it was as if she were running on a treadmill, unable to close any distance. Billy went to step toward her but he was stuck, as if he were knee-deep in mud.

Behind Ellie, a vague form was slowly taking shape. The darkness was altering and turning a flickering reddish-yellow. Upon it was a blurry silhouette that reminded Billy of an octopus. Dark tentacles writhed and squirmed, reaching out into the air as if seeking prey.

Ellie stretched out her arms to Billy, her mouth agape and eyes pleading. In the distance he thought he could hear faint screams of anguish, like a crowd panicked by something terrifying.

The obscure vision was slowly sharpening into focus. The rippling tentacles that were bobbing up and down like a sine wave were beginning to look like fabric—like torn strips of undulating black cloth. They appeared to emanate from the silhouette of a tall, thin man who was calmly walking toward them. Behind him, distant flames were licking into the air.

Ellie turned back again to look at what was advancing upon her and let out a silent scream. She looked back to Billy with resignation on her face, and stopped trying to run, as if she realised the futility of her actions.

Behind her the shadow man had stopped moving as well, but the tentacles seemed to have sensed her presence. They paused for a moment, recoiling slightly, and then rushed toward her. As they neared, they morphed from strips of tattered black cloth into thick, writhing snakes of smoke. In a matter of seconds they were upon her, smothering her body from the ground up.

Ellie stared out impassively at Billy, tears in her eyes, as the churning mass of smoke consumed her small form. Everything turned to darkness again and the great oak door slammed shut with a bang.

Billy snapped his eyes open and let out a long, slow gasp. "I saw . . . Ellie. She was being smothered in black smoke. It was wrapping itself around her. She was terrified and calling out to me for help but I didn't do anything. I just stood there," cried Billy.

"Oh my," muttered Sal, pausing to reflect for a moment. "It's been a long, long time since he was around these parts. But I had a bad feeling in my gut that something nasty was heading our way. I'd hoped it wouldn't be him. I'm afraid it sounds like he's heading to Earth. I think we need to get you prepared. And fast."

"What?" cried Billy, alarmed. "Who's 'he'? What did I just see?"

"Calls himself 'Typhon, the Destroyer of Worlds.' Kind of says it all, wouldn't you agree? What you saw was a future memory, Billy. I know that don't make no sense to you right now. How can I put this?" Sal pondered for a moment and continued, "You see, time don't always go in a straight line, like you folks on

Earth believe. Nope, in fact it never goes in a straight line. It's more like a big old bowl of spaghetti. Lots of timelines running back and forth and all over the place. Bit of a time-tangling mess, to be honest with you. You saw a glimpse into a future pathway. A very unpleasant one for Earth, by the sounds of it."

"I don't understand," said Billy, still feeling nauseous. "How can I be seeing the future? In spaghetti?"

"Don't be too literal there, pilgrim. It's complicated, and I ain't about to get into all that now," said Sal, firmly. "We can do that another time. But you appear to have some abilities. Have you looked at what you're wearing?"

Billy swallowed hard and looked down at his arms. He was wearing a long-sleeved garment that was an odd metallic silvery colour. He touched his left arm. It felt like soft metal, cold and yet insulating, tough and yet yielding. His chest was enveloped in the same material.

Billy slid out of the booth to stand under brighter lighting and gazed down at his body. His legs were covered in the same matt-finish silver material. His feet were encased in hefty boots with pipes running down the sides. They looked a little scorched around the heels. Around his waist was a grey belt supporting a holster on his left hip. In it was a silver gun. A big one.

Billy looked at Sal, fear and confusion in his eyes. He was starting to feel odd, out of his depth and frightened. It all felt horribly real but he didn't want it to be.

She was looking right back at him, knowingly. She cast her gaze down to the seat next to her. On it was a large round transparent helmet, inside of which was a pair of silver gloves.

"You're a somviator, Billy."

— TWO —
Something Stirs

Nightshade's glistening, dark-matter fuselage ripped through space like a hot knife through butter—her incredible speed and razor-sharp profile allowing her to scythe through almost any celestial object in her way.

Inside the ship, it was dark, dormant, and still. It had been so for a few decades. Ever since their last search had proved unsuccessful, yet again. Grand Overseer Oberyn had then sent them on a mission to the other side of the universe—an arduously long journey, chosen in part as punishment for their continued failure to locate what he desired so badly.

Then, finally, after such a long period of darkened silence, a discreet floor light flickered into life, casting a small beam of blue light across the reflective surface. Then another ignited. And another. Gradually numerous small lights buried in corners and crevices around the interior bathed *Nightshade's* inner sanctum in a very subtle, cold glow.

Something in the inky darkness stirred. It was ancient and almost forgotten. A tall, thin, frail figure lay wrapped in a weathered black robe. He was prone on a hard, onyx black dais, seemingly asleep, only faint breathing movements discernible as his narrow rib cage creaked up and down.

The surrounding room was a black, highly reflective, oblong chamber where the walls leaned inward at an angle, sloping up to a narrow ceiling. Every surface was made of the same material— some kind of polished mineral. It felt like a tomb, and in a way it was.

There were no windows to look out of and no other objects or furniture. At either end, triangular door frames led away to farther chambers, each illuminated by a glow no brighter than a child's night light. There were no sounds in the sterile room except the very faintest rhythmic sighs coming from the resting life form at the room's centre.

The silence was suddenly broken by a clinical female voice that echoed off the flat, angular surfaces. It spoke in a strange alien tongue. "Master, we have a reading. A Stone has been detected. We have been diverted from our original course and have arrived at our new destination," it hissed.

He awoke with a start, an emaciated hand lashing out from under his black robes at an unseen foe. Someone had been watching him. He had felt his presence—or had it been a dream? Impossible. He had never had a dream in his whole long, miserable life. He slept like the dead. But now he was awake, groggy, and irritable. He had travelled so very, very long and so very, very far—a deep hunger and yearning driving him forever onward in the endless pursuit of his father's prize.

"What is the meaning of this? Give me visuals," said the solitary figure gruffly, now sitting up and stretching—rolling his head from side to side and cracking his neck joints loudly.

"A Stone was detected in a previously scanned region," came the meek reply, again echoing off the chamber's cavernous space. "It appeared and then vanished shortly thereafter, lost on a planet saturated with organic life forms. Bringing you visuals now, master."

A thin slab of hard, black material slid vertically out of the ceiling and down in front of the sitting figure. Its wide surface flickered into life and an image appeared showing a desolate and barren planet. Overlaid on the screen were indecipherable symbols and glyphs, and an animation showing nine concentric rings, upon each riding a dot, travelling anticlockwise.

"What system is this?" said the shadowy figure, frowning.

"Orion-Arm 7521066/Single-Solar number 422," replied the slavish voice.

Typhon sighed. So many worlds had been encountered. So many of their voices hushed. Snuffed out in moments. Yet something about this quaint arrangement of planets and its single puny sun fired a neuron of recognition deep within his fractured mind. He had been here before, many, many eons ago. He felt certain of it. But why would he return? It was unheard of.

Typhon's *Nightshade* fired past an uneven brown planet—the outermost of this system's nine. It was a dry, cold, and arid rock devoid of life and thus his interest. Another flicker of a memory sparked in his mind. A giant gaseous world with a great collar of rings. Ah yes, thought Typhon. I remember it well—a strange, isolated beauty to the cold, lifeless orb. Then he remembered a giant planet of storms with an angry, spinning red eye staring out into the cold darkness of space. He had liked that lifeless and destructive giant too.

Nightshade sped farther toward the solar system's inner core and onward Typhon's memories took him. A smaller, sandy red planet covered in mountains and canyons came into view, and he remembered how it had once held life. Life that something unknown had snuffed out long since. Then they reached the third planet from the sun and entered into a low orbit around it. It had been a land of fire and jungle when he'd last seen it. A crude world still forming, volcanoes ripping the surface apart, tearing great canyons into its crust. Water then crashing in to form seas, and where land met water, jungles had formed.

He remembered the dumb creatures that had lived there. Huge lumbering dragons. Millions of strange, flightless, birdlike creatures, hell-bent on devouring one another. How he had laughed at their folly, and laughed again as he snuffed them out with the darkness. The darkness that dwelled deep within him. The darkness of his pitiless mind made real. His Storm of Shadows.

— THREE —
EVA

"A Somva . . . Somvia . . . what?" said Billy, a feeling of anxiety growing inside him. "I don't think any of this is making sense, Sal. I want to wake up now, please. I've had enough of this. It's just weird and wrong. I want out."

"You'll leave when you're good and ready, kid," said Sal. "Ain't no way to get out of here faster than that."

"What?" said Billy crossly. "It's time this nonsense ended, Sal. You're not real. This place isn't real. It's all a stupid dream. I want to wake up. I want to go home. Oh, never mind, I'm leaving." With that, Billy turned and stormed off toward the door with the white hand symbol above it. He'd only taken a couple of steps when Sal said from behind him, "I wouldn't do that if I were you."

"Or what?" snapped Billy, not breaking his stride.

"Or you'll be dead quicker than you can say, 'No stranger to danger.' That's the somviator motto, by the way."

"What on Earth are you talking about?" said Billy, stopping short of the doors and turning to face the alien cook. She was starting to get on his nerves. It was his dream, not hers.

Sal appeared to be stuck in the booth and so had rotated her head 180 degrees to look at him. "Well, Earth is about to be in a whole heap of trouble, son," she said, trying to maintain an air of calm. "But before we get to that—here, catch." She tossed him the clear helmet with the gloves shoved inside. "Stick these on if you're going out there. Come back in when you've had a belly full."

Billy thought for a moment, feeling his growing bad temper slip down a gear. He looked curiously from Sal to the door. Then from the door to the windows, which were still obfuscated by a rhythmically pulsing, multicoloured glow from outside. Then he studied the oddly floating cutlery on the tables around him. Then back to the doors again. They were made of thick glass. Two sets of them. One set in the diner, followed by a chamber about the size of a department store elevator, and then another set of doors leading to somewhere else.

Slowly, Billy took the gloves out of the helmet and pulled them on tight. He noticed how a metal ring around each glove's wrist clicked into and sealed against a metal ring on the corresponding sleeve. Similarly, when he placed the helmet over his head and began turning it around, it suddenly snapped into place with a satisfactory metallic clang that resonated inside. A row of small blue lights lit up around the inside of his collar and projected a vector path display onto the inside of the clear visor. It depicted what looked like a rotating planet with columns of numbers and charts that constantly changed on either side of it. Finally, a hissing sound filled the helmet and faded away after a few seconds.

"Atmosphere secure," said a clear female voice from within the helmet. "Swift GB03 standby power at sixty-seven percent. Disintegrator charge at nineteen percent. Use caution. Plasma rounds remaining: seven."

"Who's that speaking?" asked Billy.

"She's your new buddy, LAURA."

Billy looked over to Sal. She was still wedged into the booth and looking quite uncomfortable. "Who?" he asked again.

"Your suit's artificial intelligence unit. L.A.U.R.A.—*Light and Unobtrusive Reconnaissance Assistant.* She looks after all your cockamamie gadgetry in your Swift—navigation, rocket boosters, weaponry—all that sort of stuff. She can also give you tactical advice too—combat strategies, flight path information, and the like. Plus, she basically is the Internet of everything, so she can help you find the best pizza in town too, heh heh!"

Billy didn't know what to say. His mind was reaching a critical meltdown point. There was only so much jibber-jabber it could take. He simply said, "I'm going," and turned and walked up to the diner door. There was a large button in the middle of it. He pressed it.

There was a hiss, and a clank, and then a whirring sound, and the doors popped inward about ten centimetres and then split in half, like an elevator door, and pulled apart.

Billy walked into the chamber beyond. There was another set of doors in front of him; identical to the ones he'd just passed through. Like them, they had a button in the middle. He pushed it.

The doors behind him whirred and clanked and reversed their previous motion, closing back tight. Then the doors in front of him made a clank and pulled apart in absolute silence. Billy felt a little gust of air pull at him and then ease. He stepped out.

Everything was so much brighter outside. There was a night sky full of stars that positively glowed with phosphorus energy. Their density increased and decreased across the sky, forming bands of cloudy wisps.

The range of colours was mesmerising. It was as if somehow an intense fireworks display had been frozen in time—glowing embers of every colour caught in limbo.

Billy slowly panned his gaze in an arc across the heavens until he was looking at an intense spiral nebula. It had a brilliant white core that looked like it was being fed by tendrils of star clusters.

Billy felt a vibration and turned around to see the diner doors closing silently behind him. He was indeed standing outside a vintage American railway carriage. It was parked up on concrete blocks and was apparently the only building in the area.

Above him on the roof stood a vast neon sign. It ran the full length of the train carriage and was about five or six metres high. Billy walked around to get a better view, aware that he felt slightly lighter than normal.

Glass tubing formed a curved set of enormous letters that spelled out "Sleepy Sal's Star-Plucked Café." It blinked alternately between white and red. Beneath the lettering was a stylised drawing of a mountain formed of purple neon tubing. At its peak was a yellow neon boulder. It was crudely animated in three frames to show it rocking left and right.

Billy turned back to gaze at the vast nebula. It was spectacular, he thought, closing his eyes for a moment and wondering if he'd wake up in Hagnaby's class when he opened them again. He didn't. The nebula and diner were still there. As was he.

He looked down at the ground. There was no pavement or path—or even grass. It was hard, brown rock. It glinted with a subtle metallic sparkle, like iron ore. He walked out a little and noticed that it was pitted and marked with hundreds of little craters. He continued onward in total silence. His footsteps made no sound. In fact, there were no sounds of any kind. No birds. No cars. No people talking. No disturbances at all, except for the noise of his own breathing inside the helmet.

The farther he walked from the diner and the blinking neon sign, the darker everything became and the harder it was to see his feet. He started to shorten his pace until he was doing mini-steps—arms outstretched in case he collided with something unseen in the gloom.

After about a minute, LAURA interrupted him. "Advise caution. Edge proximity."

"Edge?" queried Billy.

"Edge of terrain approaching. Advise stop traversing."

Somewhat arrogantly, Billy continued, but he could feel his heart rate quickening as he nervously shuffled forward.

He didn't really have a plan, apart from getting away from the crazy alien lady. Perhaps if he kept walking he'd eventually see something he recognized, or do something that caused him to wake up.

Suddenly his left foot slipped as the ground beneath it gave way. He fell backward and sat on his bottom hard. His legs from the knees down were hanging over a ledge. Billy swore and caught his breath for a moment and then slowly leaned forward and peered down.

There was a planet far below him. It was vast and covered in an angry-looking, swirling mass of green clouds. They were turning around a colossal rocky protrusion that poked out of the atmosphere and rose up and disappeared out of sight under the ledge Billy was sitting on. He was evidently on top of a very tall mountain. He was so high up that he could see the curvature of the planet bending away behind it.

If he wasn't mistaken, he was in outer space.

— FOUR —
Déjà Vu

Typhon found it peculiar to be returning to this insignificant little planet. He had already been here and cleansed it once before but, as it transpired, not thoroughly enough. Apparently, life had found a way and, despite his best efforts, evolved into something new.

If nothing else, Typhon was a professional who took great pride in his purpose and felt tremendous satisfaction in the meticulous fashion in which he completed every search. To be returning to an old target again was disappointing, to say the least.

Millions of Earth years ago he had searched this planet's primitive geology thoroughly and the prize had not been here. It aggrieved him greatly that his father had ordered him to return and look once more. It was inconceivable that he would have missed it the first time around, and it was humiliating to come back. This time he would redouble his efforts and make sure the eradication was complete. He would do it slowly and methodically. A smile cracked his wizened face. He would savour every moment.

— FIVE —
Transference

"Don't move, Billy," said LAURA.

"What is that? I mean, is it really a planet? Am . . . I . . . in . . . space?"

"Affirmative. That is Igonosphar IV below us. We're on an asteroid called Balta, named after the Great Balta, who was the first to climb Mount Rubaz Lav . . . "

"What?" interrupted Billy.

"Igonosphar IV. It's a planet. Once mined for its ore. Formerly rich in magnesium, gold, aluminium, saleneum, barazeum, and a host of other valuable deposits—see your HUD, your heads-up display, for further breakdowns, if you wish. After a few centuries of inactivity, it was repurposed as the somviator proving grounds."

A three-dimensional wire-frame model of a rotating planet was projected onto the inside of Billy's helmet. As the diagram turned, a tall, twisting, gnarled, and jagged mountain came into view that must have been a few hundred kilometres high. It poked right through the planet's cloudy atmosphere and out into space. Upon its tip was a massive boulder, the Balta asteroid; a red dot upon it marked their position.

"Riiiiiight, okay," said Billy sarcastically. "Let's pop back in and have another little chat with Sal, shall we?" He shuffled backward from the edge and then carefully stood up. He turned around to face the distant neon glow of Sal's diner and began trudging back.

He arrived at the train carriage diner's airlock a few minutes later and went through the double-door safety procedure once again.

Inside, Billy removed his helmet and gloves and put them on the nearest table. Sal was mopping the floor down the middle of the carriage, and "Love Me Tender" by Elvis Presley was playing on the jukebox. Sal was humming tunelessly along. He could still smell fried onions from his earlier meal.

"That was fun," said Billy, in a surly tone. "So we're in outer space now, are we? Nice one. Thanks for telling me, Sal."

"Darn it, Billy, I had no choice. If I'd just come out and told you, you'd never have believed me," replied Sal, stopping to look up and lean on her mop. "You had to see it for yourself."

"I know this is all just a dream, Sal, so there's no need to pretend I'm really here anymore. I didn't tell you earlier, but I've been having these weird dreams for a few months now. In them I wake up in a place far from home. I usually just wander about aimlessly for a few hours and then wake up back in bed." Billy hesitated and added, "Mostly in bed, anyway. This is just another one of those."

"Uh-huh, honey," she said, sympathetically. "I know you're dreaming. And I know you don't always wake up at home, neither."

Billy immediately flushed. "How do you know that?" he asked. "I haven't told anyone, except . . . she would nev . . . oh, hang on, hang on . . . stupid me. This is my dream, so you know everything I do, obviously."

"Obviously," she replied.

Billy was taken aback. He wasn't expecting Sal to agree with him.

"I know all about your dreams, Billy. I should do, as I'm in this one, ain't I?" she said.

He had been expecting her to insist she was real. He said, "You admit this is a dream?"

"Of course," she replied. "Although, depends on how you look at it, I guess."

"How I look at it?"

"Sure. It all depends on what you think dreams is all about."

"Oh please, don't make this any sillier than it already is, Sal," sighed Billy, impatiently.

"I'd best keep it short then," grumbled Sal. "I can see you're one of them cynical fellas. You think dreams is just a load of old piddle-twaddle. Random thoughts thrown together in your noggin. Fair enough, I guess, but a little shortsighted, in my humble opinion. Others have a different view. They'd say dreams is like looking into another world. Another dimension, they might call it. Perhaps a parallel universe, even? It don't really matter none what name you give it. If you believe something is real, Billy, then to you, and any other believers, it is. Who's to say different?"

Billy thought about that for a moment before accepting it. "Okay. I suppose that makes some kind of crazy sense."

"Good. I ain't gonna harp on about it," said Sal. "But let's just say that in my world I'm real and you're just a dream of mine. Think about that!" She smiled and winked.

Billy smiled back. Uncertain. Questioning.

Then she added, "You're visiting with me just like you visited that Australian city the other day. The one with the funny name. What was it again? Oh yeah, Sydney."

"I see," said Billy, raising his eyebrows in surprise. "You know about that?"

Sal looked at him as if he'd asked a stupid question. She said, "I sure do. You caught the 333 bus from Circular Quay, through the city centre, up through Paddington and down to Bondi

Beach and the Pacific Ocean."

"How the heck . . . were you following me?"

"Kind of, but not in the way you think. I'll get to that in a moment."

"Right, uh, so yeah, I caught a bus up a hill and down the other side to the ocean. I didn't really know where it was going exactly. I just stayed on until I saw the sea. I've always wanted to see Bondi since watching that vet show on TV. Sydney is an awesome city."

"Uh-huh, and you walked along Campbell Parade by the ocean and bought some fries, then went and watched the surfers for a while."

"I did. They call them 'hot chips' there. They had stuff called chicken salt on them. They were great. I had a pie too. It came with sweet chilli sauce. Mmmm, I could happily live there, I really could."

"Uh-huh, and how did you buy the food, Billy?"

"I had some dollars after I went to a cash machine in the city centre to get the bus ticket. I used my ATM card to draw out forty dollars—about twenty pounds, I think. You know, their money is all made out of plastic? It's really cool."

"Uh-huh. ATMs have security cameras in them these days, don't they?"

"Uh, yeah, I suppose they do," agreed Billy.

Sal set the mop against a booth seat and skated into the kitchen, returning moments later with a thin silver laptop. She set it on the kitchen counter and brought up the video app and hit play. Grainy footage of Billy staring out of the screen appeared. His hand was up close and out of the shot at the bottom, apparently entering his PIN number and withdrawing the plastic cash.

"That's very creepy," said Billy, shocked. "You can access

security cameras?"

"I can see into just about any gizmo that has links to Earth's interwebbery, Billy. Which is pretty much every gadget on Earth these days. It's kind of my specialty. Always been good at it." Sal then pushed the right arrow key on her laptop to reinforce her comment. The video switched to a view from an interior security camera on the bus. Billy could clearly be seen seated up the back, staring out of the window. Sal pushed the key again, and it switched to a hotel roof's webcam view. Billy could be seen strolling past, eating his kiosk food and looking out over the sand toward the Pacific Ocean.

"Why would you do that? Why spy on me?" he asked, a little freaked out by it all.

"Well, shoot, I wouldn't call it spying as such, Billy. I found out that this Earth kid was making dream journeys on his own, so I thought I'd best keep an eye on him. See if I could get through to him. And here we are now. I could see you was transferring to distant locations and not just looking in on them. It's a crazy rare gift to be able to do that, Billy. One in a trillion. Maybe rarer than that, even."

"Transferring?"

"Yup, *transference*. Shifting from one world into another. It means you ain't just visiting a place as an observer, like regular dreaming folks do. You can actually affect the place you visit. Your actions have influence. Can change things. You're really there."

"That's crazy, Sal," said Billy, his heart leaping with excitement. "You're saying I've really been visiting places like Paris and Sydney? Not just dreaming about them?"

"Exactly right. You're catching on fast. Try this for size. You dream different, Billy. With more intensity. Your dreams actually send a real living, breathing version of you into the dreamscape.

We call this your Servus, or *Servo* for short—although I guess that ain't a whole heap shorter really." Sal smiled. "Your Earth body's still sleeping exactly where you left it. We call this your Primordium, or *Primo* for short. In your case, you sent a version of yourself to visit different Earth locations. Your Primo sent your Servo to Sydney and Paris and the other places."

Billy was staring again. He might be dreaming, but jeez, it was a lot to take in. A lot to be expected to believe. If only it could be true, he thought. But then it did make some weird kind of sense. When he'd woken up from the Sydney dream, he'd found his nose was oddly red and sore. His mum had said it looked like sunburn. And then there had been that time he'd dreamt of riding on a streetcar in Toronto, and then found a TTC token for the Canadian travel network in his pocket at school in Snotton the following day. He'd figured he'd got some wrong change at the canteen. Maybe that wasn't where he'd got it from after all ...

"It was mighty interesting to observe your travels," continued Sal. "They started out with little bunny hops. You'd move a few miles to a nearby city first. Some place like Cambridge or Lincoln. It was like your mind was experimenting—seeing what it could do. When it got more confident, it would take you a little farther to some place like London. Then farther still, to Edinburgh. On May thirteenth, the Paris one happened. That's when I knew you had the gift for sure. Leaping across the sea like that, hell, to a foreign country, with a different language and all— that was a big step. I've been waiting here for you since then. I knew you'd show up sooner or later. And you ain't disappointed."

"So why am I here, Sal?"

"Heh heh, well, why are any of us here?" She laughed. "There are things we'll never find the answers to, Billy. 'Why are we here?' That's the big one. Folks have been asking that one since the dawn of time." She drew out a long whistle sound and shook her head.

"Uh, no, I meant why am I here with *you*? Now?"

"Oh, right. Sorry. I don't rightly know. I think you've maybe been drawn here. Like it's your calling or some such."

Billy looked questioningly at her.

Sal pressed on, doing her best not to overwhelm him. "You see, the universe comprises dark and light, good and bad, positive and negative—your planet's Chinese call it yin and yang. They're opposing forces constantly trying to outsmart each other. It's an eternal battle for control. That's what the universe is all about. Somviators are an ancient order of protectors. Guardians of what is right. Guardians of light. The good guys, Billy. We're at war with evil sons of guns like Typhon. The dark souls. The bad guys. We like to create. To nurture. Grow. They want to destroy. To neglect. Languish."

"How long has this been going on?"

Sal made her long whistle sound again and said, "Oh my, the battle is as long as life itself, honey. It's always been going on in some form or another. But the Order of Somviators is pretty new, cosmically speaking. In Earth time, it came along about five thousand years ago. We've been coming to Earth since then.

"Trouble was, the old civilisations thought we were gods. Humans started to worship us. Shoot, it got messy for a time. We realised pretty darn quick that we were altering Earth history too much, so we became very secretive after that. But if you know where to look, there are still some ancient texts and stone markings from Earth's past that talk about us. You can read about us and even see drawings of us wearing our Swift suits.

"It's funny how most folks on Earth pays it no attention these days. But it's all there to see if you care to look."

Billy had seen TV shows about ancient aliens. He'd heard of an old book called *Chariots of the Gods?* that talked of such things. Most folks thought it was nonsense. He did too . . . although now he wasn't so sure. He asked, "How many somviators are there?"

Sal's face visibly darkened. There was an awkward, palpable silence, and then she said, "You're looking at them, kid. You and me."

Billy was shocked. He could see now why she had been keeping a close eye on him.

Sal added, "A lot of good somviators have died. Well, all of them bar me, as far as I know. A lot of good friends. Murdered by Typhon or his bitch sisters from hell. Sorry, Billy. I hate cussing, but . . . but there just ain't no other way to describe them."

Billy didn't know what to say. So he reached out and held one of her hands resting on the table.

"They killed them all, Billy. Every one of them. Finished the last of them off when I was incarcerated on Earth. When I escaped and got back here, the place was a tomb. I've been hiding out here alone in the middle of nowhere for the last forty Earth years. Forced retirement, I guess you'd call it. Hiding in plain sight. But when I ain't flipping burgers, I'm tracking space, looking for . . . well, looking for critters like you, Billy. New somviator material."

"I'm sorry, Sal," said Billy. He could see she was genuinely upset. He gave her hand a reassuring squeeze. She looked up at him. He could see she was fighting back tears. Trying to keep it together.

Then her face took on a look of steely resolve. "Shoot, look at me getting all sad and silly," she said, snapping herself out of her morose mood. "Ain't no point in crying now. Ain't going to bring them back now, is it?" She smiled at him and put one of her other hands on top of his and squeezed back.

"So then," said Billy, "What's my role in all this? I'm just a schoolboy, Sal. Not a superhero. I have no clue what the heck I'm doing. Really, I have no idea."

Sal didn't reply immediately. She studied him for a few moments and then said, "To be honest with you, I ain't sure exactly. But the universe has sent you to me—I'm convinced of it. After our little chat, I think something deep inside you has awakened. I think something has called out to you, and you've answered. I can't say what yet, but I figure there's a lot more to you than meets the eye, Billy Twigg. For one thing, you're dressed as a somviator, right here in front of me now. That's got to count for something. I think we ought to see what you got, kid. How about it?"

"Um, I don't think I'm your guy, Sal. I think there's been a mistake of some kind. I'm not a Somvatori or whatever you call it. I'm just a kid . . . "

"It's *somviator*," corrected Sal. "We've had a few names over the years, but we've been somviators for the last couple of thousand. It's a combination of two Latin words: *somno*, meaning sleep, and *viatori*, meaning traveller. Sleep-traveller. You're already doing that, Billy, because you're here with me. You can't control it, but you sure as hell can do it. So you ain't just a kid at all. You're important."

Billy considered everything that she had said. He thought about his dream travels around the world and how they might be real—sort of. He thought about how he was in space now, talking to an alien. He thought about what she'd told him about transference. And finally he thought about being asleep in Hagnaby's maths lesson and how, despite the inevitable punishment, he really would much rather wake up back there than be where he presently was.

He was getting tired and feeling increasingly irritable. Billy hadn't asked for any of this to happen to him. It wasn't fair. He said to Sal, "What is it you want me to do?"

"Go on out back, behind the diner. LAURA will take it from there."

"Okay," he said, sighing. "But I'm only doing this to try and wake up."

With that, Billy retrieved his helmet and gloves and went back through the airlock. When he arrived outside, he walked straight around to the back of the diner and to his surprise found a life-size bronze statue of a strong-looking man wearing a suit similar to his own. On its base was inscribed the motif "The Great Balta—Fear nothing but fear itself." The figure was staring off down a short runway illuminated by dim lights set every metre or so into the rocky surface.

"The Great Balta," said LAURA. "The somviator founder. He was from Earth too, you know. He was a mage, or magician. A great healer. He travelled around Europe performing incredible feats and suchlike. Then he travelled a little farther afield. But that's another story altogether."

"Right," said Billy curtly, uninterested and wanting to wake up back home as soon as possible. "So, what am I to do now?"

"Let's have you start by running down the track here. When you get halfway, put some real effort into it. At the end, jump off as far as you can."

"You're crazy!" said Billy. "You warned me about the edge just half an hour ago."

"Well, that was then and this is now," replied LAURA, a little coldly. "Things have changed."

"You make it sound simple," said Billy. "You want me to jump off the edge?"

"You'll be fine. I'll teach you how to use your suit. You may even have fun. It's just a dream, you say, right?"

"Yeah, but . . ."

"Yeah, but nothing, Billy," interrupted LAURA. "You say it's a dream. So jump off. You'll probably just wake up, anyway. It's what you want, isn't it? To wake up? For this to be over with?"

"Yes, yes I do," said Billy quietly. He paused briefly to look at the statue of the Great Balta again. He composed himself and checked his holster—the gun was still safely wedged into it. He had a feeling he was going to need it. No time like the present, he thought, and broke into a jog.

He picked up his pace and began to run down the avenue of ground lights, wondering what he was doing. He didn't have long to think about it, though, because before he knew it, he was at the rock's edge and had nowhere else to go other than off the end. He looked up into the stars for a moment, closed his eyes, inhaled deeply and yelled, "No stranger to danger!"

Billy dived headlong into the void.

— SIX —
Blue Marble

The planet was unrecognisable to Typhon now. It had been a hot, volcanic, infant world, inhabited by enormous lumbering beasts when he'd last seen it. Now it was a cool blue marble, covered mostly in water and harbouring "intelligent" life—allegedly. At least it would appear so, judging by the bio-scans he was being shown. Although the pollution levels in the atmosphere suggested they were pretty dumb for creatures dependent on oxygen for survival.

The planet's north and south poles were frozen wastelands devoid of all but the most hardy of life forms. He would likely choose one of those from which to begin the cleansing, as he often did when tackling a planet of this type.

Inside the gloom of *Nightshade's* control deck, Typhon sat on the oblong black dais, drumming his fingers impatiently. He was studying a slew of data zooming across a floating display screen in front of him, his eyes flickering and clicking as pages and pages of information were absorbed into his cavernous brain. He assimilated every language spoken on the planet—a planet the dominant humans called Earth. He at once understood their customs, laws, moral codes, levels of science and technology, medicine, history, geography, and religions—the latter a notion that made him cackle audibly. Then, near the end of his studies, he learned of a unique building hidden near the North Pole.

"How desperate," he murmured to himself. "And devious."

"*Nightshade*," growled Typhon. "Descend to the northern

pole and land at its centre."

"Yes, my master," sighed the faint voice of no discernible origin. "That is a considerable distance from the prize's location."

"I know," snapped Typhon. "I'll get there when I'm good and ready. Don't question me again."

"No, sire. Apologies."

The *Nightshade* dropped rapidly toward the planet and quickly entered the atmosphere amid a flash of sparks and flame. The craft was shaped like a shard of glass—long, thin, and sleek— narrowing to a pin-sharp tip at its nose. It was utterly black and looked to be made of ceramic or glass. It had no discernible windows, doors, ducts, or exhaust ports. Nothing. Simply a large glass shard, around a hundred metres long and forty metres high at its thickest point at the rear.

Typhon watched the screen that was now displaying the fire outside, scuffing off *Nightshade* and disappearing out of view. The image cast a fiery light across Typhon's partly bandaged, twisted face. It was wizened and gnarled and utterly disfigured. His skin was like fire-damaged wood. Dry, blackened, and cracked, his once humanoid features were now ancient genetic history. Today it was a gaunt and haunted visage scarred by fire, but more so by the trillions of lives it had seen extinguished over the millennia. The face of a soulless, remorseless killing machine.

Nightshade buffeted and rallied against the atmosphere for a few more minutes before suddenly exploding out into a brilliant blue sky. Her appearance was immediately followed by a sonic boom as she passed through the planet's sound barrier and hurtled almost vertically down, toward the frozen plateau below.

— SEVEN —
Touchdown

Billy fell like a dead weight, breathless with fear and excitement, as he tumbled out of control through the emptiness. He reluctantly opened his eyes and found his vision awash with blurred star tracks one second, and the green planet whizzing by the next. Over and over he went, his mind confused by the shock and awe of the free fall. Evidently, he had not awoken as hoped.

LAURA's voice broke into his confused state. "Pull yourself together, Billy," she scolded. "Flatten your body out and face the planet. I want to activate the rocket boots, but I can't if we're out of control. If we hit the atmosphere like this, we'll burn up."

"Rocket boots? Ha ha ha, this just gets better and better, LAURA," yelled Billy.

She sounded so human, he thought. Not like any computer he'd encountered before. He pushed his arms and legs out so his body formed a star shape—like he'd seen parachutists do on television. Slowly the tumbling decreased until eventually he was facing the wrong way—upward. The craggy sides of the enormous mountain were zipping past the periphery of his vision, and the asteroid home of Sleepy Sal at its summit was shrinking away into the twinkling abyss of space.

"That's it, good. Now turn over, Billy," said LAURA.

Billy folded one arm behind himself and another in front and deftly rotated his body 180 degrees so he faced the planet below. He wondered how he knew how to do that? Strange, he thought. It had just popped into his head. "I wasn't expecting to fall so fast," he puffed. "I thought we were in space, you know, zero gravity?"

"Igonosphar IV has a powerful magnetic core that reaches far into space. It's what captured the Balta asteroid in the first place and slammed it onto the top of Mount Rubaz Lavlaz. We're being pulled in by that force. We need to control our entry. If we create too much friction, we're done for when we hit the atmosphere. Well done, in fact—as in burnt to a cinder."

"That's not funny," cried Billy.

"No joke," replied LAURA. "And that's just for starters. Next we have to land on the ground rather than plough into it like a hunk of space junk. And then we have to face the meteorgus test."

"What? The meteo-what?"

"Let's take it one stage at time, okay, Billy? Concentrate on the planet. Control your breathing. Calm yourself."

Two hundred kilometres below Billy, the jagged surface of Igonsphar IV beckoned. The view was at once breathtaking and terrifying. Through gaps in the planet's predominantly green atmosphere he could see a gigantic array of saw-toothed mountains jutting out at erratic angles through eerie layers of mist. Liquidlike vapour trails drifted through zigzagging valleys and pulsed with a sickly green and yellow glow, strange shadows twisting and swirling within them.

"I'm going to fire up your rockets, Billy," said LAURA, interrupting his thoughts. "You'll feel your boots slam together at the ankles, locking your feet together. Don't be alarmed. They do this to keep both rockets in unison. We can't have you doing the splits or something and cartwheeling off into the unknown, now, can we?"

"I guess not," said Billy, intrigued. He heard a faint hum from within his suit, like the sound you sometimes hear when a music amplifier is switched on, and then his boots magnetised and slammed together. A sudden, uneasy force from his footwear and a low rumbling sound told him they were active. He glanced down and noticed yellow fire jetting out from the soles of his boots.

Slowly he began to move laterally over the planet's atmosphere. "Now, this is going to be tricky, Billy," said LAURA. "Hold your arms above your head like you're weightlifting and try steering yourself. The Swift suit registers your arm movements as controls and adjusts the boots accordingly. Give it a tr—"

Billy was off already, tilting his arms to steer himself around in a slow circular motion in one direction and then the other. "This is cool," he cried. "How do I speed up and slow down?"

"You're a natural, Billy. Great. Okay, throttle control is done by clenching your right hand into a fist. Fist equals fast, palm flat equals slow," said LAURA.

That was all Billy needed to hear. He punched his fist tight and immediately steered himself into a vertical orientation, which slowed his descent. He drew to a stop and then began to ascend—slowly at first, then gradually accelerating.

"Steady there," said LAURA. "We're heading to the planet's surface, remember? You're going the wrong way."

"Yes, I know," replied Billy. "Just a quick detour. I want to fly over Sal's. Say hello."

"Okay, Billy," said LAURA, exuding an air of reluctant patience. "Just a quick detour."

The sensation of flying was incredible. The freedom to swerve and duck and dive and throttle up and down and be anywhere in three-dimensions was better than any feeling he could remember having. Within a few minutes Billy was operating his Swift GB03 like a pro. He raced upward past the knobbly sides of the mysterious mountain, and then out and around the potato-like

Balta asteroid at the top. It was maybe five hundred metres wide. Sleepy Sal's Star-Plucked Café was set out on the left-hand side of it, the gaudy neon sign blinking away to nobody in particular. He could also see the little runway he'd jumped off, lit up and stretching away from the diner.

Billy sped down to the carriage and buzzed past the window side as fast as he could go. He laughed, as he was pretty sure he glimpsed Sal leaping away in fright, and possibly slipping over. He soared up into space and spun around and around, gazing at the colourful stars that surrounded him. Beautiful, he thought. Then he turned back down toward the asteroid and flew around to the far side of it. There he noticed a classic-looking silver flying saucer parked on the surface. That must be Sal's house, he thought.

"This is great, Billy," said LAURA. "You're a natural flyer. Sal is going to be so pleased with you. Now come on, let's head back down toward the planet."

"Awww really? So soon? Okay then." He sighed.

Reluctantly, Billy turned back downward and throttled his suit, returning to where minutes ago he'd been tumbling uncontrollably.

Soon the planet's outer atmosphere struck the Swift suit, and Billy began to get buffeted by increasingly powerful forces. He instinctively positioned his arms and legs against the force and tilted his body so he was aiming headfirst about twenty degrees off the vertical, making his profile smaller and reducing the impact on his body.

"Good work, Billy," said LAURA. "You're really getting the hang of flying. It's pretty cool, isn't it?"

He had to admit it was amazing. For a dream to be this realistic was fantastic. Everything around him looked so vivid, so lifelike. "It's incredible," he whispered.

"Now, let's do a few checks. Reach for your weapon," said LAURA softly.

"You mean this?" said Billy, reaching for the pistol in the holster on his left hip.

"That's it, Billy," said LAURA, sounding pleased. "It's your desintoscram weapon."

He immediately looked it over and saw that a kill selector switch on the side was set to a *steam* setting.

LAURA said, "Allow me to continue from where you interrupted me earlier, Billy. The mountain to our left that we're dropping past is called Mount Rubaz Lavlaz, and is one of the strangest anomalies in the known universe. It's an oversize, extremely steep-sided, two-hundred-kilometre-high mountain, with the huge Balta asteroid perched on its tip. It teeters there in a strange cosmic balancing act and is thought to have been drawn in slowly by the planet's powerful gravitational pull millions of years ago. At some point it crashed onto the mountain peak and stayed there. Depending on the time of year, and the orbit of Igonosphar IV, the asteroid will wobble and seemingly try to leave before giving up some months later and staying put. It has become something of a favourite with mountaineering tourists and has that railcar diner at the top, which has been run by Sally Magmajude for almost forty years ..."

LAURA's impromptu history lesson was interrupted once more, this time by a flashing red warning graphic on the inside of Billy's visor. It said "PROXIMITY ALERT." LAURA's deceptively calm voice confirmed the warning. "Proximity alert, Billy. We're heading for the ground ... very quickly. What should you do next?"

Billy stopped fiddling with the desintoscram and slotted it back into the silvery pouch on his hip and began to frantically think. What would a somviator do now? But who was he kidding? He had no idea.

LAURA began to count down, adding to the not inconsiderable amount of tension. "Ten . . . nine . . . eight . . . "

Billy acted on instinct; or maybe it was impulse. Whatever it was, he manoeuvred himself into a steeper incline with his head pointing almost straight down and accelerated his descent. The sickly green fug below him was rapidly approaching. Within its daunting, swirling mass of shadows was the ominous sounding meteorgus test.

"Seven . . . six . . . five . . . "

A new translucent display panel appeared on his visor. It had a title that read "Meteorgus fact file." Under it was a rotating diagram of a weird-looking animal that looked like a cross between a chimpanzee and a goat. Annotations pointed to various parts of its body, highlighting features like sharp teeth, deadly claws, poor eyesight, excellent sense of smell, small brain.

"Four . . . three . . . two . . . "

Billy stopped reading the display when he roared into the green tempest—suddenly distracted by vapour trails whizzing past his head. The meteorgus graphic was immediately replaced by an altimeter that was hurriedly counting backward, showing Billy that he was about one kilometre from the bottom of an area called the Dastard Valley. He was able to see his position relative to steep valley walls on either side of him. He was almost there.

"One . . . zero."

"Prepare to land," said LAURA. "Feet first, please."

Billy spun himself around so that his feet were pointing downward. As soon as he did that, bright red, then yellow flames fired out of the soles of his boots, blasting away the thick green mist. As he slowly decelerated, the cracked and barren terrain of Igonsphar IV came into view.

"What's the meteorgus test, LAURA?" asked Billy, anxiously.

"The meteorgus is a vile interstellar creature that devours anything and everything in its path. About the size of an average Earth house, they travel through space in enormous herds, searching for planets to consume and when done, move on to another. A typical herd can destroy an Earth-size world in three to four years. They have very few vulnerabilities. Waste from the creature comes in the form of a spray of rock poo, which it ejects vertically into space—hence meteorites are made."

"How nice," said Billy sarcastically, while thinking how glad he was it was just a dream. It was starting to get a little yucky.

The valley floor looked to be comprised of mostly flat, cracked, yellowish earth that was dry and compact. Billy figured it was maybe a hundred metres wide, with its length stretching out front and behind him into a thick, toxic-looking fog that was seeping in from both ends. As he descended through the murk, he observed the valley walls on either side of him soaring upward into low-lying green clouds. Looking down he could see a scattering of large boulders—ideal for cover, he thought.

Billy felt a growing need for caution. The light was not good down there, and his boots would be noisy, potentially drawing attention to his arrival—although he already had a feeling that his presence had not gone unnoticed. He hovered momentarily over the ground, his boots blasting away sand and grit in a wide circle around him. He got to within half a metre of the surface and instructed LAURA to deactivate the thrusters.

Billy dropped to the ground and immediately pulled out his disintegrator gun and tucked himself into a defensive crouch. If it hadn't all been a bad dream, he'd have been terrified out of his wits. As it was, he was half scared and half curious.

LAURA said, "Scanning for hostiles."

On his visor's wire-frame graphic interpretation of his surroundings, he saw a large red dot was already moving slowly in his direction from over behind his right shoulder. A numerical display to the side told him that it was 587 metres away and closing. As it neared, the dot pulsed and made a subtle repeating "ping" sound. LAURA said, "One meteorgus on its way. How can we survive this encounter?"

Billy stood up and looked around. Green wisps of cloud slithered along the valley floor, obscuring his vision of anything farther away than about fifty metres. He spotted a large pile of boulders over by the east valley wall. The formation was about three times taller than himself and consisted of plenty of different size rocks piled up on top of one another. As good a place as any, he thought, holstering his weapon.

The pings were becoming more rapid and urgent-sounding, and the counter now showed the approaching object was 492 metres away and picking up speed. Billy began to run to the pile of rocks. Flying would have been quicker but he didn't want to draw any more attention to himself than was absolutely necessary.

He arrived a little out of breath at the boulders a minute later. The gravity on Igonosphar IV was stronger than Earth's, and it was hard work running. LAURA told him in no uncertain terms that he was to keep his helmet on at all times. The atmosphere was deadly poisonous to humans.

Ping; the display now read four hundred metres and closing.

Billy started to climb up the rock formation. He found a pretty decent spot that gave him good forward cover, with the valley wall to his right contributing additional protection. He was really only vulnerable from the west and from behind. He also found a gap in the stones that allowed him to look straight down the valley in the direction of the advancing threat while maintaining his cover.

Ping; three hundred metres.

Ping; two hundred metres.

Ping; one hundred metres.

Then, in the distance, through the mist, he could make out an enormous shadowy form. It was indeed the height of a house, a big three-storey one, and about as wide. The meteorgus had a vaguely human form, or perhaps apelike would have been a better description. It was lumbering on legs that looked shorter than its arms, which it was using like a chimpanzee to push off the ground and travel more rapidly. It was covered in wiry grey and brown fur, and on its head were two enormous, heavy-looking, curly horns. Billy could hear it snorting and puffing as it went, looking left and right, trying to sniff him out.

The ground started to vibrate with the rhythmic pounding of its fists into the dirt, small pebbles shaking and falling off the dusty boulders around Billy. He unholstered his gun and again checked it was set for steam. LAURA quietly pointed out that the steam setting used more charge than normal and that in reality he would only have three shots at that power setting, with maybe one regular plasma shot available after that. Great, thought Billy. Now she tells me.

The meteorgus reached Billy's landing site. It snuffled the scorched ground and scraped it with a finger, which it then lifted to its snout and sniffed hard. It sneezed loudly. Thick strings of luminous yellow snot flew out and splattered onto the ground. It wiped its face and slowly turned in Billy's direction, pausing to stare, its deep-set eyes squinting to see through the mist. It let out a high-pitched and frankly terrifying howl.

Suddenly a second red dot appeared out of nowhere on the left side of Billy's map display. It was small and travelling very quickly. He turned toward it, fumbling and dropping the disintegrator gun in his panic. LAURA was starting to say something that sounded like a warning.

And that was when the large orange pencil eraser hit him square between the eyes.

— EIGHT —
And So It Begins

Nightshade swooped in from a vertical diving position to a horizontal orientation, screaming low over the ice plateau that glistened in the bright sunlight. She generated no engine noise whatsoever; only the blistering rush of snow and wind being scythed out of her way registered a high-pitched screech that sounded eerily like a distressed beast screaming in pain.

Inside, Typhon sat impatiently studying the enhanced images being relayed to him from outside: clouds, water, ice, more ice. No life to speak of. An occasional faint heat signature from a barely evolved creature. But nothing much.

No matter, he thought. The time for extinction would be upon them soon enough. He clicked his eyes shut and took a deep, rasping breath. He remembered the taste of death, and oh how he missed its acrid burn. The finality of the flavour. The pure pleasure of ending life. Soon he would savour its distinct aromas again.

"Come, *Nightshade*," he mumbled, turning his mind away from dark memories. "Speed me to the surface and ready the shadow staff."

"Yes, my master," hissed the spaceship's computer. "Landing will commence momentarily."

Nightshade swung around in a wide circle and powered down anticlockwise, spiralling lower and lower. Gently she drew to a halt a few metres above the ice and hovered. From beneath her belly, the snow and air began to form a spiral of wind. Faster and faster it became until a vortex grew into an inverted cone and descended to the icy surface below. On contact with the ground, it formed a column of impossibly fast spinning air, which quickly darkened.

A black shape descended down the eye of the twister, barely visible through the mass of swirling air. When it reached the ice, the vortex dissipated almost immediately, revealing the crouching figure of Typhon.

He was cradling a long spear of dark matter in his arms as he stood upright, reaching a height of at least three metres. He narrowed his black, empty eyes against the bitter wind that battered his emaciated frame, tattered black robes lashing out behind him.

"*Nightshade,*" he growled. "Return to orbit and follow me from there. I have no further need of you here."

"Yes, master," she whispered, her reply barely audible over the growing wind.

Nightshade floated upward a few metres, seemingly unaffected by the wintry gusts, and turned to point straight up at a patch of clear blue sky. Suddenly, she fled away at incredible speed and vanished into the distance, a faint sonic boom rocking the air.

Typhon stood alone in the freezing environment, oblivious to its harshness. Weather had little effect on him—heat or cold barely registering even a tingle of sensation. His body, cloaked in the deathly black material, was mostly impervious to elements like wind, rain, or snow. The majority of his body's nerve endings had been destroyed eons ago.

The blackness of the billowing mass of dark matter that formed his Sygma cloak was utter and complete, as though night itself lay dormant inside its writhing furls. Such was its density that no light entering it could ever escape. It reflected absolutely nothing. He looked like an unholy shadow cast against the brilliant white ice cap.

Typhon held aloft the shadow staff and then plunged it deep into the frozen ice cap. It slid in with little effort until only a few centimetres of it protruded. At its hilt was a fist-size rock that looked like a roughly hewn black diamond. It began to pulse and hum, as if energy was building up inside it.

Suddenly a crack of bright red lightning shot straight upward from the hilt and vanished into the sky. Immediately the ice around the staff's entry point blackened and cracked like an infected wound, and dark and thunderous clouds began to bleed outward from where the lightning had struck the sky.

"And so it begins," murmured Typhon, turning his back on the expanding darkness and looking out across the flat, glistening ice sheet. "So it begins."

— NINE —
Back with a Bump

"Wake up, boy," bellowed Mr Hagnaby. "This isn't beddy-bye time. Get up, you idiot. Up!"

Billy was lying prone on a grey, tiled floor, an overturned school chair beside him. There was a pencil eraser next to his head. He could hear kids laughing. One was even complimenting someone on what a good shot they were.

"Shut up, Bates," barked Hagnaby, turning to a large, red-haired boy near the back of the classroom. He swung back to Billy and glowered. "Come on, Twigg. Get up, get up!"

Billy felt stunned and quite odd, as if he was lying on the bottom of a swimming pool looking up at people standing by its edge. He mumbled, "Help me, LAURA."

The class erupted into further laughter and Hagnaby snapped, "That's it, Twigg. Detention. Again. Stay behind after class."

Billy slowly got to his feet, blinking hard and looking around at the twenty or so laughing faces. His school uniform of grey slacks and navy V-neck jumper was covered in floor dust. He patted himself down as best he could, righted his chair and sat down. Further laughter indicated something was awry, and looking around, he realised he was facing the wrong way. He sighed and corrected himself to face the front of the class as the laughter slowly died down.

Thank the stars, he was back at school, he realised. No more aliens. He'd never been so happy to be in trouble and humiliated before.

Somebody muttered, "Oooooh, who's Laura? Kissy kissy." The class erupted into further laughter.

"What a muppet," somebody else shouted from behind him, and a soggy piece of chewed-up paper slapped into the back of his head.

"Bates," barked Hagnaby. "You've just booked yourself a desk next to Mr Twigg."

"Aw, but sir. Come on, I didn't fall asleep . . . "

"Silence," growled Hagnaby. "That's enough, that's enough. Calm down. Be quiet, all of you." He waited a few seconds for the class to settle down. "Now, let's return to page thirty-eight of your text books, Pythagoras's Theorem. As you may remember from yester—"

Just then the school bell began ringing, and the children leapt from their seats and started packing their bags. Hagnaby grumbled something unintelligible and then pointed to Billy and Bates. "You two stay put."

Detention had become almost the norm for Billy in recent months. He was finding it harder and harder to stay conscious at school. To him it didn't feel as if he was falling asleep, though. It felt more like he was . . . leaving. Like he was visiting another place. What was happening to him? Why was he doing this? At first he'd thought it was perhaps just part of growing up, but it didn't appear to be happening to the other kids at school. Once, when he'd asked a friend if they'd ever found themselves having daydreams that felt very, very real, he'd just cocked his head to one side, frowned, and told him he was a bit odd. He hadn't felt much like discussing it with anyone after that.

Until he met Ellie, that is. She was the only one he had confided in, and the less his parents knew about it the better. He was just hoping it would go away or that he'd grow out of it. But if anything, the dreams were becoming more vivid and occasionally very hard to snap out of.

***

Mrs Coldstream peered down her narrow, hooked nose and through half-rimmed spectacles at Billy Twigg and Russell Bates. "My, my, my, what a surprise to see Billy and Russell in my detention hour. It must be . . . now let me think . . . oh, two days since Billy was last here and, hmmm, about a week since Russell was here. It's nice to have a fan base. You two can't stay away from me, can you?"

Billy knew better than to answer her. She wasn't really asking them a question. Rather, she was looking to goad them into saying something stupid so she could make their stay even more unpleasant. Russell followed suit, but Billy could see he was twitching and trying to stem a snarl.

"This afternoon I'm going to give you both lines to do," she said. "A somewhat old-fashioned punishment, but one that I'm rather fond of. Billy, you will write out one hundred times, 'I must not fall asleep in my wonderful maths class.'" Russell, you will write out one hundred times, 'I must never throw things at other people unless it's a sports lesson.'" She then chuckled a little at her own joke and adopted a contented smile.

"That's so not fair," said Russell, unable to contain his fury any longer. "Mr Hagnaby threw an eraser at Billy because he was sleeping again, and I don't see him in here writing, "I must not throw erasers at kids." How come he gets to do what he wants, and I'm in here getting these stupid lines?"

Billy flinched. Mrs Coldstream was starting to change colour. Her normal clammy white, almost blue-hued pallor was starting to warm up. He could see scarlet veins appearing under her tightly drawn skin. Her eyes widened and then scrunched almost shut, while her nostrils appeared to be flapping slightly. Billy gulped and got cracking with his lines and tried to ignore what was about to happen.

Mrs Coldstream stood up and stared at Russell as if he was something very unpleasant stuck to the sole of her shoe. "What did you say, Bates?" she screeched. "Did you dare talk back to me? To your teacher? To your superior?"

Russell immediately realised the error of his ways and gulped audibly. He looked away as her face continued to redden. She walked around her desk and down to where Russell was sitting.

"Bates," screamed Mrs Coldstream, grabbing hold of one of his ears and twisting it practically upside down. "Once you have finished those first one hundred lines, you will then do a further two hundred lines of this: 'I must never talk back to my teachers in a surly manner.' Do you 'ear?" She then erupted into cackling laughter at her own terrible humour and returned to her desk.

Russell turned to Billy and mimed a finger being drawn across his throat.

— TEN —
A Storm is Coming

The weatherman from the TV network looked at his computer screen curiously. He tapped at the keyboard and clicked a mouse. He waited for the screen to update and stared. This can't be right, he thought. He picked up the phone next to him and hit four digits in quick succession. "Hi, Bob. Matt here. I'm having a few issues with GeoSat Nippon number twenty-two's data. Have you had any problems with it this morning?"

"Can't say I have, Matt," replied Robert Dyson, a meteorologist at London's Met Office. "But then I haven't been compiling any Arctic data this morning. What seems to be the problem?" Dyson had a face for radio, as he had once been impolitely told at an interview for a TV weatherman position, despite knowing more about meteorology than all of their vacuous fool presenters put together.

"I'm getting really weird readings at the pole," said Matt somewhat nervously, fearful of sounding like an idiot. "Says temperature has dipped about fifty degrees, and, uh . . . well, the wind speed is off the chart. Literally. It's saying some kind of tornado hit it and then vanished. Was there for about five seconds, then pow, it disappeared. Oddly, it left a cumulonimbus that's not moving."

"That's not possible, Matt. Let me take a look at the data myself and get back to you."

Dyson hung up the phone and muttered, "Moron."

Matt popped his phone back into its cradle and stared at the map on his PC. It showed a live satellite feed of the northern hemisphere—a few black pixels indicating a growing storm cloud at the pole.

An uneasy chill ran down his spine.

— ELEVEN —
The Bridge

Billy was released from detention at precisely five o'clock, after making suitably sad and remorseful faces to Mrs Coldstream. Unable to stop himself, he winked at Russell on the way out, knowing that he would no doubt regret doing that later. As he swung around the corner and out of the main doors, he saw Ellie Roundtree sitting on the low school boundary wall, playing with her phone. She looked up and smiled.

He gave her a little smile back. It was all he could manage. He had a lot on his mind. But seeing her pretty face and sparkling green eyes did lift his spirits some. Her black hair was swept across her face and deliberately cut to be shorter on one side than the other. She was wearing a dark purple hoodie over a tee for a band he'd never heard of and tight black jeans, tapering down to a pair of scuffed red Vans.

"Detention again then, eh?" she said, laughing, in her familiar Canadian accent. "What was it this time, reciting Latin verbs again?"

"Nope, not this time," said Billy. "It was lines today. She does like her vintage punishments. She gave Russell a right earful too. I think I'm going to have a problem with him tomorrow." Billy frowned at the thought of having to avoid him and his cronies during break times.

"Come on, Billy," said Ellie, jumping off the wall and smiling at him. "I'll chum you home. Let's walk together."

They sauntered along in no particular hurry, side by side and in silence for a minute or two. Ellie was studying Billy out of the corner of her eye. She could see he was pretty down in the dumps and seemed overly miserable for a simple detention. After all, he normally had one or two detentions a week. He was a pro. "What happened today?" she enquired softly.

Billy was frowning and looking down at his feet. Looking really uncomfortable.

"Was it one of your daydreams again? Have you told your mum and dad about them yet?" she asked.

"No, no. God, I don't want them to find out I'm having them at school. They think I only have them during the night. I don't want anyone to know." He looked across at his friend. "Well, nobody but you. I can trust you, Ellie, right?"

"Of course you can," she replied, placing a hand on his arm. "You can always trust me, Billy. We're friends for life, remember?"

Billy relaxed a little. "Good," he said, remembering their first encounter four months ago, and smiling for the first time in hours...

It was a damp, grey morning in mid-April. He was bouncing on the old trampoline in the back garden and

pondering his lot in life. He was too old for it really, but he liked the brief feeling of sailing through the air without a care in the world. Each time he bounced he could also see over the fences into the neighbours' gardens. That was when he first saw her.

A smarmy-looking guy in a suit carrying a clipboard was showing a tired-looking woman in her mid to late thirties around the garden of a neighbouring house that was for sale. Beside them was a girl with dark hair, wearing an eye patch.

She immediately noticed Billy bouncing, and when the adults turned around and went back into the kitchen, she remained there, looking at him curiously. It was hard to tell what her expression was, given that one eye was obscured, but he did manage to blurt out a "hi" and a "what's your name" really quickly between bounces. "What happened" and "to your eye" followed when his first attempt at contact proved unsuccessful.

The girl said, "Can I come bounce with you?" She had a strange accent. Perhaps American, he thought. He didn't think he'd met an American before. "Can I come and hang out with you?" she asked again.

Billy nodded and panted, "Come out your gate" and "then in mine." He gestured by flapping an arm over to his left. The eye-patch girl duly obliged and exited through her garden gate and in through his. Billy was still bouncing but trying to make room for her to get on at the same time. He nearly toppled off, making the girl giggle. "Come on up. It's really soggy, mind you. It rained all night."

She regarded him oddly for a moment and then announced that she was Ellie and that he was to help her up onto the trampoline.

"What are you doing on a wet trampoline?" she asked, as they both started to bounce in rhythm. "If it's not really trampoline weather?"

"What are you doing on one?" he replied, to which she cracked a little smile. Sensing the ice was broken a bit now, Billy ventured, "What happened to your eye?"

Ellie stopped bouncing, so Billy did the same, and they let the elasticity spend out and come to a stop. "I had an operation on it two weeks ago. It needs to be kept clean for a while."

"What's wrong with it?" asked Billy.

"I was seeing funny out of it," she replied, adding, "Seeing things a bit cloudy. Seeing weird shapes. They gave me a new lens or something."

"Gosh," he said. "That must have been sore."

"It wasn't very nice. I had some pretty bad headaches afterward.

It's not too bad now."

"I see weird things too," said Billy. *"But not blurry. Quite in focus actually."*

"Really?" said Ellie.

"Yeah. I have a few problems of my own. My mum calls them 'sleep issues.'"

Ellie looked at him, a glimmer of concern in her visible eye. A hint of compassion. He didn't know why he was telling her this. He really hadn't told anyone about it before. It was a bit of a family secret, to be honest. Perhaps it was because she sounded foreign, and her appearance might have been fleeting.

"You can tell me anything," she said. And he did. He told her everything. He thought she took it quite well, all things considered. To begin with she had seemed a little incredulous, but as his story unfolded, the more she believed his sincerity. He couldn't put his finger on it exactly, but he felt like he'd known Ellie for ages already.

"Come on," she said, suddenly snapping Billy out of his thoughts and back into the present. "I'll race you down to the Old Dairy." She took off down the street, squealing. Billy sighed and took off after her, jogging.

The Old Dairy was in fact a sweet shop, run by a couple of dear old ladies, although it did sell milk too, in a token gesture to its former purpose—on sale next to a huge array of milkshake powders, of course. When Billy arrived, Ellie was already at the penny tray counter, picking out a selection of sugary delights from a large yellow tray of assorted sweets. She paid and turned around. "Here, I got you some of those rice-paper-sherbet UFO thingies you like."

"Ha, thanks Ellie," said Billy, perking up a little and taking a couple out of her paper bag. She took out some cola bottles for herself.

The two teenagers walked on together in silence again, simply enjoying each other's company . . . and her bag of sweets. They arrived at an old wooden footbridge spanning a canal, ambled up one side of it and stopped in the middle. Below them were some ducks paddling around, waiting for people to feed them.

"So what happened today?" asked Ellie again gently. "You never did tell me."

Billy paused a tick and then said, "Well, I nodded off in Hagnaby's double maths lesson—of all the lessons to pick, it had to be his." Billy rolled his eyes and sighed. "I dreamt I was in space, talking with an alien. Apparently, I was some kind of a spaceman with a ray gun. It was really stupid. Not worth going into. Anyway, Hagnaby threw a pencil eraser at me and woke me up. That's when I fell on the floor in class. Then I got detention and so did Russell Bates, who's now gunning for me. Life sucks at the moment."

"God, Hagnaby is such a doofus," said Ellie. "And never mind about Russell. He hasn't got the brain capacity to remember to come after you tomorrow."

"Ha, I wouldn't be so sure. There's a rumour he managed to tie his own shoe laces this morning!" joked Billy, before pausing a beat. "They're getting more frequent, you know? The dreams. They used to just happen at night. In bed. These daytime ones have got to stop, Ellie. They're driving me mad. It's so embarrassing. Plus, they used to be realistic jumps to real places. Cool places mostly. Today, it went into this weird sci-fi world. Scary at the end too. I don't want to go back there."

"It'll just be a phase, I'm sure of it. You'll grow out of it, I bet. Be patient. Ride it out."

Billy didn't reply. They stood on the bridge and watched a couple of ducks make an ungainly splashdown landing on the canal. As water ripples rolled to the sides of the waterway, they both noticed the moon's reflection appearing and disappearing as miniature waves made crests and troughs on the surface. They looked up together and stared at the moon for several seconds; its upper right quadrant was still showing a silvery haze of debris stretching out into the blue sky.

Ellie had a sudden thought. "I've known you for how long? Let's see, um, four months. Right?"

"Sounds about right," said Billy, sounding distant.

"And the moon thing happened six months ago, right?"

"I don't know."

"Well, it did. It was six months ago. You told me when I first met you that you'd been having weird dreams for six weeks I think you said. So that is a bit of a coincidence isn't it?"

"How's that?"

"Oh, come on, Billy, I'm on to something here. Your weird dreams started about two weeks after an asteroid hit the moon. What if the two events are linked?"

Billy straightened up. She had a point.

"Well . . . I suppose. It was a comet, though, not an asteroid," he corrected her.

"Okay, whatever. A big chunk of space rock or ice or something hit the moon and showered Earth in stones and goodness knows what else. Remember the shooting stars we had for a couple of weeks? And remember how everybody went nuts searching for moon rocks? Sites like eBay are still full of them. What if something is affecting you? What if something from the moon is making you have these dreams?"

"Well, that's a pretty far-fetched notion, Ellie," said Billy. But he sounded brighter as he thought about the dates. "Although, you're right about the time. The moon collision was on February the fifteenth. I'm pretty sure I had my first jump experience in early March. That would be when all the meteorites were lighting up the sky. Or had just finished."

"Uh-huh, exactly. I think there's a connection. I think something fell from the moon and is affecting you. We need to find it."

"And how do we do that?"

"Well, you said you used to have them in your sleep at home, before you started having them at school. So it's got something to do with your house. When are you at home the longest? What part of the day?"

"I guess the evening and nighttime."

"Exactly. When you're asleep. It makes sense, right? There must be something in your house or nearby that's causing your crazy dreams. It's too much of a coincidence. Don't you think?"

"It's an interesting idea, I'll give you that. But it sounds a bit far-fetched to me. And it doesn't explain the daytime dreams I'm suffering at school now."

Ellie knew it didn't, but she seemed to feel there was something to her theory. "Don't dismiss it straightaway, Billy. Think it over. It's worth doing that at least."

"Okay. You might be right." He felt a little bit picked up. Despite playing it down, it was hard to completely rule out what she was saying. "Come on, let's head home. And let's talk about something else."

They turned south to continue crossing the bridge but stopped dead in their tracks after only a couple of steps. Russell Bates was standing at the foot of the exit ramp, with his mountain bike propped up between his legs. He was out of breath.

He'd taken his red chequered shirt off and tied it around his waist, leaving him wearing a plain white T-shirt with the sleeves ripped off. On the top of his left arm was a crude tattoo of his own name, spelled out, R-U-S-E-L, where the "S" was backward.

He'd done it himself when he was eight years old by repeatedly stabbing his arm with a narrow fibre-tip pen.

When Billy had last seen him in detention, Russell had been doing his extra two hundred lines. It should have taken him ages to finish them. He must have rushed like mad and then pedalled like crazy to catch up with them. Not to mention cycling the long way round to be able to cut them off on the bridge.

Ellie instinctively reached out and took hold of Billy's hand. She was more frightened than she wanted to admit. If truth be known, Billy wasn't far behind her.

Russell was big for his age. Tall and broad, he had a large head with a freckly complexion topped with wavy ginger hair. Of course, it helped that he'd been kept back a year at school due to mucking about and not learning anything the previous year. He was fourteen going on twenty-four, shaving already, and known for his brawling. He'd once taken on a sixth-form student, four years his senior, in a dare that involved him not using his fists or feet. He'd repeatedly head-butted the poor bloke into submission —fracturing his eye socket and putting him in hospital.

"Hi ya, Billy," said Russell, grinning psychotically. "Fancy meeting you here."

Billy said to Ellie, "Come on. Let's go the long way." They turned around to leave the bridge the way they had come up, but found to their dismay that they couldn't. Two of Russell's moronic goons, Aaron Beck and Dave Mere, were blocking the access from that side too. They were trapped. Billy could take a beating, he supposed, but knowing them, they'd smack Ellie around too. He wasn't about to let that happen.

"Maybe you can swim for it," said Russell, guffawing. His two lackeys on the other side of the canal joined in, laughing on cue.

Billy had fleetingly considered that very thing, but it would knacker the iPad in his bag and it would be freezing in there. And it wasn't the cleanest looking canal he'd ever seen, either. And no doubt the three imbeciles would follow them along the canal paths and not let them climb out. So instead, Billy said, "Let us pass, Russ. You got yourself into detention, not me."

"Bull," shouted Russell. "I'd never have got stuck in there if it wasn't for a freak like you in class. Why don't you just leave school? Nobody wants you around. Better still, why don't you just kill yourself, Billy? Save me the bother of doing it for you."

Ellie squeezed Billy's hand. She was getting a bit panicky now. Behind them they could hear Aaron and Dave walking up the wooden footbridge ramp, chuckling to themselves. Russell had climbed off his bike and dropped it to the ground and was walking up his side of the bridge as well. They were trapped.

"I see you still have your charming bedside manner," said Billy.

He figured he might as well be rude to him. He was going to get thumped no matter what happened. But how could he spare Ellie from a beating as well? He was running out of options. He had to think fast. What would a somviator do in a situation like this, he wondered? Vaporise them with that silly ray gun, was the obvious answer. Shame it wasn't real.

Billy quickly eyed up Russell's physical appearance. He had a big head. Wide shoulders. He must do weights. Biceps were pretty well developed too. Skinny waist, though. Narrow hips. Even skinnier legs. He suddenly had an idea of how to get out of this.

"I'm not killing myself, Russ. Well, only killing myself laughing at you, you dim-witted chimp. You know, you look quite like a chimp, when I think about it. Maybe an orangutan is more apt, given that ginger barnet of yours."

"Keep talking, Twigg," yelled Russell, starting to get riled up. "These are your last words, pal, so make them count."

"You like beating up younger kids, don't you? Makes you feel like a real big man, right?"

"I like beating up kids of any age," snorted Russell. "Or men. Or women. I don't dezcriminant."

"Wow, that's a big word, Russ. You almost got it right too. How long you been trying to learn that? Let Ellie go. She's got nothing to do with it. This beef is between the two of us."

Russell stopped walking and looked at Ellie and Billy's hands, clenched tight together, and said, "Aw, ain't that sweet. True love. Look, boys."

Aaron and Dave had stopped too. Aaron, a very tall and lean kid the same age as Russell, called back, "Yeah, Russ. They're so in love. I think I'm going to puke, ha ha!"

"Come on Russ," said Billy. "Leave her out of it."

"You know what? I think I won't leave her out of it," said Russell, enjoying the mental torture. "I think I'll teach her that she needs to stop hanging out with a nerd like you and start over with a man like me. Maybe she needs a good slap to bring that home to her."

Aaron chipped in from the other and said, "Yeah, Russ. Way to go."

Russell continued, "Maybe she wouldn't be so keen on you if she knew about you and . . . Laura?"

There was a moment's silence. Ellie turned to Billy, confusion adding to the look of terror in her eyes. "Who's Laura?" she whispered.

Russell answered before Billy could. "He called her name out in class today, Ellie. Called it out in his sleep, ha ha. 'Pillow talk' they call that, don't they?" The three pursuers laughed, enjoying the lull before the imminent takedown of Billy Twigg and Ellie Roundtree, the school weirdos.

Ellie looked hurt and confused. She and Billy weren't an item or anything. They didn't go out with each other in that way. They were mates. But she had, perhaps wrongly, assumed that it would develop into something more serious over time. Now she wondered if she'd been silly to think that way.

Billy squeezed her hand and whispered, "LAURA is a computer, Ellie. I'll tell you about it later. When we get out of this fix." He squeezed her hand again, reassuringly. She gave him a slight, nervous smile back. He then whispered to her, "I've got a plan. When I shout 'top heavy,' hunker down into a ball on the deck, okay?" Ellie frowned, looking really scared and confused, but nodded to signal that she would.

"So, Russ, tell me what happened. All those years ago. How did it unfold?" said Billy.

"What?" said Russell. "What are you talking about, you freak?"

"I was just wondering how you became such an insecure, pathetic waste of air. What's the story? Mummy not love ikkle Russy baby?"

Russell's face darkened as if a thundercloud had slid over it. "You leave my mum out of this," he shouted, starting to walk purposefully toward Billy and Ellie again. He cracked his knuckles and snarled.

"Poor Russy. No mummy love," goaded Billy again. "It's quite the sob story. Did daddykins beat you? Maybe with his belt, yes? Or maybe you had an uncle who loved you just a little bit too much? In a wrong sort of wa—"

"That's it," screamed Russell, breaking into a run. "You're dead, Twigg."

Russell was really moving now, sprinting up the gradually levelling incline of the footbridge's curved span. Billy had seen Russell fight numerous times before, and this time it looked like he was going to go for a flying head-butt to start with. Perfect. Billy let go of Ellie's hand. She was standing next to him, visibly shaking. "Almost there," he murmured.

"You know what you are?" shouted Billy. Then Russell was upon them, springing off his right foot, fists clenched by his sides, leading with his head.

"Top heavy!" shouted Billy, immediately crouching down. Ellie dropped down beside him too. Billy saw everything unfold in slow motion. He looked up. Russell was airborne and staring down at him, a look of pure hatred morphing into a look of bewilderment. When Russell's chest was above him, midflight, Billy thrust upward, pushing Russell's body up and away from himself with both hands, while twisting slightly to his right. It took surprisingly little effort. Russell's forward momentum and top-heavy body mass were redirected over the side railing of the bridge, and he quite elegantly sailed over it in complete silence.

Time returned to its normal speed again. Billy stood on the bridge, watching Russell plunge five metres headfirst, arms still by his side. A dozen or so ducks fled noisily in every direction as the bully splashed into the murky water below. Billy couldn't contain an incredulous laugh. He'd just thrown Russell Bates, the hardest kid in Snotton, off a bridge.

"Russsssssell," screamed Aaron, disbelief in his voice. He ran to the railings and looked over. His great leader was flapping about in the water with gooey green water plants stuck to his face. He still hadn't said anything, apparently too shocked by what had happened, and far too busy trying to get himself to the side.

Billy bent down and offered Ellie a hand up. She took it, rose to stand next to him, and peered over at Russell. Then she burst into nervous laughter too. She said to Billy, "How did you do that? You moved so fast."

"I'm not really sure. It's kind of to do with my dre—"

"Look out!" shouted Ellie. "Behind you."

Billy spun around to find Aaron towering over him. Right

arm raised high and pulled back. Fist clenched. About to swing. Quick as a flash, Billy kicked Aaron as hard as he could between the legs. Aaron crumpled like a high-rise building demolition—straight down. He curled up into a tight ball and began whimpering like a baby.

"Let's hope that takes you out of the gene pool," quipped Billy. He then looked over to Dave, but he was backing away with his hands up in the air, as if Billy was pointing a gun at him. "Go home, Dave," said Billy.

Stunned into silence, Dave managed to nod back.

"And Dave," added Billy. "Choose better friends."

He then turned back to Ellie and said, "We'd better go. You all right?" He took Ellie's hand again and led her down the south side of the bridge. When they reached Russell's bicycle lying on the ground, Billy stamped hard on the back wheel a couple of times, breaking some spokes and severely buckling the rim. It would be unusable until the wheel was changed.

Billy and Ellie stepped off the bridge and turned and walked along the canal side, heading for their street. On the other side, Russell had managed to clamber out and was lying on the towpath, covered in slimy green weed, spluttering and shivering.

After a few minutes of silent walking, the euphoria of not being pulverised by Russell Bates was ebbing away for both of them. Ellie was beginning to feel decidedly uneasy. She took her hand out of Billy's and looked at him as they walked. She was thinking the same thing Billy was. That fight could have been deadly for Russell. What if he'd drowned? What if he'd hit the side of the canal rather than land in the water? What if he'd hit his head on an underwater object?

After a moment she said, "Who are you, Billy Twigg?"

Sadly for Billy, he wasn't entirely sure anymore.

— TWELVE —
Sygma Awakens

Typhon snarled at the approaching polar bear, a lopsided grimace that bared a scattering of black, broken teeth. He had sensed the bear following him many hours ago when it first picked up his trail. The bear was female, and hadn't eaten for many of Earth's day and night cycles.

The tall, thin humanoid sensed the bear's muscles tense before she sprang forward. She was about fifty metres away when she broke into a lolloping, ungainly run, head low and a steely look in her eyes. Rather than flee, Typhon faced the creature head on, bracing himself for the kill. He stooped over slightly as if to gather up some unseen force and then thrust himself upright, arms outstretched, a low growl emanating from his cracked lips. Then his black eyes rolled backward and exposed flaming hot orbs that glowed like melting pools of lava.

Behind Typhon, the nine tattered strips of fabric that formed his Sygma cloak leapt into life, the billowing material transforming into a thick mass of churning black gas. It streamed forward, flowing over and around him, as he pulled and pushed against the smoke with outstretched fingers like a mad orchestra conductor. He steered and manoeuvred the increasing mass of dark energy toward the rapidly advancing bear.

Typhon roared and narrowed his flaming eyes to stare in wonder at the sight before him. The once great bear was enveloped within Sygma's swirling death shroud, her twisting form disappearing into the churning mass with a horrifying crunching sound. He looked up and saw a shimmer of lightning ripple through the growing storm above him, as if emboldened by the bear's demise.

Quickly the smoke tentacles calmed and slid back along the ice toward the withered man in black. He was leering skyward, with his head tipped back and his arms pointing to the rolling mass of clouds high above him. His eyes rolled forward in their sockets to shield the inferno that dwelled within them, as Sygma's limbs thinned out and returned to form the billowing shredded cloth cape.

The polar bear's oversize footprints stopped a few metres in front of Typhon. Where she had once been, black ash was blowing away into the Arctic squall. He let out a sigh of pure pleasure, opened his eyes and turned south again to continue his walk.

Far behind him in the snowy vastness, two bear cubs mewed pitifully for their mother, sensing that something had gone terribly wrong with her hunt. Who would love and protect them now? Typhon felt their grieving and fear too. He soaked it up, feeding the darkness that infused his twisted, ancient frame.

— THIRTEEN —
You Got Mail

Dinner was a subdued affair. The late afternoon's events were playing on Billy's mind. He'd found it surprisingly easy to dispense with Russell and his cronies. But it had been completely out of character—and totally unplanned. He tried to imagine what would have happened had he not dreamt of being a somviator earlier that day. Would he have got beaten up? Would Ellie have too? Did his newfound toughness come from his dream of being a somviator? Was Sal right? Had something been awakened in him? Maybe. That was about all he could surmise. Maybe.

As soon as he'd arrived home and his mother had asked how his day had gone, he'd lied and told her all the usual stuff about his lessons, but had omitted the parts about falling asleep in class, his subsequent detention, and throwing a boy off a bridge. It was at times like these that he was glad to be an only child and not have a kid brother or sister to come barging in and tell his parents otherwise. Not that he'd ever had times like these before.

After the evening meal, Billy told his mum and dad that he had some homework to do, and that he was also going to try out some new code on his Raspberry Pi computer for an upcoming computer studies class. He said he'd pop back down at suppertime for the obligatory cheese and crackers bedtime nibble. They seemed fine with that.

When he got upstairs to his bedroom, Billy dressed his desk to look like it was messy with homework assignments and then lay down on his bed and began surfing the web on his iPad. He was looking up medical conditions whereby people might fall asleep and hallucinate nonsense.

He came across narcolepsy, a condition that can hit kids his age. But his symptoms seemed way worse than those. Then there were ailments that strike when people get much older, such as dementia, and things to do with low blood pressure, emotional trauma, and diabetes. But nothing quite fit the bill for what he was going through.

Next he image-searched the term *aliens*. There were a lot of photos and a lot of rubbish out there. An unbelievable amount. From eyewitness drawings to fake autopsy videos and numerous shots from Hollywood's finest efforts. He'd figured Sal's physical appearance must be influenced by a movie or comic book he'd seen somewhere once—even if he couldn't remember it. But he found absolutely nothing that even came close to the alien from his dream.

After a couple of hours of fruitless searching and pondering and worrying, his thoughts were disrupted by his mum shouting up the stairs. "Suppertime. Come and get it before your dad eats it all."

"Coming," he called back. He was about to put the iPad down when he had another thought. "Just a couple of minutes, please," he shouted down the stairs.

Billy quickly Googled, "what is moon made of?"

It turned out not to be cheese. Instead it was comprised of the same stuff as the Earth. So not very exciting. No mystical dream stones or hallucinogenic crystals. However, it had apparently been heavily bombarded by asteroids and suchlike four billion years ago. Any manner of foreign content could have hit it, he supposed. Or maybe there had been something in the Hex-27 comet that had collided with it at the beginning of the year? Oh what did he know? He had no idea. He was clutching at straws and getting nowhere. He tossed the tablet to the end of the bed and got up.

Billy joined his parents in the lounge. They were watching the news and doing their usual moaning at politicians and shaking their heads at the latest world atrocity. What was it with parents and always watching the news? It only made them mad. Why did they bother?

On the coffee table were a few cracker biscuits, pickled onions, and chunks of mature cheddar—anything involving cheese was a Twigg supper essential and pseudo-religious affair in their household. Next to the plate was an envelope carrying a bank logo, addressed to Billy.

He carefully stepped over the large slumbering dog on the floor and took a seat on the couch. "What's this?" he asked, pointing at the envelope.

"Oh, sorry," replied his mum. "Forgot to give you that earlier. Came this morning. Looks like your statement."

Billy was immediately suspicious. All his banking was done online. He didn't get statements in the post. It wasn't as if he had a high cash flow. He had pocket money going in and wages from his Saturday job. That was it.

He tore open the envelope and read the enclosed letter. It wasn't a bank statement. Statements didn't have large text in red ink. It was a letter informing him that his bankcard had been rendered inactive. A new one was being issued and was on its way to him in the mail. Apparently, his old card had been either copied or stolen by crooks and used to make a withdrawal in Australia a few days ago. It blabbed on about how card copying was a common crime and that they were combating it with several initiatives, but he had stopped reading by then.

Billy turned pale and put down the cracker he was munching

on. His mother noticed. "Are you okay, love?" she said.

"Uh, yeah, yeah, fine," lied Billy, his mind racing at the ramifications of what this might mean. "My, uh, ATM card's been copied, and they're sending me a new one."

"You need to be more careful with your money. Thieves everywhere. Just look at these clowns," his father mumbled through a mouthful of cheese and biscuits, while gesturing at the television.

But Billy wasn't watching. "I'm really tired, guys," he said. "I'm off to bed. Thanks for supper. Good night."

His mother gave him a strange look and checked her watch. His father barely noticed.

Billy climbed the stairs while whispering to himself. "It could be just a coincidence . . . it could be just a coincidence . . . it could be just a coincidence . . ."

Once back in his bedroom, an incoming message alert on the iPad's mail icon caught his eye. He pushed it. Up sprang a "downloading video" notification; under it a blue pie chart slowly filled up and then a video appeared. It was the clip of Billy operating the ATM machine in Sydney—from his dream. A time and location stamp in the corner said it was on Bent Street at 4:14 p.m. on Saturday. Under the video was a short message. It read: "Proof of transference, Billy!!!"

He looked up to the email sender's address: sal@starplucked.cafe.

Billy ran to the bathroom and threw up his cheese and crackers.

— FOURTEEN —
America Calling

"Are you seeing the same figures?" barked Robert Dyson down the phone. He waited, listened to a reply, then continued. "No, no, no, I've checked the data, and it's accurate. Nippon number twenty-two was the originator, but I've pulled up readings from seventeen and eighteen, which are in the vicinity. They confirm the information to be accurate, albeit from a less reliable vantage point."

Robert paused to listen to a further reply. "Uh-huh. Well, I don't care if he's asleep. Wake him up, goddamn it. This is important. Get him to phone me back ASAP. *Sayōnara.*"

Robert slammed the phone back into its cradle and slumped back into his chair with a frustrated sigh. For the first time in as long as he could remember, he was genuinely stumped. After a tip-off from a TV network, he'd spent the entire day chasing crazy meteorological data centred on the North Pole.

Japanese satellites had recorded weather anomalies that were quite simply impossible: huge drops in temperature, an impossibly fast tornado, and a growing storm cloud that was now starting to look like a hurricane.

The problem was that several different satellites corroborated the information, meaning that either they had all malfunctioned at the same time or there really was something weird going on in the Arctic. To compound things, the Japanese were not being very cooperative—hence Dyson was still at work well into the evening, chasing a lead that nobody else wanted to touch.

The desk phone rattled and let out a shrill ring. Dyson grabbed it immediately. "*Konnichiwa.* Is somebody there finally going to listen to m—"

"Good evening, Mr Dyson. My name is Agent Entwistle of the CIA," said a no-nonsense, but very polite American male voice. "I wonder if I may speak with you, sir? I apologise for the late hour of my call, but it's regarding an urgent US national security matter. Are you alone, sir, and at liberty to speak?"

"Uh, okay Mr . . . um, Agent Entwistle," replied Dyson, completely taken aback. "Yes, I'm alone and can talk."

"Excellent. Thank you. We've picked up some chatter that indicates you have found something inexplicable in the Arctic Circle today. Is this the case?" asked Entwistle, getting straight to the point.

It most certainly was. Dyson went on to extol his amazing meteorological abilities throughout a fifteen-minute synopsis of his day, Entwistle interjecting just enough *I sees* and *how clevers* to keep Dyson babbling like a brook. By the time he'd finished, Dyson had told him everything he knew and emailed him twenty megabytes of data and satellite imagery to back up his claims.

When Dyson finished his report Entwistle said in rather dramatic fashion, "The United States of America thanks you for your cooperation," and rang off.

— FIFTEEN —
Land Ahoy

Having walked for several hours to stretch his legs that had been idle for so long, it was now evening, and the earlier blustery weather had subsided. Typhon was gliding a few metres above the ice, its surface bathed in low-lying sunlight that cast enormously long shadows from even the smallest of undulations and protrusions.

At this time of year the Arctic Circle experienced no nighttime, the sun never sinking below the horizon. The opposite would be in effect in a few weeks, though, dipping the top of the world into perpetual darkness for several months.

Typhon liked the idea of continuous darkness. It was, after all, what he was going to implement on this ridiculous planet himself. He looked forward to completely smothering it, and watching its life ebb away.

But to reach that point by walking about its surface would take years. And besides, the planet's surface was mostly composed of water; so flying was going to be a necessity anyway.

Behind him the sky was gravely dark, crimson lightning cracks and thunder claps heralding his progress. As he moved south, the storm expanded behind him—his position forming the circular storm's radial distance. The shadow staff he'd pushed into the North Pole a few hours earlier formed the Storm of Shadow's epicentre. The farther away he traversed, the farther the storm expanded.

When he reached the South Pole, Earth would be engulfed in

complete darkness. Plant life would be dead in three or four weeks. Animals would starve to death a few weeks after that. The planet would be cleansed. Then Typhon would be free to search for the Remnant Stone unimpeded, although he himself would not be able to detect its peculiar radioactive biorhythms. Instead he would rely on *Nightshade's* advanced scanners to seek out the stone's weak life force.

He realised he had to find it this time or face the wrath of his father—an encounter he would most likely not survive. He'd barely escaped with his life after their last altercation—hence his present physical appearance. Being cast into a dying star will do that to you.

Typhon squinted his black eyes. A habitation was coming into view, the faintest blobs of light reflecting off windows and metallic objects in the extreme distance. It would be the first to fall, and soon the human detritus would bear witness to his wrath.

— SIXTEEN —
The Evidence

The knock at the door of the White House Oval Office was met by an immediate "Come" from within.

Agents Ramone and Entwistle entered, closing the curved door quietly behind them. They walked in reverently and stopped dead centre in front of the huge, solid oak Resolute Desk. They looked like twins in all but skin colour—Ramone's a healthy, sun-kissed Hispanic shade, while Entwistle's was a slightly sickly, pallid, Chicago-Irish hue.

They both wore identical service issue black suits and complementing brogues. The lights in the president's office had been deliberately dimmed, so that President Mitch Swanson could look out at the night sky. He was standing at the windows just to the left of his chair, looking out at the moon through the six-inch thick bulletproof glass.

"She's a real beauty tonight, isn't she, boys?" said the president. "We owe her a lot too. None of us would be here today had it not been for our beautiful celestial partner. She stopped that comet from hitting our planet and killing us all. Come take a look. See, she's a blood moon tonight. The red umber comes from an effect called Rayleigh scatter—"

"Excuse me, Mr President," said Ramone, clearing his throat nervously. "We have something important here you need to see."

Just then, the door swung open and chief of staff Reggie Watson almost fell in, clutching a bunch of loose paper files. He had a pen in his mouth and was trying to talk into a cell phone at the same time. "Gotta go, Walt," he mumbled. "We're going to brief him now." He fumbled over to a couch by a small coffee table and slouched down, exhausted, files spilling everywhere. "Damn things weigh a ton," he muttered. "And of course they were miles away, about seven floors below us. Why can't they just digitise this stuff?"

Agents Ramone and Entwistle regarded each other for a moment before Ramone piped up, "The Internet, sir. The less these files can be transmitted electronically, the better. Safer to keep it old school. Avoid another Snowden."

"Ahem," came the voice of President Swanson. "Did I miss a meeting? I am here, you know? Last time I checked, this was, in fact, my office. Unless I missed an election?"

"No, sir. Sorry, sir," replied the two agents almost in unison. Reggie Watson mimed the word *sorry* and began to tidy up the files.

The president raised an eyebrow and smiled wryly. "So, what's up, fellas?"

"We think he's returned, Mr President," said Ramone somewhat hurriedly. "We think he's come back to Earth. It's not good, sir."

The president frowned. "Who's 'he'?" he said, losing at little of the cool public demeanour he was renowned for.

"Climate anomalies were picked up by the Brits looking at Japanese weather satellite data twelve hours ago. Our boys then retasked NASA satellites and hacked everybody else's in the region. They show a craft landing in the Arctic Circle, dropping off a passenger and taking off again. It's currently in a low geostationary orbit over the pole. What's causing immediate concern is the abnormal storm that is developing up there. It's moving south, spreading evenly in a precise circle, centred on the North Pole. The passenger was walking south toward Europe, but seems to have speeded up in recent hours, so must be now utilising a vehicle of some kind. The storm is, uh, ahem, well sir, the storm appears to be following him—expanding to match his position."

President Swanson looked confused. "What have you boys been smoking? What craft? What passenger?"

"Uh, Mr President," interjected Reggie. "Remember those classified files you were given to read over when you took office? The ones pertaining to extraterrestrial life?"

"Oh, come on, Reggie, I didn't read that nonsense," replied President Swanson. "I don't go in for practical jokes, as well you know."

The three men stared impassively at the President. Reggie said, "I wish you had, sir."

"What? You're going to tell me extraterrestrials exist now? Come on, don't waste my time," said the president.

Reggie opened the top file in his lap and took out a photograph. He stood up and walked it over to the president's desk and placed it there, turning on a desk lamp as he stepped back. President Swanson took a step forward and looked at it. His hairline slid back half a centimetre and then rolled forward again. He took an unsteady step to the left and sat down heavily in his tan leather swivel chair.

"This was taken in New Mexico on July eighth, 1947. Commonly referred to as the Roswell incident," said Reggie, pointing to the black-and-white image on the desk. The picture was large and very distinct. It wasn't fuzzy or grainy like the type you find on the Internet. It was crystal clear, sharp, and in focus. In it, a massive, saucer-shaped craft lay partly submerged in the dirt. The front half of it had crumpled after a huge impact and had been torn to pieces.

Reggie put more photos on the desk, some taken on

Kodachrome colour stock. In one photo the craft looked to have slid about five hundred metres, carving a wide ditch into the earth. Broken and bent metal pieces were scattered all around. Smoke could be seen wafting out of the main hull and numerous small craters.

In another colour photo taken from the air, the mangled bodies of humans and peculiar, multi-limbed green animals wearing silver suits could be seen lying around the forward impact crater, as if they had been flung out during the crash.

President Swanson picked up a glass of mineral water on his desk and shakily took a sip.

"I thought you'd taken it all pretty well when you took office, Mr President. I guess that explains it if you didn't read these," said Reggie, gesturing to the stack of files.

"I . . . I had no idea," mumbled the president. He pointed to one of the green creatures in the photo and said, "They're really here? We have these creatures in confinement somewhere, right? I want to see one right away."

Entwistle glanced at Ramone and then spoke for the first time. "One alien creature survived, Mr President. Four others were killed in the crash. Plus five dead human crew. We have their bodies in the Nevada facility. Some of the spaceship parts are there too. Unfortunately, the surviving alien escaped in 1977, sir."

"Escaped?" whispered President Swanson. Reggie Watson flicked through some more files and deposited a few more photos on the president's desk, as if to annotate the agent's description. They depicted unsteady, hurriedly taken photos of a smaller disk-shaped craft flying off into a summer sky.

"That's correct, sir," continued the agent. "She had been helping us build a test vehicle—reusing some parts from her original ship. She had convinced us that she was an affable creature. Convinced us that she was perhaps a little slow-witted, sir. Anyway, she had us complete enough of the ship to make it functional and then, when we were least expecting it, she stole it and took off. We never saw her again. All that's left of her is a severed arm that she lost in the crash. It's in the Groom Lake facility too. Back in the 1940s, our medical knowledge was too poor to reattach it for her."

"Riiiiight, so let me get this straight. A UFO crashed in the New Mexico desert seventy years ago. You captured a one-armed alien who you then helped to escape by building 'her' a new spaceship out of 'her' broken flying saucer? I just want to be clear. Have I left anything out?"

"I wouldn't have put it in quite those terms, Mr President, sir, but, um, yes, we underestimated her abilities and intentions. As an aside, she had three arms remaining. Her species have four upper limbs and two legs. We have thousands of hours of surveillance and interview footage with her, if you'd like to . . . "

President Swanson interrupted Entwistle midsentence. "What was she doing here? What was she called?"

Ramone interjected. "She chose the name Sally, Mr President." He cleared his throat and looked at the Seal of the United States of America emblazoned on the carpet beneath his feet. "We were unable to understand her for many years. Her vocabulary consisted of high-pitched chirps and whistles and, uh, other less harmonic sounds and gestures." He looked back up at the president. "The scientists and psychologists of the day eventually gave her access to a television, in the hope that she would learn to communicate with us. And in 1959 she began to speak English. She watched programmes like *The Debbie Reynolds Show* and *I Dream of Jeannie*. She became especially fond of a show called *Rawhide*—the western series starring a young Clint—"

"Goddamn it, Agent Entwistle, I know what Rawhide is. Get

to the point," snapped the president.

"Sorry, sir. I'm trying to, sir," replied the agent nervously. "Let me cut to the chase. Sally learned to speak English from TV shows and adopted a cowboy twang accent because she became fixated with the show *Rawhide*. It became one of her endearing qualities. As it transpired, all part of a long-term escape plan.

"Anyhow, during the subsequent hours of interviews she did with researchers, she talked about being on a recruitment drive—looking for what she termed 'new somviators.' She also warned us about an entity called 'Typhon.' She described him as a—well, I'm using her words here—'intergalactic pest-controller.' This Typhon sees life forms such as ourselves as we would see mosquitoes or cockroaches.

"Our scientists now have pretty solid evidence that he was responsible for the dinosaur extinction at the end of the Cretaceous Period, sixty-five million years ago. We think this is who may have arrived in the Arctic Circle earlier today, sir."

The room fell silent for several long, awkward seconds. Reggie was the first to speak. "We're sorry, Mr President. We know this must be a lot to take in right now, but we need to act quickly and decisively. We have two spy satellites heading to the Arctic region from the Middle East now, so we should get hi-res visuals very soon. But we have every reason to believe that this single entity, known as Typhon, is currently there. And we believe he is planning another extinction event."

President Swanson stared at the scattered photos on his desk and at the three trusted men around him. *This is complete and utter madness*, he thought. "You guys really aren't kidding, are you?"

"No sir, Mr President," replied Reggie and the agents in unison.

"Well, we'd better get started," said the president after a

reflective pause. "Let's get to the War Room."

"Walt, the secretary of defense, and the rest of the boys are already there, Mr President," said Reggie. "We can join them now."

"In that case we appear to have no time to lose," said President Swanson, standing up. "Let's go."

— SEVENTEEN —
Insomnia

Billy woke with a jolt and sat bolt upright. The glowing alarm clock by his bed read 3:44 a.m. He turned his bedside lamp on and checked he was at home. It appeared he was, so he turned it off again. It was the second time he'd woken up in four hours. He felt exhausted, scared, and most of all alone.

He picked up his smartphone and texted Ellie next door:

Hi. Having terrible night. Don't suppose u r up r u?

He put the phone down and lay back down, staring at his bedroom ceiling, a Taylor Swift poster just visible in the gloom.

Billy was now too wired to sleep properly. He was afraid he'd dream travel to that godforsaken planet again. Plus, his mind was trying to unravel how he had received an email from Sal. She was a dream. He was real. It didn't make any sense at all. Not unless you believed what she had said about transference. But that was impossible dream jibber-jabber and couldn't be real. Right?

I'm a complete nut job, he thought. *What is happening to me? Why am I like this? Why can't I just be normal like everybody else?* He scrunched his eyes shut, made fists, and groaned to himself quietly. "I'm so messed up," he murmured out loud, while punching the duvet.

Just then, his phone vibrated and lit up, shaking him out of his self-loathing. Ellie had texted a reply:

I was asleep until u texted! That'll teach me to not switch it off at night! What's up? U OK?

Billy smiled. He really liked Ellie. She just seemed to "get" him. She was usually around when he needed a friend. She was fun and intelligent. And she was cute too, but also kind of an oddball and a bit weird. He didn't know how he'd have got along these last few months without her to keep his spirits up. He texted a reply:

Usual stuff. Actually, no. Not usual stuff. Things have taken weird turn tonight. Appears funny dreams may not be dreams!!! Think I may be going insane.

Ellie: Cool. R u going to start drooling and shouting out in class?

Billy: Don't I do that already?

Ellie: Oh yeah, you do! Forgot!! U need a new ailment then. Extreme flatulence perhaps? Up the hilarity factor.

Billy: Will work on it! Thanks, I think!! See u in morning. Night. Parp!! Whoops!!!

He put the phone down, rolled on to his side, and stared at his clock—3:57 a.m. Despite being stressed out, fatigue took over, and slowly the red clock numbers smudged and faded, and eventually sleep took him back into its uncertain folds.

— EIGHTEEN —
Bunker Briefing

President Swanson and his entourage, consisting of chief of staff Reggie Watson, the two CIA agents Entwistle and Ramon, plus vice-president Carol Stead, and two armed secret service officers who they'd picked up on the way, swung into the White House War Room. It was a large, grey, boxy chamber buried several floors underground in what was nicknamed "the Bunker"—a reinforced network of offices and accommodation designed to keep the heart of government alive in the event of a nuclear attack from an enemy state or terrorist group.

A long, wide conference table stood in the middle of the room with a couple of dozen chairs placed around it. Each one was occupied, bar three at the top end. Seated around the table were the secretary of defense, various military commanders (representing the army, navy, and air force), war strategists, reconnaissance operatives, intelligence officers, and technical experts from every division of the nation's defence arms.

President Swanson, Vice-President Stead, and Chief of Staff Watson walked around the table and took their seats; whispered conversations amongst the group died down immediately.

"Good afternoon," said the president, taking his seat at the head of the table and depositing a leather folder in front of him. Carol and Reggie pulled up seats on either side of him but remained a few centimetres back from the table, a visual acknowledgement of the pecking order. "I believe we have some business to attend to."

"Yes sir, Mr President," came a unified reply.

"Walt, why don't you kick off proceedings," said President Swanson, nodding to a scholarly looking elderly man down the table. "Reggie's filled me in on the basics. Give us more details."

Walter Albright, an uncomfortable-looking old man with a white beard, stood up from the other end of the desk, using a walking stick for support. He adjusted his thick-rimmed glasses and said, "Yes sir," while picking up a remote control from the table and pressing a button. Enormous flat-screen display units fastened to the walls all around the room illuminated.

"A little over twelve hours ago a British meteorologist by the name of Robert Dyson started making investigations into reports of odd climate conditions in the Arctic Circle," said Walt, eyeballing his wristwatch and pressing the next button on the remote to bring up a satellite image of the polar ice cap. "He'd been tipped off by a UK TV channel weather reporter called Matt Cornish," said Walt, pushing the slide button once again to bring up a still image of the broadcaster in full weather forecasting flow. "He'd come across odd-looking data from the Nippon number twenty-two weather satellite—part of a Japanese funded research progra—"

"Perhaps we don't need quite that much detail, Walt," interrupted President Swanson. Walt was an excellent science officer, but could be too thorough. "Get to the important data, please. We're on the clock."

A stern-looking army general in a jacket emblazoned with medals and colourful ribbons coughed, signifying both his agreement and annoyance.

"Of course, Mr President. Sorry, Mr President," said Walt, pushing the remote button a few times to zip past some apparently superfluous slides. He stopped at a pixelated satellite image showing a black, shard-shaped object pointing downward at the Arctic Circle. "This is a spacecraft of unknown origin descending to our planet," he said matter-of-factly.

"Nonsense! How do you know it's a spacecraft?" butted in the army general. "Could be a bit of space junk. An asteroid. Just about anything."

Unfazed by the interruption, Walt pushed the button and loaded another image onto the screens surrounding the War Room. The shard moved downward. He repeated the action a few times, the view zooming in on each press to follow the shape in a crude animation. The shard started to turn and level out and move across the ice before stopping at what looked like the exact centre of the top of the world. "Space junk doesn't behave like an airplane, General," said Walt, dismissively. "And it certainly doesn't travel upward." At that, Walt continued the slides to show the shape moving back up into space, turning around, and pointing back down to the surface, remaining in orbit. A few murmurs escaped the mouths of some of the assembled staff.

"Could be a Russian experimental plane of some kind," said the general, refusing to be defeated by a pencil pusher.

"I guess it could," said Walt. "But I think you'll find it probably isn't, if you let me continue."

"Get on with it then," snapped the general.

"Cut the man some slack, Jim," interjected President Swanson, directing a beady eye in the direction of the general. "Carry on, Walt."

"Yes, sir. These images come from the Nippon satellite and some other commercial vehicles we hacked into up there. Here we zoom in a little closer. There, see that mark there? That's the start of the weather anomaly. It starts to grow now. Watch closely."

A pixelated cloud was clearly visible at the pole, and it began to spread like a blot of ink with each press of the remote button.

"The time frame here is just a couple of hours. The storm is not a natural phenomenon and quite outside the realm of anything the Russians would be able to do. It's beyond anything humankind can do. Otherworldly, you might say."

"Oh, this is preposterous," said General James Hunter. "You really expec—"

"With all due respect, Jim," said the president sternly. "Shut up. I've been through all this earlier. Aliens exist. Get over it. Walt, proceed."

Some of the assembled defence force specialists gasped and looked around at one another.

"Yes, sir," said Walt, pushing a channel button on the remote. The images on the monitors switched to a video. "This is a live feed from one of our birds over the Arctic. It's just arrived, having been retasked there from a Mideast geostationary orbit. It shows a composite radar, heat signature, and night vision view. Notice the dark figure in the lower right?"

Walt then zoomed in on the shape to make it clearer. The experts around the table gasped in unison. The silhouette of a humanoid figure, arms outstretched, and with some kind of flapping cape trailing behind it, was clearly visible against a green moving background.

"That is an alien occupant deposited by the spacecraft we saw in earlier still images," he said. "Beneath it the green moving surface is ice, as perceived by our satellite's night vision camera. The more astute of you will know that the Arctic region should be in perpetual sunlight at this time of year. The fact that we need to use a night vision camera to see him should indicate to you the denseness of the cloud bank up there, and how it is completely blocking out the sun. And it's only getting thicker.

"We fear we may lose all visuals soon if it continues to expand and strengthen at its present rate. You can see the traveller is moving at considerable speed and, as I can tell from your reaction, you've all noticed it's flying a few feet off the surface."

The people around the table were shaking their heads and muttering amongst themselves, the army general now quiet and subdued.

"Okay, okay," said President Swanson. "I know this is all very shocking for most of you. But really we have no time to waste, people. Quiet down. Walt, where is this thing heading?"

The old scientist pushed some buttons on the remote again, and the image zoomed out until the figure was all but a pixel or two in size. Expanding storm clouds could be seen following him like a volcano's pyroclastic flow. It was an unnerving sight. The image zoomed out farther still, until a small cluster of man-made structures could be seen nestled against the side of a natural harbour, several miles ahead of the alien figure.

"Looks like that's the town of . . . Longyearbyen, in Norway," said Walt, cross-referencing the image against a map on the desk in front of him. "He appears to be aiming directly for it."

"Get me the Prime Minister of Norway on the telephone immediately," barked President Swanson to Reggie, who instantly picked up a red telephone on the desk. "Tell her aides it's an urgent life and death matter. Walt, how long until that thing gets there?"

"Judging by its velocity, I'd say around fifteen minutes, sir," said the scientist.

"Jesus, that's not enough time to do anything," said the president, turning to the head of the air force. "Emmett, sounds like it's over to you. What assets do we have nearby? We need to kill this thing. This Typhon, as he's called."

Heads around the table looked to US Air Force General Emmett Wainwright and then back to Swanson, who cast his eyes around to the room and acknowledged their reaction.

"This thing is very likely a crazed menace called Typhon," said the president. "A one-man holocaust machine, from what I've heard. Although he ain't no man."

He glanced at Reggie and the two CIA agents, Entwistle and Ramone, who were standing in a corner of the room. They nodded sagely.

"This Typhon is here to kill us all, ladies and gentlemen," he continued. "We are now, all of us, all the world, fighting for our very survival."

USAF general Emmett Wainwright, who had maintained a quiet, sombre demeanour throughout proceedings, said, "We have an F-35B Lightning II covertly stationed at a former RAF base in Scotland, sir. I can scramble it immediately. It's about one thousand, six hundred miles away from the target."

He was looking at a tablet computer in front of him, tapping and sliding a finger over a world map scattered with blinking icons.

"Hmm, it's going to take about, let's see now, eighty minutes to get there. Could well be too late to save the town, but we'd get the SOB when we arrive. We won't be able to fly the plane back, though. It'll have gone beyond the point of no return. Best I can do in terms of speed, Mr President."

"It'll have to do," said Swanson. "Make it happen."

He turned to Admiral Kilburn, sitting opposite Wainwright, and said, "Bob, what can the navy do for us in a hurry?"

Kilburn chewed the corner of his mouth and studied his laptop.

"We have the *Abe Lincoln* carrier out on manoeuvres up near Greenland. We can have her set a course for Longyearbyen now. Could launch a plane full of Special Forces from her deck on a long haul, but they'd take, um, about seven hours to get there. Too late for what you need right now, sir."

"Okay. Send them, anyway. We've got no idea what we'll need in seven hours. In fact, send two teams in two planes."

The admiral nodded.

"Mr President, the prime minister of Norway," interrupted Reggie suddenly, passing the red receiver over to him.

"Hello, Prime Minster Hagebak?" said President Swanson, quickly taking the handset from his chief of staff.

"Yes, Mitch. What's going on?" replied the Norwegian prime minister, a note of trepidation in her voice.

"I'm sorry to call at this late hour, Eidi. I have so much to tell you and no time to say it. I swear to you that what I'm about to say is the God's honest truth."

"Okay, Mitch. You're scaring me now."

"Sorry, Eidi. Okay, you need to send everything you've got up to Longyearbyen. There is an alien creature on its way there right now. It's travelling from the north. We're tracking it with a spy satellite now. The only asset we have up there that can be of any use is an F-35 fighter, which we're sending from Scotland now, ETA eighty minutes."

The phone line was silent for a moment before Prime Minster Hagebak responded. "Mitch, when you say alien, do you mean an alien as in an outer space alien?"

"Yes I do, but it doesn't matter. We can discuss all that later. What you have to do is get your air force up there, ASAP. This creature is incredibly powerful and incredibly dangerous. He's creating the storm cloud brewing in the Arctic."

"Yes, we are aware of the peculiar storm activity there."

The president looked up at one of the wall-mounted monitors displaying a map of the region. "Uh-huh, well, that storm cloud has now reached Spitsbergen and shows no sign of abating."

"Mitch, I can't scramble my air force on the crazy whim of the US president. How will that look? Are you sure you're well,

Mitch?"

"Then call it a surprise joint US–Norwegian military exercise, but please do it. Look, Eidi, our F-35 is going to get there in a little over an hour, and when it does, it's going to hunt this monster down and kill it. I'm sorry, but I don't give a damn about whose jurisdiction or air space I'm in. But over an hour is going to be too late to save Longyearbyen. You must have planes closer than ours. You have to get them there."

"Okay, Mitch, okay. You sound sincere. I'll send some F-16s to take a look. But so help me, Mitch, if this is a prank, I'll—"

"No prank, Eidi. I have to go. Good luck." Swanson slammed down the phone and turned to his air force commander. "Emmett, we need to draw up Plan B in case Typhon takes out our plane."

General Wainwright looked unfazed. "Not going to happen, Mr President. That bird is practically indestructible."

"Make the plans, Emmett," said President Swanson coolly. "Make them."

He then stood up and addressed the whole room. "Listen up, people. We need to draw up contingency plans for every eventuality. Imagine that after Norway this thing heads west and keeps going. Imagine he's in DC or Wyoming where your dear old grandma lives. Imagine he's breaking down your children's bedroom door." The president paused for a second. "Get the picture? Right, now let's kill this monster before it's too late."

The room erupted into a hive of activity. People grabbed phones and laptops and frantically began calling colleagues or plotting scenarios.

The president caught Walt's eye. "What's the population of Longyearbyen?"

"About two thousand, sir."

The president sighed. "Sweet Jesus. God help them."

— NINETEEN —
The First to Fall

Typhon approached the old former coal-mining town from the west, a descending gloom following in his wake. The Arctic ice was giving way to a slushy thawing sea the farther south he ventured but was starting to freeze behind him as the trailing Storm of Shadows smothered the light.

He'd detoured out wide to get a better view and was now gliding in via the cove. The coastline was covered in dozens of identical red, green, and yellow wooden cabins, now illuminated by street lighting that wouldn't normally need to be on at this time of year.

He pictured each cabin as a refuge for human vermin and therefore something to be destroyed. "I'll make an example of this festering hive," he snarled to himself.

The emaciated figure came to a halt over an icy street near the waterside, his tattered cape fluttering to a standstill and hanging down to his feet. He was levitating half a metre off the ground and looking up and down the road. There were no people about —no doubt hunkered down for the approaching storm. The only signs of human activity were empty cars and snowmobiles parked along the roadside.

The area was becoming illuminated with cones of light from street lamps attached to wooden telegraph poles that were flickering on all around him. The sky was filling with black, liquidlike clouds.

He pondered where best to begin. He wanted somewhere

public. Somewhere his powers could be demonstrated to maximum effect. Someplace where panic could spread like a cancer.

Just then, Typhon noticed faint music coming from up ahead. It had a kind of tribal beat and was broadcasting from somewhere behind the colourful cabins. He set off, gliding down the street, trying to locate the source of the sound. At a road junction, he took a left turn and travelled silently past another long row of houses, the pulsating musical rhythm growing louder.

After a few minutes of searching, he found the source—a long, low building with a red roof. Outside, it had raised timber decking and a wooden sign that read Mjölnir. Under it was a low-relief carving of a hammer emitting lightning bolts. Ironic, thought Typhon, slowing to a stop across the road from its entrance. The frontage was constructed of large sheets of glass held in place by a thick white wooden frame. Inside were at least a hundred revellers, drinking and cavorting with one another.

Suddenly the music increased in volume as the front door flew open and a big man stumbled out onto the wooden patio. He was holding a bottle of something intoxicating in one hand and trying to set fire to something in his mouth with the other. The bar door eased shut behind him, dulling the music and party sounds once more.

Albrecht wandered forward, burped loudly, and then fell down a short flight of wooden stairs, landing in a pile of snow by the roadside. He swore and then laughed at his clumsiness; that "one for the road" had become four, or was it five? He pulled himself up and opened his trousers to urinate onto the snow, chuckling as he did so.

The drunkard was lifting his head to look up at the weirdly dark sky and take a swig from his beer, which he'd somehow managed to keep hold of in the fall, when he saw a shadowy figure looking at him from the opposite side of the road. He opened his eyes wide and blinked twice, hard.

It looked like some kind of a ghost. It surely can't be, he thought, his urine stream immediately running dry.

Typhon observed the fool for a few moments, as if studying a spider trapped under a glass. So this is a human, he thought. What pitiful creatures. It will be a pleasure to annihilate them.

"What are you?" called out the thickset man, zipping himself back up and staggering backward a step or two. "Hey, Jurgen," he shouted over his shoulder toward the front door of the bar. "You should come and see this weird guy. He's like flying or something."

Nobody inside could hear him because of the club music pumping out of the bar's impressively powerful sound system.

"Hey, Jurgen," he bellowed again, louder, just as the music fell silent between tracks. "Jurgen, you've got to come and see this flying guy."

A moment later the front door swung open again and another broad-shouldered male came out. "What are you talking about, you idiot?" shouted the blond, bearded man, strikingly similar in appearance to Albrecht. He stepped unsteadily out onto the decking and immediately frowned at the unusually dark sky. Then his eyes found Typhon.

"Oh my God. What the hell is that?" he gasped, instantly sobering up and pointing a shaking finger at the floating figure on the opposite side of the street. It reminded him of the angel of death.

"Jesus, Albrecht, get back inside quickly," he pleaded.

"Cool, so you can see it too," slurred his brother, losing his balance and falling forward into some yellow snow. "Get your smartphone out and video it. I bet we can make some money selling it to that DMM news channel, aye?"

Typhon stared at the bumbling men as they argued about whether they should video him or run back inside. He cast his black eyes up to the bar full of partygoers, and then back down to regard the idiotic men.

"Yes, you should video me for your DMM," growled Typhon, speaking perfect Norwegian. "Record the first slaughter. The cleansing."

"What?" said Jurgen, terrified. "I'm recording nothing. What the hell are you anyway? A ghost? A demon? Get away, whatever you are. Albrecht, get up here now."

Albrecht threw his beer bottle toward the floating apparition but it fell woefully short.

Typhon shook his head from side to side very slowly and wagged a bony finger at him, like a parent might do to a naughty child. The sky was continuing to darken. The low sun had disappeared behind thick banks of cloud, making the town feel smothered, claustrophobic, and even colder.

"Record the slaughter of the many . . . or add to their number," said Typhon.

"No way," shouted Jurgen defiantly. "Go back to hell."

He ran down the steps and grabbed his inebriated brother.

The alien sighed. "Always so defiant."

He brought his arms up into the air in an action that summoned Sygma, the dark strips of material fluttering into life once more. They arched over him like talons for a second and then writhed and danced like flames before mutating into tendrils of smoke once again.

Typhon gestured his right hand toward Albrecht, who was still being helped up out of the snow pile. A single thick smoke snake shot across the street and twisted around the fallen man's legs. In no more than a second, Jurgen went from helping his brother up by the arm, to being alone, losing his balance, and tipping over backward.

When he righted himself he could see Albrecht dangling upside down over the street a few metres away, crying out for help. A thick, twisting coil of smoke was holding him by his feet, arching up into the air and back down into the dark figure's shoulders.

"Record the slaughter," demanded Typhon once more. "Record it or die . . . like this."

The smoke rapidly consumed Albrecht's wriggling body like a python eating a rat. Albrecht's screams were quickly muffled as the smoke engulfed him, crushing his body like a beer can—his bones noisily cracking and shattering before completely disappearing into the tumultuous black cloud. It then rapidly thinned out and slithered back into the black creature's cloak, where it writhed like a frustrated beast.

Where Albrecht had once been hanging over the street, a fine dark ash was floating to the ground, discolouring the snow.

Jurgen screamed, "You've killed my brother. You ba—"

"Record the slaughter or meet the same fate," said Typhon firmly. "It's a simple offer. I'll not repeat it."

Jurgen sobbed uncontrollably for a few seconds and then forcibly composed himself. There was no way he was going to be able to fight a foe of such superior power. He had no choice but to agree. For now. But maybe the collective might of the bar crowd could overpower it, or at least maybe they could escape out the back way?

"Okay, okay," he wailed, holding his hands up in a sign of capitulation.

"You have chosen wisely. Go back inside and await me," said Typhon. "Ready your video device. You are to record my actions for the world to witness."

Jurgen's shoulders slumped forward in defeat, and he wiped

away snot and tears from his face. He took out his smartphone, switched on the video camera, and reluctantly climbed the steps back up to the patio bar entrance.

Once inside, and as soon as the door had shut behind him, he jammed a chair against the handle, ran to the music system behind the bar and yanked the plug out of the wall.

"Hey, what are you doing?" shouted the barman, as the music went dead. "You can't do—"

"Shut up. Listen to me," shouted Jurgen. "Albrecht is dead. Some kind of flying creature outside killed him. We have to prepare. It's going to come in here. We must send the women out back. Tell them to spread out and run to the hills and hide. The men should prepare to fight—"

"Christ, Jurgen," shouted the barman. "Have you been smoking your brother's weed again? I think you've had enough for tonight, fella. Go home before I throw you out."

Unperturbed, Jurgen turned to the crowd and shouted, "Ladies, please, you have to leave right now. No time to explain. Get your coats and get out the back way . . . *now.*"

Most of the crowd who could see the bar were now booing Jurgen for turning the music off, but the barman had had enough. He grabbed Jurgen from behind, and the two began to tussle. The crowded pub starting to cheer and shout at the spectacle.

Jurgen turned around and shoved the barman hard against the drink optics. Several large, expensive bottles fell out of their holders and bounced off the bar to smash loudly on the hardwood floor.

The barman heaved back, furious at the drunken fool, and knocked his phone out of his hands. It cartwheeled along the floor and came to rest in amongst some tables and chairs in a corner of the lounge.

Suddenly an enormous crashing sound came from the front of

the building. Everyone turned around in unison to see a terrifyingly tall figure, wrapped entirely in jet-black material, smashing in through the windows and front door, shattered glass and splintered wood flying everywhere.

People screamed and tried to run to the back of the bar, but they were too many in number and rapidly blocked the way through. Some customers nearest the back had fallen over and were now being trampled on by dozens of panicked revellers, who themselves then tripped and fell, causing a large crush of yelling people.

The terrifying black apparition glided into the wrecked lounge area. His arms were outstretched, churning smoke clouds pulsing around his hands, and small crackles of strange red lightning snapping out of each fist. Amongst the broken glass and splintered wood on the floor, the Mjölnir bar sign was spinning on an edge. It slowed and toppled over, displaying the hammer of Thor wooden carving uppermost. Typhon laughed again at this apt portent of doom, and then looked up at the scene of panic and destruction.

Most of the people had tried to run out back and were now caught in a tangle of drunken limbs, fighting to clamber over one another. A few of the men were grouped together in the centre, some of them wielding broken chair legs or pieces of window frame.

At the front, Jurgen gripped a length of wood with a triangle of glass sticking out of the side, like a rudimentary axe, a look of pure hatred in his eyes.

Typhon hissed at the group of men like a demented cat and lowered himself to the floor, assuming a position ready for attack. His stone black eyes rolled backward once more, revealing blazing orbs of fire.

From the back of the bar came a yell and some bottles and

glasses were thrown at him. He batted them away with ease, but during that momentary distraction, Jurgen lunged with surprising vigour, a lot more nimble than his size should have allowed. He swung his makeshift weapon at Typhon, who saw it coming just in time to sway backward but not quickly enough to avoid contact.

The glass blade struck his chest, tearing through layers of material and into his body. Typhon screamed out in pain and shock and glanced down. Black material flapped open on either side of a long, curved gash running down the centre of his chest. Filthy-looking smoke vented out from the dry wound. The torn material looked like thin, patchy black bandages. His whole body was wrapped in the stuff. However, the torn section was now alive with activity, the frayed ends wriggling like bisected worms, intertwining with their severed counterparts to reform and patch the tear.

Jurgen stared at Typhon's bloodless, self-healing injury in astonishment, the tiny pause just enough time for the dark demon to lash out with his right arm. Jurgen's feet left the floor. He was launched through the air and smashed straight through a cracked lounge window, and out into the gloom.

Bolstered by Jurgen's astonishing strike against the creature, the rest of the men screamed in anger and ran forward in a united attack. But before any of them could strike the monster, thick columns of smoke flew forth from it and into the advancing men, snatching at them randomly.

The smoke limbs made short work of defeating them all. It threw the men into the air and then caught and crushed them into nothingness, sounds of crunching bones and screams of despair adding to the terrifying cacophony.

Sygma's nine shadow tentacles then made grabs for the chaotic throng of wannabe escapees at the rear of the building and continued to grab people at an astonishing rate, tossing four or five of them into the air at a time. Within a couple of minutes, the bar was empty, black ash filling the air and drifting to the floor. The room fell eerily silent.

Typhon floated back into the air and scanned the wreckage for movement, but could see none. The bar had been cleansed. It had begun.

He glided out of the broken frontage, turning to look at something on the floor that made him grin, before continuing out into the street below.

On hearing the commotion, some alarmed residents had come out of their houses and were standing, staring at him in shock, a few of them holding up mobile devices or talking into them. He smirked, chose a dwelling at random and flew toward it.

— TWENTY —
Testing Times

Billy woke up again. He didn't feel like he'd slept much at all, and he hadn't moved a muscle. But at least he was at home, because the red digital alarm clock numbers were right in front of him, just as they had been when he'd fallen asleep. He wondered what time it was and tried to focus his eyes on the display. The blurry digits slowly took form. They looked different, though. They didn't form a time at all. They formed a word. They spelled out DANGER.

The word was being displayed on the inside of Billy's helmet. Other alert symbols were flashing around, indicating he had fallen, had been unconscious, was trapped, and was being hunted.

He tried to sit up but found he was stuck fast—trapped lying on his side. He tried to kick his legs and arms but found he could only move his left arm and leg sideways. He panicked and was about to shout out when a familiar voice spoke to him.

"Wake up, Billy," whispered LAURA. "Don't make a sound. Wake up, Billy. Come on."

"I am awake. What's happened? Where am I now?" he asked, his voice trembling. But he knew where he was. He wished he didn't know, but in his gut he knew he was back on Igonosphar IV, being tested in the somviator proving grounds. He appeared to be failing.

"Ssssh, be very quiet, Billy," LAURA instructed. "The meteorgus is just above us. You passed out a few seconds ago, and you've fallen into a fissure in the rock pile. We're wedged in tight.

It's up above, sniffing around for you."

Just then a thick, viscous drool slid down the rock wall and plopped onto Billy's helmet. He could hear snuffling noises above and felt small stones falling onto his suit. A few beams of light were shining into his dark location from above, but flickering in and out as the meteorgus moved about.

Billy looked around as much as he could within his helmet. He was wedged in pretty tight, lying on his right side. It looked like his whole body was in a narrow crevice, about two metres deep. "Okay, LAURA," he said, trying to focus his mind and not panic too much. "How do we get out of here? And why is it looking for me? I thought you said it ate rocks."

"It eats anything, I'm afraid to say, Billy," replied LAURA. "Organic matter—like you—is an added bonus. As for getting out: I've scanned the immediate rock formations. Here, look."

Thoughtfully, LAURA displayed a three-dimensional model of the rock pile they were in onto the inside of Billy's visor, but did so using the dimmest projection possible so as not to give away their exact position to the slavering beast above them. "Pretend you're holding the graphic in your left hand," she whispered. "Twisting your hand about will move the model."

Billy tried what she said, and it worked beautifully. Under normal circumstances he'd have commented on how cool it was, but since a massive planet-eating monster was trying to kill him, he kept quiet. The model could be pinched and zoomed with finger gestures in a similar way to using a tablet computer, only without touching a surface. The three-dimensional model showed his body lying on its side on the floor, with rock walls in front and behind him. At his feet the walls joined together and were blocked, but at his head end there was a thin vertical crack between the boulders that ran all the way through to the outside. A little light was bleeding in.

"LAURA, I need to blast through that crack and get out of here. Give me options," whispered Billy, hurriedly.

"Plotting scenarios," said LAURA. There was a brief pause and then she came back with, "Three rounds fired at the locations I've indicated on the model, followed by an immediate and maximum rocket boot launch could get us free. Probability of success is below forty percent, but best option."

Thankfully, the desintoscram was wedged between his stomach and the rock wall, and so he was able to reach it. The three-dimensional model highlighted three points in the fissure that LAURA said were the optimum targets. "Use the atomiser setting to reduce the stone to sand at these points, and we should be just able to fly through the gap before the rock above collapses. Timing the rocket boots to the shots is going to be crucial, so use the auto-target assistant—marked ATA on the side of your weapon. Then we need to be lucky and not get caught by the meteorgus."

"Okay, I'm going to need to have the rocket boots fired up and ready to go, which means the noise is going to indicate our location to Mr Nasty up there ahead of time. It's going to be tight, like you say, but I think we can pull this off."

"Right you are, Billy."

He held the desintoscram, adjusted the setting to atomiser, selected ATA, and aimed it at the big crack in the rock. On his helmet display, LAURA had overlaid an augmented reality layer that highlighted exactly where he should fire the shots. He aimed at each one and pushed the now glowing ATA button. The gun immediately logged the x, y, z coordinates of the target into its memory banks. Now all he had to do was aim at approximately the correct location, and the desintoscram would make final adjustments so the shot would hit where it was supposed to.

"Okay, LAURA, the targets are locked in. Start up the boots.

As soon as the third blast hits, give me everything we've got and push us the hell out of here."

Billy's rocket boots magnetised together once again and the motors ignited. He aimed at the crack, held his breath, and steadied his hand. There could be no missed shots. It was all or nothing.

Up above the meteorgus had become very agitated and excited. It had heard the muffled whump sound of the boots igniting and had turned around. Moments ago it had suspected that a creature was hidden in between the big boulders, but unable to locate anything, it had moved on.

Now, it leapt back from another rock pile it was investigating and landed with a heavy thud on top of Billy's hiding place, sending more grit and pebbles tumbling onto him. The meteorgus started screeching and scraping at the crevice, desperate to get in.

Billy aimed his weapon at the fracture, lined up the first shot, and mentally rehearsed moving on to the two others.

"Here goes," he whispered.

The three shots fired off extremely quickly. And their effect was immediate. The crack instantaneously exploded into a cloud of sand particles. Billy could see it happening in slow motion, the rocks above giving way to the sudden void under them. LAURA was on the ball though, and had given the boots full throttle before the first shot had even made contact.

Billy felt the immediate g-force push his body down into the suit. The thrust was immense. He flew out of the sand cloud like a jet plane then LAURA cut the power a split-second later. Billy watched the gritty terrain shoot by under him, just centimetres from his face. Then he walloped into the ground and tumbled over a few times before coming to rest lying flat on his back. His boots demagnetised, and his feet flopped apart.

He sat up quickly and asked LAURA to silence the alarm that was ringing in his helmet and turn off all the alert visuals on his visor.

A large cloud of dust was slowly clearing away to reveal the meteorgus. It appeared to be stuck but furiously trying to get to him, its long powerful arms batting off the ground and trying to grip on to something. Luckily the ground there was smooth and offered it no purchase.

As the sand and dust settled, Billy could see what had happened. The meteorgus had been standing directly over them when he'd fired the blaster. Its left foot had fallen straight into the void and wedged itself tight, exactly where he had been stuck seconds earlier.

Bit of a role reversal, thought Billy, standing up and calmly checking his gun. It indicated it had power left to fire one regular plasma shot, and nothing more. He adjusted the ammunition selector to that type.

"I take it we're done here, LAURA?" asked Billy.

"Yes, I think so. You've proven your mettle," replied LAURA, sounding quite pleased with the way things had turned out.

"Before we go, I just have to do something," said Billy, calmly walking over to the meteorgus, which had, as expected, begun to bite chunks out of the heavy rocks that were trapping its foot. He stood as close as he dared, raised the gun took aim, and blew the meteorgus's brains right out the back of its skull, sending a spray of pasty grey material skyward. The giant animal immediately went limp and slumped over the boulders. Dead.

"Good heavens, Billy," said LAURA. "You have a ruthless streak in you."

"Well, the way I see it is this. The meteorgus would have eaten itself free of the boulders in a matter of minutes, and then it would come after me again. You could argue that we'd have been gone by then so I didn't need to kill it. But what if my boots had malfunctioned? What if we had crash-landed back here just after take-off? It would have been after us again, and we'd have been stuck here with one round of ammunition. Better to take it out of the equation now."

"Like I said, Billy. A ruthless streak," said LAURA.

"I prefer to think of it as cautionary and efficient. Come on, let's go. I have an appointment with Sal."

He blasted off into the thick green atmosphere above them, the boot's yellow flames carving a twisting path through layers of cloud as they roared back into space.

— TWENTY-ONE —
The Secret Mission

The pilot, Lieutenant James Randolph, ran from his old, rusty command centre building and into the gloomy evening drizzle, darting across the runway and into an unassuming hangar on the other side of the civilian airport. It still amazed him how the rain here was horizontal, and how often it occurred. Scotland was not the natural habitat for a man born in Bakersfield, California. Still, it was a beautiful part of the world to hang out in for a month, albeit a soggy one.

Machrihanish Airport, on the west coast of Scotland, was a former British RAF base. It was also a former NATO base, ex-home of a Navy SEAL commando unit and, with a three-kilometre long runway, had been an emergency landing strip for the Space Shuttle, should it have ever needed it. Which it hadn't.

Now it was called Campbeltown Airport, hosting small domestic flights to Glasgow. It was a rather dull evolution of a once important and busy military establishment. But it still had a trick or two up its sleeve.

For one, it was the secret home of a single USAF F-35B Lightning II vertical take-off and landing fighter jet—the most advanced military fighter plane in the world.

It was stationed in a modest hangar just south of the two runways and serviced by a small team of undercover USAF personnel who kept to themselves. Their cover was that they were an executive private jet company called Xcelsior Charter, so locals would accept aloofness as par for the course.

They flew a black Learjet 60 in or out every few days to reinforce their cover that bigwig executives of some kind were coming and going, to play golf or sample whisky or some other such baloney. In reality, the plane was bringing in supplies from a USAF base in England or rotating staff in or out. The crews dubbed the assignment the "Tartan Tour," and treated it like a small vacation because nothing ever happened there.

The American powers that be had decided to secretly station several F-35s at strategic points around the world, "just in case." The Scottish one covered Europe, North Africa, and western Russia. If they needed to perform a little covert undercover action of some kind, they could use it, rather than go through official air force channels. It made absolute deniability far easier.

Lieutenant Randolph went quickly through his preflight checks, making sure weapons were stowed safely, fuel was maxed, his anti-grav suit was inflated correctly, various pressures were at optimum levels, and that he was A-OK to go. Everything checked out fine, so he taxied out of the hangar and onto the main runway.

A colleague of his on the ground was radioing the domestic airport tower, pretending to be the pilot of a departing Xcelsior flight, and thus leaving Randolph free to talk with USAF Command back home to find out what was going on.

Apparently, due to the nature of the emergency, he would be briefed in the air. He was given a heading and instructed to get there ASAP.

The F-35 roared westward down the runway toward the Irish Sea and rocketed into the sky. Randolph turned the plane immediately north and aimed it at Spitsbergen Island, in the Svalbard archipelago. He opened up the throttle and accelerated away as fast as he could go. Within seconds he broke through the sound barrier, sending a loud shockwave down to the picturesque sea inlets and Scottish countryside far below.

"Bravo one, Bravo one, this is Yankee-three-eight. Do you read me? Over," said Randolph into his helmet's mouthpiece.

"Roger Yankee-three-eight, this is Bravo one. Proceed to Spitsbergen as instructed. Over," came the reply on his radio.

"Roger Bravo one. Affirmative, heading to Spitsbergen. ETA seventy-seven minutes. Bravo one, what is mission? Over."

There was no reply from USAF ground control.

"Bravo one, Bravo one, this is Yankee-three-eight. Repeat. What is mission? Over."

Still no reply.

"Bravo one, Bravo one, this in Yank—"

"Yankee-three-eight, this is Bravo one. Maintain heading. Transferring you to DC Command."

There was a noise like static interference and then a very recognisable voice came over the intercom. "Am I speaking with Lieutenant James Randolph?"

A pause. "Roger that. Please confirm identity."

"I'm your commander-in-chief. You're talking with President Mitch Swanson."

"Oh gees . . . I mean, yes sir . . . "

"Look, Lieutenant, for the remainder of our conversation, I want you to call me Mitch. I'd like to call you James, if I may. We're just two men having a conversation. You cool with that?"

"Yes, sir."

"Well, we'll try and nullify protocol."

"Yes, sir. I mean yes, Mitch."

"We have a situation brewing in Spitsbergen, James. More accurately, Longyearbyen, the main habitation there."

"I understand."

"Good, good. Okay, James, listen up. Longyearbyen is under attack. Most likely going to be wiped out. We estimate two thousand-plus fatalities."

"I see," said Randolph, feeling his pulse quicken but not knowing quite what to say.

"It is being destroyed by a single individual. Goes by the name of Typhon. I'm not going to go into too many specifics about what he is, because frankly we don't know a whole lot. But what we do know is that he is extraterrestrial in origin . . . "

"Holy cra—"

"Don't interrupt me, son. We know he is extraterrestrial in origin. He is humanoid in appearance, but we think about ten feet tall. He wears black clothing with some kind of a wild cape attached. We know he is extremely dangerous. He has flight ability and appears to be doing so without needing a vehicle. He has control over the weather, and, as I'm sure your radar is showing you, there is an enormous storm system over the Arctic, which has engulfed Spitsbergen. That's his doing."

"Yes, sir, I understand, sir."

"Call me Mitch, son. Are you a family man, James?"

"Yes, Mitch. I have a daughter, Gabby. My wife Helen is expecting our second in November."

"Very good, James. Let's make sure you get home then. Sounds like some folks need you. But be under no illusion, this is a very risky mission you're undertaking. We need you to terminate Typhon. He absolutely must not be allowed to get away from that island and do any more harm. Do you get me, James? He absolutely must not survive. Under any circumstances."

"Yes, Mitch. Thank you for your candour. I understand the mission."

"Good, son. Good. Okay, James, I need to go attend to other matters of state. I'm going to hand you over to General Wainwright for further briefing. God bless you, son."

"Thank you, sir."

There followed brief static interference on the line and then a less familiar voice came on. "Lieutenant James Randolph, this is General Wainwright. How are holding up, son? This must all sound nuts." said his superior officer.

"Good, sir. Thank you, sir," said Randolph, more comfortable to be talking in a formal manner again.

"I'll tell you what we know thus far, Lieutenant. Give you an idea of what may be required of you. But I ain't going to tell grandma how to suck eggs. I see you're one heck of a pilot. Your file says you did a stint with the Thunderbirds display team. Correct?"

"Yes, sir, three years based out of Nellis. Formation flying F-16s. You may have seen me fly at Falcon Stadium during one of the commencement ceremonies. Just as the cadets throw their hats into the air, we fly over, sir."

"I have indeed, Lieutenant. Low-level flying skills may be particularly useful to you this evening."

"Yes, sir. I see."

"You heard the president talk about Typhon. The SOB was attacking a bar in Longyearbyen, the last we saw him, then his goddam storm clouds got denser and obscured our spy satellite's view.

"The cloud is weird stuff. At first we could read thermals through it—follow Typhon via satellite. Now it's thickened up, and we can't anymore. Nothing. Seems to be impenetrable. We basically don't know what the heck is happening up there on the ground, but we have pretty good intel that he is going to destroy the town and kill everyone in it.

"The Norwegian Air Force is sending some F-16s up there now to take a look. They should be getting there about now. They're based much closer than you. Trouble is, the F-16 can't exactly fly slow—two hundred mph is about stalling speed, as you will be aware. And we can't get an Apache chopper up there fast enough, either. Even if we could, the weather would probably ground it. The damn cloud is making it really cold up there. Like winter's arrived early.

"No, Lieutenant, your F-35B is our best bet. You can hover and manoeuvre like a chopper or move fast, like the F-16. We need your bird and your expertise to find this monster and destroy it."

"Yes, sir," replied Randolph, pausing for a moment. "Am I to assume this is a one-way trip, sir?"

"Hell no, Lieutenant," said the general. "Although, I guess that depends on your meaning, exactly. It's a one-way trip for your plane. Once you get there, you'll only have enough fuel to hunt him down for about twenty minutes. Then you'll have to land it at Svalbard Airport, or if worse comes to worst, eject and dump the aircraft. Then we'll come get you. Kill him quick, son, and everything will be fine."

"Yes, sir, General," Randolph replied, now more convinced than ever that he would not be returning to the United States alive.

"One more thing, Lieutenant," added the general. "Fly low. Our lab boys here don't think you should enter the storm clouds at all. They think they'll suffocate the engine and bring you down."

"Roger that, sir."

"Oh, and I almost forgot. Our resident alien expert here, Walt, thinks he might know why Typhon is targeting this particular island. He thinks he's after a very specific target."

"I'm listening, sir."

— TWENTY-TWO —
Hunting the Beast

Two Norwegian Air Force F-16s screamed out of the night sky like banshees, skimming low over the mountains toward Longyearbyen. Tonight's low altitude flying was particularly dangerous because their radars were only working intermittently because of a strange interference pattern, which was breaking up the display.

Radio contact with Ørland Main Air Station had become equally unreliable the farther north they advanced from their base of Bardufoss. At least local communication between the two aircraft seemed to be still working, but to all intents and purposes, they were alone.

Through their canopies the pilots could see the strange and menacing weather front up ahead—an alarmingly solid-looking bank of dense black cloud. Behind them the night sky was crisp and illuminated by the never-setting sun, the gently undulating snowy mountains below them accentuated by the long shadows they cast. Up ahead there was a different vision. The cloud bank was vast and completely obscured the sky, rendering the terrain dark and invisible.

Flying side by side in tight formation, the pilots pushed onward, thousands of hours of flight time experience giving them courage, despite trepidation building in their hearts. Each aircraft was armed with six Maverick air-to-ground missiles and two Sidewinder air-to-air missiles—ready to engage whatever they found.

During a very hurried preflight briefing, they had been shown unbelievable surveillance video provided by the Americans that revealed a bizarre flying man, apparently making a beeline for Longyearbyen.

Suddenly the pilots saw it. An orange glow emanating from behind a row of mountains silhouetted in the distance. As they neared, they began to see flames licking into the air. The two pilots instinctively looked across to each other, clearly alarmed.

The planes flew low and as slowly as possible, banking hard to the left so the pilots could look down at the scene. It looked as if every building was on fire. All the wooden huts, scientific research facilities, port buildings—everything was ablaze. Some structures looked as though they had been torn to pieces, with heavy chunks of roofing tossed into the streets. Cars were overturned like toys, some of them ablaze too.

Only occasional streetlights were working—others flickered randomly. Oddest of all, there was no sign of any people. Not even bodies. Nothing. Just wrecked structures and fires consuming fractured gas canisters and pipes. Both pilots had served as peacekeepers in war-torn parts of the world, but neither of them had witnessed anything like this before.

"Jesus," said Captain Ericksen over the radio. "Where is everybody? Where are the casualties?"

"It's really odd," replied Lieutenant Steffensen. "Everyone's gone. Are you picking up any heat signatures?"

"Nope, I got nothing. Sensors are shot. I'm blind up here."

"Me too. How are we supposed to find a target like this?"

"Keep circling, Lieutenant. We keep looking until our fuel reaches critical."

"Roger that, Captain."

The two planes screamed over the wrecked town in a wide arc, their wingtips almost touching. Typhon watched them from inside a wooden cabin. He was looking up through the gaping hole where the roof had been just moments before. Now the house was a smouldering shell.

Despite the darkness and poor visibility, his keen eyesight could quite clearly make out the shape of two warplanes soaring above the town. *What fun! The humans have sent some toys.*

Moments earlier, Typhon had completed the cleansing, and was still riding high on a wave of euphoria. Everything had begun wonderfully. It had been such good sport. He'd even given them a fighting chance, but they'd failed to take advantage of his generosity. Although the big man who'd lacerated his chest had been a surprising encounter.

He couldn't remember the last time he'd been struck by a hostile. He was getting rusty and would need to take better care. But wait a moment . . . what had become of the big man? Jurgen was his name. He recalled hitting him out of a window but didn't remember Sygma consuming him.

Oblivious to the circling warplanes, the alien floated out into the burning street and began to track his way back to the bar where the massacre had started. After a short search he found it —one of the few buildings not on fire. He levitated outside and replayed the fight in his twisted mind.

There, that was the window. Typhon scanned a broken pane of glass on the gable end of the wrecked bar. He tracked along and down, calculating the flight path Jurgen's body would have taken. There, a pile of snow had been levelled on the pavement, and blood spilled. But there was no sign of a body. *Dammit, he got away. The cleansing was not complete.*

He looked around keenly. A few metres down the street was another small pool of blood. *He's left a trail,* he thought. He glided down to the stain and saw a footprint in it. He seemed to be heading in the direction of a blue van. *Was he hiding in there?*

Typhon gestured one of Sygma's smoke tentacles down the dark street and to the vehicle, whereupon it poured into its engine and immediately caused it to catch fire. A few moments later the whole vehicle exploded, sending fragments of twisted metal and molten plastic across the street. There was no sign of Jurgen. No severed body parts. The van had been empty. Where could he be? He scanned the street again, looking for clues.

Lieutenant Steffensen immediately saw the explosion as he rolled his F-16 around the carnage. It had occurred near a long, damaged, white building. Maybe a bar, judging by the decking and overturned tables and chairs outside it. Then he saw him. A dark silhouette against the frozen ground. Tall and lean, he appeared to be floating beside a burning van. He looked like the character in the American spy satellite video. "Captain, I have a visual. My nine o'clock, sir. Burning car. Figure, um, floating next to it."

"Roger that, Lieutenant. I see him too. That's our guy. I'm locking on a Maverick now."

The underside right wing of Captain Ericksen's F-16 lit up as a missile engine ignited and tore away. It arced downward at tremendous speed and exploded in a monumental fireball directly where the figure had been. The planes flew out of the area, turned and flew back in to survey the damage.

Typhon was completely cocooned in the Sygma cloak. Fortunately for him, it had sensed the threat and instantaneously enveloped him in its nine layered strips to form an impenetrable protective sphere. The blast had barely moved him, but had destroyed everything immediately around him. The cape then opened and returned to his back. He was now floating over a street-wide crater, the mangled remains of the van lying at the bottom. Any telltale signs of where Jurgen might have gone were now obliterated. Enraged, Typhon rose high into the air, looking for the aircraft.

The two F-16s flew back over Longyearbyen, tipped at an angle again so the pilots could look at the target area. There was a flaming crater where this so-called Typhon had once been.

"I think we have a strike, Captain," said the younger of the two men.

"Maybe Lieutenant, but let's not be too . . . Jesus, he's directly ahead of us."

The planes separated and narrowly avoided colliding with the enraged alien, who was now hovering a hundred metres above the town. As the planes sped past him, Typhon spun around and fired two Sygma smoke trails straight at them. The columns of black smoke separated and chased after the two F-16s, catching them both after only a couple of seconds. Before the pilots had a chance to react, Sygma punched directly into both jet engine exhausts, immediately choking and shutting down their Pratt & Whitney turbofans, and shorting out all the planes' electronics.

The pilots screamed into their radios as their aircraft plummeted into the foothills south of town and exploded. The detonating ordnance and fuel tanks created an enormous flaming mushroom cloud that rolled skyward. When it reached the storm front overhead, it was absorbed into the blackness, faint bloodred lightning crackles momentarily illuminating the cloud from within.

— TWENTY-THREE —
Rules of the Game

Billy swept up and over the Balta asteroid, around the enormous Star-Plucked Café neon sign a couple of times, and descended in front of the airlock. As he touched down, he noticed for the first time that there were scorch marks already scarring the rock. They looked old and established.

He pushed the big door button and went through the entrance procedure. The inner door hissed and clanked open, and he strode in purposefully, twisting his helmet off and uncoupling his gloves as he went.

Sal was sitting in a booth looking at him. It was the same one he'd woken up in a few hours before. The jukebox was turned off and the room was silent and dimly lit. She was holding an e-reader in one hand, the screen glow highlighting the underside of her chubby face.

"How you diddling, Billy?" she said. "I'm mighty glad to have you back. LAURA's told me how you got on. Pretty creative thinking down there. Bold, even."

"It was a bit touch-and-go to be honest with you. And LAURA helped me out lots. But I'm back here in one piece. Oh, that reminds me, I need to charge this up," he said, pulling out his depleted desintoscram and expertly twiddling it around in his left hand.

Sal pointed to a wall unit at the end of the carriage.

"Thanks," said Billy. He strode over and found an empty rack mounted on the wall to the left of the airlock door. It was pretty obvious by the shape of the moulded trays what he was to do. He pushed his depleted gun into a charging bay. It slotted in snugly and then made a small beeping sound. Tiny red lights along the muzzle began to flash in a repeating sequence, acknowledging the weapon was charging. He walked back and slid onto the bench opposite Sal. There was another tall glass full of raspberry milkshake on the table.

"Have a drink, honey," she said. "It'll refresh you."

Billy took a huge swig of the pink drink, downing three-quarters of it. He smacked his lips and wiped his mouth with the back of his hand.

"I feel better for that," he said, "and oddly invigorated by the whole experience. Don't get me wrong. It was very frightening, especially toward the end there, but . . . I dunno, I think I'm just riding the glad-to-be-alive adrenalin wave at the moment. Normal service will resume shortly, and I'll probably burst into tears or something."

"I don't think so, Billy Twigg," said Sal slowly. "I think you're a bit of an odd fish, right enough. And you can't talk the talk. But you sure as heck can walk the walk."

"I beg your pardon?" replied Billy, confused.

"Ha, there you go again. What I mean is, you don't seem to have no clue what you're doing, son, yet somehow you instinctively do exactly the right thing. I don't know quite what to make of you. Ain't never seen a candidate like you before. You sure you ain't got military training, sonny?"

"I'm thirteen, Sal. The nearest I get to military training is through my Xbox."

"Hmm, well, whatever you got going on in that little Earthling noggin of yours, it's untamed somviator material through and through. You performed outstandingly down there, kid. I mean it. I applaud you."

Billy beamed. "Just lucky, I guess."

"Nope, I don't think so," said Sal, scrutinising his facial features. "I think you're one tough hombre under that silly posh English kid veneer of yours."

"Excuse me, I'm not posh."

"See, I rest my case!"

They burst out laughing, both happy the test was over and that Billy had performed so well. Sal was also mocking his accent (somewhat hypocritically, given her linguistic skills), while he was just laughing at the absurdity of the whole experience. Whatever that was. What was real? What wasn't? Did any of it really happen? If so, did it matter at all? His mind boggled.

Eventually, their laughing fit died down, and Billy ventured, "So, tell me how you emailed me on Earth. In the real world? And don't just say 'transference' and go all mystical on me."

"Heh, heh. Okay, Billy. Well, I just kind of willed it into being . . . just like that," said Sal, loudly snapping the fingers on her three hands and grinning mischievously. "I wrote the message, and I have your email address, but up here in the back of beyond, I'm too darn far away from Earth to be connected to your interwebbery thing so can't really send an email.

"Instead, I willed it there. Imagined it right into existence and right into your inbox. It's how I kept tabs on you in Sydney too— by imagining I was picking up digital camera surveillance feeds. Interwebbery stuff works particularly well. There's nothing physical there, you see? Just electrical impulses. You'll learn that ability in time too."

"Wow, just like that? You make it sound so easy, but it's not, is it?"

"It becomes second nature soon enough. You just got to keep trying stuff out. Keep practising. The real hurdle is believing you can do it in the first place. Without belief, you got nothing, kid.

When you can manage that, you're off. Then you can travel anyplace using your mind to penetrate other worlds in the dreamscape."

"That sounds awesome. So at the moment I'm just randomly jumping into dreams—is that right?"

"Well, that there's the quandary, son. I think it used to be random and jumpy for you, but now I ain't so sure. It feels more like a kind of preordained destiny type of deal to me. Like something or someone is sending you to see me, I guess in an effort to have you learn how to control it."

"This is so crazy, Sal. The whole thing. I can barely believe it," said Billy. He then realised the irony of his remark and added, "Duh, I guess that's my problem right there."

"You'll get used to it in time. We all do. Unluckily for us, time ain't something we have a bunch of. That no-good snake Typhon has declared war on Earth and is destroying it, piece by piece. Somehow we need to get you—that being the Servo you—down there so you can kick his ass."

"Declared war?" said Billy, alarmed. "What's he doing?"

"I've been keeping tabs on things down there—listening to chatter and stuff between governments. Looks like the United States is trying to kill him with some fancy-swanky airplane of theirs. They're going to fail, of course.

"The Norwegians have tried and failed already. Shoot, they've lost an entire Arctic town already. Two thousand souls gone. I'm pretty darn sure other nations are being alerted to Typhon now and will try, and fail, to stop him as well. You see, Earth's conventional armies or weapons can't kill Typhon. He can be damaged, for sure, but they'll never truly kill him—not with their level of technology. He ain't a normal fella, see. He's protected by dark matter. Makes him much tougher."

"What's dark matter?"

"Right, of course, you guys have only recently discovered it, ain't you? Hmmm, well, best I can put it is, it's a strange and invisible substance that fills the voids in space. It's eluded every advanced species in the universe. That was until Typhon's father, Oberyn, discovered how to harness it into a seemingly indestructible material. Typhon's clothed in the stuff."

"Oh great! How can I kill him then?"

"Well, I'm thinking, we can load you up with a bunch of hi-tech killing gizmos I got, and then you can go pay him a little visit. I figure you think fast on your feet, as you demonstrated down there with the meteorgus, so you can adapt well to a fight. And of course you'll have LAURA with you."

"That doesn't sound like a plan, Sal. That sounds like you just thought that up a minute ago."

"Okay, Billy," said Sal, pausing to consider whether or not to tell him the truth. She decided she would. "I have no idea how you can kill him, Billy. And we have no way of getting you there in time, anyway. All I do know is that we have to try."

"I'm getting confused again. I'm on Earth already," he said. "The real me. My . . . what was it again? Primo? He or me is there now, right?"

"True, but, your Primo is just a regular kid. Servo Billy up here is the somviator. The one with the flying suit, desintoscram gun, and other weapons at his disposal. What needs to happen is for Servo Billy to get back to Earth with all this technology, and then take out Typhon with it."

"So, let me get this straight. Me—the Primo me on Earth—has to stay asleep so that the Servo me appears here? Then I have to stock up on gear and then travel back to Earth and kill Typhon with it."

"Yup, you got it. Your Primo is asleep now. It's how you're here, talking to me, you see? Normally, the somviators are based here. We then sleep and send our Servo selves out on missions. The Primos are always here, Billy. Always. What we got with you is a peculiar situation where your Primo is on Earth and your Servo is here. It's the wrong way round. Do you see?"

Billy did see. It sounded like a bit of a mess.

Sal then added, "It's a tricky situation. If we get your Servo down to Earth, it means your Primo and Servo will both be there. On the same planet. At the same time. Not ideal. You have to make sure you don't meet yourself. Ever."

"Why not?"

"Primos and Servos just don't meet, okay? It would be very bad."

"What kind of bad?"

"The end of time and space as we know it bad. Something like that."

"I see," said Billy, a little dismissively. He looked away, shaking his head. He wanted to wake up again. This was absurd in the extreme.

"Listen up. There are some very important ground rules you need to keep in mind. You got to try and keep your Primo on Earth asleep for as long as you can, so your Servo can stay active. You got to remember that your Primo is having the dream, and your Servo is living inside it. If your Primo wakes up, your Servo will disappear from whatever dreamscape it's in, ending the sequence. And of course your Primo is always going to wake up after a few hours anyway, unless something bad happens to your Servo."

"What bad things can happen to my Servo?" asked Billy cautiously.

"Well, you see, your living consciousness, the part that makes you who you are, moves from your Primo to your Servo during dreamtime. In the dreamscape, somviators ain't invincible; they just have great technology with them. If you're careless your Servo can die in the dreamscape.

"Don't do that. If it happens, your Primo at home will slip into a kind of irreversible coma. You can also get stuck in the dreamscape, say, if you're imprisoned or trapped, or something like that. Basically, if your Servo gets into serious peril, your Primo can't wake up. And you can't just jump your Servo out of there and into another dreamscape, neither. You have to resolve the Servo predicament before you can move on or return—before your Primo can wake up. It's just the way the brain handles it, I'm afraid. No way around it. If you do somehow get stuck, then your Primo will never wake up. It'll likely starve to death or maybe be kept alive in a hospital waiting for your Servo to escape so the dream can end, and it can wake up. I speak from experience here, Billy. It's very unpleasant."

"Great!" said Billy, rolling his eyes.

Sal got up and skated back into her diner's polished metal kitchen. "Didn't mean to scare you there, kid," she said. "We need more milkshakes while we work out how the heck we can pull this off."

Sal retrieved a large jug of raspberry milkshake from the fridge while saying to Billy, "I know it all sounds crazy, son, but you'll do great. If we can just get you back to Earth. Are you up for it, Billy? Shall we give it a shot?"

There was no reply.

Sal turned around to see what was up.

Billy had disappeared.

"Dammit," she muttered. "He's gone and woken up again."

— TWENTY-FOUR —
The Survivor

Jurgen crawled out from under the remains of the bar building. He was shivering uncontrollably—suffering from the combined effects of exposure and shock. He had a deep gash under his hairline that had stopped bleeding now, but his face was caked in dried, flaking blood. He had a couple of missing molars and one eye was mostly closed from swelling. His right shoulder felt wrong, and he figured he'd broken something up there. His right knee too, was swollen and tender. But he was alive.

His watch told him it was 6:05 a.m. The sun should have still been up but was obscured by the huge cloud bank hovering over Spitsbergen, leaving the obliterated town silent and still in the unwavering darkness.

Some streetlights still worked sporadically, though, and they were enough for Jurgen to make out the destruction around him. There wasn't a building that hadn't been set on fire or smashed in one way or another. Broken electricity and streetlight poles stood at haphazard angles all down the street.

A massive crater not far from him was still smouldering from the impact of the missile a few hours ago. There was no sign of life. The whole place smelled of burnt wood.

Jurgen was frightened out of his wits. He daren't call out in case that thing was still here, so he began to quietly walk around to see if he could find anybody else alive. Maybe there were other survivors like him?

There weren't. After ninety minutes of slow, careful, and quiet searching he was back where he'd started—at Mjölnir's. He'd scoured most of the small town and found nobody at all. No one living. No one dead. He had at least found a thick crochet blanket in the back of a wrecked vehicle and was feeling very slightly warmer for wearing it around his shoulders, but he needed some nourishment.

He limped up the steps and walked in through the enormous hole in the front of the bar, ducking around a smashed wooden beam, broken glass crunching underfoot. He could only just make out the long wooden bar in the gloom, but he knew there was a flashlight under there, having experienced a couple of Mjölnir power blackouts in the past.

After stumbling around broken tables and chairs, he made it behind the bar and rummaged around on the shelves, his fingers sifting through an unfamiliar layer of dust. It felt like it was covering every surface he touched.

Just then his fingertips located the plastic handgrip of the flashlight. He picked it up and tentatively switched it on while aiming it point-blank at the floor, keeping the beam from illuminating too much. His heart was racing. Slowly he lifted the torch and allowed the beam to spread out.

Everything was coated in a fine layer of black powder. Jurgen immediately felt sick. He realised it was the ash that was left behind each time that thing had killed somebody, like his poor brother, Albrecht. He'd seen that every time one of those devilish smoke trails had taken someone—a handful of black dust drifting to the floor, as if their last breath had turned to ash. The fact that the whole place was covered in a thin layer of it just showed how many people had died in this room only a few hours ago. Jurgen had to get out of there.

But before he fled, he turned around and snatched up a bottle of spirits, roughly removed the top, and took a swig. He coughed, almost choking on the fiery fluid, before the whisky slid down his core, warming him from the inside out. He shivered with momentary pleasure. He took the bottle with him, and using the flashlight aimed low at the floor, he quietly navigated around the broken furniture. He was almost out the way he'd come in when the torch beam struck an object that caught his attention. He went over to investigate.

Unbelievably, it was his own cell phone. It was resting screen downward, at a forty-five-degree angle, against a table leg in the corner of the lounge area. There was a little pile of ash around its base where it had fallen onto the back of the phone and slid off.

Jurgen picked the phone up and blew on it to clear away the residue. He flipped it over and pushed the home button. The screen lit up with a notification that its memory was full and that he needed to free up more space. It was then that he realised it must have been recording video the whole time, right up until its memory had maxed out—however long that was.

Jurgen righted an unbroken chair and sat down, his heart racing. He turned off the torch and pressed play on the last recorded video. The image was shaking and wobbling back and forth, recording the moment he'd switched it on while climbing the steps outside. It continued to depict blurry, fast-moving shapes for a few minutes as the audio played back sounds of the fight he'd got into with the barman. The image then spun rapidly for a moment, jerked two or three times and came to rest. It showed a view from the floor looking up at the front door of the bar with people standing and jeering at the fight he was in, unseen off to the right. Suddenly chaos ensued as the front of the bar exploded into fragments, and the devilish creature floated inside.

Tears welled up in Jurgen's eyes as he forced himself to watch the ensuing slaughter. His phone's camera had caught all the action at the front, including him striking the demon and then being batted out through the window.

Most of the remaining footage was of an empty room, with gut-wrenching audio of the rest of the attack, out of sight, farther into the back of the bar. Peoples' cries for mercy being ignored. Crunching bones. Screams and yelps for several agonising minutes—then silence. Finally, the dark creature glided back into view, turning to look directly into the phone's tiny camera. The fire in Typhon's eyes flared up, like match heads igniting, and then his cracked mouth formed a grotesque smile before he glided out into the darkness.

The injured man stopped the video and cupped his face in his hands and sighed. He rubbed his eyes for a moment and then looked up, a newfound resolve in his heart. As far as he could tell, he was the sole survivor of an impossible-to-believe attack, but one he held video evidence of right there in his hands. He tested his phone's reception but there was no signal, neither cellular nor Wi-Fi. He felt a growing compulsion to get his video into the hands of the media. It needed to be seen by the world. *People needed to be warned.*

He looked through the broken doorway and over to the smouldering research institute building in the far distance, where he worked as an IT engineer. They had many kinds of transmission systems over there, mainly antennas or dishes that were quite possibly all destroyed now. But they had an ancient ISDN cable connection that ran along the seabed to Norway's mainland. He had a hunch that it would still be connected.

Jurgen gathered up his phone and the whisky, pulled the blanket tight around his shoulders, and set off limping apprehensively toward his workplace.

— TWENTY-FIVE —
The Ark

Typhon had greatly enjoyed tearing the small island town to pieces and killing all of its residents. He'd found it a little awkward at first, even sustaining a mild wound. Hibernation had made him rusty, as it always did. But after the bar episode, he'd found his rhythm again and was back to killing as though he'd never stopped.

He calculated how long he'd been under for: in Earth orbit cycles it came to around fifty years. The equivalent of a catnap for him. He'd had some voyages that had lasted thousands of years— hauling himself across the entire universe and back again.

How a Remnant Stone had escaped his search here earlier was beyond him. Perhaps it had been hidden? Not possible. Maybe it had been brought here recently? More likely. Who was responsible? Certainly not these humans. They weren't advanced enough. And they weren't going to get any more advanced, either. He'd see to that.

Generally speaking, most life forms he encountered on his searches were barely above pond life, so the human creatures were considerably further up the evolutionary ladder than most. But they were still laughably naive when it came to their understanding of the cosmos. Having said that, they could still be formidable. He could see that now. They had a strong desire to survive and were quite warlike too. He needed to be much sharper. One of the two fighter planes that had come for him earlier had very nearly harmed him significantly. It was only

Sygma's keen senses that had saved him from the considerable pain of being reconstituted from fragments. An agonising effort he'd experienced once before and had no desire to repeat.

Typhon, having enjoyed a little sport, felt it was time to fulfil the reason for his trip to this desolate and sparsely populated island. Earlier, when he'd been downloading Earth's historical data aboard *Nightshade*, he'd learned of a highly unusual and quite ingenious storage building on this desolate island—the Svalbard Global Seed Vault. It was a one-square-kilometre underground repository for all of the planet's seeds. A backup supply, intended to kick-start a repopulation of Earth's flora in the event of an apocalyptic event.

His Storm of Shadows could indeed smother and kill every living thing in time, but it would have no effect whatsoever on chambers of seeds locked away deep inside the Arctic permafrost. To his mind, such a structure was cheating. It needed to be removed from the equation and would require a more personal touch.

The vault was just around the corner, literally only five kilometres west of Longyearbyen. It was a simple arrangement of three storage rooms carved deep inside a mountain, where the rock was permanently frozen, and high enough up to avoid potential future rising sea waters.

It had taken Typhon only a couple of minutes to fly there and find it, shortly after bringing down the two warplanes, and now he was standing outside the angled concrete entrance, oddly finding himself admiring its economical geometric construction. It reminded him of *Nightshade*'s elegant lines. Simple but strong. Above the door, an illuminated art installation shimmered like a beacon of hope in the darkness. A false hope, as it would transpire.

Typhon forced the front door open with ease, the large metal lock splitting in half as he pulled it apart, setting off a loud alarm bell in the process. He ducked under the door lintel and wandered in. There was a ninety-metre-long concrete-reinforced, tubular tunnel carved into the sandstone, sloping down to another set of doors. It was brightly illuminated with strip lights in the ceiling, and multiple security cameras capturing his every move.

In a corner above the entrance, he saw the pulsing orange light of the alarm box and heard its screeching, repetitive siren. He reached up a thin, spindly arm and crushed it like a soft drink can, silencing it permanently. He then ambled down the slope, taking his time. Savouring the moment. Knowing he was being filmed. Imagining his growing notoriety with world leaders as they frantically and futilely discussed ways to eliminate him.

When he was halfway down the incline, a side door near the bottom opened, and two men armed with Heckler and Koch assault rifles stepped out and ordered him to stop.

Typhon laughed and continued toward the inner doors.

"Halt or we'll shoot," shouted one of the men, pointing his weapon directly at the approaching alien, his panting breath visible in the freezing air. The other soldier followed suit, shakily raising his gun.

The Destroyer of Worlds had no time for such folly.

"Sygma," he said simply.

Immediately, the nine black lengths of fabric swept up and over Typhon's head like vipers. He casually flicked a finger in the direction of the men and set Sygma on them. They had no chance.

The less experienced and more nervous of the two soldiers screamed and opened fire with his HK416. His more mature colleague, now with no other options, joined in. Within two seconds they'd unleashed sixty rounds of ammunition in a deafening attack.

Not a single bullet hit Typhon. Instead, seven of Sygma's tentacles had moved with lightning speed to form a smoke shield in front of their master, the bullets entering the cloud on one side but not exiting the other.

In the following second, the remaining two Sygma tentacles flew along the floor, plucked the soldiers up off their feet and smashed them headfirst through the metal ceiling gantry that supported the lights, cables, and pipework, killing them both instantly. Their spasmodically twitching bodies were then consumed in a chaotic flurry of spiralling smoke. Within seconds there was no sign of the soldiers whatsoever, apart from two guns lying on the floor and a few grams of ash filtering down from the ceiling. Typhon hadn't even broken his stride.

When he reached the locked double doors at the bottom of the tunnel, he pushed them apart. The sound of breaking locks and hinges echoed along the empty corridor behind him. On the other side, the path divided into routes left and right. Typhon took the right-hand one and was immediately met with a dead end and another set of doors on his left, marked by a large number 3. He calmly broke through them and into a huge chamber roughly hewn from the sandstone.

It was minus eighteen degrees Celsius inside but he barely noticed. Long avenues of tall shelving units filled the room, floor to ceiling. On them were sealed boxes. Thousands of them. Inside each one were plastic sachets holding thousands of seeds and bulbs, representing all of Earth's trees, flowers, shrubs, fruits, vegetables, and even weeds. You name it, every type of plant had been carefully archived, packed, and stored, alphabetically by nation.

Typhon stood by the broken doorway and summoned the Sygma cloak once again. It slithered out from behind him, its nine tattered bands curving down low to the floor and then up and around him so they joined together in front of his chest. "Launch the Solex," he said. "Destroy everything in here."

Sygma's black material heaved in and out, morphing into the familiar pulsing dark clouds. The form rippled in a muscular-like movement until a brilliant ball of light was birthed. About the size of a basketball, it hovered in front of Typhon's face like a miniature sun, its surface alive with liquid fire. The alien pointed to the rows of shelves, turned, and ducked out through the broken door.

Behind him, the Solex zipped up into the near right corner, paused a beat, and then flew along the front, burning through every plastic box of seeds in its path. Brief fires and puffs of smoke appeared at every Solex collision, but quickly dwindled, as molten steel from the shelving units dripped onto the concrete floor. Once the Solex reached the wall at the other end, it halted, moved back one width distance behind itself, and took off back the way it had come, vaporising every obstacle in its way, in a new parallel row. It repeated this action over and over again, systematically burning away row upon row of seeds.

Meanwhile, Typhon had smashed his way into the two other seed vaults, marked 2 and 1 down the left-hand route, and was now waiting patiently at the bottom of the main passageway for the Solex to finish the first chamber. He was listening to its high-pitched whine as it zipped back and forth, seemingly getting faster and faster, when his obsidian black eyes became aware of an odd flickering light. It was almost imperceptible, even to his extremely acute vision, but there was some kind of faint red light blinking very quickly, but coming from where? Just then, the Solex flew out of the smouldering chamber and back to Typhon. He gestured to the two other chambers and said, "Repeat."

The Solex did as commanded and flew into central chamber 2

and began the whole process again—instantaneously consuming millions of seeds by fire.

Suddenly, Typhon heard *Nightshade's* voice calling to him inside his head. She sounded alarmed. But he couldn't hear her properly. Some kind of interference was disrupting her transmission. It must be the geology of the mountain, he thought. He began to walk up the slope of the main tunnel, to try and improve the reception of his inner ear radio implant, when his world unexpectedly turned a brilliant shade of white. There was brief searing pain. Then nothing.

— TWENTY-SIX —
Gotcha

"Yahoo!" yelled Lieutenant Randolph. "Gotcha."

He was shouting to himself. Pumped up on adrenalin. He couldn't believe he was still alive. His comms were down. They had been for twenty minutes or so—as soon as he'd flown underneath that slab of black cloud hovering over the pole. He was amazed it had been this easy to take out the target, Typhon, after everything he'd been told.

As he'd neared Spitsbergen Island half an hour ago, Air Force Command had relayed spy satellite video to the heads-up display in his helmet. It depicted a weird flying humanoid skimming over the Arctic ice—a truly bizarre vision. A hostile alien with designs on destroying our planet, they had told him. It was the stuff of sci-fi B movies and very hard to believe. But then he'd been shown grainy, barely discernible footage of the figure attacking a building in Longyearbyen before the video had become scrambled, like his communications systems were now.

It wasn't unexpected, though. He'd been forewarned that he could be flying solo on this mission and if that was the case, he was to use his discretion. He'd also been informed that Norway had lost two F-16s—pilots presumed dead—in an attempt to kill Typhon. Moreover, some two thousand islanders were also most likely dead by his hand. Randolph had assumed that he was heading for an unsurvivable situation but was determined to end Typhon's existence. This alien scumbag was messing with the wrong guy in James Randolph. If he had to die, then he was taking Typhon with him.

He'd flown around the smouldering wreckage that was Longyearbyen for five minutes. It was almost completely obliterated. Nothing remained intact. There was an uncanny lack of people to be seen, alive or dead. It was hard to believe that an individual had done this and not an army.

His plane's radar was unusable, its screen corrupted by zigzagging interference patterns, but its hi-tech optical scopes seemed to be working fine—including a new top-secret three-dimensional laser scanner. He'd used it to view a detailed virtual reality display of the terrain below. It had the ability to ascertain if anything was moving or not. Nothing had been. The town was dead. He'd then decided to take the analyst's advice and go and look for some seed vault place that was just around the headland, and see if Typhon was in there.

On arrival, his night vision helmet display had clearly shown him the broken entrance to the vault poking out of a low, smooth mountainside, its doors ripped off and lying in the snow. That was when he'd decided to take a gamble and use the last of his plane's fuel to wait it out there. His other option was to fly about for a few minutes like a headless chicken in the gloom, looking for Typhon. That had seemed like too much of a long shot. This was an actual lead, and thank God, Walt's hunch had paid off.

The USAF F-35B Lightning II aircraft was now positioned outside the smashed entrance to the seed vault, keeping a safe distance away. Its Pratt & Whitney F135 engine's vectoring nozzle turned downward, diverting all its thrust vertically. This, coupled with the Rolls Royce lifting fan directly behind the cockpit, allowed it to maintain a steady hover.

Randolph was making small adjustments to the roll-post air jets on the plane's wingtips, keeping her steady in the blustery conditions on the northern side of the mountain. He'd just fired an AGM-65 Maverick missile straight down the long entrance tunnel and watched it detonate. His reasoning had been simple. He'd shone the laser scanner down the tunnel and waited. Waited, as if he was fly-fishing for rainbow trout back home on the Kern River. Biding his time. Hoping to hook his prey. He'd known he had very little time left to play the waiting game, but he'd stuck with it.

Thankfully, the scanner had soon returned a positive match on Typhon. After less than five minutes it had relayed back a bright red, animated, three-dimensional model of a ten-foot-tall exceptionally thin humanoid figure wearing a weird, undulating cloak. It was pacing about at the far end of the tunnel as if it was waiting for something. That had been enough for Randolph to make a judgement call: to terminate the slimeball before he could kill anybody else, even if that meant destroying the seed vault in the process. The stakes were too high not to. He'd lifted the trigger guard and pressed the fire button on the stick. The Maverick missile had sped away instantaneously, straight down the tunnel, and right into Typhon's chest.

The flash of light had come a split second before the explosion and sounds of shattering rock. Then fire had spewed out of the entrance in a long but quickly dwindling orange-coloured jet. Farther up the mountain slope, part of the terrain had cracked and a wide portion of it had collapsed inward and sunk a couple of metres.

The dust and debris was settling now and Randolph could see on the laser scanner display screen that the tunnel had collapsed about two-thirds of the way in, leaving the rest intact. He had about four minutes of fuel left and his F-35 was carrying one more Maverick missile. He remembered a saying his British grandmother used when he was a kid: "In for a penny, in for a pound."

He quickly flicked the trigger setting over from the empty missile bay to a loaded one, aimed it down the tunnel, and fired the second Maverick. It disappeared in an instant, flew straight down the corridor and impacted on the collapsed sandstone boulders near the bottom. If anything, it created the more devastating explosion of the two.

Firstly, the tunnel fully exploded this time, propelling fire and jagged rocks out of the entrance. Secondly, the front half of the mountain completely collapsed, a square kilometre of land instantly dropping down and forming a huge concave cup shape in the mountainside. It was as if the first missile had cracked everything open and the second one had finished the job. The entire seed vault and its accompanying tunnels were gone. Obliterated. And seemingly, Typhon with them.

Randolph let out a sigh of relief and shook his head in disbelief. Had he been lucky or what? This Typhon character had sealed his own fate the moment he'd walked into the seed vault—now his tomb. There was absolutely no way he could have survived two direct hits by Maverick missiles, then to be buried under millions of tonnes of rock. He was dead, for sure.

The F-35 had three minutes of fuel remaining—just enough time for him to find a safe place to set it down and save the air force $120 million by not ditching it. Svalbard airport was less than a mile from his position. He rotated the plane on the spot and adjusted the vectoring nozzle so the aircraft gained some lateral northward movement.

That was when he saw the black arrowhead drop out of the sky. It was very far away but he could tell it had a sharp, angular profile. It was densely black too. Several shades darker than the rolling storm clouds behind it. He squinted his eyes and watched it hurtle downward far faster than any naturally falling object would have.

Randolph's heightened senses tingled with anticipation. This was not a friendly craft.

The object began to level out low over the mountains and head directly for his position. It was definitely moving far too quickly to be of human origin. He concluded it must be Typhon's ship, coming to his rescue.

"Too late, sucker," mumbled Randolph to himself.

Instinctively, he locked on two Sidewinder air-to-air missiles and fired them at the approaching black deltoid. But it was to be in vain. The target made impossibly fast evasive manoeuvres, completely confusing the two missiles' targeting systems. They promptly shot straight past the object, turned into each other and exploded.

Silhouetted in front of the spectacular fireball, the triangular craft swept back into view, returning to its original course—heading straight for Randolph's F-35.

He barely had a second to decide, but ultimately thrust both his hands between his legs, found the handle tucked under his seat, and yanked upward, hard.

There were three explosions.

The first one was his cockpit's canopy being jettisoned away—so he wouldn't break his neck.

The second one was his seat tearing free of its fixtures and thrusting upward and backward with tremendous force. He hung onto the handle, his head tucked in tight to his chest as he was catapulted out of the aircraft.

He was only a couple of metres clear of the plane's fuselage when the approaching object scythed straight through the middle of it, from nose to tail, creating the third, and loudest, explosion.

In that moment, time seemed to momentarily slow down. Randolph saw the plane tear in half, right there beneath him as he continued his rapid ascent in the ejector seat, its compact rockets pushing him clear of immediate danger.

The plane's engine had exploded, causing a ball of fire to push the two halves of the plane apart. They fell downward, thousands of small components and fragments of shattered metal spilling out of the eviscerated warplane.

Time returned to its normal pace and Randolph was rudely hurled around the sky as the parachutes deployed and brought his upward trajectory to an end.

Completely disorientated and suffering from whiplash and shock, he began to spin uncontrollably downward. All the optical scanners that had been feeding visuals into his helmet visor were, of course, now disconnected. He was unsettlingly blind, the black sky above him melting into a desolate and uncertain terrain below.

He wasn't sure when he would hit the ground or how hard the impact might be. But for the moment he was alive, and for that he was grateful.

— TWENTY-SEVEN —
Tell the World

Jurgen hobbled down the last stretch of deserted road to the research institute. It took him twenty-five minutes to get there when ordinarily it would have taken him only ten. His knee had swollen up further, locking his right leg straight. His shoulder, jaw, and eye were also causing him considerable discomfort. Still, the whisky was doing its job, perhaps too well—he was feeling a little intoxicated.

Along the way, a couple of loud explosions had rocked the ground beneath his feet. He'd had no idea where they had come from until a couple of minutes later when three smaller explosions had come echoing out of the mountains to the southwest of him. Then he'd seen a faint and tiny object propel upward and then descend again by parachute. He didn't really know what was happening, but it looked like it might be coming from the seed vault area a couple of kilometres away. He guessed the military was trying to eliminate the demon that had killed his brother and everyone he knew. *Good luck to them.*

There was obviously still a lot of violent activity going on. Jurgen needed to get inside and find shelter. And he needed to get warm. It had begun to snow quite heavily. The climate was totally screwed up.

Finally, he arrived at the metal double doors of his workplace. He slid his security swipe card over a wall panel but nothing happened. The door remained shut. The power must be out. Then he noticed that the doors were slightly askew. In fact, the whole doorframe was leaning over slightly like a rhombus. He looked up and saw that the entire metal-framed building had been warped by some colossal impact.

A closer look at the door lock showed that it wasn't connecting properly. Jurgen balanced painfully on his bad leg and gave the door latch a big kick with his good one. The lock immediately gave way and the doors smashed inward, bouncing off the inside walls and back out again.

The battered survivor limped into the institute and found it wrecked almost beyond recognition. The metal staircase to his right had been torn down, as had some of the upper level gantries and most of the central ceiling. He clambered over some broken desks and computers that had once formed the security area, noticing more ominous black ash covering some surfaces, and headed into the open-plan working area.

Jurgen made his way to his workstation via a circuitous route, carefully negotiating fallen beams and jagged metal roof sheets. His desk was tucked away in a far, windowless corner and was remarkably intact, with at least one desktop terminal appearing to be undamaged.

In Jurgen's role as an IT support engineer, it was his job to make sure the scientists and researchers had access to all the computer equipment and software they needed, and that he knew how to keep it all running smoothly. Part of that knowledge was how to supply the facility with electricity in the event of a blackout.

It didn't take him long to get a backup generator online, and his PC powered up. As he'd guessed, Internet and satellite communications were down but the undersea ISDN cable link to the mainland was indeed undamaged. After half an hour of jiggery-pokery, he managed to piggyback his system on to one on the mainland, access the Internet, and upload his terrifying phone video of the Mjölnir bar attack to YouTube and email a link to the DMM news channel.

He described himself as the sole survivor of the incident and gave them his location. Then he made a Skype call to his organisation's headquarters in Narvik and told them his story. They didn't believe him, of course, so he told them he didn't care, but that they would not be able to contact any of the hundred or so staff on Longyearbyen because they were all missing and presumed dead. Then he added that their multimillion-dollar research centre had been completely destroyed, and hung up. If that didn't get a plane sent up later that morning, then he didn't know what would.

But now Jurgen was tired. Moreover, he was completely drained. He downed the last of the whisky, pulled the woollen blanket tight around himself, and added a jacket he'd found in the wreckage. Then he curled up on the floor next to his PC tower, which was giving off some heat, and passed out.

— TWENTY-EIGHT —
Reality Check

Billy woke up on the floor. Again. What was wrong with the bed? This time he was lying on his bedroom carpet, the duvet cover coiled up on top of him. He was quite warm and cosy under there, and he'd have probably stayed put were it not for his screeching alarm clock notifying him that it was time to get up for school.

On the plus side, it was Friday—just one more day of toil and then the weekend. He needed to clear his headspace of the crazy sci-fi dreams and get back to reality. As he worked in the local market on Saturdays, he planned on spending the whole of Sunday just playing with Mungo, the family's Great Dane.

The dog had been looking at him oddly of late. He couldn't put his finger on why, but he figured they needed to go *mano a pata* and see what was up. Have a little man-and-pooch quality time. He loved that mutt and wanted to take him for a long walk somewhere. Maybe down to the riverside for a really good scamper. Maybe he'd invite Ellie along too. There was something happening between him and her. And he liked it.

On the negative side, it might be a Friday, but Russell Bates would still want to beat him up. Or possibly worse.

Having witnessed the lout charging at him yesterday, he was of the opinion that the boy was seriously unhinged, more so than a regular school bully. The look in his eyes on the footbridge had been very unsettling. Billy couldn't remember how he'd managed to throw Russell into the canal, but he was now convinced it was just a fluke. He figured their next encounter would not end so favourably.

He sighed, rose onto his knees, turned off the alarm and stretched his arms and shoulders. He remembered having another one of those nutty dreams involving Sally the alien—the one with an American diner on an asteroid. He laughed at himself. He needed to cut down on the cheese before bedtime.

Then Billy's smile slid south and disappeared. Segments of a conversation he'd had with Sal were coming back to him. Typhon was trying to destroy the world. Something about Norway and the Americans trying to kill him with an aeroplane. That would mean it was happening a little too close to Britain for his liking.

He knew it was all a dream, of course, but it didn't stop him from leaping up and bolting downstairs to see if everything was okay.

His mum was in the kitchen, feeding the dog. There was bread in the toaster, as normal, waiting for him to push it down. A jar of peanut butter and a tub of cheese spread were on the kitchen counter, waiting for him to choose one. A glass of milk stood next to a plate and knife.

Billy's mum had heard him come charging in and had turned around, surprised by the suddenness of his arrival.

As was Mungo, who was looking over at him, a long drool hanging from his chops. It was possible that Mr Goggles, the goldfish, was looking at him oddly as well.

"Are you all right there, Billy?" said his mum, a trace of concern in her voice. "You went to bed very early last night. Everything all right at school?"

Billy stood in the doorway, looking around the kitchen, then at his mum, then at Mungo and the fish. Everything seemed normal. "Fine, Mum," said Billy. "Everything's good. I, uh, just had a weird dream."

"Oh, not those again," said his mum, sounding more concerned.

"No, no, nothing to worry about, Mum. Just a silly sci-fi dream. I'm starving this morning." He walked over and pressed the toaster slider down, then carried his milk over to the patio doors and looked out at their back garden. It was grey and overcast outside. A fine drizzle was falling onto the lawn grass. There were birds flying overhead. A lot of them. All going in the same direction.

"Looks a bit nasty out there. So much for summer. What's the weather forecast, Mum?"

His mother, Janice, scrunched her eyes, looked out of the window and said, "Wet."

"Very funny," replied Billy, groaning at her sad and predictably lame parent humour.

"No idea," she said. "Not had the radio or telly on yet. Why not stick the idiot box on and see?"

Billy went over to a sideboard in the adjoining open-plan dining area and turned on the TV. It paused momentarily to tune in and then lit up with DMM's morning news show. A red banner along the bottom read:

BREAKING NEWS: Witness says Longyearbyen destroyed

Low light images that were grainy and a little hard to make out seemed to show some kind of fight going on in a bar or club. A grim voice-over commentary said, " . . . unbelievable scenes here at Longyearbyen. An entire town destroyed, and its population—some two thousand people—missing. Coming up, we have exclusive eyewitness footage of what may have caused this calamity . . . and you're not going to believe it. Don't go away. We'll be right back after these messages."

The TV then cut to commercials for cereals, children's toys, and female grooming products.

Billy stared at the screen as though he was in a trance. He slowly backed away and sat down at the dining table. He didn't hear the toaster ping.

"Toast's ready," Janice called as she tried to empty the rest of the tinned dog meat into Mungo's bowl without him slobbering all over her.

Billy didn't hear her, either. He was staring at the TV, waiting for the news show to return.

"Christ, Mungo, get back will you?" complained his mum. "You'll get it a lot faster if you just back off and let me empty this thing."

Mungo continued to push against Janice, trying to force his enormous head into his bowl, his tail wagging gently to and fro. It was the same wrestling match every morning. A battle of wills between owner and beast. Mungo was very laid back but was just so enormous and solid that he generally got his way. Billy's mother was petite but feisty and generally tried to stop Mungo getting his way—usually failing. Somewhere in the middle of their eternal struggle for dominance was a mutual respect for each other—although one got the impression that Mungo was tolerating her, rather than the other way around.

"Billy, get your toast," his hassled mother called over, glancing up and seeing Billy still sitting at the dining table. "You'll be late. Come on."

"I don't think I'll be going to school today, Mum," said Billy, sounding distant. "I think it'll be . . ."

The wall phone started ringing. "Christ, what now?" shouted Janice, standing up and getting out of the way of Mungo's frothy chops. She grabbed the wall phone while pulling a stern face at Billy and pointing over to the toaster. "What?" she snapped into the handset.

Billy ignored his mum's orders. The DMM newscaster was back on air and trying to tell her audience that the existence of life outside our planet appeared to have been confirmed, but unfortunately it had turned out to be hostile. She looked like she couldn't believe what she was reading off the autocue, as if to do so was news anchor career suicide. But she carried on, regardless, warning viewers that "the following footage is harrowing . . . " and to "watch with caution."

The image cut away from the blonde newsreader with perfect teeth, to be replaced with video of what looked like the inside of a pub. It was being filmed from floor level, looking up at a wall and ceiling, taking in several tables and chairs in the foreground. There was shouting and some sort of commotion going on out of shot, to the right. Half a dozen people in the frame were looking that way and jeering in a foreign tongue.

Suddenly, the glass frontage and entrance exploded inward, sending glass and splintered wood toward the camera, a piece hitting it and causing it to jolt. An extremely tall, strange, willowy man dressed entirely in some kind of black costume floated into the picture. He was sneering and levitating off the ground, wearing a black cape that billowed unnaturally behind him, as though it was underwater. People screamed and ran out of the frame.

He raised clenched fists that had dark clouds around them, with little crackles of lightning flashing within them. Then some men approached him and a fight ensued that saw one big man get thrown out of frame to the left followed by a sound like breaking glass. More men lunged at the dark figure, but in what were really confusing images, streams of sootlike smoke spewed from the attacker's body and overpowered the men. Everything went black, but you could hear screams for mercy and disturbing crunching sounds.

When the smoke cleared, fine ash was falling from the ceiling onto overturned and broken furniture. The room looked completely empty, its disturbed interior caught in an eerie, flickering light.

Somewhere off camera ghastly screaming continued for at least two more agonising minutes. Then there was silence. A few more seconds passed and then the terrifying black figure floated back into view. He turned and leered directly out of the television, his eyes now glowing with fire.

DMM paused the video there and zoomed in tight on his face. They applied some video enhancements to the freeze frame and his strange and horrifying face became much clearer. Although the picture was a little pixelated and fuzzy, Billy could see the face was scarred and pitted. It looked burnt and charred. Riddled with pain. Its burning eyes seemed to stare out at him, looking directly into his soul.

Billy shivered and sat back, breathless and light-headed. His ears popped and a high-pitched whining sound filled them and then faded away. He felt like he was retracting inside himself. Shrinking. He could hear his heartbeat. Feel blood ebbing and flowing through his disconnected body. The sensation was not wholly unpleasant. It felt like he was inside a suit of armour, staring out of the grille, the edge of his vision filling with encroaching shadow. Then he became aware of a voice, far away. It was calling to him. It was his mother. She was saying his name over and over. Softly. Then not so much. Then loud. A slap sound. Somewhere around his face. Then suddenly he was rushing forward. Back to light. Back to life.

When he came to, his mother was supporting him. "You're okay, darling," she said. "You're okay."

"What happened . . . Mum," he mumbled.

"I think you fainted, Billy," she said. "Everything's okay, love. I've got you. I've got you."

— TWENTY-NINE —
A Dog's Life

Mungo was very upset. What had he done? It was all his fault for fetching the strange glowing stick thing from the pond outside. Now Pack Leader was lying on the floor, being cuddled by Pack Leader Mother. Mungo backed out of the kitchen apologetically, with his tail between his legs and his head hung low. He stood in the hallway, peeking into the food-making room and tried to recall what he'd done earlier in the year . . .

It was during the middle of the dark time, in what his upright-walking pack brothers and sister called the month of March. Mungo was asleep in his big basket when he was awakened by a loud swooshing sound overhead. It was quickly followed by a sharp splashing sound from his domain out back.

Mungo needed to know what had made the strange sounds. Mungo needed to know everything that went on in his domain. It was what Mungo did.

He got out of his basket and crept down the slope that joined above to below, and walked through to the food-making room, and the invisible wall beyond. He pawed at it and waited. He repeated this a few times, but nobody came.

He woofed. A low volume one. One that said, "Give me your attention, Pack Leader." He again pawed the invisible wall and stared out at his long, narrow range.

There was something new out there, but he couldn't see it. It was dark. But he could sense it. Oh, he could sense it all right.

Something strange. It was out there, beyond the bushes. Somewhere at the back, near the wooden wall. He could feel a tingle of energy, like a minute crackle in the air. It tickled his nose ever so slightly.

He woofed again. Louder. Not an alarm, but a stronger message this time. One that said, "Come on, Pack Leader, open the invisible wall and let me go out and investigate."

A voice called out from above. Aggressive. It was Pack Leader Father. The tone indicated he wanted him to stop making noise. But how else could he communicate? None of them spoke dog. Well, Pack Leader came the closest, but even he was not very good. In fact, Mungo had had to learn some of the strange sounds his upright-walking pack made in order to understand them.

Mungo woofed once more. A higher pitch. It said, "Sorry, I know you want me to stop, but I have to get outside and find the strange thing."

There was a thump from above. Footsteps. Muttering. Pack Leader Father was coming. Mungo did not like Pack Leader Father, but if he would let him out, that was fine. Mungo pawed the invisible wall again, and made a little woof, one that said, "Over here."

A light went on at the top of the slope that joined above to below. Footsteps again. Pounding. Then another light near the food-making room. Muttering. A shadow. Pack Leader Father appeared. His posture was aggressive. Unhappy. He barged past. Unlocked the invisible wall, slid it to the side and shouted something unpleasant. Mungo didn't need further encouragement. He jumped out into the chilly night air and began to look around, sniffing for that tingle.

Various animal markings had been left since he had last patrolled his territory. Nothing out of the ordinary. He dissolved their markings with his own. This was his domain. Then something caught his eye. A streak of light across the sky. Then another. And another. The strange lights in the black were back. He had been watching them for several sleeps now. At first Pack Leader and family had watched them too. Now they did not. Perhaps this was normal, and this is how the black would be from now on? Mungo did not think it was normal, though. Neither was the strange thing hiding in his domain.

He trotted up the gravel path on his long legs, feet springing lightly off the ground and making minimal noise. He was looking around and sniffing. It was very dark. He could only just make out faint shapes of things. The bench. The shed. The pond . . .

Wait a moment. The pond looked odd. Mungo skipped over to the water. It was glowing slightly. His nose tickled more than ever. There was something under the water. This was a problem. He did not like getting wet. What to do? He woofed at it softly and wagged his tail to say, "I've found you, but I don't know how to reach you, whatever you are." I shall come back in the light time and find you properly, he decided.

Mungo trotted back to the den's invisible wall and pawed and woofed at it again until unhappy Pack Leader Father returned to let him in.

***

The next morning the pack was preparing food as normal. He was waiting for his, standing over his bowl. Pack Leader Mother was getting things ready. Mungo smiled at Pack Leader Mother. She did not respond. Mungo smiled at Pack Leader. He smiled back and gave him a good lug scrub and pat. Pack Leader was a good leader. Mungo was happy. He hoped Pack Leader would be happy too, when he brought him the strange underwater object later. But after food. Food was very important.

Pack Leader Mother approached and started to fill his bowl with biscuits and meat. She was pushing at him and trying to move him.

Mungo thought this was funny. He resisted. Pushed back a little. He smiled at Pack Leader Mother again. She did not notice, but gave him food. He loved her.

After eating food, he pawed the invisible wall. Pack Leader was eating, but he stood up and opened the invisible wall for him anyway, and patted his haunch. Pack Leader always knew what Mungo wanted. Mungo loved Pack Leader the most.

Once outside, Mungo trotted up to the pond. This time he didn't even stop to sniff the foreign markings and remove them. He had an important task to fulfill. He could not see a glow in the light time, but he knew where the strange thing was because his tingling nose told him exactly where to look. There was nothing for it but to jump into the pond and dig it out. Mungo did not like getting wet but Mungo decided he would have to.

Mungo sprang forward into the small pond, making an almighty splash. The water only came up to his chest, which he was holding as high as possible. He began digging with his front paws and immediately found what he was looking for. He then thrust his head underwater and came back out clutching an amber coloured piece of rock, about the size of a large tube of toothpaste. He clambered out. Ears back, tail between his legs. He was soaking wet and cold. He did not like it one little bit. Also, the strange object was making his mouth so tingly that he couldn't hold it for very much longer. He walked over to a shrub and dropped it in there, and then sneezed three times and shook himself vigorously.

He did not like the strange object at all. But it was out of its hiding place now. Mungo could come back for it later when he was not cold and not wet. He trotted back to the invisible wall and woofed. There was noise from inside. Sounds of surprise, disappointment, and anger. Pack Leader eventually came out with a big towel and started to rub him dry. Mungo loved Pack Leader. He always knew what to do.

After he was dry enough to be allowed back into the den, Pack Leader Father and Pack Leader Mother scolded Mungo. Pack Leader remained by his side, stroking his head. Pack Leader always had his back.

Pack Leader Father then took Mungo to bed. He made more aggressive sounds and wagged a finger at him, before leaving him up there. Normally this was a punishment. Mungo hated being put in bed when he wasn't tired. But oddly, since fetching the strange glowing stick thing, he had become very sleepy and was quite happy to be sent there.

***

Mungo woke with a start, one of his hind legs kicking out and hitting the skirting board. He had had a strange sleep journey. Something about running away and darkness and fear. He had not liked it. He was glad to be awake now. He was lying in his basket, directly under a radiator. He was warm and cosy and dry.

He sat up. Judging by the light outside, he must have slept for quite a while. Perhaps most of the light time. The pack had gone off hunting like they did most days, leaving Mungo to guard the den. He was very tired. This was not normal. It must be that strange object from the pond. Mungo decided he must get that strange thing to Pack Leader as soon as possible. He would know what to do with it.

Mungo went below and stood by the front door and waited. And waited. And waited.

Finally, Pack Leader arrived back, carrying his bag of things. The one he left with most mornings and came home with most nights. He hung it on the wall near the slope that joined above to below. Mungo was very happy to see Pack Leader and Pack Leader was very happy to see Mungo. He knew this because Pack Leader gave him a big ear scrub and chest rub and then hugged him.

Mungo licked Pack Leader's face and wagged his tail and then skipped over to the invisible wall and woofed and pawed at it, saying, "I have something to show you. Let me out."

Pack Leader opened the invisible wall, and Mungo trotted outside and headed to the shrub where he'd dropped the strange object earlier. On his way there, he heard Pack Leader shout out a message. He was not sure of everything he said, but it seemed Pack Leader was going to leave again and would be back later.

Mungo carried on up to the shrub. His nose was tingling a lot. The strange rock-stick thing was still there. He thought he saw something move inside it and a faint glow again. He did not like it, but he needed to give it to Pack Leader. He picked it up in his teeth. His mouth immediately began to tingle again. He would not be able to hold it for long. He ran back to the den. The invisible wall had been left open a little bit, just enough for Mungo to squeeze through.

He trotted through the food-making room and into the hall. Pack Leader had gone. Sometimes he would go to the nearby shop to hunt food after school. That was where he must be. But Mungo's mouth was tingling unbearably now, and he could feel a huge sneeze building up. He needed to get rid of the strange object NOW.

Then he saw Pack Leader's bag hanging on the wall.

The top was open. It was full of stuff. Cluttered with things he did not understand. He put his head over it and dropped the strange, tingling object into it. He heard it hit a few items and fall to the bottom. He then sneezed a few times and shook his head. He was glad to be rid of it. Pack Leader would know what to do. But now Mungo was tired again. He lay down on the hallway floor and closed his eyes.

That was all Mungo could remember of that day. Since then Pack Leader had carried the strange tingling stick with him in his bag everywhere he went. He assumed Pack Leader knew what he was doing. But Mungo was now having doubts. What if he didn't? What if he didn't realise it was in his bag at all?

— THIRTY —
Waiting Game

Nightshade was confused. What had happened? Typhon, the master she was sworn to serve, protect, and obey had disappeared. She had been sitting in a geostationary orbit over the planet's icy northern pole keeping an eye on things, when she'd been suddenly alerted to a potential threat to her master.

There was a lot of space traffic orbiting this world. Most of it appeared to be redundant junk from vintage launches, but there were a fair number of operating devices around her too. None of it as advanced as her design, of course, but some of the satellites could pose a threat, although most of them seemed to be communication transceivers.

Some of them were observation devices, looking back to Earth or out into the vastness of space. A very few of them were weapons platforms carrying crude nuclear fusion devices, clearly intended for mass destruction of targets on Earth. These she paid particular attention to. These were potential hazards to her master.

Interestingly, there was one very large satellite that came around the planet every ninety-two minutes, carrying six human creatures. It was much larger than her, but was of a frail and weak design. She would need to inform Typhon of its existence, as he would surely seek to destroy it.

It was during this spell of scanning and analysing the thousands of objects around her that *Nightshade* had perhaps become distracted and taken her eye off Typhon. Regardless of what exactly had led to the present situation, she had quickly become aware of a human flying weapon hovering near her master's last known location.

He had entered a structure inside a mountain a few moments ago. Then an alien ship had appeared, hovering directly outside the entrance. She had tried to warn Typhon through his radio implant but had only been able to make a stuttering, infrequent connection—the mountain's geology most likely interfering with the signal.

At that point she had enacted emergency evacuation mode, and sped down to his location as fast as she could. During those short minutes of travel, she had sensed the alien craft firing explosive weapons directly into the mountain and Typhon's location. By the time she had arrived at Longyearbyen, the alien vessel was turning around and preparing to leave, and she could pick up no signal from her master at all.

Nightshade had then come under attack from the alien craft herself, but had easily avoided its simplistic projectiles. Unable to fire her own weapons without Typhon's direct authority, she had done the only thing she could do—collide with the aircraft and destroy it. It was no longer a threat.

Now *Nightshade's* glassy black, angular form was hovering outside the collapsed and smouldering mountainside, the snowy landscape below reflecting off her hull. Frantically she scanned for signs of life, but Typhon was gone. She could find no trace of him whatsoever. Her scanners could see nothing, and the infrequent radio signals from earlier were now completely dead. What if he was too? It didn't bear thinking about. Oberyn would have her melted down for spare parts. But what could she do? Nothing. To wait was her only course of action now. Wait and see if Typhon would emerge from the mountain again.

Remaining there was not an option, however. The Earth

creatures would come for her now, and without the authority to use her own firepower, she would be constantly hounded. No, she would need to hide in space, where the humans would be less likely to find her.

She pointed her nose to the heavens and shot away into the darkness—punching a hole through the Storm of Shadows and allowing a solitary beam of sunlight to bleed through for a moment, before the wound quickly healed and utter darkness returned.

Unwittingly, this tiny aperture allowed Lieutenant Randolph's ejector seat locator beacon to transmit a vital burst of data out from beneath the smothering confines of the Storm of Shadows.

— THIRTY-ONE —
Truth of the Matter

The doorbell rang, followed by feverish banging on the front door that refused to let up. Then the doorbell rang three or four more times, and the banging started over. Mungo was in the hallway, growing more and more anxious by the second. He looked to the front door and then back into the food-making room at poor Pack Leader, lying on the floor. Then back to the front door. And then back to Pack Leader. On and on it went.

Janice ignored the front door commotion. She had her hands full—literally. She was sitting cross-legged on the floor cradling her son's head in her lap and stroking his hair. He was lying on the tiles, dazed but semiconscious.

Moments ago the school had telephoned to say it was closed due to security concerns. Pupils were to stay at home. They said that it was unlikely that anyone would go to work that day, either, for the same reason, so hopefully Billy could stay home with his family. She had been about to ask what kind of security concern could stop school and work, when she'd seen Billy tip over and fall out of a dining chair. She'd immediately flung the phone back into its cradle and rushed to his aid.

The door banging continued. Then a voice shouted, "Billy. Billy. Come on. Open up, will you? Have you seen the TV news?"

Janice recognised the voice as belonging to Ellie Roundtree from next door—the slightly odd but nice enough emo girl from Canada. She figured Ellie would try the back door in a minute so left her there at the front door, unanswered. She was kind of busy after all. Her world had momentarily unwound. Well, she hoped it was momentary. One minute she'd been feeding the dog. The next thing she knew, school was cancelled—work too, by the sounds of it—her son had fainted, and the telly was talking about an alien attack in Norway, of all places. Who attacks Norway, for God's sake? Don't aliens always attack New York or Los Angeles in the movies? Her mind was wandering. It always did in times of stress. She needed to focus.

"How are you feeling now, Billy?" she asked her son.

"Groggy," he replied quietly. "But better. I should get the door. That's Ellie."

"No, no, stay put," said his mother. "You can see her later. You've had a funny turn."

The door knocking stopped. Then they heard the side gate latch click open and shut. They both turned to the patio doors and watched as Ellie rounded the corner; she placed her hands up to the glass and peered in. She immediately flinched back in surprise when she saw them both on the dining room floor. Then she immediately tried the sliding door, which was unlocked. She slid it open and ran in, a look of genuine concern on her face.

"Billy, Mrs Twigg. What happened? Are you all right?"

"It's okay, Ellie," said Janice. "Billy's had a bit of a fall."

Billy smiled weakly. "It's okay, Mum. Ellie knows about everything." *In fact, she knows a lot more than you do*, he thought.

His mum looked at Ellie for a moment but decided it wasn't the time or place to start discussing what she knew about Billy's condition.

Ellie glanced up at the DMM news broadcast on the TV. They were repeatedly looping clips of the alien bar attack video together with footage of a strange black cloud. Being voiced over the top was a debate with so-called experts about what this could all mean. Suffice to say, there was a lot of nonsense being spouted by ill-informed journalists, ex-military people, somebody who claimed to have looked after top-secret British Ministry of Defence UFO cases, and a religious scholar.

"Turn that rubbish off, would you please, Ellie?" said Janice, putting on a controlled smile.

"Of course," she replied, marching over to the television and switching it off at the wall socket. "Let me get him some water." She trotted over to the sink and filled a tumbler with water from a filter jug on the counter top and brought it over to Billy. She sat down opposite his mother on the floor.

"Thank you, Ellie," said Janice, touched by her thoughtfulness.

"Yeah, thanks, Ellie," mumbled Billy, forcing a smile and then adding in a mock American movie actor voice. "Got anything stronger?"

"Someone's feeling better," replied Ellie, tapping Billy on the nose, pretending to scold him. She then felt immediately self-conscious because of Janice's presence, and blushed.

Janice smiled. She could clearly see that these two kids had something going on between them. They were more than just neighbours or pals. There was a little spark of something else there. It was nice, she thought. Billy needed somebody like her in his life. It was just a shame about her emo look. Still, she'd most likely grow out of it.

"Can you sit up yet, Billy?" asked his mum.

"I think so," he replied. "Actually, I'd like to stand up."

"Let me give you a hand, guys," added Ellie, standing up herself.

Together, Janice and Ellie hauled Billy onto his feet and kept hold of him while he got his bearings. After a few moments of unsteadiness, he said he was okay and to let go. There was an anxious few moments as Ellie and Janice waited to see if he'd collapse again. When he didn't, their minds eased and turned to other worrying matters, like what the hell was going on in Norway and what was happening there in Britain?

Billy walked over to the TV and turned it back on again. "We'd better find out what's happening."

"Take it easy," said his mother. "Eat something, please. I'm going to call your father. Actually, Ellie, can you make sure he eats his breakfast, please?"

"Of course, Mrs Twigg," she replied earnestly.

She then set about making some peanut butter toast while Janice went back over to the wall phone to try and get in touch with Billy's dad, Simon, who was working an early shift in the cardboard box factory a couple of miles away.

Yet another annoying DMM commercial break came to an end, and the news channel had an update to its "fast-paced developing story." It said that the prime minister of Norway and the president of the United States would be making a joint, live televised address to the world via satellite at nine a.m., UK time, to be followed by a localised address by Britain's prime minister. Citizens were advised to stay at home.

Clearly, something epic was afoot. Synchronised globally televised addresses by world leaders weren't something Billy could ever remember seeing before. He was also going to have to face the fact that everything Sal had told him in his crazy dream last night was quite likely true, which in itself meant that Sal was real, and therefore his dreamscape travels were also real.

There was a peculiar blurring of the line between reality and imagination going on here. It was a surreal concept, but he couldn't argue with what he was now seeing on the TV and with what he'd been told in his dream. As mad as it sounded, this somviator stuff was looking increasingly authentic.

"Ellie, this . . . this attack that's happened. This Norway massacre," said Billy, in a low, hesitant voice. "The alien. Everything. I knew about it last night . . . from a dream."

"No way," gasped Ellie, in a tone that expressed her unequivocal belief that what he'd said was completely true.

Billy wanted to hug her. She was the only one in the world who understood him.

"Was it like a premonition or something?" she asked.

"Sort of, I suppose, although it was more of a conversation I had with an alien called Sal. Sally Magmajude. The weird dreams I've been having this week have all been about her. She's been telling me all kinds of crazy stuff, including information about him." Billy gestured to the TV that was yet again showing a still image of the alien looking at the camera. "He's called Typhon. Calls himself 'the Destroyer of Worlds.' He means to kill us all, Ellie. And he'll do it too, unless I stop him. Sal told me our military weapons are no use. We're not advanced enough to stop him."

"Jesus. What can we do then?"

"Well, as stupid as this sounds, Ellie, I have to go back to sleep. I have to get back into that same dream. Back to Sal. Then I have to get back here and . . . well, I have to kill him. Kill Typhon."

Ellie looked puzzled and scared. "I'm sorry, Billy, but I'm confused. You're going to have to explain more to me."

"Of course, of course. Sorry. Let's go into the garden."

"Take your toast," said Ellie.

Out they went, into the fine drizzle, a steady stream of birds flying overhead. All flying south. All different shapes and sizes. All different species. A mass exodus.

"Do you see that?" said Billy, chewing on his toast and pointing at the sky.

"Yeah. Weird. All flying south," acknowledged Ellie, looking up.

"Weird perhaps," said Billy. "But not inexplicable. I'll bet you anything they're flying away from Typhon. I bet if you drew a straight line back from their direction of travel, it would take you straight to that Long Beard, or whatever it's called, Norwegian island that was attacked last night."

They both fell silent for a few seconds as they watched the unusual bird migration overhead. Finally, Billy said, "So, I'd better tell you what's been happening to me the last few days, hadn't I?"

"It would be good to know," replied Ellie. "I've been concerned about you, Billy. Especially after the bridge thing yesterday. That was intense."

Billy and Ellie wandered about in the back garden, ambling up and down the meandering stone pathway through the centre of the lawn, up to the small ornamental pond at the rear of the property and back down to the dining room's sliding glass patio doors. He told her everything he knew. All about Sal, LAURA, the Balta asteroid, Igonosphar IV, the meteorgus test, and Typhon, with his horrific intentions for Earth. Last, he explained Sal's theory of sending the dreamscape Billy back to Earth to confront Typhon.

When he was done, Ellie remained silent. Contemplative. Confused, most probably, thought Billy. He looked at her and wondered if she was considering running away from this lunatic. Somewhat surprisingly she didn't. She was about to say something when the patio door slid open, and Billy's mum stuck her head out. "Your father's coming home," she said. "Let's not mention what happened in the kitchen this morning, okay? Ellie, you'd better go home to your mum too. And Billy, you'd better be inside when your dad gets here."

The two teenagers nodded. Janice disappeared back inside and closed the door.

"So," said Ellie. "How do we get you back into the Sally dream then?"

"I have no idea," said Billy solemnly.

"Perhaps we should re-create your surroundings from yesterday?" she suggested.

"How do you mean?"

"Sit in the same classroom and see if you pass out again. Like you did in Hagnaby's lesson yesterday."

"School's closed, Ellie. They called my mum this morning and told her."

"Mine too. So, let's break in."

Billy regarded Ellie coolly for a moment then said, "Okay."

— THIRTY-TWO —
Spasm

The strand of black fibre twitched in the darkness, like a wriggling caterpillar, jerky and spasmodic. It had very basic self-awareness and a primary objective: find more of itself. It began to search blindly amongst the rubble.

— THIRTY-THREE —
Bag of Tricks

The two teenagers sneaked back into Billy's house before his dad came home. He collected his bag and a coat from the hall and then they scuttled off next door so Ellie could get a coat from her house too. Then they scarpered before they would be spotted by anyone.

The streets outside were eerily silent. There was nobody going about at all. They imagined people glued to their televisions, watching reruns of the Norwegian attack and waiting for the press conference at nine a.m. It was the ideal time for them to be sneaking about.

Billy and Ellie were taking a short cut through a children's playground, talking about how best to break into the school's main building via a fire escape door that had a dodgy locking bar. Suddenly Billy crumpled into a heap on the rubberised safety pavement beside a kids' slide. Ellie stood over him in complete shock. She'd heard about Billy's sudden collapses from other kids who'd witnessed them and from Billy himself, but she'd never seen one for herself. It was quite upsetting.

Her first instinct was to wake him up. Maybe slap him in the face and get him upright. Then she remembered how important he said it was for him to return to Sal. He'd explained how the plan was for him to load up on futuristic alien weaponry and haul it back to Earth so he could take on Typhon and ultimately destroy him.

Even for open-minded Ellie, this would normally have been a

preposterous idea, but the TV news coverage that morning, and yesterday's incident on the footbridge, had convinced her that Billy was the real deal. Somehow he'd been unwittingly dragged into a major conflict, and just might be the key to winning it.

So instead of giving Billy a wake-up slap to the face, Ellie made him a little bit more comfortable. She took hold of his arms, dragged him a couple of metres, and arranged him so that he was lying under the diagonal slope of the children's slide, sheltering him from the elements as much possible. She placed him so his feet were under the bottom of the slide and his head was beneath the roomier, higher end.

She intended to pop his bag under his head as a makeshift pillow. His "Indy bag," as he called it—so named after the hero's satchel in his favourite *Indiana Jones* movies. It was a brown leather record bag with a great big flap of leather that folded over the front and a long shoulder strap, so that when worn it hung by his hip. It was a really nice bag actually—very well worn, beautifully soft leather. Billy never went anywhere without it. She'd asked him before what was in it, and he'd just said "stuff" and never elaborated.

Ellie sat down next to him and picked up the satchel, only to find she had an irresistible urge to look inside. It would be so wrong to do that, of course. It was none of her business. But . . . but she just couldn't help herself. She gently folded the leather flap back, and as quietly as she could, dragged the zip back across the top. The bag went slack and the top opened right up. Ellie peered inside.

There was a lot of "stuff" in there, right enough. On the top was a folded-up sweater. She took that out and laid it over the top of the thin shower-proof jacket Billy was wearing. It would help keep him warm. Now she could see that poking out of the bag was the edge of his iPad. It was a second-hand mini model that he'd saved up to buy on eBay.

Ellie remembered how Billy had told her that his dad had said iPads were just a fad and that they were too expensive. He would not be getting one from them. So instead, Billy saved up his birthday and Christmas money and added to it by working Saturdays in Snotton Market Square, where he was a general dogsbody, running errands for stall owners.

He'd help them to set up and pack up their stalls. And look after them when they went on loo breaks or went for lunch. That type of thing. It paid cash and had perks like free leftover food at the end of the day. His mum always welcomed the exotic breads he usually brought home.

They were long days, but Billy had really wanted an iPad, so motivation was not a problem. But once he'd bought his tablet computer, he'd decided to stay on working at the market. By then he'd struck up a rapport with many of the stall owners and was developing an interesting circle of friends. He'd grown to like it, and the extra cash meant he could now afford to buy apps and things for his new gizmo.

Next, Ellie found a really old Nintendo console—an original Game Boy from 1989, loaded up with Tetris. Billy always said you couldn't beat the original classic machine. Then she found a textbook on World War II and a small jotter full of quotes and notes about the epic war against Hitler and the Nazis. She knew Billy was really enjoying that module in his history lessons.

There was a yo-yo and a Rubik's Cube, tucked up against a plastic water bottle. She also found a battered old paperback called *Baaawhooo the Weresheep*. It looked like utter twaddle to her, but then Billy did like to read fantasy nonsense like that.

There were some other bits of battered paperwork, like a Lego model kit's instruction booklet and some small origami models. Then she found a strip of three photos and smiled for the first time in a while. The photos were of her and Billy goofing about in a coin-operated photo booth. She remembered them giggling and pulling faces at each other behind the curtain. She thought he was really sweet to have kept it with him.

The remainder of the contents consisted of his iPad's charger, some conkers, elastic bands, and paper clips rattling around the bottom, along with crumbs from sweets and snacks, and a few small Lego bricks. That was basically it—a messy bag full of *boy stuff*.

Ellie was putting things back where they belonged when she realised she could feel the weight of something else still in the bag, despite it looking empty. She squinted and peered into the satchel again. There was something under the lining at the bottom. A tubular object. She could feel it on her thigh too, where the bag was resting. It was hard, like a stone of some sort.

She felt up the inside of the bag and at the top came across a wide rip in the lining right by the zip. Curious. She pushed her hand down the space between the lining and the leather and, right at the bottom, found the object. It was slightly warm and felt like glass. She pulled it out.

In her hand was a crystal about twenty centimetres long and four wide. It was amber in colour and seemed to have a faint glow to it. For a moment she thought she saw something move inside it that caused her to drop it silently onto the cushioned play surface. Billy immediately murmured something in his sleep and frowned. Ellie's spine snapped her bolt upright. Billy and the crystal seemed to be linked in some way.

She carefully picked the crystal up and looked it over. It felt a little lighter than she would have expected, as if it was perhaps hollow. It felt a little tingly too—as though it had an inner power source. It gave her the creeps.

I was right all along, she thought. I bet this is what's making him dream. But why had he never mentioned it before? Why the secret? She felt a little wounded. What was he up to?

Ellie yawned unexpectedly and placed the crystal back inside the lining of the bag; she put everything else back in its place, except the sweater. Then she gently slid it under Billy's head to form a pillow.

She stared at him, wondering where he was now and what he was doing. How long was he going to be asleep? She felt vulnerable and exposed, but at least they were sheltered from the drizzle, which had become a little heavier. Their position under the slide was also out of the way of prying eyes.

Not that there would be anyone out there prying at the moment, surely.

— THIRTY-FOUR —
Rage

Russell was still angry. Really, really angry. He'd woken up roughly twelve hours after skinny geek Billy Twigg had somehow managed to throw him into the canal, and he was still furious about it. He'd hardly slept, his mind rerunning the episode over and over again all night long. He just couldn't understand what had happened. How could the little runt have moved so quickly?

Twigg should be in the morgue, or at least recovering in hospital this morning. Instead, Russell was at home, in his grandmother's run-down flat, starting with a cold and feeling anxious about ever seeing the canal again. This was not how it was supposed to be.

How could his head-butt attack have failed? Russell's secret was to strike the opponent with the thick bone on the top of his head. Not his forehead, like in the movies. The top of his head hurt him less and them more. Russell had spent the last few years perfecting this particular variety of thuggery. It struck his opponents hard and usually took them out with the first blow. He figured it looked cool too. It had never failed him before. It unnerved him that it had now.

One thing was for sure, though. Twigg was going to pay for it. Russell would make sure of that. He was giving serious consideration to ending him, if he could get away with it. Maybe Billy could *fall* down the stairs of the main building at school? Better still, perhaps Billy could be playing around with the handrail at the top of the four-storey staircase and then tragically lose his footing and plunge down the central stairwell—splattering his brains all over the stone floor. That might be possible.

Russell's scheming and plotting was interrupted by his chain-smoking grandmother, who shuffled in and rasped that the school had just called to say it was closed because of some big news event happening now. He was to stay at home.

Yeah, right. He was going to do that.

Since his gran only watched soaps and quiz shows all day, and he only watched violent action movies, neither of them knew of the seismic events unfolding a couple of thousand kilometres north of them. His grandma lit another cigarette off the smouldering end of the last one and shuffled back into the lounge.

Russell grabbed a jacket from the back of his bedroom door and a long metal screwdriver from under his bed, the tip of which he'd sneakily sharpened to be like a chisel blade during metalwork class a few weeks ago. Then he stole some of his gran's money out of a jar in the kitchen and left. If Billy wasn't at school today, then he'd have to find him elsewhere, and he'd need some help.

It was remarkably quiet outside. There were no pedestrians or cars going about. It was like a mild weather version of Christmas Day. Russell laughed at this notion. It was going to be his Christmas Day all right, and the big present was going to be Billy Twigg's hide.

— THIRTY-FIVE —
Digit

The small patch of black material flexed and undulated in the dust and grit. Another couple of strands of dark thread had just inched their way across the ground and woven themselves into it. It was now four or five centimetres square. Thin, fragile, and dirty looking.

The material flicked up into the air and quickly rolled into a tube. Where the edges met, the fibres wriggled frantically for a moment like tiny worms, and intertwined to form a hollow cylinder. At one end, more fibres unwound slightly and pulled together to create a tiny closed dome. A few dozen more fibres crawled out from under rocks and over rubble and joined the other end of the tube to lengthen it. Then two equidistant creases formed around its circumference, and it folded up and down on them slightly. It was beginning to look like something recognisable. It was growing into a finger.

It rolled over and twitched some more and then began to crawl by bending and straightening at the two joints. The finger became more nimble. Faster. More eager. It searched amongst the shattered rock fragments for more.

— THIRTY-SIX —
Zap

Billy woke up. Unsurprisingly, he was sitting in a booth in the space diner again, wearing the now familiar silver somviator onesie. Sal was sitting opposite him, still reading her eBook.

She looked up and said, "Ah, finally. Please don't take off midconversation like that again, Billy."

He frowned and looked at her. He could tell immediately that she had a grump on. His memory was a little groggy at first but it began to clear, allowing him to recall what had happened.

"Sorry, Sal," he said. "My alarm clock at home went off and woke me for school. Turns out it's cancelled anyway. Seems Britain has shut down, awaiting a press conference from the Norwegians and Americans. Typhon is all over the TV news. They have video of him killing people and destroying a town."

"I'm real sorry to hear that," said Sal, sounding concerned and frustrated. "It's going to get ugly. Dammit, we need to get you down there, Billy, or it's game over for Earth. Everybody will die, including you. You're only here because your Primo is asleep back there. If he dies, you're dead too. Gone for good. Do you get me?"

"Come on, Sal," gulped Billy, forcing a smile. "We can work it out. You'll think of something, right? We can use your flying saucer to take me back, can't we?"

"It can't get there fast enough, Billy," she snapped. "We're twelve light years from Earth, and my ship can't travel at light speed. It would take us twenty Earth years or more to get there.

The only way to get back in time to stop the son of a gun is to use transference and shift yourself right back to Earth. But you got to believe in the dreamscape before you can move around in it at will like that, Billy. And you don't believe in any of this yet, do you? You think it's all madness. Nonsense. Shoot, I'm amazed you're even here at all. Whole thing's a mite peculiar." Sal sighed and shook her head.

"I'm sorry," replied Billy, mumbling. Then he protested, anger rising in his voice. "I can't do what you want, Sal, because I'm the wrong guy for this stupid nonsense. I told you before. I didn't ask for any of this to happen. I didn't wake up one morning and suddenly say, 'I know, I'd like to meet up with Sal in her space café and save the world from a homicidal lunatic.' I told you, I'm just a kid with no idea what I'm doing. Don't start blaming me for this mess. It's not—"

"Whoa, whoa, simmer down there, son," interrupted Sal, holding up three palms toward him in a gesture of peace.

He stopped shouting and sighed, rubbing his forehead.

"I'm sorry, Billy. I shouldn't have lost my temper," said Sal. "Forgive me. It's just . . . I was worried you weren't coming back, is all."

"I'm sorry too," he said slowly, nodding and accepting her apology. "I'm a bit freaked out by all this, to be honest with you. I suppose I don't really know what's going on. There's a part of me that refuses to accept this is anything other than a dream. Then there's a growing part of my mind that believes it is true, especially after the attack in Norway showed on TV. That's when I deliberately tried to come back here. To you."

"I'm mighty glad you did. How did you?"

"My friend Ellie suggested we recreate the surroundings of my last trip. We were heading back to my school, to try and emulate yesterday, but . . . I'm not sure. I was walking there and then . . .

then I was here."

"Hmm, sounds like something triggered your return earlier than you planned. Is Ellie a good friend?"

"The best."

"Good. She'll be looking after your Primo then, hopefully."

"Yeah, she will be. I just hope she isn't freaked out by it and wakes me up. But she knows that I need to be here."

"Well, let's assume she's a smart girl and lets you finish what you need to finish. Besides, your dream time on Earth is way faster than the time you spend out here."

"How's that?"

"Just one of those weird cosmic things. You ever fallen asleep and dreamed a big dream that feels like hours of activity, and then you wake up to find you've only been asleep for ten minutes?"

"Yeah, sometimes that happens."

"Same thing. A few hours up here is only a few minutes of sleep time back on Earth."

"Okay. That should make it less awkward for Ellie."

There was a natural pause to their conversation. They both knew where it was going next.

"So," said Billy, verbalising their thoughts. "How the heck do we get me from here to Earth?"

"I don't know if we can," replied Sal. "We might be too late."

"So, you say that the only way for me to get there is if I have such an unfaltering belief in this whole dreamscape business that I simply choose to be on Earth and jump there?"

"Exactly," said Sal, her face brightening up. "That's exactly what you need to do. Do you think you can?"

"No," said Billy, flatly. "I don't believe in it enough to do that, Sal. I'm so sorry. I still have nagging doubts."

"I figured as much," she said, her face falling. "It's asking a huge amount in a very short space of time. We hadn't even met until yesterday. Most somviator cadets take a few weeks to come around to it all being real. No reason to presume you would be any quicker at it."

Billy nodded. There was another brief pause in the conversation as they both pondered their dilemma. Then Billy had an idea. "Why don't you zap yourself to Earth, and you take on Typhon? You can do that, right?"

"I could 'zap' myself there," said Sal, smiling a little. "I like 'zap,' by the way, Billy."

"Sounds a bit better than *transference*." He smiled, putting on an exaggerated posh accent for the last word.

"It does that," she said with a laugh, the atmosphere relaxing more. "So, yes, I could zap myself to Earth right now. But I don't think I'd blend in very well." She held up her three hands, one of them plucking at her purple sprout of head hair. She then popped out a little smoke ring from her left nostril, for added effect. "I don't think jittery humans would take too kindly to me," she said. "Hell, they'd probably think I was Typhon and shoot me down dead before I could walk ten feet."

"Good point. How about you zap yourself and the flying saucer into an Earth orbit? Could you do that?"

"Could do, I guess. But again, a flying saucer ain't going to go down too well with your species. They've shot them down before!"

"What? When?"

"You heard of Roswell?"

"Of course. Supposedly a UFO crashed in New Mexico or Arizona or somewhere like that, back in the 1950s."

"Foster homestead, near Roswell, New Mexico, July the eighth, 1947. That was me. An air force P-80 Shooting Star fighter jet shot us down. We'd been having some engine trouble anyway, and then we got taken out. That's how I ended up with three of these instead of four." Sal held up her three arms and waved them at him. "But that's another story."

Billy was utterly amazed. "You're not just an alien, Sal, uh, you know, an alien to Earth people, I mean. You're not just an alien, Sal. You're a famous alien. *The* alien!"

"Gee, that's swell," said Sal sarcastically. "I didn't feel so welcome after being held prisoner there for thirty years, I can tell you."

"I had no idea," said Billy, somewhat in awe.

"Hardly anybody did. Was all hushed up. US military called it Project Sign. Then Project Grudge. Finally, it became Project Blue Book. They investigated UFOs for years. Eventually, they gave up. Most of them were fakes. They held me for three decades at a remote part of Edwards Air Force Base in Nevada, commonly known as Area 51."

Billy's jaw went slack. In an odd way, these latest revelations made it all the more believable. Rather than sounding crazy, it made more sense.

"What were you doing there, Sal?" he asked.

"Recruitment drive, mostly. Looking for somviator candidates. For some reason, humans make particularly good somviators. Naive, underdeveloped brains most likely accounting for that. No offence. And we were harvesting cows. Can't beat prime beef, my friend."

Billy stared. "Cows?" he repeated, incredulously.

"Yup. Earth's greatest contribution to the universe thus far—the humble hamburger. Why do you think I opened this joint? Everyone loves them. Where do you think all those cow abduction stories come from in America? They're true. Caused by rival hamburger enterprises from across the universe taking cows for breeding and cloning. It's funny, you know? Humans spend so much time and money trying to further their exploration of space, when the whole time cows are the most experienced intergalactic travellers in history. There are cows on just about every advanced world in the universe. Ha ha, and you guys have no idea!"

Billy laughed. "That's bonkers, Sal. Absolutely mental!"

"Yup, the universe is full of surprises, ain't it?"

"Sure is," agreed Billy, wistfully. "So, getting back to more important matters, you say you could zap yourself and your saucer to Earth if you wanted to?"

"Yup. It just wouldn't do much good, is all."

"Why don't you take me with you, then? Put me in your saucer and zap us both there?"

"Ah, because I can't take anything living with me, Billy. Nothing alive can accompany a somviator during transference. It's one of the issues with doing this. Somviators can send themselves and inorganic stuff like weapons and vehicles to any place they like. But they can't take another living creature with them. They don't make it. They disappear. Nobody knows where to, but they just don't arrive at the other end."

Billy frowned and thought for a moment. Then his eyes almost popped out of their sockets. "But I'm not here," he cried. "What I mean is, I don't really believe I'm here, right? I'm asleep on Earth, really. A Primordica, or whatever it is you call it. So it's different for me. This is just *dream Billy* right here with you now. A Servo as you called it, right?"

"Well, I, uh . . . don't know about that, Billy," said Sal, sounding slightly confused. "I, uh, hadn't thought of it quite like that. Besides, you are here, in most ways. You have a physical presence." She patted him on the shoulder to reaffirm her point.

"Okay, try this for size. If I don't fully believe I'm here to begin with, can I be in any real danger? How can I die if I don't think I'm here in the first place? Isn't it worth a shot?"

"Um, I don't know, Billy," said Sal hesitantly. "I'm not sure . . ."

"I think it's worth a go," he cut in. "Take me with you, Sal. Let's try it. It's our best shot."

"It, uh . . . could be very dangerous for you. I don't know if it would work. It's a risky thing to try." Sal paused a moment to ponder the idea and then mumbled as she thought out aloud. "Zap a nonbelieving Servo back to his home planet where his Primo is located. Do it by transferring my own Servo-self, inside my ship, with you as a passenger—loaded up with all the weapons we can carry."

"Exactly."

Sal thought about it for a moment longer. She took out a notepad and pencil from her apron pocket and did some quick doodles depicting spirals and arrows, with little equations scribbled around the edges. When she finished, she still looked uncertain. "It sounds like a recipe for disaster to me. I'm not convinced it can work, Billy. Not convinced at all. I think you'll probably just disappear like the others who've tried similar stunts. It'll most likely kill you."

"You say I'm going to die anyway. Typhon's going to kill me and everybody else back home very soon. What's to lose by trying?"

"When you put it like that, I, uh . . . guess we haven't got any better ideas, have we?"

"Nope, we don't. Come on, Sal, let's get the gear we need and get going."

Sal paused for a moment, deep in serious thought, then hunched her shoulders and said, "Okay. I'd better give you the tour, then."

— THIRTY-SEVEN —
A Helping Hand

It had grown larger, gaining two more digits. Now it consisted of a right thumb, index finger, and middle finger. They were attached by a quarter of the back of the hand and part of the palm.

Now it had much more manoeuvrability. It was quick too—able to scurry like a crab over some of the smaller obstacles, long tendrils of tattered thread dragging behind it. Increased digits and agility meant it could access more parts of the collapsed tunnel. Likewise, more and more dark, wriggling threads were able to locate it. The hand's growth began to accelerate at an exponential rate.

— THIRTY-EIGHT —
Shelter

The precipitation had picked up. It was no longer drizzle. It was rain. Billy was still out cold under the children's slide. He had been for about ten minutes, but it felt a lot longer to Ellie. She was still sitting by his side, looking at him, making sure he was breathing. Every minute or two she'd look around and make sure they weren't attracting any undue attention. So far, so good. She could have done without the rain, though. Their shelter was long and narrow and didn't offer much protection from the sides. They were both going to get wet if this kept up.

She looked at her smartphone. It was 8:56 a.m. The joint Norway–United States TV news conference was about to begin. Ellie opened the DMM app and watched it log on to the news agency's servers using a 4G connection.

The familiar and annoying news anchors appeared on her device's small screen. They were still wittering on about who or what the alien creature was and why it would be doing the things it was. They had no idea and were just making rubbish up and generally killing time as they waited for the satellite feeds to begin. Then the show went to a commercial break.

Some enterprising movie studio had managed to place an advertisement for *The X-Files* TV show into the ad slot already. Ellie rolled her eyes and shook her head. Billy would have done the same. She missed him.

She stroked his mop of blond hair, wiping a few strands away from his eyes. They were frantically rolling about under his eyelids like he was having a nightmare. She hoped not.

— THIRTY-NINE —
The Tour

Sal escorted Billy through the kitchen to the large walk-in refrigeration unit at the back of the train carriage. She skated up to the door, stopped on her brake pads and pulled it open. There was a soft clunk sound and some cold air flowed out along the tiled floor. She gestured to Billy to enter ahead of her. With a little trepidation, he did. Sal followed behind and pulled the door shut on them both. It went momentarily black and then a red light illuminated the interior space.

It was very chilly in there but seemed like a regular cold room. It contained the types of things you'd expect to see, like packets of cheese, boxes of burger buns, and baskets of vegetables. Sal pointed to one such basket by Billy's shoulder. It contained a lettuce, some onions, and a cucumber that was poking out vertically.

"Yank the cucumber," said Sal, with a mischievous wink.

Billy narrowed his eyes in puzzlement but did as requested. It was a fake rubber cucumber, locked in place at its base. When he pulled on it, it hinged forward and then lit up bright green. The floor vibrated and then descended like an elevator, leaving the stainless-steel door, walls, and ceiling behind.

They were travelling down into a new chamber. Lights were flickering on in a random pattern, gradually revealing a large, clinically white, circular room. It was far wider and taller than the diner car above them, and dominated by a strange array of white pods radiating out around the floor from a central circular platform.

"Welcome to my somviator hideout. These are the lay-bays," said Sal, pointing over at the pods.

The refrigerator elevator drew to a stop on the floor of the secret room. Sal skated out and waved at Billy to follow her. There was a thin countertop running around the curved wall. Sal went up to it and began tapping at a concealed keyboard. The top of one of the pods hissed and hinged open, levering upward from the end nearest the centre.

Inside was a sculpted, white plastic seat in a reclining position. Billy walked up to the other pods as the elevator behind him quietly rose back into the ceiling. There were twenty lay-bays in all. They formed a large circle. In the centre was a raised, white platform. Upon it stood a small mount holding an amber-coloured crystal about the size of a half-litre soda bottle. It had some sort of faint light inside it that glowed and pulsed. Just for a moment he thought he saw something squirm within it.

"What is this place?" whispered Billy.

Sal turned around. "This is where the somviator Primos slept, while their Servos went out on missions. It was our lair. Reminds me of those old James Bond movies I used to love. Say, do they still make those?"

"Um, yes. They're up into the twenties now, I think."

"Wow. Ain't Sean Connery getting too old to make them?"

"Ha ha, yes, Sal. They use different actors. I think they're on about Bond actor number six now. You get sidetracked way too easily, by the way. You know that?"

"Sorry, Billy, I miss my time on Earth sometimes. Well, I miss the TV down there. They used to let me watch movies, if I'd been, uh, cooperative. It was my only escape from the hell of that military base."

"It's awesome in here," said Billy, trying to get back on point.

"Are we inside the Balta asteroid?"

"I'd sure like to watch me one of them there new Bond movies . . ."

"Sal! Give it up, will you?"

"Mmm? Oh, sorry. Right, yes. Now, where was I?"

"Are we inside Balta?"

"Yup, yup, yup, we sure are. We got a few chambers like this in here. It's our secret base. It ain't been used for a while now, though. Ain't been anyone around to use it for years. Just little old me."

"What's that in the middle, there," said Billy, pointing to the glowing amber object in the centre of the room.

"Ah, that my friend, is a Remnant Stone. It's what gives us our power. Not our ability, though. Somviators can, and do, enter the dreamscape at will. But this crystal acts like an amplifier to boost our ability. Like a stabilising antenna to send us further. When we're close enough to it, it allows us to maintain a strong and steady connection to our Servos on the other side, to the places we're visiting."

"Amazing," said Billy, impressed by the whole setup.

Sal continued. "The somviators would lie in these lay-bays and project themselves to wherever they needed to go, with the aid of the Remnant Stone. It could handle as many somviators as we threw at it. Never seemed to falter."

"What is it?"

"It's a very powerful, indestructible piece of ancient universe geology. Maybe the very first. A sacred object. There are three of them, so they say. All part of one bigger piece. Supposed to all fit together somehow. They ain't been that way since the Big Bang, as you folks call it. They're believed to be the origin of everything. Maybe even caused the Big Bang in the first place. The creation of the universe. During that eruption, they were cast far and wide. We have one. Two are missing. Well, I think you might have one actually, Billy."

"Huh?"

"You might not know it, but I think that one of the other stones could be on Earth. And given your recent adventures, I'd say it's very close to where you live."

Billy was stunned. "Ellie was right the whole time," he whispered.

"What was that?" asked Sal.

"Ellie has a theory," said Billy, in a clearer voice. "She thinks my dream travels started right after the moon collision."

"Moon collision?"

"Yup. A comet hit Earth's moon about six months ago. It sent a lot of debris down to Earth. Was pretty spectacular for a couple of weeks. My odd dreams and travels began shortly afterward. She has a theory that something came down in that shower and set my dreams off. She thinks there's probably something in my garden."

"Of course! How did I miss that?" said Sal excitedly. "That makes a lot of sense. One of them Remnant Stones could have been frozen inside the comet and been thrown clear when it hit your moon. I want to meet this Ellie girl. She sounds like a real smart cookie."

"She is pretty amazing," he said, smiling proudly.

"No wonder he couldn't find it."

"Huh?"

"Typhon. No wonder he couldn't find it, if it's been trapped inside a frozen comet all this time. He's looking for all the Remnant Stones, you see? Has been all his life. For millions of years. His father wants all three. He must never get them. They have untold power. If the three are reunited . . . " Sal paused and shook her head, adding, "Well, the three must never be allowed to fall into his hands. NEVER."

"Right," said Billy solemnly. "I guess that explains what he's doing on Earth then."

"Yup, most probably. His ship, *Nightshade*, could have picked up a trace signal of the stone when it was freed from the comet. He's likely looking for it on Earth now. You see, the Remnant Stones are unique in many ways. One of them being that they have a life force. They're alive."

Sal pointed over to the stone in the centre of the room and said, "Sometimes you can see something move inside. Nobody knows what the heck that is, by the way."

Billy stared at the stone but didn't see anything move this time.

"Typhon's been searching for these things for so long now, he's probably forgotten why," said Sal. "Probably doesn't care, neither. He's obsessed with death. Just kills for the sake of it. But there is actually a reason for his brutality.

"The stones give off a life force energy reading, just like you and I do, and every animal and plant does. *Nightshade*'s scanners can pick up these signals. But by Typhon's reasoning, the best method for locating a Remnant Stone is to kill every living thing on the target planet and then only have to look for one life sign, which would, by default, have to be a Remnant Stone. There's a brutal logic to it, I guess. It's why we hide our Remnant Stone inside this hollowed out asteroid. Mostly made of iron, see? Blocks out *Nightshade*'s scanners. Well, we hope so."

"Oh God, which means he's heading to *my* house."

"Shoot, yup—I'm afraid that is a possibility."

"I have to wake up, Sal. Get back to the house and warn Mum and Dad. I can't be here doing . . ."

"Hold on there, son," interrupted Sal evenly. "Let's just think this through for a second or two, shall we?"

Billy paused for breath. "Right, okay, yes," he said. "What shall we do?"

"First off, if you wake up and run home, all that'll happen is your parents won't believe you and then they won't let you out of the house again. Ellie's will be the same. Our best solution is to get you—this you, your Servo—down to Earth. You're the only one with a hope in hell of defeating Typhon."

"Yes, yes, you're right. So, how are we going to do that?"

"Well, I'm going to get in this here lay-bay and transfer, or zap, out of here," said Sal, smiling. "You're going to wait for me upstairs in the diner."

She sat on the edge of the open pod, untied her roller skates and dropped them onto the floor. She then reversed her large bottom in backward, lay down on the seat, and put her feet up.

"Why upstairs?"

"Remember what I said about meeting yourself? Not a good idea if I meet myself, either. I'm going to transfer up into the diner. Understand that somviators used to lie here and then zap out their Servos into distant realms. We never sent ourselves anywhere near as close as upstairs. That's risky in itself. What we're doing here is all topsy-turvy. Your Servo's on Balta. Your Primo's twelve light years away on Earth. It's never happened that way before. It's always been Primos here and Servos out there. We're all backward and mixed up now."

Sal gestured all three of her arms in a swinging motion aimed at the heavens. "Now go on, off with you," she said. "Push the wall tile that's a little darker than the rest over there, and the lift will come back for you." With that, Sal pressed a discreet switch beside her leg and the translucent white lay-bay hatch slowly closed over her.

Billy quickly moved to the elevator area and saw a light grey tile on the wall. He pushed it and stepped back. Above him a whirring sound told him the platform was on its way back down. He stood alone in the somviator hideout and regarded the strange crystal in the centre of the room. It was visibly brighter than when he'd first entered the chamber. It was faintly pulsing up and down as though it was working on a task, presumably helping to transfer Sal into the diner upstairs. It made him think of where there might be one at his house, but he couldn't remember seeing anything like it before.

The lift arrived and Billy stepped on to the platform, being careful not to trip over a box of cabbages. The fake cucumber on the shelf was lit up and leaning over as before. Unsure of quite what to do, he pushed it back upright. It stopped glowing and the lift juddered and rose up into the diner above. When it docked back into the refrigeration unit, the red light came back on and Billy pushed a lever on the door and stepped back out into the kitchen.

Directly ahead of him in the dimly lit seating area stood a plump silhouette, legs akimbo. Three hands were spinning Desintoscram guns like a cowboy spinning six-shooters from an old Clint Eastwood spaghetti western.

"Howdy partner. What took you so long," said Sal, slotting the weapons into two hip holsters and one strapped diagonally around her bust. "Shoot, I'd clean forgotten what fun this is."

Billy had to stem a laugh. "Hi, Sal," he said. "What're you doing?"

"Fine-tuning my reflexes, sonny. It's been quite a spell since I saw any action."

"You got enough guns there?"

"I'd have had four if it weren't for Roswell, darn it. Anyways, we need to get you armed up. I got a container of weapons in my saucer. Come on, let's hightail it over there."

They picked their clear helmets up off a table near the exit and screwed them into place simultaneously. Then they fitted their gloves. Sal looked at Billy and made three thumbs-up signs. Billy reciprocated with two, and then they both exited the diner and stepped out onto the rocky surface of Balta.

"Let's fly there, Billy," said Sal, pointing over to the left. "It's not far."

"Good idea. And yes, I know, I saw it on the way down to the planet earlier."

A familiar voice cut into Billy's audio feed. "Prepare for boot ignition."

"Hi LAURA," said Billy, smiling to himself. "How you doing? I've missed you."

"Glad to be reunited with you, Billy. We have a big mission this time."

Then their respective rocket boots magnetised together and launched the two of them upward.

"Follow me," yelled Sal as she unsteadily undulated toward the far side of the asteroid.

Billy didn't remark on her flying. But LAURA did. "She's a little rusty, Billy. It'll come back to her."

Billy smiled as he soared over the pitted and scarred surface of Balta. Off to his right, he noticed several rows of small, sandy mounds, and his smile faded. They were subtle and barely noticeable. Perhaps he saw them only because he was flying so low over the surface. He guessed they were the graves of the dead somviators Sal had spoken of earlier. With the Servos being killed in action, the Primos had died there on Balta. It gave him a little chill.

He banked left by making minor adjustments to the position of his arms and caught up with Sal. She was still bobbing up and down like a sine wave. He wondered if having an uneven number of arms was causing her suit to malfunction or if she was just a lousy pilot. He hoped she could fly the saucer better.

— FORTY —
Piece by Piece

An arm flopped over the top of a large boulder. A second later, the other did the same. They pulled themselves up and then both of them rolled over the top and down the other side, separately. They tumbled into a shallow pit full of grit and small rock fragments and lay still for a few moments, as if catching their breath, before separating to carry on the search in opposite directions.

The left arm pulled itself out of the pit and on into the semidarkness of a new chamber—a collapsed cavern consisting of large boulders and smaller broken chips of concrete. Somewhere at the back, a flickering orange glow radiated through cracks between stones, partially illuminating the stone surroundings.

The hand's fingertips gripped on to anything it could find while the wrist and elbow hinged in unison to form an effective, if ungainly, method of movement. Where the bicep should have joined on to the shoulder, there was a ragged hole. Smoke wafted out of it and hundreds of tiny black threads wriggled and squirmed to weave themselves together.

At the other end, the fingers had stopped gripping and pulling. They were now delicately feeling around under a slab of sandstone, seeking something out. They spent a few minutes on this task, being extremely careful and thorough. Then there was a sudden flurry of activity and the hand began to reverse out of the gap.

When it was clear of any obstruction, the arm reared up on its elbow, raising its forearm vertically. The clenched fist at the top slowly opened, allowing fingers to manoeuvre a sticky black eyeball until it was facing outward. Slowly an eyelid rolled backward to reveal a fiery glow burning within it. The wrist then twisted left and right to let the eye stare into the gloom.

It saw things it liked. It saw many, many fragments of itself scattered around the cavern. They were busily assembling themselves back into recognisable forms. There was most of a foot, not far away over to the left. A piece of lower back and buttock was weaving itself together on top of a pile of boulders right in front it. Then, over toward the right, a skull was taking shape.

Wispy black smoke tendrils seeped through narrow gaps between boulders and flowed along the floor, seeking out hosts. When they encountered body parts, they hurriedly flowed into them, breathing dark energy back into the malevolent life forms.

It wouldn't be too much longer now.

— FORTY-ONE —
Search Party

The deathly silence that had descended upon the devastated town of Longyearbyen some hours earlier was finally interrupted by a distant and rapid whump-whump-whump sound coming from the south.

The US Air Force Bell Boeing V-22 Osprey tilt-rotor aircraft swept into the bay, swift and low, its tandem rotors producing a unique and unmistakable rhythm. A second Osprey quickly followed it. Both of them carried a platoon of elite troops, medics, field hospital apparatus, and small off-road vehicles.

Both aircraft were operated by the CIA Special Activities Division—a hard-ass outfit of handpicked personnel recruited from Special Forces—and sent to Longyearbyen at the express orders of President Swanson.

Their mission: establish if Typhon was dead or not and recover his remains if he was or kill him if he wasn't; recover their downed pilot and, if alive, find out what had happened; search for any extraterrestrial technology and retrieve it.

They had one lead, a fleeting partial transmission from Randolph's ejector seat beacon some hours ago disclosing it had been launched close to the seed vault entrance.

Assuming Randolph was still alive, he'd need assistance ASAP after enduring several hours in seasonally unusual freezing temperatures. Time was of the essence.

Sea landing craft from Norway were on their way, but the American Ospreys would just beat them to it, carrying the first ground forces to reach the scene since Lieutenant Randolph had ejected from his aircraft.

Being on Norwegian sovereign territory meant things could get a little dicey, politically. It was imperative to get in and get out as quickly as possible and avoid any unwelcome entanglements. Do it right and Norway would never know the United States had put troops on the ground.

They had flown some two thousand kilometres from the deck of the USS *Abraham Lincoln*, a Nimitz-class aircraft carrier, retasked from a training exercise in the north Atlantic and now steaming at full power to the Svalbard islands.

The Ospreys pulled up over the town, rotating their enormous prop rotors into a vertical position and shining powerful searchlights through the darkness onto the ruined settlement below. Snow blew around in crazy spirals under the powerful downdrafts as they probed the devastation, looking for the Mjölnir bar. When it was finally located, one aircraft descended and the other peeled away westward, heading for the Doomsday Vault location.

The crews were tired and irritable, having been in the air for over seven hours, and having performed two risky midair refuelling manoeuvres. Despite the dangerous nature of their location, they were glad to reach solid ground, intact and without incident.

The Osprey touched down hard, the rear cargo door immediately lowering to allow over a dozen stealth snowmobiles to launch onto the uneven, snowy terrain. The sixteen-man Special Operations Group squad converged their vehicles into a circle and regarded one another for a moment. The leader then held up his right hand and made some coded gestures that they all understood.

In unison, the riders flicked their Warrior Systems night

vision goggles down, fanned out, and sped off on their machines, vanishing into the unnatural darkness.

The terrain was rough and barren, and with no sunlight getting through, it was becoming colder and colder by the hour. The team were going to have to quickly search several square kilometres in the hope of finding the ejector seat.

Unfortunately, their assorted scanners and devices for pinpointing the downed pilot were not working properly. They'd been warned that this might happen. Something to do with the bizarre cloud formation above them. Instead, they would have to do the search the old-fashioned way, by sight. Adding to the confusion, they had no communications, either. Radio interference was off the chart.

With night vision goggles in place, the men began the laborious task of looking for their downed comrade. The terrain, however, was not what they had expected. The vault entrance was gone. In fact, the mountainside, as they knew it from detailed maps, was completely gone. In its place was a rough scree slope, peppered with larger chunks of shattered rock and a few inches of fresh snow, giving it a brilliant green appearance through their visors. Something monumental and catastrophic had occurred here.

Adding further pressure to the dangerous mission was that nobody knew what had become of Typhon. He'd simply stopped being active at the same time as the beacon broadcast had been received, leading analysts to believe Randolph had somehow killed him and then been forced to abandon his aircraft. This theory was further bolstered by the weird storm cloud, which had simultaneously stopped expanding and now appeared to be dormant.

Ensign Ben Southgate skilfully handled his snowmobile over the uneven terrain, steering left and right to avoid larger pieces of sandstone. It was like driving through a quarry, his transport only just able to maintain traction on the loose ground. He should have brought a scrambler motorbike, he thought. Never mind—get the job done whatever the situation, he reminded himself. Make the best of things. Nothing was unsurpassable. He looked down at his Tissot watch. They were to rendezvous back at the Osprey in thirty-seven minutes. There wasn't a second to lose.

His predetermined route took him north by northwest, downhill and away from where the Doomsday Vault entrance had once been. He was driving relatively slowly, trying to concentrate on his immediate hazardous surroundings as well as focus on the middle distance and out as far as his night goggles could reach.

Southgate liked to consider himself a relatively positive guy, with a can-do attitude and aptitude for being lucky. He believed you could make your own good fortune by remaining upbeat at all times and imagining the best possible outcome. Sure, it didn't work out like that all the time, but he had a funny knack of being in the right place at the right time more often than not.

Today was going to be no exception.

After less than three minutes, something fluttering in the far distance caught his eye. He pulled the brake levers, skidded to a halt, and stared hard into the dark-green image in his display. Nothing. It was gone.

He waited patiently for a few moments, convinced he'd seen something real. He thought encouraging thoughts. Put out good vibes. There it was again. Something large, flapping, in a tone ever so slightly lighter than the darkest shades around it.

Southgate gunned the snowmobile's engine and shot forward at speed, flying over the shattered mountainside with little thought for his own safety.

Again, the flapping shape returned, brighter now and making

more sense. It was billowing fabric, undulating and rolling in the wind. It was hooked around a large chunk of rock, with fine strings attached to its edges that led away into the darkness.

The ensign slowed his approach when he was ten metres away. He could tell by the patterning that it was a US-issue nylon parachute canopy, of the type fitted to military aircraft ejector seats. He throttled up a little and steered onward, now following the direction of the tethers.

A few seconds later, he found it.

The seat was lying on its side, the occupant still strapped in. It looked pretty mangled—as if it had been bounced and dragged over the boulders a lot.

Southgate pulled up near the seat, leapt off his vehicle, and ran over to the figure. He wiped an inch of snow from the helmet, flipped up his own night vision goggles, and shone a torch light directly into the face. The closed eyes immediately scrunched tighter at the sudden brightness. Lieutenant Randolph mumbled an expletive and lolled his head from side to side.

Southgate calmly introduced himself as a friendly rescuer while shining his torch down Randolph's body. His legs looked misshapen, the shins clearly broken in several places. He was in a bad way and would need immediate medical treatment. It was a miracle he was alive at all. Lucky then that his seat had tipped over like it had and shielded him from the worst of the wind chill, which was striking the back of the apparatus. Also his flight suit had remaining mostly inflated, which meant he'd had just enough insulation to keep him alive.

"You're going to be all right, sir," said Southgate. "We're going to get you out of here. Hang in there."

Randolph smirked and mumbled an incoherent line.

"Say again, sir," said his rescuer, leaning in close.

"I killed him," croaked the pilot. "I put two Mavericks up his ass. Inside the vault. Hell of shot. Wish you could have seen it . . . "

His voice trailed off.

Southgate cracked a smile and ran back to his snowmobile, where he opened a side pannier. Inside were five different coloured flares, lined up in a row. He pulled out the blue one first, thrust it into the air and yanked the ignition cord. It screamed skyward with an ear-shattering whistle, stopping short of the brooding clouds above, and casting a brilliant blue hue all around it. Then he repeated the action with the red flare, before returning to attend to Randolph.

The other Special Ops unit members heard the nearby flares going off and immediately stopped their vehicles and killed their engines. They flicked up their night vision goggles so they could see the normal colour spectrum and looked around until they saw them.

The highest flare in the sky was a blue one. That meant Randolph had been found alive and to get their asses over there and help him. The second one was the red one. The one that told them Typhon was dead and that they could all relax a little.

— FORTY-TWO —
Joint Announcement

Ellie turned her attention away from Billy and back to her smartphone. The press conference was starting. She cupped her hands around it to keep occasional rain splatter from hitting the screen and to boost the sound level from its tiny rear speaker.

It began with a silent title screen that read in bold, white serif lettering on black:

JOINT PUBLIC ANNOUNCEMENT FROM THE PRIME MINISTER OF NORWAY AND THE PRESIDENT OF THE UNITED STATES OF AMERICA

The title card stayed on screen for several seconds before fading to a head-and-shoulders view of Norway's prime minister, Eidi Hagebak, in her office. She looked solemn and wore clothes to convey that sentiment—a black suit jacket and dark purple blouse. The lighting was dim and subdued, with drapes pulled across windows behind her. It was not going to be a joyous announcement.

She made a statement in Norwegian, with English subtitles running along the bottom of the screen. "Good morning citizens of Norway and the world. I'm afraid I come to you this morning bearing grave news. As you are no doubt now aware, there is a strange and threatening storm developing over the Arctic Circle. It has been spreading outward for the last twenty-four hours and now covers the entirety of the Arctic region.

"We do not at present understand what the cloud formation is or how it can behave in the manner it does. But we do know that it cuts off all sunlight to the ground below it. And alas, one of our settlements lies within its bounds.

"It is my gravest of duties to inform you that the town of Longyearbyen on the island of Spitsbergen in the Svalbard archipelago has been destroyed and with it, we fear, two thousand lives."

She then paused to allow the gravity of her words to sink in with her audience.

Hagebak continued. "To be more accurate, they are missing and presumed dead. The town has been razed to the ground."

She paused again.

"As you may have already seen via news media reports, there is a video circulating that purports to show a single individual that can be seen attacking a Longyearbyen bar and murdering the people inside it. I can confirm that we believe this video to be authentic."

Hagebak paused again, imagining the fear her words were instilling around the world.

"This mutation of all that is good goes by the moniker Typhon—the Destroyer of Worlds. I think it's plainly obvious what his intentions are."

Prime Minister Hagebak audibly gulped and added, "He is extraterrestrial in origin. That is to say, he is not born of this planet. I repeat—he is not from Earth."

Hagebak looked visibly ill, as though she could not believe what she had just said. She added, "Now, I'm going to hand you over to US President Mitch Swanson in Washington, DC, who will expand further upon this information. Do not panic, dear citizens. Stay in your homes and keep your loved ones near until told otherwise. Rest assured that your government, and its powerful military, is doing everything in its power to protect you. Remain calm. Remain courageous."

The screen faded to black and then back up to a new view. President Mitch Swanson was sitting at his desk in the White House Oval Office. The windows behind him were black. It was 4:03 a.m. in DC.

"Good morning, my fellow Americans," Swanson announced in a sombre tone. "Good morning citizens of Norway and the rest of the world. You have just heard Prime Minister Hagebak disclose some of the awful events that have occurred in Longyearbyen, Norway. The United States of America stands strong with our friend and ally, Norway. We will do all we can to help in their hour of need, and our thoughts and prayers go out to all the fallen of that coastal community."

Swanson paused a respectful duration and then announced in a more confident tone, "Overnight, our air force was involved in a seek and destroy mission, and I'm pleased to say that we believe we have eliminated the abomination referred to as Typhon."

He paused for effect before continuing. "The target entered the Svalbard Global Seed Vault, or Doomsday Vault, as it is also known, during the night but was spotted by an exceptional US pilot who discharged multiple ordnance directly at him. He has not been seen for several hours now, and the Arctic weather phenomenon that had been expanding ever since his arrival yesterday has stopped moving. We are quietly optimistic that he has succumbed to our attack and has been eliminated."

President Swanson paused, imagining whoops and cheers as if he was at a campaign rally, before continuing his statement. "The United States will pay for a replacement seed vault to be constructed at a new location of Norway's choosing. The previous site has been destroyed and shall, we hope, forever mark the tomb of this tyrant."

Swanson next put on a questioning face and said, "Now, I imagine many of you will be asking how we know who this creature is and where he's from. How we know that it is a "he" even? The answer to that is simple, but will surprise many of you. We've known about the existence of life on other planets for many decades. And we have been communicating with some of it since the 1950s. It is through these tentative conversations that we first learned of Typhon.

"Now, allow me to hand you over to an expert in this matter, Dr Walter Albright, who will elaborate far more eloquently than I on this information, which I'm sure will have come as quite a shock to most of you. But rest assured, there is no reason to panic."

The camera cut away to a shot of Walt standing by a large video display screen. The analyst proceeded to explain how Typhon and his craft had been tracked from space and showed all the video evidence he'd showed to the president and key staff in the bunker the previous evening. He was meticulous and expansive, showing the craft depositing Typhon at the pole, the storm's creation and his subsequent travels to Svalbard, and even included censored sections from the DMM pub attack video. Then, in a somewhat hollow afterthought, Walt told people not to panic and to stay calm. The threat was likely over.

When he was done, the camera cut back to Swanson.

"People of America, Norway, and the world, be assured that we are not resting on our laurels and are working around the clock to protect you from any further alien threats. Following this broadcast there will be a website link that you can use to receive up-to-the-minute details, as we disclose them. We are here to protect you. Good day. God bless the United States of America. God bless you all."

The broadcast ended and a government website link was displayed on-screen for thirty seconds before the programme returned to the DMM studio. The journalists were in raptures. There was enough information in that fifteen-minute broadcast to keep them waffling on for years, and they didn't hesitate to get started, cramming in as much jibber-jabber as they could before Britain's prime minister was due to come on air.

Ellie had heard enough. She switched off her phone and looked back at Billy, who was still asleep, or unconscious, or whatever he was. She was a little stunned at hearing the news come from the lips of the US president, but not really surprised. She'd heard most of it from Billy already. She felt truly sorry for her friend. He was cursed.

— FORTY-THREE —
The Recruit

Russell's first stop was Aaron's house, which wasn't too far away on foot. His bike was still broken and unusable, so he was going to have to walk for a bit until he could steal another one.

He wasn't allowed into Aaron's house because Aaron's parents believed Russell to be a "disruptive influence," so instead he Facebook-messaged him and they met around the corner at their usual bus stop rendezvous point.

They'd both tried to get in touch with Dave, but he wasn't answering their texts, chats, or calls. Coward, thought Russell. The pair of them would deal with Billy together then. They didn't need Dave. The hunt was on.

Russell suggested to Aaron that they walk into town and see if Twigg was at the old video game arcade. Everybody knew Twigg was oddly into vintage computer games with rubbish graphics, so it stood to reason that he'd go there on a day off school. But Aaron told him that he doubted it would be open because of what was happening in the north.

Russell had no idea what he was talking about.

"Haven't you seen or heard any news programmes?" asked Aaron, somewhat perplexed.

"Naw," said Russell. "I was playing GTA until two this morning. Practising some killing. Getting in the mood, yeah." He laughed and pretend-punched Aaron in the gut, except it wasn't so much pretend and it hurt quite a bit. Great, thought Aaron, doubling over. Another bruise to hide from Mum and Dad.

"Why, what's happened?" said Russell.

Aaron took a moment to get his breath back and pretend it hadn't hurt. "You won't believe it, but some kind of alien creature has attacked a town up in the Arctic, somewhere foreign, and killed a lot of people."

"Bollo—"

"No, really, Russ. The US president's just been on telly saying how they've killed it with a fighter plane. Blew it up, apparently. That's why school's closed. Why the shops are shut too. The PM came on telly afterward and said Britain was in lockdown. Called it a *curfew*. Said the army was mobilising and that people had to stay indoors until further notice. My mum and dad think I've gone back to bed. They'll kill me if they know I'm outside."

"What?" said Russell, incredulously. "It's a wind up."

"It's not. Check the web. Search for 'news.'"

Russell brought out his smartphone, stolen from a kid three years younger than himself a few months ago, and opened up the browser. He typed in "nooz" and hit search. Fortunately, Nooz happened to be the name of a Greek news website and so even though he couldn't spell "news" or understand the resulting text, he saw the images and videos that showed Typhon's despicable handiwork.

"This is so cool, man," said Russell, laughing. "You know what this means, right?"

"Uh, no," said Aaron, a little nervously. "What?"

"It means we can do what we want. People are all inside their homes. Afraid. Hiding. The town is ours, mate. Ours."

"But what about the army? The prime minister said the army was being deployed to keep an eye on things."

Russell laughed out loud. "You muppet, the army's not coming to Snotton. They're going to the cities where the big trouble might happen. Hell, they closed Snotton's police station a few years ago, remember? We're like a lawless Wild West town out here. No one gives a damn about us. This is the best news I could have heard. Billy's dead meat, and I'll get away with it too, because nobody can nick me for it, ha ha!"

"Yay, cool," said Aaron, feeling decidedly uncertain about things and wishing he'd been more like Dave and not answered his Facebook message earlier that morning. "So now what?"

Russell slapped Aaron around the head and said, "We find Twigg, you numpty. Come on. Let's go find his house and see if he's there."

"Right, gotcha," said Aaron meekly. "Cool. Let's go."

The two idiots, one certifiably psychotic and the other just stupid and easily led, set off toward Billy Twigg's house. Russell led the way, taking a slightly longer route that avoided going anywhere near the canal. Aaron followed along behind, hobbling and still tender after Billy's well-placed kick on the bridge the previous day.

— FORTY-FOUR —
UFO

Sal and Billy glided down to a graceful landing next to the flying saucer. Well, Billy did. Sal, on the other hand, bounced a couple of times on her bottom before tipping forward and face-planting into some loose dust at the bottom of a small crater. She sat up and wiped her visor.

"Shoot, my rockets have got a hair trigger on them," she said, clearly embarrassed and looking for an excuse for her accident.

"Come on, Sal," said Billy, quietly giggling to himself and helping her up. "So, this is your saucer then?"

They stood side by side and regarded the machine. According to Sal, it was quite small for a flying saucer. It consisted of a metallic sphere around six metres across, with a tapering metal disc flange around its diameter that brought the total width to approximately ten metres. It stood on three spindly, pointed legs that protruded from its belly at forty-five-degree angles, raising it off the ground a couple of metres.

To Billy, it looked like something out of a 1950s B movie or an old Looney Tunes cartoon. "Are you sure this thing can fly, Sal?" he queried. "It looks like an old movie prop."

"Cheeky monkey," said Sal. "She's got what it takes under the hood. That's what counts, kid. You got to bear in mind that it was cobbled together from the wreckage of my saucer crash in Roswell. I managed to harvest enough of the core to build a new gyro, and then the hull had to be made out of what was left of the original ship's skin. I'll tell you all about it another time. We need to get going."

Sal reached up and confidently slapped the underside of the rim with her hand. Nothing happened. She did it again, still nothing. "Shoot, where is that panel?" She tried a few more spots and then, on the seventh attempt, there was a dull thud from inside and a door opened in the bottom of the central sphere. A metal ramp slid out. "Ah, there we are," she said. "Let's go in."

Inside it was cramped and, frankly, very untidy. Billy had to stoop a little to stand, which drew his attention to the floor. There were crumbs everywhere, stains here and there, candy bar wrappers, empty drink bottles, an old newspaper—that kind of thing. The mess reminded him of his mum's car, although here the interior was circular and there were only two seats stationed right in the centre. The rest of the space was just dull metal with a weird-looking control panel in front of the chairs and a big storage box behind them. There were no windows at all.

"Sorry about the mess," said Sal, smiling meekly. "Wasn't expecting company. Ain't ever had a need to clean it out since escaping Earth. I, uh, lived on Twinkies and sodas for a few days."

Billy laughed. "I can see that," he said. "When was the last time this thing flew?"

"Well, I guess, in Earth's calendar, it would have been in 1977."

"Jeez, you're kidding, right?"

"Nope."

"It's an antique, Sal."

"Well, so am I, son, and I'm still going, ain't I? Now sit down and shut up. I got to remember how this thing works."

Billy rolled his eyes and did as he was told. He swiped away some junk food wrappers and removed an old glass Coke bottle that was wedged down the back of the left-hand seat, and sat down. Both seats were sculpted to fit humans and were quite comfortable. A bit like sports car bucket seats.

He reached behind himself, looking for a harness or seatbelt of some kind, and noticed again the large cuboid container strapped to the floor behind him.

"What's that?" said Billy, pointing to it.

Sal was standing up by her seat, fiddling with some wiring behind a panel in the curved ceiling. She looked over.

"That's the weapons stash," she said. "Got a little bit of everything in there. Hopefully there's something to Typhon's disliking."

"Right," said Billy, his mind beginning to wander and imagine what kind of trouble he was headed for.

Sal seemed to sense his emotions and said, "Don't bother trying to figure out what we're going to do, son. We're flying by the seat of our pants, remember?"

She then winked at him, closed the ceiling panel, and sat down. She pulled two straps over her shoulders and locked them into a clasp on the seat between her legs. Billy copied her actions with his own seat harness.

"Oh my, I'd forgotten how uncomfortable this darn thing was," she said. "I swear these chairs have shrunk."

Sal wiggled and squirmed and forced her bottom deeper into the narrow seat. Just then a green light lit up on the wide console in front of them. It was covered in dials, buttons, knobs, and switches.

"We can take our helmets and gloves off now, Billy. We got air."

They both did, putting them into a storage compartment under the metal dashboard.

Billy was starting to feel nervous. The jovial bravado of earlier was rapidly dissipating. He was scared. Sal knew it. She turned, smiled, slapped him on the thigh and said, "You're going to be fine, kid. Right, let's get this puppy off the ground, shall we?"

She took hold of a lever that looked like an old car's gear stick and pulled it toward her. Then she pushed and held down a red button on the console. A slow, grinding sound started from beneath them. It gradually increased in volume and pitch, as though something was spinning around increasingly quickly. The noise moved from under them and out to the sides and all around them.

"Gyro's filling up the anti-grav tanks around the edge. Won't be a minute," said Sal.

The ship started to vibrate and its balance seemed to move. Billy could feel the weight of the saucer shifting upward and outward and his own weight increasing ever so slightly. It was as if it was shedding its own mass—no longer succumbing to the gravitational forces exerted on Balta. It wobbled a little bit and then calmed again, the engine sound changing into a quiet hum before fading away altogether.

"There we are," she said. "We have onboard gravity now. We're all set to go. You'll like this next bit. Watch."

She let go of the red button on the console and slowly turned a dial next to it anticlockwise. The lights inside the cockpit began to dim, and at the same time the grey walls of the capsule started to fade. Billy could see Sal, their seats, and the console controls in front of them. Everything else appeared to be getting replaced by the view outside.

"Don't worry, the saucer's still here," said Sal. "It's a visual trick, really, but it's a hell of a view."

The lights finished dimming, leaving Billy with an extraordinary spectacle. He looked down and was surprised to see the Balta asteroid, now far below them. They'd been rising the whole time. Behind it and dwarfing Balta, Igonosphar IV glowed bright green. Billy looked up. Myriad colourful stars were all around them and the nebula was still there, frozen in time, consuming thousands of stars.

It was an uncanny feeling. It was like being in space without your helmet on. It felt wrong and crazy and bewildering and awesome, all at the same time. Like when he was a kid and seeing his first three-dimensional movie in an IMAX cinema.

"It's amazing, Sal. That's so clever. I love it," gushed Billy, genuinely impressed.

"I know. Takes a little bit of getting used to, but it's handy for flying. It's great to see what's coming at you from every direction, particularly in the heat of battle."

Gosh, thought Billy. Space battles. He could barely imagine what they must be like. He looked down again and saw his feet seemingly dangling in outer space. Balta and Igonosphar IV were now quite small and continuing to shrink.

"So, what do we do next, exactly?" he asked.

"Just want to get clear of the base," replied Sal. "Gives us plenty of wobble room. I've never transferred, sorry, zapped this thing anywhere with a passenger before . . . I, uh, don't know what's going to happen."

Sal was trying to keep the conversation light and laid back, but in reality she was pretty frightened that Billy wouldn't make it through the transfer jump. She figured there was at least a 75 percent chance he'd simply not be in the capsule when they arrived at Earth. If they arrived at Earth at all.

Back in the early days of somviator training, long before even Sal had been recruited, experiments had been done with the Remnant Stone. Groups of somviator Servos had tried jumping together to the same location, only for them all, bar one, to disappear without a trace. Alas, all the Primos back on Balta and paired to the missing Servos had fallen into comas and died as a result. It was deemed far too dangerous to repeat, and it never had been.

"Okay, so we're ready to go now?" said Billy, nervously.

"Yup," she said. "Let's stop here and try it out. See if we can pull this off."

The saucer immediately ceased climbing, but kept its anti-grav gyro spinning at maximum revolutions. Inside, Sal closed her eyes and mentally prepared herself to jump. She favoured the elastic band technique. An unglamorous sounding, yet simple and clever meditative solution to leaping about the universe.

She pictured planet Earth in her mind, then mentally reversed backward through space from there, imagining herself, the saucer and, most importantly, Billy, zooming out past the other planets in its solar system. Then out farther and farther, leaving the solar system far behind and speeding through open space, past other systems and galaxies, until she was at her present location, hovering over Balta. She imagined she was attached to Earth by a huge long piece of elastic and that she was struggling to hold on to where she was because of the tension.

"Okay, take a hand," she said through gritted teeth, extending both her left arms out to her passenger.

Billy grabbed hold of one tightly with his right hand. Bare flesh to bare flesh. Sal gripped his hand very tightly back, painfully even. With the other left hand, she reached out a little farther and grabbed on to his forearm too. And with her single right arm, she held on tight to the saucer's control stick, completing a chain whereby she was in the middle, holding on to the saucer and Billy.

It was time. She relaxed her mind and allowed the imaginary elastic line to whip them from where they were, twelve light years away, to being in orbit around planet Earth.

It didn't work. But it came close.

From the perspective of the occupants of the saucer, a brightly coloured tunnel of light instantly appeared around them, and they flew down it at incredible speed, bands of spectral colours shooting past in a blur.

The saucer rattled and banged, fearfully at times, but held together. Billy looked over at Sal, but she had her eyes scrunched shut, and her head tilted back.

Then, suddenly, the tunnel of light vaporised, and they were thrust into a cluster of floating boulders. Their ship tumbled through it, stones clanging off the hull every second, sending it careering off in different directions.

"What's happened?" shouted Billy over the sounds of heavy collisions.

"Hell, I don't know, but we're alive, ain't we?" called out Sal. "But not for much longer if we don't get out of here."

"Where is 'here'?"

"No idea," she yelled. "Unless ... unless ..."

They both stopped talking and looked around at the thousands of rock fragments hurtling past them. They were both having the same terrible thought. Another rock struck the invisible hull right in front of them and shattered into fragments.

"We're too late, aren't we?" shouted Billy. "This is all that's left of Earth, isn't it?"

"We don't know that," yelled back Sal, yanking the control stick hard and sending the saucer spiralling upward.

"Earth's gone, isn't it, Sal?" shouted Billy again, tears welling up in his eyes. "It's all my fault. I should have believed. Dammit, what have I done?"

Racked with guilt, he started to cry.

Sal didn't say anything further. All she knew was they had to fly out of the debris field quickly, before they collided with something bigger than them and got wrecked.

— FORTY-FIVE —
Resurrection

High on a boulder, silhouetted against a faint orange glow, the upper torso tried to manoeuvre into a more comfortable position but was unable to.

The two arms were now joined together in the middle by a chest, shoulder blades and abdomen. However, there was something wrong. One shoulder was much higher than the other. And the back was humped and contorted into an ugly looking distortion of its former self.

Not far away, a pair of legs was dragging itself over the rubble and grit to join the rest of the body. The legs too, were newly joined together by a still-forming pelvic area.

One leg's knee seemed loose and able to swing the lower limb around in any direction.

Something was definitely wrong. And the head knew it.

It was lying on a flat boulder next to the arms, watching the building work progress. The arms had put the almost finished skull and eyeball down there a little earlier. The eye, and its attached optic nerve, had then slithered up the front of the skull and slopped noisily into place in the left socket. The other eye had been found soon after.

They were now both set in place and blazing like spheres of lava, flicking left and right, observing every minutiae of reconstruction. The head was distressed at the sight before it. The body was not coming together as it should.

As if to confirm the observation, the head's own mandible was not attaching correctly, either. One side was on, the other was not. It was as though a small but vital piece was missing. The head organised a quick fix.

The arms began to wrap a narrow strip of black material to the jaw, rolling up and over the head and back down again several times, holding it in place. Then more dark material enveloped the head, leaving gaps for the burning eyes to stare out of.

Despite these setbacks, the rebuilding work progressed apace. Soon the legs and waist had joined the upper body—thousands of fine black strands along the tear, squirming and wriggling like maggots, joining the two halves together.

At last, the body was all but complete, except for one vital component. It sat awkwardly on a boulder like a decapitated ghoul, its back hunched and right shoulder pushed up and forward. Black smoke was seeping out of the severed neck and flowing down the chest like a small and putrid waterfall.

The deformed creature turned to the left, its hands fumbling over the neighbouring rock to locate the head. The arms then held it aloft and lowered it into place over the seeping stump, the jawbone rattling with the motion.

The final strands worked quickly to secure the head in place, sewing and threading the various vessels together and finally uniting all the body parts. It sat for a moment, leaning over, elbows on knees, face staring down at the floor, then slowly it rose onto ungainly feet.

The left knee was dislocated, causing the figure to sag over to that side. It raised up its head, cracking sounds coming from its ancient vertebrae. The loose and skewed jawbone waggled from side to side like a broken ventriloquist's dummy. The eyes raged with fear and anger, jagged flames bursting forth from their sticky black sockets.

Typhon let out a choked and anguished scream that echoed

off the caved-in chamber, causing dust and small stones to fall from above. He sucked in a huge, rasping breath that caused him to grip his chest in agony. His body was broken, disfigured, and lame.

He had felt pain like this only once before, and that had been when his father had tried to kill him, several million years ago. His loyal ship, *Nightshade*, had saved him. She had swept down to the exploding sun and extracted him, just in time. She had then encased his dying remains inside a fine cloth bodysuit spun from dark matter. This protective garment had sustained his existence up until today. But now, clearly it and he had been severely damaged by some crude human attack.

Yet again, Typhon had underestimated the tenacity of the human vermin.

He lurched forward, confused as to what had happened. He could remember only standing in a tunnel, then a brilliant white flash of light that burned. Then nothing. But his humped back, broken jaw, and dislocated shoulder and knee were testament to the desecration of his body by something that could only have been man-made.

But in a strange way, Typhon was grateful for the absolute agony he was being forced to endure, for it fuelled his impetus for retribution.

He needed to get back to *Nightshade*. Get himself patched up, and find out who had done this to him. Then he would unleash revenge unlike anything he'd ever done before.

He turned to look at the light source leaking out from small gaps in the shattered rock debris and at once knew what it was.

"Solex," he slurred through his broken mouth.

The light pulsed brighter and dimmed again.

"Solex," he tried again, louder this time. "Return to your master."

The light pulsed brighter again and remained intense. Then a familiar high-pitched whine began, and then a sizzling, bubbling sound came from behind the boulders.

Typhon watched as the miniature sun melted through the rocks and exploded into the cavern amid a burst of sparks and molten ore.

"Come to me," said Typhon, his long, spindly arms outstretched.

The orb floated up to the strangely shaped figure and presented itself to him, hovering directly in front of his face, its brilliant glow filling the chamber with a revolving light that cast abstract shadows across the uneven surfaces.

"Find Sygma. Bring it to me," he said, a black tar oozing from the broken corner of his mouth.

It immediately zipped away to the side and hovered. Then it shot upward and waited a moment. Then down. And so it continued for a couple of minutes as the drone scanned for any sign of Typhon's cape.

Suddenly it shot away into a corner and then continued straight on, melting its way diagonally downward and noisily disappearing into the molten, smouldering hole.

The cavern fell back into almost complete darkness, and Typhon slumped down clumsily, coughing and then screeching at the pain it caused his malformed chest. He wondered how much time he had left. Was this the end? Was he finally to die on this ridiculous little planet? Maybe so.

Perhaps that was to be the irony of his life—to be almost consumed in the fire of a dying sun, only to perish in the freezing wastes of an insignificant planet far away from home.

Home. Now there was a thought. He hadn't seen his in eons. He'd been banished to the outer reaches of space ever since that fateful day. Alone. Unbearably alone. All communication with his father conducted through *Nightshade*. She was now the only home he knew.

He wondered if she was still alive? Well, in operation. Alive was a stretch. Her artificial intelligence didn't go as far as to provide her with a personality, or conversational company. She was just a vehicle to take him from one target to the next. But she was the nearest thing he had to a family. A nurturing shelter where he could feel safe. And now he didn't know where she was. He longed for the quiet seclusion and solace of her shadows.

Such was the toil of Typhon. Racked with continuous pain in a body held together with dark matter and living a life of enforced solitude, he had been Oberyn's minion for longer than he cared to remember, scouring the universe in search of Remnant Stone fragments and growing increasingly twisted and mad in the process. Life for him had no meaning or justification anymore. He was essentially dead himself, so why should anything else be allowed to live? He was the bringer of death. The Destroyer of Worlds. Utterly devoid of pity.

If this was to be the last planet cleansed by him, then so be it. But cleansed it would be.

Typhon was pulled from his thoughts by the chamber beginning to illuminate once more. A whining sound indicating the imminent return of the Solex.

It burst forth into the cave, filling it with brilliant undulating light, and hovered near the hole it had emerged from. Close behind it, a dark flying creature that resembled a jellyfish fluttered out into the room, long cloth limbs rippling up and down like tentacles treading water. It slowly turned toward the seated Typhon, glided over to him, and gently lay across his lopsided shoulders.

He shuddered and yelped, then relaxed, seemingly soothed by the garment's arrival. Sygma fluttered and fidgeted, and allowed

Typhon's suit of dark matter to stitch itself to it. Then, once in place, it spread its dark bands outward like an angel's wings, fluttered them a few times, and came to rest down his back.

Invigorated and empowered by its arrival, Typhon rose unsteadily to his feet once more and looked to the Solex.

"Get me out of here," he commanded.

The Solex immediately flew straight upward in a spiralling motion, drilling a wide hole in the rock above—one big enough for Typhon to fit through.

The crippled alien stood back, allowing molten rock and debris to fall from the hole and onto the floor. After a few moments he felt a cold blast of air rush into his rock tomb. The Solex had punctured through to the outside world.

Typhon crossed his arms around himself, instructed Sygma to wrap a protective shroud around his body, and flew gently upward through the white-hot tunnel and out into the frozen landscape above.

— FORTY-SIX —
Radio Chatter

Nightshade was sitting completely still, orbiting high above the planet's northern hemisphere, listening to Earth's unrelenting chatter. She was way above the man-made satellites orbiting the planet. Far away from prying human eyes.

She had all of her scanning equipment activated and directed toward Earth, concentrating all of her resources on finding her master, lost somewhere in the north polar region. He had last been seen inside a mountain on the island of Spitsbergen. Then he had been attacked. Now nothing. No trace of him.

Her gigantic processing power was listening to every phone conversation and every radio signal being relayed by the planet's primitive but vast satellite network. She was watching every single television broadcast passing through the airways. Observing every single Internet transmission. Analysing every single detectable signal for any mention or sign of Typhon.

All she was picking up were chatter echoes saying that Typhon had been killed by a double-missile strike from an American warplane originating from a country called Scotland.

Nightshade was unable to feel emotion and so could not feel remorse or anxiety. But she could feel a close, synthetic approximation of it. She knew, for example, that she was to make a report to Grand Overseer Oberyn soon. If she informed him that his son Typhon was missing—possibly even dead—she would probably be neutralised herself.

This made her very aware of time, and the narrowing window

of opportunity in which to locate his son and render him safe. Not that *Nightshade* had any understanding of life or death or any emotive feelings either way. She was, however, programmed to protect Typhon and shelter him and transport him safely to places of Oberyn's choosing.

Being neutralised would go against these coded instructions. It would create an Error 4414 system crash. She was programmed to avoid one of those if at all possible. So, although she was just a machine, to all intents and purposes she was afraid that Typhon was dead, and she was afraid that she would be held responsible for it.

What was that? She sensed a rise in tension on the island. There were explosion sounds. Gunfire. She picked up snatches of confused radio transmissions: " . . . back from the dead . . . the sky, the sky . . . it's alive . . . tornadoes, they're everywhere . . . the lightning burns . . . "

It sounded like Typhon's handiwork all right. *Nightshade* was relieved. She swivelled her nose fractionally toward the precise origin of the signals and accelerated closer to the planet, listening hard for more details as she approached the cluttered space junk surrounding Earth.

An increasing amount of military band communications made it clear to *Nightshade* that Typhon was alive but under attack once again, this time from human armies, using archaic weapons to fire thousands of projectiles at him.

It sounded like he had invoked the Storm of Shadows to defend himself and was apparently unable to communicate with her and call for assistance. His inner ear radio implant must have been destroyed in the earlier attack.

She would have to get down there, extract him to safety, and probably perform some medical procedures to injuries he was bound to have sustained.

Nightshade sped toward the blackened polar ice cap, the vast storm system churning over the planet like a jet-black hurricane. Uncanny bloodred flashes of lightning burst forth from the phenomenon like bursts of lava. *Nightshade* had never seen the Storm of Shadows behaving so violently before. She accelerated.

— FORTY-SEVEN —
Mushroom Cloud

President Mitch Swanson leaned back in the swivel chair, kicked off his shoes, and placed his stockinged feet on the Resolute Desk. He carefully snipped the tip off a Cuban cigar with a monogramed pearlescent cutter and rolled and moistened the end in his mouth. He lit the other with a slightly vulgar butane lighter in the form of a miniature brass world globe—the flame jetting out of the Arctic region. He smirked, the irony not lost on him, and placed it next to his feet on the oak tabletop.

"Well done, people. Well done," he said, puffing eagerly on the fine tobacco and applauding.

Around him in the Oval Office, his key aides and members of staff were sitting on chairs and couches or standing around the edge of the room. To the left side, his media people were packing away a camera, autocue machine, and audio equipment. Everyone applauded politely, but none too enthusiastically. The general feeling was it was perhaps too early to be confident of victory. A view not shared by the president.

Outside, the sun was just beginning to rise, spreading warm rays into the room through numerous windows and highlighting the pall of cigar fumes. Smoking was, of course, absolutely forbidden in the historic Oval Office, but who was going to stop the man who'd just saved the world?

"How's he doing?" asked the president, withdrawing the cigar from his mouth and plucking a tiny flake of tobacco from his lips. "Randolph, I mean. How is he? Is he going to make it?"

Chief of Staff Reggie Watson replied. "He's pretty shook up, sir. Took quite a whack on landing. Got a touch of hypothermia too. Neck injury from whiplash. Both legs broken from hitting the mountainside. But he'll make it, Mr President."

"Excellent, excellent news. That boy's a Goddamn hero," said Swanson, taking another big draw on the cigar and blowing the smoke up toward the ceiling. "Whatever that man needs, he gets it. Understood?"

"Yes sir, Mr President."

"He's going to be my ticket to a second term. He's getting the Medal of Honor. Hell, I want him on a stamp. We need to capitalise on this opportunity, people. Let's get him back here ASAP. Make sure the news networks cover him reuniting with his pregnant wife. Got it?"

"Of course, Mr President," acknowledged Reggie.

President Swanson was feeling very pleased with himself. His ace pilot had killed the marauding alien scumbag Typhon before he'd had a chance to lay waste to any large populations. It was unfortunate about Longyearbyen and the Doomsday Vault, but they were acceptable losses. In the grand scheme of things, two thousand deaths were a drop in the ocean compared with what could have been.

Lieutenant Randolph was the man of the hour, but Swanson would be the man of the millennium. Forever remembered as the president who took on the alien invader and won. He could even envisage himself on a future hundred-dollar bill or even adorning Mount Rushmore.

Suddenly there was brief, loud, double knock on a curved door at the back of the room. It flew open, narrowly missing a young female political advisor who was leaning against the wall.

Agent Entwistle ran in unannounced.

"Bad news, sir," he blurted out, breathlessly. "He's not dead . . .

He's risen again."

"What?" exclaimed Swanson. "How the hell? . . . "

"No idea, sir. We're just getting reports of a firefight by the ruined seed vault. Seems our infantry has engaged the enemy."

Swanson cast a glance at General James Hunter, seated on the end of a delicate-looking yellow settee, to see if he knew anything about it. Apparently not, judging by the frown on his face. Then the general's cell phone rang and he answered it immediately. He listened, mumbled a reply, and stood up.

"The agent's correct, Mr President," said the general. "Our army is under attack. Started with the Norwegians. Then we went in to help them. It would appear Typhon has emerged from the hillside. He's apparently using the weather against them, sir. Tornadoes and lightning, by the sound of it."

President Swanson jumped to his feet and stubbed out his cigar directly onto the antique desk's woodwork, giving Reggie cause to wince. He looked around the assembled group of experts who were standing there in utter silence, staring back at him. He frowned, thumped a fist onto the desk and bellowed, "Well, don't just stand there gawping. Go kill me an alien!"

The aids and advisors in the room scattered like startled crows, back to their offices and meeting rooms, as much just to get out of President Swanson's line of fire as to work out what to do next.

As the room cleared, the president slumped back into his chair and stared at the smouldering remains of his cigar. It had just expelled a last puff of smoke in the shape of a miniature mushroom cloud, which was now rolling up to the ceiling in a doughnut shape. He looked across the Oval Office and saw his top military men gathered in a huddle, whispering amongst themselves.

Swanson said in a loud and clear voice, "Gentlemen, I think

it's time to discuss our nuclear options."

— FORTY-EIGHT —
False Alarm

A moment before, Billy had been blubbering about how he'd destroyed planet Earth. Now he was crying with laughter. "It's not Earth, Sal," he managed to say, stifling another giggle.

Sal was still concentrating hard on piloting the saucer out of the rock field, which was at last starting to thin out—boulders becoming rocks, becoming stones, becoming pebbles, becoming grit. "So where are we then, Mr Smarty pants?" asked Sal, swerving to avoid another large chunk heading directly for them.

"It's Saturn, Sal. Pretty sure, anyway. Looks like photos I've seen. And the sun, it's too small. Too far away. This can't be Earth. And these rocks, I think we're inside its—"

The saucer suddenly burst clear of the detritus and back out into clear space. Sal slowed the ship and spun it around so she could see what Billy was talking about.

"Wow," she said, looking up and down at the vast planet. "That's massive. I've never been this close to it before." She looked down. A huge ring of crushed rock was orbiting the planet. She could see the hole her ship had punched through it, boulders cartwheeling away from the aperture in every direction. "Whoops, we made a hole in that," she said, laughing and pointing. "They'll have to update the astronomy books!"

"Ha ha, yeah, maybe. I think I read once that the rings are made of ice and rock. Something about being fragments of asteroids that have collided with its many moons. It has sixty of them or something crazy like that."

"You know what? I think you're right, Billy," she said. "I remember something like that too. It's a gas giant. It and Jupiter exert tremendous magnetic forces throughout this solar system. That would explain it. It must have interfered with our transfer. Somehow pulled us out of it before we'd reached Earth. Thank goodness for that. For a moment back there, I thought you were maybe right, and Earth was gone. Instead, this means we're real close now. We only have about one and a half billion kilometres to go, yay!"

"What?" yelped Billy. "One and a half billion kilometres? How's that close?"

"Oh, shush, we'll be there in about two hours, if I floor it. I'm not going to risk another jump. I'm amazed we survived that one, frankly. I'm mighty glad you're still here, by the way. Surprised, maybe. But mighty glad. You got all your fingers and toes, sunshine?" Sal grinned.

Billy checked himself over. He felt okay. Fingers, toes, and other appendages all seemed to be where they should be. "All present and correct," he said. "That was incredible, Sal. Absolutely incredible. You did it. You really jumped us here."

"Why, thank you, kind sir," said Sal, fluttering her eyelashes in a mock flirtation. "I always knew it would work!" She spun the saucer around to face the distant sun and added, "Let's get going, shall we?"

She aimed the stick forward, turned a dial, and flicked some switches on the console in front of her. A few lights flickered on and off here and there, and then the ship rapidly accelerated. Billy looked back at Saturn as it shrank away at an ever-increasing rate.

"Right then, young man," said Sal. "Let's take a look at that box of goodies back there. It's time to introduce you to some future-tech armaments." She unbuckled her seatbelt and heaved herself out of the tiny sports seat, groaning with discomfort. Billy hopped out of his a little more athletically.

They walked around to the back of the saucer and together lifted up the wide container lid to reveal an interior filled with equipment. There were several guns, a sleek backpack, fist-size, glasslike orbs, and a few other gadgets that looked slightly familiar to Billy, but also new and confusing, as if somebody had taken Earth's standard army weapons and pumped them full of steroids.

Sal reached in and pulled out one of the orbs, told Billy to pay attention, and began explaining what it did.

The battered silver flying saucer sped away from Saturn at a velocity slightly south of light speed. In two hours they would arrive at Earth—if there was anything left of it by then.

— FORTY-NINE —
The Test

The streets of Snotton were deserted. The earlier rain had stopped, leaving the roads dark and reflective. Not a single vehicle or pedestrian had passed Russell and Aaron in the twenty minutes they'd been walking. There'd been the occasional curtain twitch from a house window as they passed by and a generally uncanny feeling that they were being watched, but that was about it. Nature too, seemed to have taken the alien story seriously and all the birds had vanished. It was like somebody had hit Earth's mute switch.

"Come on," said Russell. "Let's cut down by the school and over to Billy's side of town."

Russell knew Billy lived in one of four identical semidetached new builds in the older, slightly more well-to-do part of town. They had been sympathetically styled with features like wooden sash windows and Welsh slate roofs to match the surrounding period homes. Their idea was to knock on each one, pretending to be a concerned friend of Billy's until they got the right house. Then they would wing it from there and grab any opportunities that came their way.

The boys walked through the bigger of the school's three playgrounds and out into the teacher's car park. Like the rest of town, it was completely deserted. Not even the caretaker had turned up.

Russell felt like testing the water. He walked over to the edge of the parking area and kicked around for a moment until he loosened a palm-size stone at the edge where the tarmac was breaking up. He fetched it up and bounced it in his hand a couple of times. It had a good weight.

"What you doing, Russ?" asked Aaron.

Russell smirked. "You'll see," he said. He walked over to the blocky old Georgian main building and stopped a few metres short of it. He picked a window—the chemistry lab up on three would do—and pulled back his right arm, took aim, and launched the stone as fast as he could.

It shot through the air and smashed straight through a large upright window with a loud crash, angular pieces of glass tumbling out of the old metal frame and shattering into fragments on the ground near Russell's feet.

There was a second's pause, and then the alarm tripped and sounded a loud, wailing klaxon. Russell grinned, looked to Aaron, and took off running.

"Jeez, Russ, wait for me," shouted Aaron, breaking into an ungainly, painful jog to try and catch him up.

They ran out of the parking area entrance and turned left, running as fast as they could, Russell laughing and screeching the whole way. They carried on a short distance to a T-junction that abutted a park, leaping right on over a low boundary fence and landing on a damp, grassy escarpment and tumbling down it. They slid to the bottom and came to a halt, giggling and cheering.

The boys took a moment to compose themselves, lying on their backs just inside Sunnybank Park, the town's main area of green space. It was spread out in front of them for hundreds of metres in three directions and was full of trees, football pitches, and playgrounds.

Russell turned over, crawled back up the slope, and peeped over the top at the road junction. They could see the road they'd just run down, leading back to the school parking area gates about fifty metres away. They were in the perfect spot to observe it.

"What was all that for?" asked Aaron.

Russell closed his eyes and shook his head, as if dealing with Aaron's chimplike IQ was an exhausting, thankless task.

"I want to see if the pigs come, idiot," chided Russell. "We'll lie here and watch the school driveway. It's the only way the cops can get a car in there. Or the army, if what you say is true."

"Oh right, yeah, cool. Good idea, Russ."

"If they're not here in half an hour, I think it's safe to say the town is ours, mate. Bring it on!"

The two hooligans lay in wait, listening to the distant alarm bell ringing.

***

The boys weren't the only ones lying in wait and listening to the school alarm bell. Ellie could hear it too. It had given her a real jump and now she was super-edgy. She could hear two boys talking in hushed tones over by the roadside.

They were planning something and goofing around a little bit, but generally keeping their voices down. She guessed they were responsible for the alarm bell, which sounded like the school one from her memory of fire drill practices.

After ten minutes she dared to peak around the corner from under the slide and gasped silently at what she saw.

Russell Bates and Aaron Beck were lying on the grassy slope that separated the park from the roadside, sheltered beneath a canopy of ash trees. They were only a few metres away, looking the other way as if waiting for something to happen.

Ellie couldn't believe her bad luck. Of all the people to come across right then, right there. This was a major screwup. Hurry up, Billy, she pleaded inwardly. Whatever it is you're doing, get it done quickly.

— FIFTY —
I See You

"Well, well, well, look what we have here," said Sal, her voice sounding bittersweet. "This has been a real long time coming."

"What?" said Billy.

Sal pointed out in front of her at the view. Earth filled most of it, with Europe and North Africa bathed in sunlight. The eastern fringes of North America were just beginning to join them, the shadow of night slowly pulling back westward.

Silhouetted in front of the brilliant blue of the planet's Atlantic Ocean was a jet-black triangular shape. It looked to be moving away from them.

"I do believe that there's *Nightshade*. Typhon's ship," said Sal. "A flying coffin, more like."

Billy gulped. "Right. I see it."

"Looks like she's heading down to the surface. Let's find out what she's up to."

As they followed *Nightshade* closer toward the planet, a filthy black hurricane rolled into view. It completely covered the Arctic region and flashed red sporadically with some sort of lightning storm.

"What is that awful cloud over the North Pole?" asked Billy. "It looks very odd."

"That, I'm afraid to say, is Typhon's Storm of Shadows," replied Sal. "Wherever he goes, the storm is sure to follow. It'll eventually flow over the entire planet and smother out the sunlight. And just like your dinosaurs before you, all life will eventually die out. He'll then be able to locate the Remnant Stone and retrieve it."

"I had to ask, didn't I?" said Billy, shaking his head.

Sal executed some more button-pushing on the confusing instruments in front of them and a display panel appeared on the right, superimposed over their view of Earth. It showed interference patterns and squiggles of static for a moment, and then flashed up a distant aerial view that clearly showed Typhon standing on a snowy hillside, battling soldiers armed with tanks and cannons. He appeared to be responding to their shells and gunfire with lightning, tornadoes, and some kind of smoke weapon.

"Ah," said Sal. "Looks like Typhon is in a spot of bother down there."

"How are we seeing this?" asked Billy.

"I've hacked *Nightshade*'s receiver array. We're watching what she's looking at. My guess is she's been up here on standby. Waiting until she was needed down there. I'd say by the way she's tearing off in that direction, Typhon's in a bit of a pickle. He don't look too good, neither."

Sal turned a dashboard dial and the image magnified and stabilised on a close-up of Typhon. He looked deformed. Broken. Weary.

"He's hurt bad, I think. Good," said Sal. "Look at his posture. He's all bent over and leaning to his left. That ain't normal for him."

Sal was right. Typhon was hurting badly. Since coming out of his mountainside tomb, he'd been under constant bombardment from a seemingly endless supply of human warriors. Their weapons were crude, but their numbers were many. He was having trouble fending off the horde and was feeling weak and out of sorts. He wasn't himself. He needed help and could only hope that *Nightshade* had seen him and was on her way.

"Let's go say hello," said Sal, grabbing the stick and pushing her saucer on at speed.

"Won't *Nightshade* see us?" asked Billy.

"She might," answered Sal. "But hopefully she's all tied up monitoring Typhon."

The battered and dented flying saucer sped on after the sleek and shiny shard. They flew through a layer thick with man-made satellites and onward to the top of the world. The leading craft glowed red as it pierced the atmosphere, inadvertently leaving a helpful fiery trail for the second to follow.

Nightshade was completely oblivious to the fast-approaching saucer giving chase. She was far too preoccupied monitoring Typhon's predicament. Sygma was doing its best to protect him from bullets and missiles, while he directed lightning bolts and tornadoes down from the Storm of Shadows to attack the numerous military vehicles and personnel closing in on him.

Her master was vastly outnumbered by the aggressive human animals but was dealing savage blows to their numbers. Red lightning was striking forth to tear their tanks and trucks apart, and black tornadoes were whipping in to devour soldiers and debris alike. It was joyous pandemonium, but she could see he was struggling. He needed to be evacuated immediately.

"I've waited a long time for an opportunity like this, Billy," said Sal, gesturing to the glowing hull of *Nightshade*, and then reaching down to grab her helmet from under the control deck. "Suit up. You're going to have to get out here. I'm going after her. If she picks up Typhon, she'll heal him. If she doesn't, you'll have a much better chance of killing him."

Billy didn't question her. As the saucer rattled and banged, he unsteadily undid his chair harness, bent forward and retrieved his helmet and gloves too, and like her, hurriedly put them on. Then he gathered up his new backpack from behind his seat, the one Sal and he had put together ninety minutes ago, slipped it on and moved back to perch on the edge of his chair.

They flew on for a while longer until they exited Earth's outer atmosphere, and the burning and turbulent conditions outside their saucer had ended.

Sal turned to Billy, vigorously shook his hand, and said, "It's been a real pleasure knowing you, kid. Now, I've told you what you need to know. And I've given you all I can give you. Go get that A-hole. With any luck, I'll see you soon. Now go on, get out of here."

Billy stood up and made his way toward the exit hatch. Then he stopped and ran back to Sal, leaned in and gave her a hug, their helmets bouncing off each other. He didn't want her to go on without him. He'd grown to love the crazy old alien.

Sal closed her eyes for the briefest of moments, enjoying the feeling of Billy's embrace, then popped them open again and said, "No time to get soppy, kid. Go get him. And don't worry about me, neither. I can look after myself."

With that, Sal opened the outer door and a huge gust of air swept in and blew all the old food garbage around inside the saucer. Billy carefully made his way through the blustery wind and flying food wrappers to the exit hatch.

He turned to Sal, waved, and said, "No stranger to danger." Then he leapt out into the fast-moving air and disappeared out of sight. Sal closed up the hatch again and watched the litter flutter back down to the floor. Then she narrowed her eyes and returned her focus to *Nightshade*.

The two spaceships roared toward the Storm of Shadows, the leading craft on a rescue mission, the other out to destroy the first. Billy was already far behind them, trying to use his rocket boots to stabilise himself in the air turbulence left behind by the two spaceships.

When he'd gained control and righted himself, LAURA and he began discussing tactics and how best to deal with the enemy.

"But why shouldn't I go for Typhon now?" said Billy.

"Because it's chaos down there. You're just as likely to be attacked by friendly human fire as you are by Typhon. Not a good combination. We need to play it smart. Try and get Typhon on his own or when there's less of a firefight going on. I suggest we leave Sal to try and destroy *Nightshade*, and we go to Britain. Sal's been observing things down there and keeping me informed. I'm concerned about how vulnerable your Primordium is right now. We need to fix that."

"How? Sal said I must never meet myself. Ever. Would end the universe or something."

"Yes, she did say that. But, strictly speaking, she isn't correct."

"How come?"

"Well, she said that to keep you from wanting to meet yourself. The difference now is you have to meet yourself. Listen; there are a few theories about what might happen if you do. Some scholars say it could cause the universe to collapse. Others say nothing will happen at all. Some say it can't happen and that one of you will simply disappear. Truth is, nobody has any idea. Nobody's tried it because of hokum theories like the one Sal told you.

"Speaking as an artificial intelligence unit, built upon purely mathematical principles, I calculate there to be a 2.10816 percent probability that the universe will disappear because a Servo and Primo occupy the same event. Low enough to risk it."

"Right. So I should meet myself?"

"You're going to have to, Billy. Your Primo is in a child's playground, completely exposed. Ellie is with you, but she's frightened."

"And what else? You're keeping something from me."

"Russell Bates and Aaron Beck are looking for you. They're going to really hurt you. Or worse. At any rate, the very least they're going to do is wake you up. Which, of course, will end your involvement in this dreamscape. You'll disappear. Essentially allowing Typhon to finish his business on Earth."

"Christ," said Billy. "This is such a mess."

"Let's get back to Snotton, ASAP. You're going to have to meet yourself, because you have to save yourself."

Billy turned around and accelerated his rocket boots, aiming himself toward the United Kingdom.

Back to Cambridgeshire.

Back to Snotton.

Back to himself.

— FIFTY-ONE —
Look Who I Found

Aaron was bored. Staying still and not messing about was not his strong suit. Russell, on the other hand, seemed perfectly happy to lie there in hiding. They'd been there about twenty-five minutes, and the alarm was still ringing. No vehicles had gone by. No police cars with screaming sirens. No truckloads of soldiers. Nothing.

He rolled over on to his back and looked out over the park. The grass had been cut recently. It smelled fresh. Close to them was an infants' playground consisting of a few swings, a couple of slides, and a wooden climbing frame in the shape of a pirate ship. The swings consisted of toddler safety seats and regular flat boards. He decided to kill some time and have a swing. What harm could it do?

Aaron slid down the slope quietly, stood up at the bottom and walked over to the play area. He pulled open a spring-loaded metal gate and stepped into the play zone. A wide slide was directly in front of him, swings to the right. He walked over to them and chose the only flat seat without bird droppings on it. He sat down, pushed back the swing, and immediately saw Ellie Roundtree from school, hiding under the slide. She was peeking out at him, a petrified expression on her face.

Ellie saw him notice her. She immediately pulled up an index finger to her mouth and mimed silence, her eyes pleading.

Aaron grinned, silently got off the swing, and began walking over to her. He brought an index finger up to his own mouth and copied Ellie's signal. He looked over to Russell. He was still lying on the slope and facing the other way, unaware Aaron had even gone.

Ellie felt a little relieved to see Aaron's gesture but didn't trust him as far as she could throw him. He was an easily led twerp with a misplaced loyalty to Russell.

As Aaron drew closer he could see Ellie was not alone. There was somebody lying on the ground beside her, beneath the slide. It didn't take long for Aaron to realise who it was. Bingo, he thought to himself. The guy who'd kicked him in the sack yesterday.

"Please, Aaron," whispered Ellie, as he approached her. "Please go away. Don't tell Russell you saw us. Please. You know what he's capable of."

Aaron did know what Russell was capable of. "Sure, okay," he whispered back to the odd emo girl. "I won't say anything. Stay put." He grinned and nodded, making a "shhhhhh" sound against his index finger.

Ellie's heart rose. She silently mouthed thank you back at him and slouched down in relief. Who would have thought that Aaron Beck could be reasonable like that?

Aaron was still nodding his head, but it was going on a little bit too long. It looked peculiar. Then it slowed down and changed direction, gradually morphing into a shaking head. Ellie's expression switched to one of confusion. Then fear.

Aaron knew what Russell was capable of, all right. He knew what he'd do to him if he ever found out that he'd known of Billy Twigg's whereabouts and not told him.

Aaron shouted, "Hey, Russ, look what I found over here!"

Ellie swore at Aaron and jumped to her feet. She'd have to fight them. No choice now.

"What the hell are you doing over there?" said Russell,

turning around angrily. Get back over here, dummy."

"No really, you're going to want to see this, Russ."

"No really, get your ass back over here and stop being a baby."

"Russell, Billy's right here, under the slide."

"Christ alive," shouted Russell, getting up and marching over to the playground. "You must think I was born yesterday. You're going to get a slap, you know that don't you?"

As Russell approached Aaron's position and his line of sight changed, he suddenly saw Ellie Roundtree standing behind the ladder of the slide. Impossible! Aaron wasn't kidding. His day just kept getting better and better. Then he watched her call out Aaron's name, and when he turned to face her, she hoofed him in the groin as hard as she could.

Predictably, Aaron screamed out in pain and fell to the ground, clutching his nethers. "Not again," he howled.

Russell burst out laughing. He was starting to like this girl. Aaron was a mindless idiot, but he was good comedy value to have around. He arrived at the slide and then saw Billy Twigg lying on the floor. Asleep again. Ellie stepped in front of him, her fists held high in a boxing-style stance, protecting her friend. He had to hand it to her. She was a feisty wee thing.

Ellie swung for Russell's head with her right but he quickly pulled away and then jabbed her hard with his left. It smacked her in the eye and she fell straight down, stunned and moaning.

"Grab her, Aaron. If you can manage that?" said Russell.

He reached into his jacket and pulled out the long, sharp, red-handled screwdriver.

"Payback time, Twigg," he said, with a grin. "Time to say bye-bye."

— FIFTY-TWO —
Shootout

Sal was 100 percent committed to destroying *Nightshade*. She'd lost count of the number of times she'd seen Typhon escape from justice inside that infernal machine, and she'd seen far too many good somviators perish because of it.

It was time to get even.

Nightshade was going to try and remove Typhon from the battlefield without causing him further injury. No easy task when your weapons system is locked down, awaiting a voice activation command from a master who cannot supply one. She was in a quandary.

She decided the best course of action would be to drop a replacement inner ear radio implant down to him. He could install it and then grant her permission to fire her weapons at will, giving her a fighting chance to clear away enough enemy troops to initiate a safe extraction.

Nightshade sped down to the northern hemisphere of the troublesome little planet and skirted under the edge of the vast, choking storm cloud. Soon she reached the island. Then the mountain. Then him.

Her master was still holding his own, although it would not be something he would be able to do indefinitely, especially as he appeared to be unsteady and needing medical assistance.

She skimmed down low over the snow-capped mountain and buzzed over Typhon so as to make sure he saw her and knew help was at hand. Around him, the firefight was still under way. Shells and bullets were being absorbed into Sygma's protective smoke shroud or exploding on the mountainside behind him. In retaliation, Typhon's black tornadoes were plunging up and down into the ranks of Norwegian and American soldiers, decimating their numbers. So too were frequent bolts of red lightning.

Typhon glanced up briefly as his beloved *Nightshade* swept silently into view and over the battlefield. At last she was here. "Good girl," he muttered to himself. As much as he hated to admit it, he was not functioning well and his judgement was off. He urgently required her assistance.

Then he frowned. A strange flying disk rattled overhead a few seconds after *Nightshade* had. It looked like a toy. But a familiar one. If his tired eyes weren't deceiving him it was a miniature version of an old somviator craft he knew well, except it looked homemade and quite battered.

The human gunfire desisted for a moment as gobsmacked soldiers looked up in renewed fear at the two alien spacecraft hovering above them. Then they trained their weapons on them both and began firing.

Somewhat unfairly, Sal's ship was the first to be struck, delivering it a severe blow and giving her quite a shock. Sal cursed and swerved around to try and avoid other incoming shells. Her ship's shields were not in great shape and wouldn't be able to take too many direct hits like that, especially after the pummelling it had taken around Saturn.

Nightshade too was under attack, but her shields were very much more powerful and able to better repel most of the crude explosions. She'd slowed and was turning back toward Typhon, when she noticed the small flying saucer tailing her. She gave it little thought, instead deciding to deal with it later. She had far more important matters to attend to right then and so accelerated swiftly back to her master and, when close enough, launched a storage tube from a small, round hatch in her smooth underbelly.

The cylinder was tall, narrow, jet black, and capped by a strobing red beacon. It sailed silently through the air, avoiding munitions shooting past it in all directions, and slammed into the soil at Typhon's feet, its two-metre length sticking out of the ground.

He looked at it curiously for a second, then reached down and popped it open. The front panel pinged off to reveal its tiny cargo—a black conical device the size of a fingertip. He knew what it was at once and immediately pushed it into his right ear. He winced as it quickly drilled down his ear canal and into the centre of his head, connecting directly with his cerebrum.

Typhon heard her speak straight away. "Master, activate my weapons system," she implored, her voice sounding as thoughts within his depraved mind. "Allow me to assist you."

"Granted," barked Typhon. "You may fire at will."

"Thank you, Master."

Nightshade immediately opened fire with a blistering attack of red energy pulses from the angular tip of her nose. They pounded into the human army positions, inflicting catastrophic death and injury.

"Oh no you don't," shouted Sal, spinning her rickety old flying saucer around and wobbling on after *Nightshade*. Her ship may not have looked like much, but she still had a surprise up her sleeve. Sal pushed a button on her dashboard and looked on, grinning, as a panel slid open and a second control stick rose out.

Simultaneously, the domed underbelly of her saucer jettisoned away to reveal a short, fat cannon. It clanked and banged as various shiny metal components unfurled and extended from it. When it was finished, it was twice the size it had been when stored. The chunky barrel lit up green and began to glow.

"I been saving this bad boy just for you," guffawed Sal. She grabbed hold of the new gun stick and guided a graticule over her view of *Nightshade*. When they lined up, she smirked and pulled the trigger.

A huge pulse of bright green energy shot away from under her craft and smashed into *Nightshade*'s side.

Typhon's ship was sent reeling. She twisted away and almost crashed into the mountainside, before righting herself and turning to face Sal's saucer. Whatever had hit her was a new weapon she was not familiar with. It was playing havoc with her navigation systems, sending them haywire. Clearly she was going to have to deal with the ridiculous flying saucer first.

"What you think I been doing for forty years?" mumbled Sal, to herself. "I ain't just flipping burgers, no siree. Been tinkering around, building me a gun to take you on."

Nightshade fired back at the saucer but Sal dodged nimbly sideways to avoid the strike, and at the same time returned fire and struck *Nightshade* for a second time.

Typhon was enraged. He pulled down more red lightning and black twisters to try and take down the little saucer, but Sal could see everything coming from her 360-degree viewpoint and was able to skip away from most strikes.

"*Nightshade*," screamed Typhon. "Deal with the saucer pest, then come back for me."

"Master, I have located a faint signal from the Stone," she hissed back. "It's in England. Go there now. Go to Snotton. I'll clear a path for your escape and come and help you find it, after I've dealt with these fools."

Nightshade swerved out of the way of another flying saucer blast and then fired an almighty red pulse straight downward to the hillside. The huge shockwave knocked over every soldier and piece of artillery like toys, sending them tumbling backward for several metres. All the firing temporarily stopped.

Finally, Typhon was free to move away without being shot down. He leapt into the air and sped away south as fast as possible. Then he had a thought and asked *Nightshade* another question. "The craft that nearly killed me. Where did it originate?"

"Scotland, Master. Machrihanish Airport, to be precise."

He consulted the Earth map in his head and made a course adjustment.

Time to pay a little visit to this Scotland.

Nightshade ended the conversation abruptly. She'd just taken another wallop to her flank from the tiny saucer's incredibly powerful gun. She returned fire, but with her navigation computer spitting out erroneous coordinates, her shots veered off in crazy directions. She was taking a beating that could in theory eventually wear down her shields and destroy her, as unlikely as that seemed. She decided to take the fight out into space, where she would be free of the humans and more comfortable. Perhaps she could lure the saucer into the debilitating Storm of Shadows?

Sal watched as the sleek enemy ship twisted and turned, green crackles of lightning running over her hull. She looked to be having trouble moving properly. She wobbled and vibrated until her nose was pointing upward and then accelerated up and into the brooding storm clouds above.

Sal immediately pursued, her hearts pounding in her chest. Her new gun was the business. *Nightshade* was on the run. Sal had the upper hand. She could almost taste the victory. After all these years, revenge was almost hers.

Suddenly Sal yanked back on the control stick and brought her saucer to a complete stop, just metres from the thick clouds. *Almost. She almost had me in there. Crafty.*

Sal turned her ship south and flew it fast under the expanding cloud bank until she found the edge and daylight again. The saucer then soared around it and back out into space.

The chase was on.

— FIFTY-THREE —
A Death in the Family

Billy broke through the cloud layer to the sight of the mostly flat, arable countryside of Cambridgeshire far below him. The weather was fine, if a little hazy. It looked like it had rained until only moments ago and was now clearing, the sun slowly evaporating excess water.

LAURA was helpfully projecting a vector map onto his visor but he didn't need it. He'd spotted Cambridge in the distance, its clutch of cathedral-like historic universities unmistakable, even from a couple of thousand metres away.

Snotton was just a few kilometres west of the city, so he squeezed his right fist tight and powered the Swift's rockets to maximum and hurtled down to his hometown.

He shot over the railway line that led to London, and screamed in low over the many red and brown brick houses lining the eastern belt of the commuter town. Within seconds he'd flown over his own house and was heading out toward the high school, covering the path he'd walked with Ellie earlier that morning. His own memory was a little vague on where his Primo was exactly, but LAURA had said he was lying in a kids' playground, so he was pretty confident he knew where that was.

Billy opened his right hand and immediately pulled up to a hover over Sunnybank Park's children's play area. He couldn't see anybody—just the swings, two slides, and a climbing frame. Then he spiralled outward to give himself a more oblique view and saw somebody under the widest slide. They were crouched over.

He set his boots for landing and blasted down a few metres away from the figure. Now he could see it was Ellie. She was hunched over another person lying flat on the ground. His sleeping other self, presumably. She turned her head around, saw Billy, and screamed in terror.

Billy held up his hands in a gesture of peace and then slowly reached for his helmet, unscrewed it and placed it on the ground. A building alarm was ringing faintly in the background, adding an edgy air to the oddly quiet atmosphere. Then he undid the additional armaments backpack and dropped it to the rubbery floor as well. Ellie was sobbing hysterically. She looked back to his Primo beside her and then over to him. She was shaking her head and shivering uncontrollably. Something was wrong.

"It's me, Ellie," said Billy. "It's okay. Don't be afraid. Remember what I said about there being two of me?"

"It ca . . . can't be," she stammered. "You're . . . you're . . . " Ellie paused, unable to compute what she was seeing. Billy started walking toward her very slowly, his arms still out to try and show her he meant no harm. He noticed now that she had a black eye. He got a sinking feeling in his gut.

Ellie looked back at the body beside her then to the strange boy in the spacesuit again. "Is that really you, Billy?" she called out, her sobs ebbing away a little.

"Yeah, Ellie. I made it back," he smiled. "Sal brought me. Remember what I told you about the somviators and the Balta asteroid? All true! Who'd have thought it, eh?"

Ellie laughed nervously for a second and wiped her nose. Then she suddenly said, "Oh God, don't come any closer, Billy. You shouldn't see this."

Billy frowned and said, "It's okay, Ellie. I know it's the other me under there. I'm going to be okay."

"No, no, you don't understand. You're, uh . . . look, just stay there."

Billy continued his slow approach to the slide. Time was of the essence, but he didn't want to frighten Ellie any more than she already was.

"I need to come over there, Ellie. I need to protect my Primo," he said. "I'm going to move him—well, me—somewhere safer. Out of the way. It's the only way to keep this me here. He mustn't wake up."

"No!" shouted Ellie. "He's not going to wake up. You don't understand. It's too late."

"What?" said Billy, the hairs on the back of his neck prickling and standing up.

"It's too late, Billy. You're too late. He's . . . you're . . . "

Ellie couldn't finish her sentence. She started sobbing again.

Billy ran over, crouched beside her and gave her a hug. He felt her body loosen up slightly and then go rigid again, as though she didn't want him there. She was blocking the view of his Primo so he gently pushed her to the side and looked round her.

He finally saw why she was so upset.

Primo Billy Twigg was lying flat on his back, the sweater from his bag laid over his body, put there by Ellie to keep him warm, no doubt. The red plastic handle of a screwdriver was sticking out of his chest, the metal shaft embedded deep into his body. The garment was soaked dark red with blood. Primo Billy's pallor was as white as snow. His mouth was agape in a silent scream, trickles of drying blood running down both cheeks from the corners of his mouth. His eyes stared straight up, fixed and lifeless.

"You're already dead, Billy," cried Ellie. "You should have stayed away."

Billy felt numb. He couldn't breathe properly. Nausea set in. "I'm dreaming," he mumbled. "I must be. This is all one long, terrible nightmare."

"Then I'm having the same one," sobbed Ellie. "What's happening?"

He stared down at himself, his face just a few centimetres away from his Primo's. It was surreal. Like looking into a mirror, only not seeing yourself as you are, but as a macabre, unrecognisable version of yourself. He touched the other Billy's cheek. It felt cold and waxy. He reached down along its nearest arm and checked for a pulse. Nothing. It wasn't looking good.

Then the first of two really peculiar things happened. Even more peculiar than the regular peculiar things that had been happening lately.

Billy saw a faint glow emanating from inside his Primo's open mouth. It was as if a miniature lightbulb was rising out of its throat. The tiny sparkle of light drifted past his Primo's bloodstained teeth and out into the air.

Ellie made a little gasping sound and whispered, "What's that?"

Billy had no idea and said nothing. He couldn't stop staring at it. He was transfixed.

The glimmering light bead floated between Primo and Servo for several seconds. Billy's mouth slowly fell open in awe. There was something utterly bewildering and captivating about it.

Then, suddenly, the light shot into Servo Billy's mouth.

He jumped back in surprise, spluttering and flapping his hands at his face. After an initial second or two of panic, he realised there was nothing to cough up. No irritation in his throat. Nothing at all. He appeared to be okay, so he sat down again, a couple of metres away.

"That was weird," said Ellie, making a small involuntary laughing sound to disguise her fear.

Billy did likewise and said, "You saw it too, right? I didn't just imagine that?"

"Maybe we both imagined it," she said, sounding exhausted.

Billy looked at his friend properly for the first time since touching back down on Earth, and began to wonder how she was. Her left eye looked swollen and painful. Her cheekbone too. She'd obviously taken a smack or two from Russell or Aaron. He wondered what it must have been like to watch himself being murdered? He realised she must be deeply traumatised and was just about to go to her when delayed shock finally hit him.

His Primo was dead.

He. Was. Dead.

Billy's bottom lip began to quiver. He looked up and around as if trying to find some rational explanation somewhere. There was none. Tears started to trickle down his face. If his Primo was dead, then how could he still be alive? Sal had been very clear about that when she'd explained how it all worked. Servos were the dreamscape manifestations of sleeping Primos. The former couldn't exist without the latter.

He began to feel a strong rising emotion deep inside himself. Something unknown. It frightened him. He had never experienced anything like it before. It was so intense he didn't know how to stop it. How was he supposed to react to seeing himself dead? He fought a rising surge for a few moments, standing up and taking a couple of unsteady steps away. Then he succumbed. It was too strong and all-consuming. He let it take him.

A searing pain surged through his body from his chest outward, leaving him feeling torn and ragged. Then he suddenly threw up, violently. An angry, aggressive puke that cast the contents of his stomach far out across the playground. It felt like he was spewing fire. He crumpled to the ground on his knees and screamed into the earth. Then he arched his back and screamed at the sky until his throat felt damaged and bleeding. Tears gushed from his eyes.

Snot poured from his nose. Spit and phlegm flew from his mouth. He dug his gloved fingers into the ground and ripped patches of rubber from it.

Ellie crawled farther away. She had never seen such raw grief before. It was extremely powerful and very frightening. She watched Billy convulse and roar for two or three minutes, until she saw signs of him calming. Then she inched back toward him, desperate to console him.

Billy had crawled along the ground back to his dead Primo and was kneeling next to it, staring. He'd stopped crying and cursing and drooling and spewing. He wiped the back of a hand across his face to clear away most of the mess, his composure returning.

"Who did this to me?" he whispered, his voice hoarse.

"Russell," said Ellie, quietly. Stupidly, she felt guilty for saying so. She didn't want to be responsible for anything else bad that might happen. She just wanted everything to be back to normal. For her to be the weird foreign kid at school. To not give a damn what anybody thought of her. To hang out with Billy and be happy.

"Why?"

"Said you'd embarrassed him. Couldn't let you do that. Said you had to pay."

"Did I have any chance?"

"None. He did it as you slept."

"Did you try and stop him?"

Ellie pointed at her eye and said, "Of course. He wouldn't listen. Aaron held me back as Russ . . . "

She sobbed again.

"Finish what you were going to say."

" . . . as Russell killed you."

Billy's eyes made an involuntary blink. He stood up, turned his back to Ellie and stared at the patch of ground he'd torn up with his fingers.

"How did he do it, exactly?" he growled.

"He pressed the screwdriver to your chest and then threw his full weight behind it. It was horrible. I don't want to think about it."

"Did I wake up?"

"Yes, for a moment," Ellie sobbed. "You just opened your eyes, sighed a huge sigh and . . . and slipped away."

"What happened next?" asked Billy, a steely resolve beginning to set in.

"He swiped your Indy bag, with the weird rock in it."

"Weird rock?"

"You know, the glowing amber stone thing? It was hidden down the lining of your bag."

"A Remnant Stone," mumbled Billy.

"What?" said Ellie, standing up too.

"Sounds like a Remnant Stone," he said again more clearly, turning around to face her. "Sal was right. So were you. You figured something weird must have come down after the moon collision."

"What's a Remnant Stone?"

"It's the *something weird* in your theory. Too long a story for now. Let's just say it's very unique and very powerful. It's what Typhon's come here for. It's why he's trying to kill us all. So he can locate it and leave."

"What were you doing with it?"

"I didn't know I had it. No idea how it got there. Unless . . ." Billy paused a beat and then continued. "Unless Mungo had something to do with it."

"Huh? Your dog?"

"Mungo. He behaved weirdly for a few days during the moon meteor showers. Threw himself into the pond one day. Wanted to go out into the garden at weird times during the night. Kept falling asleep everywhere for a while. We just figured he was upset by all the moon junk raining down."

Billy paused for thought again and then said, "When he was a puppy, he used to bring me trophies. Things he'd found. Sticks. Discarded plastic bottles. Stuff like that. He used to bring them to me, or leave them by my toys or clothes. I wonder if he found the stone in the garden? Doesn't matter, I guess. What's done is done. Explains why my dreams could strike at any time though, if I was carrying the thing around with me all the time."

Ellie looked confused.

Billy clarified. "The stone—it helps somviators to travel into the dreamscape. Sal has one on Balta. She used it to bring me back here."

"Well, Russell's got it now," she said. "Lord only knows what he's going to do with it."

Bet he doesn't, thought Billy.

Then the second of two really peculiar things happened.

Primo Billy's corpse moved slightly. Or deflated might be a better term.

"Look," said Ellie, pointing a finger over to the body.

Billy flicked his head in that direction and saw it too. His Primo was sort of collapsing inward. Shrinking. Exposed body parts like the head and hands seemed to be fading while his clothes remained visible and collapsed downward.

Ellie and Billy both took tentative steps toward it. They watched, dumbfounded, as the body of Primo Billy slowly faded away. When it had finally disappeared, his shoes, socks, jeans, jacket, and sweater were lying flat on the ground, the long-shanked metal screwdriver sticking straight up out of the soft surface of the playground.

The two teenagers looked at each other. They'd just witnessed something utterly impossible. Billy opened his mouth as if to speak but then thought better of it and closed it again. What was there he could say? At least the universe hadn't imploded and ended all life, or whatever it was Sal had said would happen if he met himself. Although something else very weird and horrible had clearly occurred.

Ellie spoke instead. "How are you feeling?"

"Like I'm not here," said Billy, hesitantly. "Like I'm not anywhere. Where do I belong now?"

It was Ellie's turn to not know what to say. Her mind was racing. What was Billy now? Had he changed? Was he even Billy at all? The memory of seeing him die was thankfully feeling less like a memory and more like a bad dream. After all, Billy was standing there right in front of her, albeit wearing a dull silver spacesuit. But still . . .

Billy suddenly pointed up at something behind her. She spun around and followed his gaze. An ominous bank of dark cloud was rolling south across the sky at an oddly unnatural pace, like time-lapse movie footage. Like it shouldn't really exist in their world.

"That doesn't look good," said Ellie.

Billy agreed. He was scrutinising it. It looked artificial. Too dark. Moving at too regular a speed. In a direction counter to the wind. It completely blocked out the sun and sky—the Earth below it cast into immediate darkness. Automatic streetlights were turning on in the distance, adding an umber glow to the ground.

As it neared, they could see strange bright red veins of lightning crackling within its tumultuous black mass. The more Billy stared at it, the more he sensed it. Felt it. It was calm, calculating and economic. There was an arrogance to its arrival, as if it knew it had nothing to fear. It wasn't a cloud, thought Billy. It was alive and had but one purpose. It was death. It was the ender of days.

"The Storm of Shadows," said Billy.

Ellie looked at him quizzically.

"Typhon's method for getting rid of us all. It'll smother out the sun and eventually we'll all die. Takes a few months, apparently."

"How nice," said Ellie, her tone sarcastic.

"Yup. He's a real charmer," added Billy. "If the cloud's moving our way, it means he is too."

Just then, they heard LAURA's voice crackle from inside his helmet, which was lying on the ground next to his backpack, "Billy, Billy, are you there? We need to get going."

"That's LAURA, keeping me straight. I have to go and stop him, Ellie," said Billy.

He picked up the backpack of hi-tech weapons and swung it over his shoulders. Then he pulled on his helmet and turned it until it magnetically clanged into place.

Ellie watched the boy from next door prepare his flight suit with an emotional cocktail of fear, awe, anger, envy, and pride. As his helmet locked into place, she saw blue computer graphics scroll around the inside of the glass dome and faintly heard the female voice talking to him.

"LAURA's my computerised assistant," said Billy, his voice now coming from a loudspeaker grill on the front of the helmet and sounding deeper. "The one I mentioned before."

"Right, of course," said Ellie, suddenly feeling like a spare wheel.

"Sorry, Ellie, I have to go and get the Remnant Stone and stop Typhon now," he said, sensing the awkward atmosphere. "I haven't got time to talk. Do you know where Russell went?"

Ellie pointed northeast. "Toward Market Square, I think."

"Thanks. Get home and hide, quickly. Please tell my parents to do the same. Things could get really nasty out here. Is that okay?"

"Yeah, sure, fine. Off you go. Good luck."

Billy waved to her and then soared into the air, riding on the yellow flames of his rocket boots. He turned his body and arched away toward the town centre in a graceful parabola.

Ellie watched him go and then turned her gaze to the rolling storm front, now only a kilometre or two away. The wind was getting up. An unpleasant breeze ruffled her hair. She looked toward the side of town where she lived and then turned the opposite way and began walking in the direction Billy had flown.

— FIFTY-FOUR —
On His Way

Typhon was travelling down the British mainland, enjoying occasional random acts of terror. He'd reached the Scottish mainland less than an hour after escaping the island of Spitsbergen, the thick black Storm of Shadows trailing behind him, laying its smothering blanket over land and sea, continually expanding and thickening as it grew.

Earlier he'd arrived in Scotland in a place called Fraserburgh, where he'd run amuck, slaughtering a few dozen innocents as a warm-up for Machrihanish Airport—the source of the aircraft that was causing him so much pain.

After Fraserburgh, other towns along the way, chosen at random from the map of Scotland stored in his photographic memory, he had also hit. The likes of Forfar, Perth, Auchterarder, Stirling, Lennoxtown, Erskine, and Largs were now shadows of their former selves—many, many families left grieving for loved ones murdered and absorbed by Typhon's terrifying cloak.

Eventually he'd reached the small airport *Nightshade* had told him about. It was a minute installation but had offered him the greatest resistance of all the towns visited thus far. A hangar, marked as belonging to Xcelsior Charter, had opened its doors and several heavily armed individuals had then tried to kill him.

He'd sparred with them a little before slowly inflicting unmentionable pain and suffering on them all, until they were incapacitated but conscious. He'd lined them up, broken and whimpering on the runway, and then allowed Sygma to consume them greedily, one by one—the vermin to be dealt with last having to observe the full horror of what was to befall them.

It had gone some way to relieving his anger at what had happened to him, but only a little. There was still plenty of rage left seething inside that damaged, cruel mind of his.

Typhon had then cruised down the Pennines mountain range, the backbone of England, and was now travelling over flatter, less interesting geography, heading to some place called Snotton. According to *Nightshade*, there was a Remnant Stone somewhere in the area.

Not long now, he thought, a little excitement making his gut squirm.

— FIFTY-FIVE —
Getaway

Aaron was a mess. Completely freaked out and sobbing like a baby. He was pedalling hard and trying to see where he was going through a veil of tears. He couldn't stop thinking about what had just happened.

Russell had made him grab on to Ellie and stop her from protecting her friend while Russell had murdered him right there in front of them both.

He knew Russell hated Billy, but this was an outcome he hadn't seen coming. Sure, Russ was always saying stuff like, "I'm going to kill that Billy" or "We'd be better off if Twigg was dead," but he hadn't taken it seriously. Kids always say stuff like that about other kids they hate. But it's just pent-up aggression and frustration being expressed. Nobody actually means it for real. Nobody acts on it.

Russell had.

He'd impaled the boy through the heart with a long screwdriver, right there in front of Ellie Roundtree and himself. Billy Twigg had died almost immediately, but not before opening his eyes, staring accusingly at his killer, and letting out a long agonising groan.

It was the most horrible thing Aaron had ever seen in his whole life. It had made him sick. Physically sick. Actually made him vomit right there and then, down the front of his own shirt. Maybe it was also to do with being kicked in the plums for a second time. He wasn't sure.

What he had been sure of was that he had to get as far away from Russell Bates as he possibly could. The guy was a maniac. Totally off the rails. And the curfew had just given him licence to do whatever he wanted to whomever he wished.

What was to stop Russell from killing him next?

That was why Aaron Beck was now huffing and puffing loudly and cycling away from Russell as fast as he could. Cycling for his life down a leafy suburban residential street. His crotch was aching terribly on the narrow bicycle seat, and he felt like throwing up all the time, but it was nothing compared to his desire to be as far away from his "friend" as he could possibly get.

After killing Billy Twigg, Russ had smacked Ellie in the face again and told her she was lucky he wasn't killing her too. She was being spared because he'd grown to like her, if you can believe that. Then he'd grabbed hold of Billy's Indy bag and dragged Aaron off with him toward Snotton town centre. Russ figured there would be more fun to be had with the closed shops. A little looting fun.

As Aaron had been limping on after Russ, trying to keep up, he'd spotted a racing bike parked mostly out of sight behind a hedge, just inside the driveway of a posh-looking house near the park. He'd acted in a nanosecond. Convinced that Russell would soon want to kill off any witnesses to Twigg's murder, he'd grabbed the bike, which was thankfully unlocked, turned it around and taken off in the opposite direction.

Russell had heard the commotion of the bike being pulled out from the garden and given chase, shouting expletives at Aaron as he ran after him. Luckily, Aaron had had a long enough head start from lagging so far behind Russell that he'd been able to escape.

Now he just hoped Russell didn't steal another bike and come after him. Aaron didn't know where to go, but he was just smart enough not to go home. That would be the first place Russell would look. But then that made him fear for his parents. What Russell could do to them didn't bear thinking about. What an unholy mess he was in.

Suddenly Aaron heard an engine revving behind him. It sounded especially out of place under the current curfew. He managed to cast a furtive glance behind him. A large white four-by-four vehicle was racing down the road, heading straight for him. If he wasn't mistaken, Russell was at the wheel.

Aaron looked back to where he was going, trying frantically to remember where he could pull off the street, when he was suddenly airborne. There was a brief sensation of flight and freedom, and then he thudded hard into the tarmac road surface, rolled over a few times and came to rest, the buckled and flimsy racing bicycle cartwheeling past him. He heard the sound of car brakes screeching and skidding tyres and then fell unconscious.

***

A faint, rhythmic tapping sound brought Aaron back from a peaceful land he'd just been visiting. There had been clouds and snow-peaked mountains and birds singing. It had been a beautiful and relaxing place.

Now he was back in the horror of his own reality. His eyes focused and his worst fears were realised. He was lying in the middle of the road. His head throbbed. His knees and hands stung. Russell Bates was sitting on the edge of the pavement, flipping a coin up and down, making a tapping sound as his thumbnail pinged it up into the air and another when it returned and was caught.

Russell said, "Do you like *Batman*?"

"Huh?" said Aaron, confused. "How . . . how did you drive

that car?"

"GTA. The game has a lot to give. I told you before."

Aaron sat up painfully. He felt groggy and confused. He looked at his palms. The upper layers of skin had been ripped away and grit and dirt was pushed into the bleeding, fleshy inner parts. He was shaking. He touched his head. There was a lump the size of half an egg over his left eye. It was so big that he could just see it if he looked up and left. "What happened?" he said.

"Have you heard of a *Batman* character called Harvey Dent?" asked Russell.

"No, I haven't. What're you talking about?"

"Dent is Gotham City's district attorney. Gets disfigured by acid and becomes a supervillain called Two-Face. He has a cool gimmick. Decides the fate of his enemies by flipping a coin. On one side they live. On the other, guess what? They don't."

Russell caught the spinning coin and flipped it onto the back of his left hand.

"I wonder what your fate will be?" said Russell, menacingly. "Shall we see?"

— FIFTY-SIX —
I'm Back

Billy was flying low over Snotton. The town was deserted and eerily quiet. Nobody was about. No vehicles were on the roads. Not even the police or army. Nothing.

He scanned the empty streets and gardens, looking for anybody at all. Under the present emergency, every sensible person was sheltering at home, so it was quite likely that anyone moving around outside would not be sensible and therefore quite likely to be Aaron Beck or Russell Bates. They were both idiots and either of them could have his Indy bag, and, more importantly, the Remnant Stone.

Snotton was a pretty small town and it hadn't taken him long to fly over all the routes leading from the park to the centre. He'd found nobody. Now he was spiralling outward in ever widening circles, looking for the pair.

The wind was still picking up and the streets were becoming darker and darker as the storm continued to drag south. At this rate it would be as dark as night in about quarter of an hour, he estimated.

Then, on one of his southern arcs around town, LAURA piped up with a message saying she'd detected a car engine sound nearby. She located the area on a map display, and Billy flew there immediately.

LAURA was right. Two people were up to something on North Road, near the junction with the main A1 southern route out of town. It looked like a fight. There was an upended red bicycle in the middle of the road and a white car, parked haphazardly across it, twenty metres away. In between the two a couple of boys were fighting each other.

Billy immediately swooped down, his boots getting louder as he squeezed his fist and throttled the rocket motors. As he neared, he saw it was indeed Russell and Aaron squaring off to one another in the middle of the road.

LAURA had recommended he darken his helmet glass, and he'd complied, allowing her to lower a jet-black veil through the dome, rendering him anonymous.

Russell had just thrown Aaron to the ground and was about to start kicking him, when Billy's arrival stopped them both in their tracks.

"Oh God," spluttered Aaron. "That must be him. The alien guy from the news."

They both stared up in slack-jawed surprise as a flying humanoid descended out of the darkening heavens, circled them twice, and landed a few metres away. It looked to have rocket-powered boots, which had left a trail of smoke up into the sky, now dissipating in the increasing squall.

"What the hell do you want?" shouted Russell, fearful yet defiant. "Get lost."

Billy remained where he was and silently studied the two. He could see perfectly well through his visor, but from the outside it looked like black marble. It was having the desired effect. Russell was unnerved and not looking as full of himself as normal. In fact, he had that nervous, doubtful look in his eye that Billy had glimpsed when he'd sailed over his head and into the canal the day before.

"What do you want, alien scum?" Russell shouted. "Why are you here?"

Billy took a step forward and pulled out his Desintoscram

gun. He wasn't really aware of how powerful he looked as he'd never clapped eyes on himself wearing the full somviator getup. But to Aaron and Russell he was very imposing.

For one thing, he looked taller than his real height, the thick-soled boots and roomy apex of his helmet adding at least thirty centimetres. And the Swift suit itself made him look bulkier too. Add to that the blacked-out visor, dull metallic finish of his outfit, seeping smoke coming out of vents on his boots, and a pretty mean-looking gun, and Billy Twigg looked just how you'd imagine a hostile alien to look.

Aaron broke first. He held up his hands and started gabbling like a panic-stricken toddler.

"He did it," he stammered, pointing a bloody hand at Russell. "He killed Billy, not me. It was all his idea. I was just . . ."

"Shut up, maggot," screamed Russell, turning around and punching Aaron in the abdomen, making him fold over and gasp for breath.

"Enough," shouted Billy, his hoarse voice sounding even more distorted and mechanical through the helmet grille. "Enough from both of you."

He aimed his gun slightly to the right of the boys and fired. It made a loud whump sound and blew a molten, smouldering, metre-wide hole in the street, sending chunks of grit and stone skyward. His gun whined and recharged instantly, ready to be fired again as dozens of pebbles and a cloud of grit fell back down on the two boys.

Russell turned back to face the advancing humanoid, brushing dirt from his shoulders and shaking it out of his hair. "Okay, okay," he said. "Look, there must be some kind of arrangement we can come to, right? I'm not worth killing. I'm just a stupid kid with . . ."

"Shut up, Russell," said Billy coldly. "Where's the bag, you moron?"

"That can't be good, man," wheezed Aaron, now sitting on the ground clutching his stomach. "It knows your name. You've had it."

Russell didn't know if he should be flattered or frightened that the alien knew his name. Maybe the alien knew everybody's name.

"What bag?" said Russell, trying the cocky, tough-guy routine again.

Billy had no time for such games. He twiddled a dial on the side of the Desintoscram and fired it again, this time directly at Russell, who promptly flew up into the air, somersaulted backward several times, and smashed back first into the asphalt road surface. He groaned in shock and pain, clearly badly injured.

Billy ignited his boots and gently glided toward Russell.

As he cruised past Aaron, sitting upright on the ground a metre below him, he said, "Run away home. Hunker down somewhere with your mum and dad and stay there until the storm passes. Got that?"

"Right, okay. Thanks, uh, Mr Alien," said Aaron, still clutching his gut.

"He's a murdering coward, and you're not much better," said the flying figure, gesturing over to Russell. "But he's a nasty piece of work, and you're just an idiot hanger-on. He's never going to bother you again, but I will if you ever step out of line again, do you hear me?"

"Yes, th-thank you," said Aaron, pausing a moment to reflect on something and then continuing. "Don't I know you?"

Billy didn't answer. Instead, he moved on to Russell, who was lying squirming in the street. He touched down by his feet, rocket boot smoke clouding around Russell and making him cough and splutter.

Russell tried to back away by shuffling along the ground but he was in no shape to do anything. He thought both his arms might be broken and his bottom hurt like hell. Maybe he'd broken something in his pelvis too. It was agony to try and move at all.

"Leave me alone," he screamed in terror. "Just . . ."

Billy bent down, grabbed Russell by the scruff of the neck and yanked him to his feet, surprised by his own surge in strength. Russell hollered out in pain and surprise, broken humerus bones rendering his arms limp and useless to fight back.

"Where's my bag," growled the anonymous voice again.

Russell's face was up close to the alien's blacked-out visor. All he could see was his own distorted reflection, the expression contorted into one of fear and submission. Russell hadn't seen this look on his own face for years. Not since his mother's boyfriend had beaten him half to death when he was five years old. It resurrected an old, painful memory and frightened him further.

"Your bag?" he burbled. "What do you mean your bag? It was Twigg's bag. He's, uh . . . he no longer needs it."

"I know that," snapped the stranger. "You killed him, Bates. And in cold blood, when he was asleep. You're a filthy coward."

Billy tightened his grip and shook Russell back and forth, aggravating his broken limbs.

He yelped in pain and shouted, "Twigg was a freak. You'd have hated him. He was so annoying you'd have killed him yourself." He then laughed nervously and began to grovel. "Maybe I can serve you? You know, become your assistant or something? Your deputy on Earth, perhaps?"

Billy yanked Russell even closer, until his nose was squashed against his visor. He then quietly instructed LAURA to clear his helmet tint.

The black oily coating slowly drew upward like a curtain within the glass. Russell's eyes widened as he peered in, anticipation and fear making him momentarily forget his broken arms.

First he saw a collar of blue lights, then a neck. A human-looking neck.

Then a chin.

Cheeks and a nose followed.

Russell was beginning to think he knew the face. But that was impossible.

Last the eyes and blond hair were unveiled, and the inky tint drew away to the top and vanished.

Russell's mouth fell open. Billy Twigg was glaring out at him from behind the glass.

"You . . . c . . . can't . . . be," stammered Russell. "You're . . . y . . . you're dead. I killed you."

"You did," snarled Billy, looking coldly at his murderer. "But you didn't kill me hard enough. Now I'm back."

— FIFTY-SEVEN —
Taking a Beating

The forty-year-old, jerry-built flying saucer was getting licked. Its shields were down to 20 percent as *Nightshade* flew in fast orbits around it, firing pot shots into the weakening hull and slowly chipping it away. Outside the dampening effects of Earth's atmospheric conditions, Typhon's transport was able to move with incredible agility.

Sal was responding by firing back with her new cannon, but the gun could not fire quick successive rounds and needed a moment to charge between blasts. She was trying to hit *Nightshade*, but the enemy vehicle was moving far too quickly for her to calculate when to fire—meaning she was randomly pulling the trigger, hoping to get lucky.

So far, she hadn't been.

Sal sat helplessly inside her beat-up old saucer and tried to follow the dizzying blur that was *Nightshade*, as she spun relentlessly around and around her. The saucer's marvellous 360-degree viewing screen, clever as it was, now only succeeded in making her feel light-headed and nauseous.

She tried to lose *Nightshade* by flying around erratically but it had no effect whatsoever. Sal's flesh-and-blood brain was simply no match for *Nightshade*'s computerised reflexes—the sleek black ship was able to anticipate every move Sal made and stick to her like an angry wasp.

Survival prospects had rapidly become very low.

With radio reception knocked out by the Storm of Shadows,

Sal just hoped Billy was having better luck than her.

— FIFTY-EIGHT —
Face-to-Face

Russell couldn't believe what was happening. It was like a bad dream. Billy Twigg, the pest he'd killed only hours ago, was back. And not only was he alive, he was now some kind of an astronaut or something. It was crazy.

"Where's my freakin' bag?" said Billy angrily.

Russell went to gesticulate behind him but his arms were so painful he yelped out again. "In the car. In the bloody car, behind me," he screeched.

Billy cocked his head to the side and saw a white Range Rover Evoque abandoned sideways across the road, its driver's door open. He dropped Russell back onto the asphalt and walked over to it, quietly enjoying the sound of Russell screaming out in pain again.

His leather Indy bag was lying on the passenger seat.

Behind him, Russell started whimpering again. "What are you? Please don't kill me. Look, I'm not worth it. I'm a nothing. A nobody..."

Billy pulled open his beloved bag, tore the contents and lining right out of it in one swift movement and said without looking, "I'm not going to kill you, idiot. Although you deserve to die."

In the bottom of the bag, the roughly tubular Remnant Stone flickered and glowed slightly. Billy grabbed it out, looked it over curiously for a moment, and then stowed it in a discreet side pocket on his suit's right thigh.

Russell cried out again. "Oh my God, get away from me. Leave me alone . . . "

Billy noticed it was getting markedly darker. A nearby streetlight flickering on. Then a few more, farther along the street.

"You're not worth the effort," said Billy, sliding a strip of photo booth snaps of himself and Ellie into the same thigh pocket. "Or the guilt. Besides, I'm a somviator now, and we don't do that sort of thing. Not unless absolutely necessary."

Then a different voice, with a strange and otherworldly tone, hissed from behind him. "A somviator? Really? Here? How fascinating. I wonder what the odds are of that happening?"

Billy spun around in surprise and stepped out from behind the car door. Russell hadn't been talking to him at all. He'd been speaking to a new arrival—a dark, cloaked figure floating above him.

Typhon, in the flesh.

He was unbelievably tall, perhaps twice Billy's height, and unhealthily slender. He was disfigured too—his right shoulder pushed up and forward awkwardly. His left leg looked to be bending the wrong way at the knee, and his face appeared to be partly held together by fabric tape of some kind.

Typhon was black. Not in the racial sense, but in the colour sense. As in his colour was completely jet-black. The darkest black Billy had ever seen. His body was wrapped in a kind of black bandage material. It looked tatty and frayed.

But what gave Typhon the most frightening and ethereal look was his cape. It ebbed, flowed, and rippled behind him. It was formed of several long bands of material that moved independently of one another, in a manner not dissimilar to ink drops in water, or smoke from a fire.

Hovering there above Russell, Typhon certainly knew how to

make an entrance. But then, Billy supposed, he'd had lots of practice.

"You wouldn't happen to know the whereabouts of the Remnant Stone, would you?" said Typhon in faintly old fashioned English, smirking slightly and being darkly playful. "Been looking for the item for a while now."

Billy didn't reply. He was trying to think fast. Russell was in grave danger. One would think he wouldn't care about that, given their history, but Billy genuinely didn't want to see him dead. Jail, yes. Dead, no.

Typhon was obviously an adversary not to be trifled with, but he really didn't look that strong. On the contrary, he looked tired and frail. Billy figured he should try and draw Typhon away from Russell, so he ignited his boots and rose up until his head was level with his adversary's.

"Ah, the boots," said Typhon, continuing the banter. "I'd forgotten about those. Crude, but effective, I suppose."

Billy began to fly backward, over the abandoned car and on down the dark street, hoping Typhon would follow and leave Russell behind.

It didn't happen quite like that.

A gently undulating band of Typhon's cloak suddenly became aggressive. In an instant it thickened up, mutating into a flexible, rippling column of black smoke, and swooped down over Typhon's shoulder. It wrapped itself around one of Russell's feet and unceremoniously yanked him into the air, letting him dangle upside down, screaming in pain as his broken arm bones swung around wildly.

Typhon then matched Billy's sedate speed and followed him, enjoying their game—their dance of death.

Billy asked LAURA to black out his visor again, and she did so immediately. He felt it would be to his advantage not to let

Typhon see his face. Keep any emotions it might betray from the enemy.

"What are you bringing him for?" called out Billy, uncomfortably aware that he had what Typhon wanted in his pocket. "And what makes you think I'd have this Remnant Stone you speak of?"

"Don't trifle with me, boy," countered Typhon. "You're obviously here for the same thing I am. I wager you know of its whereabouts already. Give me its location."

"I don't know what you're talking about," said Billy, surprised and relieved that his enemy seemed unable to detect it was right there in front of him. Typhon's ravaged appearance apparently more than skin deep.

"Come now, you know what I want. You're a somviator, you say? Then you know all about the Remnant Stones. The original core of our universe, and the key to creating others."

Billy didn't know much about Remnant Stones at all. Sal had been rushed and quite vague about them. So Billy pretended. "Yes, of course," he said. "Remnant Stones. Yeah, the three stones."

Typhon frowned, sensing the somviator was out of his depth. Inexperienced. Frightened even.

"From whence do you hail?" asked Typhon. "What name do you go by?"

Billy didn't answer. He was still flying backward down the unnaturally dark street, partly illuminated with orange street lamps. There was a bend in the road coming up. This was going nowhere. He needed to make a stand.

"You're one of Magmajude's boys, aren't you?" said the alien, slightly increasing his velocity. "I recognise the suit. Funny, I thought they were all dead."

"Enough chit-chat," said Billy forcefully, coming to a

complete stop. "You need to leave now. Put the boy down."

Russell was still swinging around underneath Typhon. Still held in his cloak's smoky grip. He was no longer screaming, just whimpering and groaning. Close to passing out.

Typhon gestured his arms down to his captive and said, "You're just a boy, aren't you? Like this one. A friend of yours?"

"Hardly," snapped Billy, losing his cool a little.

"Pity," said Typhon. "Sygma, do what you must."

The cloak leapt into action. Russell was dragged up higher into the air, whereupon the rest of the cloak's strips of fabric morphed into smoke tentacles and hurriedly joined the first, wrapping their long trails around him.

Russell regained consciousness and yelped out, "Billy, help meeeeeeeee . . ."

But it was too late. The combined force of the Sygma cloak quickly smothered the injured youth, spiralling around his body until just the top half of his head remained visible. He stared out in terror at Billy's blacked-out helmet, before letting out one last muffled, gut-wrenching shriek.

Billy was stunned by the aggressor's speed and power. He was raising up his gun to aim it at Typhon, and in that brief second watched in horror as Russell's body was sucked into the mass of pulsating smoke. It crushed him down noisily, shattering bone and pulverising organs. Then, just as quickly, the cloud dissipated and returned to its fabric form; Russell's body had disappeared like a sick magic trick. The cloak withdrew meekly and returned to its rightful place behind Typhon. Where Russell had once been, a curious scattering of dark ash was drifting to the ground like dirty snow.

Billy fired his Desintoscram just as Typhon seemed momentarily delirious from the kill, as if he'd consumed some tasty morsel that had stupefied him.

The energy beam hit him a glancing blow to the face, brutally knocking his head to the side and sending him cartwheeling to the left. Typhon screamed out in pain and shock, but quickly righted himself in midair and charged forward. He swooped down low to just above the road surface and rocketed along at incredible speed, his eyes ablaze once more.

Meanwhile, Billy hadn't been wasting his time. He'd quickly reached around and unloaded from his backpack one of the devices Sal had given him. It was called an Orbotron Time Bomb. Fist-size, round, made of some kind of glass. It looked just like a crystal ball with a small metal cap embedded in it. As Typhon came flying at him, Billy hurled the device to the ground and then flew straight upward, to be out of the way of what he'd been told would be coming.

The Orbotron hit the street below and immediately exploded into a brilliant hemisphere of expanding energy. Blue and white light beams soared outward until a dome of light as wide as the street and as tall as a double-decker bus occupied the space.

Typhon couldn't react in time and collided with it, entering the light fully. His actions immediately became incredibly sluggish, like slow-motion video. His speed dropped to a crawl, with his limbs moving as though he was submerged in molasses.

Billy couldn't believe it had really worked. Sal had told him the Orbotron would slow down time for every living thing that happened to be inside it. To them, time would appear normal but everything outside it would look to be moving ridiculously fast.

Typhon was slowly raising his hands up, his expression turning into one of utter surprise. Even his Sygma cloak couldn't move quickly within the prison of light.

Billy didn't waste any time. He immediately drew his Desintoscram, turned the dial to its most powerful setting and began blasting Typhon with it. He glided closer in and aimed for his head and chest. Bolts of blue energy flew from the weapon and tore into the Orbotron dome. Unlike Typhon, they continued at speed within it and impacted on the unguarded foe.

The blasts entered his body, making it ripple in slow motion and glow like fire. Each impact chipped away at Typhon's strength and stamina. He was already ill, but these new blows were hurting him plenty.

Billy kept firing the gun, its energy cell whining and reenergising after each shot, ready for the next. After about thirty hits the gun failed, its power cell completely depleted. Billy threw it down and pulled another Desintoscram out from his backpack and continued the onslaught.

Then the Orbotron dome began to flicker and crackle, its lifespan almost expired. Billy quickly unloaded another one and threw it to the ground too, encasing the evil menace in a second time trap.

Again he unleashed a blistering attack of Desintoscram rounds into Typhon's slowly recoiling body. The frail-looking alien was taking the hits and weakening, but refusing to succumb completely.

Billy was a little unsure how to continue. He had one more Orbotron and one spare Desintoscram left in his backpack. Plus a third weapon of last resort. If the current tactic was not going to kill Typhon, then using up the last of his munitions trying would be a wasted effort. He decided to hold off using them and save them for a potential later opportunity when he might know better what to do. It was a tough decision to make. He had no way of knowing if it was the right one or not.

But he did have one last idea on how to maximise the Orbotron's effect.

Billy turned around and quickly flew down to the abandoned four-by-four. He got into the driver's seat, thankfully finding the keys still in the ignition. Without even bothering to close the driver's door, he started the engine and tried to remember what to do next. He was thirteen. The biggest thing he'd ever driven was a dodge 'em car at the travelling fair.

He remembered the pedals went A, B, C, from right to left—accelerator, brake, clutch. He pushed the right pedal. The car lurched and stalled. Dammit, the gears, he thought. He looked down the street at Typhon. The second Orbotron dome was beginning to flicker. No time to waste.

Billy turned the ignition key and gunned the engine again. He pushed the clutch and roughly crunched the gear stick into the number one position. Then he eased the right pedal down as he released the left pedal up, and the Range Rover lurched again, but didn't stall this time.

He steered the car clumsily down the street in first gear until he was right in front of Typhon's direction of travel, facing the flickering dome of light. It was fading now and would deactivate at any second. Inside, Typhon's movements were jerking between slowed-down time and normal time, sliding him forward and almost out of the dome.

Billy released the accelerator, yanked the handbrake up and jumped out. Then he fired up his boots and shot vertically into the dark, while looking down at the chaotic scene about to unfold below.

The Orbotron flickered one last time and extinguished, returning Typhon to a normal time frame, and to what he'd been doing immediately before being encased in the Orbotron hemisphere.

He suddenly flew forward at enormous speed and straight into the front of the parked vehicle. His thin body tore through the vehicle's bodywork and into the engine block with an enormous crash. There was a sudden flash of yellow and the engine tore to bits amid an explosion of fire. Typhon continued uncontrollably onward, ripping through the passenger compartment and straight out of the back of the vehicle, rupturing the fuel tank as he went.

The car exploded into a huge fireball, sending chunks of metal and burning plastic in all directions. Typhon tumbled out of the wreckage as a ball of fire, somersaulting several times along the road until he flopped down, spread-eagled on the ground, his body burning fiercely.

Billy quickly flew back down and unleashed the remaining shots he had left in his second Desintoscram. It managed nine more blasts before it too died. He threw it at Typhon and hovered a few metres away, wondering if he'd actually managed to kill him.

He had not.

Like an indestructible B-movie monster, Typhon lurched to his feet, his body still on fire but seemingly otherwise unaffected. On the contrary, if anything, the flames appeared to have reinvigorated him slightly, as if he was happy to have them there.

The petroleum fire dwindled away to nothing, leaving Typhon smouldering like an extinguished matchstick. He looked around unsteadily for a moment and then quickly spotted Billy's noisy rocket boots glowing several metres above him.

He called up. "I see you know a few things . . . Billy." Then he coughed loudly and hacked up a mouthful of a sticky tarlike substance, which he spat onto the road. It sizzled and bubbled for a few moments before congealing. "You've learned a few tricks," said Typhon. "Magmajude's given you some nice toys to play with, I see. So who are you, Billy? I should know my enemy."

"Twigg. Billy Twigg," he replied coolly.

Typhon looked to the south and said, "Well then, Billy Twigg. London. Capital city of the United Kingdom. Eighty-one kilometres that way." He pointed a scrawny arm southward. "Has a population of eight-point-seven million souls. I'm going to go there now, and I'm going to exterminate every last one of them. Unless you tell me the whereabouts of the Remnant Stone. Do you understand?"

Billy didn't know what to say, so he said nothing and remained hovering above tree height, looking down at his evil nemesis.

"Come and find me when you're man enough," said Typhon. "Follow the fires."

Typhon then rose skyward and glided away into the darkness.

— FIFTY-NINE —
Double-Crossed

Billy descended to street level and landed with a bump, his rocket boots falling silent. The whole area was pin-drop quiet except for crackling flames coming from the car wreckage. Aaron had obviously fled. Russell was dead and gone. Billy was alone. Dreadfully alone.

"Are you okay?" said LAURA. "Are you injured?"

"No, no. I'm okay. Physically. Not so sure about mentally, though. Lift the helmet tint, will you, please?"

"You're a strong lad, Billy. You'll be okay. And you're doing really well," encouraged LAURA, doing as he asked. "We still have a Desintoscram and an Orbotron left . . . and the PI device, of course . . . if we must."

"I wonder if Sal is still alive?" said Billy wistfully, withdrawing the last gun from his backpack, checking it over and stowing it in his hip holster.

"I cannot detect her radio signal. Impossible to read anything through this cloud layer. Last record I have of her is from fifty-seven minutes ago. She was leaving Earth. Chasing *Nightshade* out into space. I have no further data."

Billy was silent for a moment, considering events. "What am I going to do? I don't think I have the stamina to . . . "

"Quickly, draw your gun. Something is approaching from the northeast. There. In those bushes."

Billy snatched up his last gun. It auto-charged and whined to signal it could be fired. LAURA projected a moving three-dimensional arrow on his visor display, indicating where to look.

Then a voice came out from behind the deciduous trees by the roadside ahead. "I can't believe you let him go. What's the matter with you?" Ellie stepped out into the light cone of a street lamp and stared at Billy, hands on hips, clearly annoyed.

"Are you mad?" he shouted, guiding the gun into its holster. "You could have got yourself killed. What are you doing here?"

"Like I was going to walk away from my superhero neighbour . . ."

Billy frowned. "This isn't a game, Ellie. You need to get to safety, now!"

"I'm not a little girl or a damsel in distress, you know? And I don't take orders from—"

"This is real, Ellie. You can't handle what Typhon can do. He's . . ."

"I wonder what he is? You know, really? What his purpose is? Why is he doing what he's doing?"

"Ellie, Goddamn it, you can't psychoanalyse this guy. We're not in a reality TV show. He's going to kill us and everyone we know. And everyone we don't know, for that matter."

"Why didn't you kill him when you had the chance then?"

"Because it wasn't—"

"Because he's afraid," interrupted a gravelly voice from high above them. They shot glances upward.

Typhon was back.

Sygma immediately plucked Ellie off the street by an arm and pulled her high into the air. She shrieked in surprise but was quickly silenced by further bands of smoke wrapping themselves around her until her mouth was obscured.

Billy snatched out the Desintoscram and took aim at Typhon. But it was impossible to get a clear shot with Ellie being held out in front of him like a human shield. It was stalemate.

"Give me what I seek," said Typhon calmly. "Or she dies. Just like the rest of them. You've seen what that's like."

"No! No, don't kill her," shouted Billy, holding up his arms in a gesture of surrender.

"The Stone then. Tell me its location."

Billy couldn't give it to him. Not ever. "I . . . I don't know where it is," he lied.

"Enough of this nonsense," bellowed Typhon.

Sygma's smoking limbs puffed up and writhed and rippled over Ellie's squirming body. She stared back at Billy, eyes pleading as if saying, *give him the Stone, for heaven's sake.* Then they squeezed down and compressed their cargo until it disappeared. It only took a second and Ellie was gone. Billy failed to notice that, unlike when Russell had died, there was no sound of crunching bones this time, nor was there a cloud of ash left in the air.

"Nooooooo," he screamed, firing his gun wildly in Typhon's general direction. "You killed her!"

LAURA too returned to battle mode and automatically drew the black tint down over Billy's helmet glass once more.

Sygma quickly pulled itself around Typhon as the majority of shots flew past, shielding him from the occasional one on target. Billy flew into the air and tried to get around behind him, but Typhon just rotated on the spot, constantly shielded by his cloak. It was no use. Billy was wasting ammo. He stopped firing and holstered his weapon again.

"Why kill her?" he shouted, rage making his voice shrill. "She was nothing to you. Just a girl. A nobody."

"And your friend," replied Typhon evenly. "She was a route to hurting you. But if you must know, she's not dead. Not yet, anyway."

Billy breathed hard and stared at the alien, rage burning

inside him. Slowly they both descended to the road again until they stood facing one another from several metres away, like a scene from an old western—as if ready to draw guns and see who could shoot the other one dead the quickest.

Behind Typhon, the car wreckage sizzled and popped, orange flames licking into the air and adding an unholy glow to his gaunt silhouette.

Just then a roaring sound filled the northern darkness. A deep rumble that reverberated through the Earth and rattled house windows on either side of the street.

Billy knew what the sound was almost immediately. He recognised it from years of seeing them fly practice missions overhead. For as long as he could remember, he'd watched or heard them every single day. To him they were as much a part of growing up as going to school. In fact, most of the kids in Snotton could identify every warplane by their engine sounds alone.

These were almost certainly British RAF Tornado GR4 fighter planes. Probably out of RAF Marham, or perhaps RAF Wittering, both short flight times away. It sounded like three or four of them were flying in formation. A bombing run. Given recent events, probably *not* a practice mission.

The steady thunderous sound grew in intensity. They were definitely heading their way, fast and low. Then they growled overhead, a barely glimpsed shadowy blur under the blanket of darkness.

The jet engine sounds faded for a few seconds and then slowly swung back around Billy and Typhon in a sweeping arc. They'd found their target and were coming back.

The alien invader looked up, wary but not overly concerned. He stretched his lean arms into the air, and then drew them down forcefully, his fingers curled into claws as if pulling down on invisible strings.

Incredibly, the sky above them rumbled and thundered, red lightning flashing and crackling from horizon to horizon. Then, impossibly, the entire black cloud mass began to rapidly plunge.

Billy looked on in surprise as the sky literally fell. It was surreal and hard for his mind to process. It felt dizzying, as though the ground was rising on a giant elevator. But of course it wasn't. The sky really was crashing down.

It fell lower and lower until it was only a hundred or so metres above them, swamping Snotton in its smothering, claustrophobic shroud. More blood-red veins of lightning crackled and rippled through the mass of black.

Then the planes' engine noises began to splutter and rattle and after a few seconds fell silent. There was an agonising pause, and then four close-by explosions rocked the town and shook the ground. A cluster of orange fireballs rolled up into the darkness and were immediately extinguished in the Storm of Shadows.

It appeared military air power was no longer an option for tackling the alien invader.

Typhon arched an eyebrow and looked at Billy. "Where were we?"

"Where is Ellie?" said Billy, after a pause, sweating and feeling considerably more respectful of Typhon's power, but no less determined to defeat him. "What have you done with her?"

"She's in Abaddyon now. With all the others."

"What? Where?"

"She's lost in Abaddyon Field. With the empty eyes. Awaiting her turn. Ticktock, ticktock."

"What do you mean? Bring her back at once."

"I don't know how long she'll survive out there, Billy. There is some air, but time is most certainly not on her side."

"Bring her back, now!"

"The Remnant Stone," snapped Typhon. "Give it to me quickly, and I'll give you back the girl. A fair exchange," said Typhon, grimacing and allowing his eyes to ignite for a moment and pulse with glee.

Billy absolutely would not do that, so he tried to buy a little time to think. "What's Abaddyon Field?"

"Magmajude hasn't told you anything, has she?" scoffed Typhon. He laughed maniacally for a few seconds before continuing. "You really don't know who I am, do you?"

"You're a psychotic, homicidal nut job, is all I know."

"I see, go on."

"You're pathetic. Sad. Wretched. TV news calls you Typhon, the Destroyer of Worlds."

"Ah yes. I am indeed. But so much more, Billy. So very much more."

"So what is Abaddyon Field?" asked Billy again.

"Also known as the Plateau of the Pit."

"What pit? What is this mumbo jumbo?"

Typhon sighed with impatience. "Magmajude should have told you all this, boy. Abaddyon Field is where they go. The fallen. The dead. The ones Sygma and I relieve of life. Their animas are sent to the purgatory of Abaddyon Field."

"Animas?"

Typhon sighed again and shook his head. "Their souls, fool. Their spirits. Their inner selves. Whatever you want to call them. The plateau is overcrowded with them. Millions of lost entities searching for a way out, but there is only one—the pit at its centre. The more souls that arrive, the more souls tumble into the pit, a shaft of endless dark, where the fall is for eternity. Their whimpers and cries echo through time in perpetuity as they wait to hit a bottom that never arrives." Typhon smiled.

It sounded like Hell. Billy's mouth had gone dry. He said,

"And you put my Ellie in there?"

"Of course," Typhon chuckled. "But I didn't kill her. No, she's my bargaining chip, after all. She's there . . . how shall I put it . . . intact. But how long until she falls into the pit, Billy? How long dare you leave her there? Ticktock, ticktock."

"Why are you doing this, you creepy scumbag?"

"Because I require the Stone, Billy. This is why I do what I do. It's the only reason you're not with her. Awaiting your turn to drop. You know of the Stone's whereabouts. Besides, you know who I am," growled Typhon mysteriously. "You've always known. You've felt my presence since the very beginning. Since your earliest days. Every one of you have. It's in your nature to fear me."

"That's nonsense. I don't know where you got that idea. I don't know you from Adam."

"Adam? Interesting. I reside in the darkest recesses of your mind, where the most terrible thoughts skulk and mutter. I am the self-doubt you're feeling in your gut right now, Billy. I am the fear that dwells deep within fearless men. I am—"

"A self-deluded nut job, is what you are," scoffed Billy, attempting to wind Typhon up. To unsettle him. "You're off your rocker, mate. And what a right misery you are too. You must be fun at parties."

It wasn't going quite how Typhon had envisaged. The Twigg boy didn't appear to be afraid of him at all. He decided to step up his rhetoric, setting his eyes on fire again and saying, "I go by many names, on many worlds. To some I am a deity." He paused to cackle and spit more tarlike gunk into the street. "You may know of me as Samnu, Nihasa, Mormo, Gorgo, or Dagon?"

Billy smirked. "Nope. Can't say that I do. You're not as famous as you think you are."

"Perhaps Azazel, Beelzebub, Loki, Lucifer, or Satan have more meaning for you?"

Unseen by Typhon, Billy's face had turned a deathly pale shade inside his covered helmet and stopped smiling. "You're . . . you're the devil?"

"Your planet's numerous religions speak of me often. But they're confused. Rambling. I suspect some kind of muddled, inherited genetic memory that somehow survived from our first encounter. In truth, though, I am far worse. So many, many worlds have I destroyed. And now I am here to claim yours . . . again." He grinned at Billy and Sygma ruffled its bands, as if to punctuate his declaration.

This was beginning to freak out the teenager. He'd done remarkably well so far, all things considered. But the idea that he was actually fighting the *devil* was, pardon the pun, a revelation he found hard to come to terms with.

He'd been putting on a false bravado, like he'd done when he confronted Russell on the footbridge. It had worked there, luring Russell into making an error and handing the chance of victory to Billy.

This was an entirely different bag. Facing off against Satan was not quite how he'd imagined his week was going to end when he'd gone to school the previous day. So much had happened in the last twenty-four hours.

"First encounter? You've been here before?" queried Billy.

"Why do you think your dinosaurs disappeared? Because I killed them, of course. Darkened your world for years and wiped them off the face of this rock. And I'm going to do it all again, now. Eradicate your dismal species and every other bizarre creature that lives here. Then the prize will be located and be mine at last."

Typhon erupted into spasmodic, painful-looking laughter that made him grimace. His mouth distorted, and his eyes blazed brighter. Then his jaw cracked and dislodged at one side, forcing him to crack it back into position by hand. He cursed and mumbled incoherently.

"You should get that seen to," quipped Billy. "There's a dentist just around the corn—"

"Silence!" bellowed Typhon. "Enough of this nonsense." The clouds above exploded with red lightning, bathing the surroundings in a crimson light show.

He outstretched his hands and fired two bolts of bright fire at Billy, sending him somersaulting backward into a parked car. He thudded into the passenger door, back first, his helmet whipping backward and smashing the window.

Billy shook his head and leapt out of the way just as another two bolts flew past, narrowly missing him but setting the damaged vehicle on fire instead. He immediately ignited his boots and sped away upward and backward, disappearing over a nearby house.

Typhon cursed and flew up into the artificial night. He gazed down at a row of long, narrow rear gardens nestled behind the roadside terraced houses. He couldn't see Billy anywhere. The coward had fled. No surprise there. He was just a child, after all. So he shouted down to the ground below, to anyone that might hear him, "To London then. For a little sport."

He then turned south and disappeared in a blur of shifting darkness, a red flash of lightning signalling his departure.

— SIXTY —
Mum and Dad

Billy was gathering his thoughts. He'd blindly fired his rocket boots and catapulted himself over a row of houses during Typhon's sudden unexpected attack, unceremoniously landing in a large patch of rhubarb plants at the back of somebody's garden. It wasn't the coolest of exits, but at least he hadn't crashed through a greenhouse or conservatory, so it could have been far worse.

Fortunately for him, the large green leaves had sprung back up and covered him, rendering him hidden when Typhon had flown up above the houses to look for him. Billy had heard him again say that he was going to London. Population: 8.7 million. That was a lot of death waiting to happen.

Billy got to his feet and brushed off the worst of the soil and dirt from his suit. He checked his weapons cache. There wasn't a lot left. A gun, an Orbotron, and the unthinkable PI device.

LAURA's familiar voice broke into his train of thought. "Are you okay, Billy? Vital signs appear slightly up. Anxiety levels . . ."

"I'm fine," cut in Billy. "No need to fuss. Look, I have to go and see my mum and dad now. Just for a minute or two."

"I don't think we have time, Billy. We must go after Typhon."

"I know, I know. It'll only take a moment. They'll be worried sick about me."

Billy ignited his rocket boots and blasted up into the air.

"Okay, Billy, but I'm going to hold our altitude below the cloud layer. Mechanical apparatuses doesn't seem to survive an encounter with it," said LAURA. Her comment lent more weight to the four large fires burning on the outskirts of town—the wreckage of the four downed RAF jets.

They flew on in silence for a few seconds, Billy feeling conflicted and selfish by going to see his parents when he should really be dealing with Typhon. But he didn't think he stood much of a chance against him anyway. Typhon was probably going to kill him. Everyone. This was likely the last time he'd ever see them.

Billy's street came into view. A gently winding narrow road mostly occupied by grand old buildings, several of them with sagging, weathered thatched roofs. A little block of four new builds was nestled in the centre. He hovered over the second one, number 196, and landed outside its front door.

He immediately heard Mungo barking inside and then a shush sound from his mother. He smiled at the thought of them quarrelling as usual. It was reassuring.

Not wishing to scare them to death, he knocked on the front door, rather than just walk in, dressed as he was.

Besides, he didn't have his keys anymore. He'd stupidly left them in the left-front jeans pocket of his old clothes, lying over in Sunnybank Park. He was still really confused by what had gone on there. But he still felt *normal*. Well, as normal as he'd felt before all this madness had begun.

He thudded again on the door with his fist. Come on folks, he thought, it's just me.

There was no reply.

He banged his fist on the door for a third time, louder. As he was rapping on it, the door suddenly flew inward; his dad stepped out, and bang, walloped him hard on the top of his helmet with the cricket bat from the hall.

"Bloody hell, Dad, it's me," shouted Billy, falling backward and sitting on his bottom, hard.

"Alien lies," his dad muttered, promptly walloping him on the top of his helmet again. "Go away. You're not welcome here."

"Wait, wait, wait," shouted Billy, his ears ringing. He'd forgotten about his blacked-out visor. He deactivated it quickly, just before his dad bashed him again.

"Crikey," exclaimed his father, looking at the face of his son lit up inside the helmet. "What are you doing dressed up like that?"

"Help me up, and I'll tell you."

His dad lowered the bat, pulled Billy up by his gloved hand, and quickly ushered him inside. Billy walked into his house as his mum and Mungo nervously peeked out from the kitchen.

"Billy, is that you?" said his mother nervously.

"Yeah, Mum," said Billy, walking down the hall. "Just wanted to let you guys know I was okay and see how you were doing."

She looked him up and down as he walked toward her, then her face turned to one of complete horror. "Look at the mess you're making."

Billy looked down. His boots were each leaving double-ring burn marks in the carpet.

"Whoops, sorry," he said, jumping the last two steps into the tiled kitchen. "It'll brush out ... probably." He smiled meekly.

"And what kind of time do you call this?" she said. "You missed lunch. We've been worried sick about you. Take that silly helmet off and let me take a look at you."

"What's going on, Billy?" added his dad from behind him. "The telly stopped working ten minutes ago. And why are you wearing that daft costume?"

Billy did as he was told and removed his helmet. Soon he was perched on a kitchen stool, having his earlier uneaten lunch—a cheese salad sandwich and a glass of milk that his mother had produced from the fridge. Mungo was standing by him, taking great interest in an obscure object hidden inside the thigh pocket on his suit. He sniffed it, then sneezed and stepped back, ears folded back.

Billy told them a quick, abridged version of events, leaving out anything too complex, like the part about there being two of him—the other one now dead. All in all they took it pretty well, his mother summing it up with an understated, "Well, I never."

Then his dad said, "Monica Roundtree from next door was around earlier, asking about her daughter, Ellie. You wouldn't happen to know where she is, would you?"

Billy's face fell. "I, uh . . . she's not with me right now."

"Where is she, Billy?" asked his mother, concerned.

"Typhon's taken her. Hidden her somewhere. I need to get her back." He stared at the last quarter of his sandwich, his appetite suddenly gone. "But first I have to get to London and stop this maniac. I can't stay here chatting to you guys, sorry. I really have to go now."

"Oh, Billy, do you have to?" said his mum. "You look tired, dear."

Billy quickly hugged his parents and lug-scrubbed the dog, before putting his gloves and helmet back on. He went out through the patio doors and into the back garden. He turned to his anxious-looking parents. "Close the doors, guys. This'll be smoky. Love you. Bye."

He then blew them a kiss and launched himself skyward, curving away to the south.

Inside the family kitchen, his mum and dad embraced each other and looked on nervously, just before a belch of rocket boot smoke rushed up to the glass and obscured their view. In that last brief moment, they caught a final glimpse of their son. Were those tears they could see in his eyes?

— SIXTY-ONE —
Into the Storm

Billy was flying south as quickly as possible. He was mostly following the East Coast Main Line train route, zooming over numerous small towns on his way down to London. He was skimming along dangerously close to the ground, to stay out of reach of the Storm of Shadows, aided by LAURA's navigation systems, so as not to collide with electricity pylons or green energy windmills in the dark.

The closer he got to the capital, the more built-up the landscape became. Soon the sporadic settlements nestled in flat plains of arable countryside gave way to bigger industrial complexes and larger, more extensive areas of housing.

He felt uncomfortable. LAURA was telling him something he didn't want to hear. "Abaddyon Field is a myth, Billy. Just more Typhon lies. Don't believe a word he says." She then paused as if her computerised consciousness was having trouble deciding how to phrase something. "Ellie is dead, Billy. I'm so sorry."

"I don't believe that, LAURA. Not for one moment. I can't. I must have hope. Or there's no point to any of this."

"Okay, Billy. But your priority must be to destroy Typhon. Not to try and rescue Ellie. You must save this planet first."

Of course Billy knew LAURA was right. He had to protect Earth above all else. He chose not to counter her remark and tell her of the vision he'd had in the diner, way back in the beginning. He'd seen snatches from a string of future events, including something that very much fit Typhon's description of the pit and its plateau. Billy believed it was real. He believed Ellie was still alive.

He remembered too what Typhon had said earlier—*follow the fires*. And sure enough, there they were, at least a dozen of them, zigzagging across North London. Billy flew east a little to investigate the nearest one. LAURA was helpfully displaying a map on his visor again.

The first blaze was in an area called Wood Green. An office block on High Road was burning brightly. There was nobody about, and Billy hoped it had been evacuated and empty when it had gone up in flames.

Then Billy spotted another fire burning south of his location. LAURA's map said it was in Stoke Newington. As he neared it, he could see it was a church that was burning, its steeple now a pile of bricks strewn across a leafy street. Fire danced and rippled inside, illuminating stained glass windows as they cracked and fell apart.

More senseless destruction followed as Billy spent close to half an hour hopping around from fire to fire and atrocity to atrocity. The devastation varied greatly. Sometimes infernos consumed modest homes, other times whole warehouses. One time a multi-storey car park was ablaze, with vehicles randomly exploding every few seconds.

But as different as all the targets were from one another, they all shared a common trait. Each one was bereft of life. Not once did Billy encounter another human being fleeing the fire or trapped inside a building. Not a soul alive, wounded, or even dead.

Occasionally, Billy flew over a fire engine driving to a blaze, or a military troop carrier deploying soldiers to a fire-hit area, but that was it. It seemed even Londoners had battened down the hatches and were waiting it out, praying that their thinly stretched emergency services could cope.

It made him recall his World War II history lessons at school. All those people sheltering in London Underground tunnels to escape the Nazi blitz. He was mindful too that the word blitz was an abbreviation for *blitzkrieg*, meaning *lightning war* in German.

It was a strangely prophetic thought, because just as he left the site of a football stadium blaze in an area called Holloway, the clouds above flashed a violent shade of red, and a spear of lightning crashed into the city about two kilometres southwest of him. It was followed by a burst of flame rolling out of the orange streetlight glow on the horizon, like a solar flare arcing off the surface of the sun.

Until now, Typhon had always been one step ahead, seemingly wreaking havoc with impunity. Perhaps now Billy would have a chance to catch him in the act. Even stop him dead. Billy flew in the direction of the lightning at once, mentally preparing himself for what could be the final showdown. Make or break. Kill Typhon or allow Earth to suffer the end of days.

Before he knew it he was there, his helmet map informing him it was a residential area in Islington. Thornhill Road, to be precise. A three-storey Georgian period terrace was on fire, flames licking out of broken sash windows and up the exposed brickwork outside. The ground floor's painted façade was peeling and beginning to crumble, bright yellow paint on its front door bubbling and popping like lava.

It was noisy too. The flames had a life of their own and sounded as if they were taking loud breaths. As its two-hundred-year-old timbers succumbed to the heat and flames, they moaned and creaked, adding further noise to a cacophony of wailing fire alarms.

There was no way Billy could get anywhere near it. The heat felt tremendous, even inside his protective Swift suit. Besides,

LAURA informed him she could detect no life signs inside the inferno. Dammit. As usual, he'd arrived too late.

But then Billy noticed something out of the corner of his eye. He spun ninety degrees and looked down the street to see what had caught his attention.

He frowned. He thought he'd seen a shadow moving to the right, slipping behind a large tree on the opposite side of the street, just a few houses away.

Billy immediately jogged down the pavement on his side of the street, stooping low, using parked cars as cover. He stopped across the road from a semidetached house, similar in style to the one on fire behind him, except it had a small lawn at the front, ringed by a low brick wall.

At last. There he was. Standing on the dimly lit grass in front of the house was Typhon, his back toward Billy. His arms were outstretched into the air and his head thrown back, as if in worship. He was staring up at the tumultuous low-lying black clouds, ripples of red lightning rolling across them as if the tempo were increasing, building up to some kind of an event.

Sygma's fabric limbs were arching out of his shoulders and around him, flowing up to the front door of the house. En route to the entrance they had morphed into tentacles of smoke. Billy then saw to his horror that they had pushed through the letterbox. They were inside the house.

Suddenly Billy heard a woman scream out in terror from upstairs, followed by crashing sounds, like objects being thrown. Then a man's voice shouted out in alarm too.

Billy crept silently out from his cover and headed across the road. He knelt down behind the garden wall and quietly drew out his Desintoscram.

More crashing noises came from inside the house, like pots or pans being thrown. Then a sickening crunching sound that Billy had heard once before, when he'd witnessed Russell Bates's murder.

The somviator made sure his weapon was set to the maximum level of destruction and pointed it at the back of Typhon's head. He was shaking and taking a moment to steady his aim, trying to hold his breath, when suddenly a top floor window exploded outward in a shower of glass shards and splinters of white wooden window frame. A man had leapt out. He tumbled through the air screaming and smashed face first into the grass at Typhon's feet with a sickening thud.

The alien leapt to the side in surprise just as Billy fired his gun, the brilliant blue energy bolt whizzing past Typhon's head and hitting the front of the house between the ground floor and first floor windows. It exploded in a shower of cyan sparks and punched a wide hole into the building, blowing brick fragments and chunks of plasterwork out into the garden.

Typhon immediately spun around, his eyes igniting into spheres of fire once again, only to be struck directly in the face by a second blast from Billy's Desintoscram. He screamed in pain and was thrown backward, crashing loudly straight through the front door of the house.

Billy stood up and walked cautiously forward, his gun trained on the gloomy rectangular entrance. Then he heard a groan from the lawn, and momentarily looked to his right at the poor man lying broken on the grass. He looked up at Billy with a smashed and bloody face, tears welling up in his swollen eyes, and mouthed, "Why?"

It was just the distraction Typhon needed. He sprang out of the doorway at incredible speed, clutching the central column of the broken wooden front door. He smashed it down hard on Billy's helmet and battered him to the ground. Then he raised it up and battered it down on his head again and again and again.

Inside the Swift suit, Billy was in a state of complete disarray. He had his eyes screwed shut against the pummelling he was taking, his ears ringing with each strike to his helmet. He'd dropped his gun in the confusion. LAURA was shouting something at him, but he couldn't make it out in all the chaos.

He looked up briefly and watched the wooden front door segment smash right on to his faceplate again, a large, thick, metal number 33 emblem making a terribly shrill pinging sound off his glass visor. Then the unthinkable happened. His helmet cracked. A hairline fracture right down the front.

Billy tried to get up, but the repeated onslaught was too rapid, and he didn't have a chance to roll away or get to his feet. Another crack forked off the first one, wavering away diagonally.

LAURA was repeatedly trying to tell Billy something, but still he couldn't make it out. Then Typhon's makeshift wooden club succumbed and shattered into fragments over his helmet. The nonstop bashing ended, and Billy heard a snippet of what his assistant was saying.

" . . . got to use the Orbotron. It's the only way to . . . "

Then Billy was suddenly off the ground and being pulled up into the air, upside down. Sygma had him by the legs and was dangling him over the dying man on the lawn. Billy's head was in a spin. He stared out through his fractured helmet and saw Typhon, upside down, glowering at him.

"Ah, there you are," said Typhon, pleasure evident in his tone. "How nice to see you again."

LAURA whispered to Billy that his blacked-out visor had failed and that Typhon could now see him. He also noticed how her voice was crackling and intermittent, as though she'd been damaged too. Billy said to her, "Are you okay? You sound hurt."

Instead Typhon heard him and replied, "I'm not too bad, thanks for asking." Then he erupted into his familiar cackling laughter.

Quick as a flash, Billy pulled the last remaining Orbotron grenade from his backpack and lobbed it up and over Typhon into the garden next door.

Typhon gave Billy a bemused look and said, "Missed."

Then the device exploded and formed a large expanding dome of rippling blue light that engulfed the neighbour's garden and half of the one they were in. Sygma instinctively dropped Billy and gathered its coils of dark-matter material around Typhon to form a protective shield.

But before Typhon could get away, he was engulfed in the rapidly growing hemisphere and immediately slowed down to an incapacitating level.

Billy had just got to his feet and was about to run away from the blast wave when he tripped over the body on the lawn and fell forward into a bordering flower bed. He frantically tried to get back on to his feet, only to find that the Orbotron had trapped him from the waist down. He was stuck fast, his body captured in two different time periods. He was immobilised— just like Typhon.

Except not quite like Typhon. His upper body was still functioning at full speed. He flailed around, trying to twist out of his predicament but it was no use. Then he had an idea.

Fire his boots.

LAURA immediately acted on his order and initiated a maximum throttle ignition of his rocket boosters. After a delay of a second or two, Billy saw his feet start to slide together, and the boots flash a couple of times to ignite in slow motion—yellow flames gradually extending from the soles of his feet. He clenched his throttle control fist tight and glanced up at his nemesis.

Inside the time-trap bubble, Typhon was cursing his stupidity. This was the third time bomb he'd allowed himself to be captured in that day. It was ridiculous to have let it happen again.

From his perspective, time inside the bubble was normal, and Billy had just ignited his boots to try and fly out of the light and potentially to freedom. He had to be stopped. He leapt forward, Sygma launching its tentacles to try and snag the boy.

From Billy's point of view, Typhon had slowly begun moving toward him, his spindly arms starting to reach down. Sygma too was partly unfurling a slow-moving ribbon of death.

He frantically looked about the garden. His head and shoulders were shoved into a rose bush in a narrow, oblong flower bed separating an empty driveway from the modest patch of lawn grass. Then he saw it, over by the household wheelie bins on the drive. Lying next to the recycling bucket was his Desintoscram. It was maybe three metres away. There was no way he could reach it now, but if his rockets would just . . .

Suddenly, he felt it—movement. He glanced at his feet.

The thrust was in full force, long yellow flames now fully extending from his boots. He was ever so slowly beginning to move out of the Orbotron dome. He looked back to the gun and then reached out to the thick rose bush trunk with his free hand and grabbed it, trying to steer himself out toward the weapon.

He looked back. Typhon was getting closer. He pulled harder on the rose bush, his body gradually sliding across the grass. After a few seconds his thighs were passing through the outside edge of the glowing dome. He was ever so slowly withdrawing from the light.

But Typhon was closing in, and so was his Sygma cloak monster. It was definitely gaining on him. He squeezed his fist tighter until it really hurt with cramp, trying to squeeze every iota of thrust out of the Swift.

"Come on, come on," he cried. "Can't you do anything to speed it up, LAURA?"

" . . . egative, Billy . . . uit is . . . apped in there until . . . tron has expired . . . " she crackled back.

She didn't sound good at all, her voice fading up and down.

"Are you damaged LAURA? You're breaking up."

" . . . es. Comms . . . oken . . . ot much time le . . . "

"Time left? Time left for what?"

" . . . ower cell damag . . . my . . . ime limited . . . "

"Are you dying?"

" . . . am . . . achine, Billy. I don't . . . ant you . . . upset . . . "

But Billy was upset. LAURA was the one steadfast companion he'd had throughout his somviator missions. She'd saved his life on Igonosphar IV and helped him out in hundreds of other ways. He didn't want her to go. Didn't want her to die.

He looked back at the Orbotron. It had just flickered. Billy had to get out of it ahead of Typhon, so he could get to his gun and blast him. He was almost free. His lower shins were passing through the circumference of the Orbotron field, and he was beginning to move a little faster. Accelerating.

But so was Sygma. One of its smoky tentacles was nearly at his left boot.

Seeing it up close and in slow motion allowed Billy a chance to observe Sygma's peculiarities. The snake-like form was like a tubular tornado of twisting, pulsing black smoke. Similar in a way to the storm clouds above them. And as in them, Billy could see tiny crackles of red lightning weaving around inside. But there was more to it than that.

The longer he stared at it, the more detail he could see. Deep in the furthest shadows of its murky innards, Billy could see twinkling stars, as if he were looking down a telescope into the furthest, darkest reaches of space.

Billy blinked hard. Startled. Was Sygma some kind of portal? A doorway to somewhere else in the universe? To Abaddyon

Field perhaps?

Suddenly, the Orbotron hemisphere flickered, and Billy was jolted free. He flew out too fast. His grip on the rose bush swung him around forty-five degrees and crashed him into the wheelie bins with a painful wallop.

He scrambled for his gun, picked it up, and spun around just as the Orbotron extinguished. Typhon was catapulted out like a jumping spider, Sygma thrashing its ghastly limbs around. One of them grabbed Billy around his middle and shook him so violently that he bashed his head on the inside of his fractured helmet and dropped the gun again.

Typhon skidded to a stop and watched as Sygma thrust Billy up into the air like a trophy. It then swung him around in two or three tremendous loops and hurled him into the air.

"What are you doing, you fool?" shouted Typhon, as Billy sailed past the height of the streetlights and disappeared into the darkness. "Dammit, we need the boy alive ... for now, at least."

Billy was dazed but quickly snapped out of it when he saw the glowing lights of London disappearing beneath him. "Activate rocket boots, LAURA," he said, slightly panicky.

Silence.

"LAURA? You there?"

Silence.

"LAAAAUUUUUURRRRRAAAAAA!"

No reply.

Billy looked about him. He was gently somersaulting upward, rapidly approaching the low-lying Storm of Shadows. He could do nothing except attempt to stabilise his tumbling and try and raise LAURA. His boots could be activated only by a voice command given from him to her.

He needed her back, pronto.

He spent the next few seconds manoeuvring his body until he

was pretty much travelling straight upward, headfirst. He was calling out her name over and over, but to no avail. Then he was plunged into choking darkness.

Inside the alien cloud a twisting maelstrom of vapours enveloped him, strange crackles of red lightning growing in intensity and beginning to snap and crackle over his suit. They became more violent and began to scar its organic metal alloy skin.

Thankfully, after only a few moments he exploded out of the top of the storm and was immediately bathed in brilliant sunshine, surrounded by a crisp blue sky. He'd no concept of time whatsoever but guessed it was probably late afternoon now. His momentum slowed as he approached the peak of his trajectory's parabola. Soon he would fall back to Earth and most likely die on impact. So this was it, then.

"Billy, Billy . . . alk to me . . . " said LAURA in a clipped and damaged voice.

"LAURA, turn boots back on."

" . . . oger that . . . "

The rocket boots coughed and spluttered, ignited for a few brief seconds, and then died. They repeated this process several times, stopping and starting over and over. Billy was bobbing up and down above the Storm of Shadows, one second succumbing to gravity, the next defying it.

" . . . orm cloud . . . amaged boosters . . . unable to repair . . . "

Billy considered his predicament. It was pretty obvious that his luck had run out. He said matter-of-factly, "Then save yourself, LAURA. I'm done for. No weapons left. I'm not using the PI device. No way. I'd be no better than Typhon if I did that."

" . . . LAURA stay . . . Billy Twigg . . . "

"No. LAURA go," said Billy emphatically. "Can you detect Sal now that we're above the clouds?"

" . . . es. She's . . . attle with . . . *ightshade* . . . erious . . . trouble . . . "

"Upload yourself to her ship now, LAURA. That's an order. Not a request. You must obey it. Go and save Sal."

Silence.

Billy continued to flap around uncontrollably above the deathly blanket of cloud. It looked so dense and solid that he wondered if he could actually land on it and walk about.

"LAURA, go and help Sal. That's an order."

Silence. Then a reluctant decision from his electronic assistant: " . . . oger . . . at . . . Billy. Uploading . . . aucer in . . . three . . . two . . . one . . . farewell . . . avest of . . . brave . . . dear . . . iend, Billy . . . wigg,"

There followed a brief static crackle, and she was gone.

The rocket boots powered down completely and demagnetised, separating his feet.

He dropped like a stone and roared back into the dark tempest, tumbling uncontrollably through its heaving, polluted layers. Like his trip upward, he was again attacked by bolts of powerful red lightning that burned into his protective suit and further cracked his helmet glass.

He wasn't sure how much more punishment his suit could take.

— SIXTY-TWO —
Nuke Him

President Mitch Swanson had an itchy trigger finger.

Like everybody else on Earth, barring those trapped under the Storm of Shadows and cut off from the rest of the world, he had watched the television in horror as the evil black cloud had descended farther and farther south. Now it was devouring London, England.

The menace known as Typhon was allegedly setting London ablaze at a rate that emergency services could not keep up with. If only the British government hadn't sold off its nine hundred Green Goddess fire trucks a decade ago, maybe now it would have stood a chance of saving the city.

As it currently stood, it had none.

The cloud bank was sweeping down through Canada too and had almost reached the US border. It was only a matter of time before DC got hit and he would have to evacuate. He, the president of the United States of America, sent scurrying for safety like a common rat. He couldn't allow that to happen. What would his poll numbers do? No, he needed to take action.

Swanson had watched in vain as military intervention after intervention had failed to tackle Typhon. Planes, missiles, infantry, artillery, you name it. Nothing had been able to kill the evil SOB. Several nations had tried to take him down, including the might of the US military machine. But even their greatest pilot and most ingenious aircraft had failed to stop him, despite two direct hits from Maverick missiles.

There was only one option left to try, in the president's opinion: nuclear annihilation. Nothing could withstand that. He'd consulted with US Air Force General Emmett Wainwright, and two volunteer pilots had been found for what would be a suicide mission. They figured they could just about glide a B-52 Stratofortress heavy bomber in under the Storm of Shadows from the south and detonate a cargo of nuclear warheads over London and take him out.

Of course this plan did have its detractors, namely the British government, now operating out of an emergency facility on the Mediterranean island of Cyprus. They were quite vocal in their objection. His European counterparts weren't too keen on the idea, either. Or Australia or Canada or Japan for that matter. *Cowards!*

Russia didn't seem to mind, though. They understood sacrifice. They knew it took a firm hand to deal with major threats like this. Not that there had ever been a threat like this before, of course.

The opposing nations were weaklings. Eight point seven million casualties was an unacceptable number, apparently. Swanson had argued that 7.1 billion casualties, if Typhon were to succeed, was their alternative, but they'd still turned him down in the UN emergency hearing he'd just convened. These bureaucrats had no stomach for war.

Swanson would bide his time for one more day, to give diplomacy a chance. After that, he was declaring open season on Typhon. He would nuke the scumbag wherever he was and to hell with the consequences.

— SIXTY-THREE —
The Plateau

Ellie was falling . . .

. . . falling . . .

. . . falling . . .

. . . or was she swimming?

The sensation felt like it could be either. But she wasn't sure. Something weird was happening, that was for sure.

She was drowsy. Barely awake. Not wholly sure what she was sensing. Was she floating on a cloud perhaps? Gradually her mind brought things into sharper focus, but only to the point of feeling semiconscious.

She was suspended in a river, but she didn't feel wet or cold. It was as if she were being swept along in a powerful current of . . . light. Yes, light. Flowing down a twisting, turning, translucent tunnel of light.

Was she with Billy? She looked around but saw she was alone. Had he abandoned her? She was frowning, trying to remember what had happened, when she suddenly noticed the view outside the slipstream.

Around about her as she sailed blissfully down the vortex, a rich canvas of stars was speeding past, diaphanous layers of spectral colours blending and merging with one other. Occasionally a large sun or planet would shoot by and disappear behind her.

At first it was intoxicatingly beautiful and highly exhilarating, but gradually it became repetitious and dull. Then unnerving. How long had she been here? She couldn't tell anymore. She took out her smartphone to try and check the time, but found it was dead and fumbled it back into a jeans pocket.

Then without warning the tunnel ended, and she was spat out into a much slower moving, duller vista of space. Ahead of her was a large, dark disk with an odd electric glow. It was far away but gradually increasing in size as she neared it. It was slowly spinning, like a vinyl record, complete with a dark hole at its centre.

She began to feel concerned. Something wasn't right with it at all. It exuded a sense of dread that made her most uncomfortable.

Ellie continued to fall toward the peculiar disk and slowly more details came into view. Its surface seemed to be alive. Things were writhing and squirming all over it. And it was massive. Maybe several kilometres across.

She didn't want to go there, but found she was powerless to alter her course, as if she was riding along on a rail.

Concern grew into fear.

Her trajectory took her to the outermost edge of the disk and then swept her low over the whole vast object. It was teeming with thousands upon thousands of creatures packed together like poorly treated livestock. On the outside edges Ellie saw pitiful human forms, but farther in, there were strange alien species that she didn't recognise at all.

As diverse as they were, they were all oddly transparent, like ghosts, and seemed to be pushing and shoving one another, trying to find room to move.

At the disk's centre it was much worse. There was mass panic there as creatures fought in vain to avoid spilling into a vast black pit, the weaker ones tumbling in en masse and disappearing from view.

Fear grew into terror.

Ellie was swept out from the centre, over the squabbling masses and back out to the outer rim. Then she was abruptly deposited, falling down onto a hard, cold, stone floor.

She got to her feet and found she was amongst hundreds of gauzy blue human forms shuffling around, trying to find room to move where there was none. One figure with his back to her looked familiar.

He turned around and stared at her with blank eyes before abruptly screaming directly into her face.

It was Russell Bates.

— SIXTY-FOUR —
Virus

It was no use, Sal conceded. The game was up. She knew that in herself, and she knew it because there were sparks leaping out of the control deck in front of her and smoke was beginning to fill the compact flying saucer passenger compartment.

The shields had succumbed to the battering and were now at 9 percent, triggering all manner of flashing red lights and sirens. Through the smoky haze, Sal could still see the speed blur of *Nightshade* outside as she whirled around her saucer, taking potshots at her.

Sal disabled all the sirens and flashing alarm lights while keeping one hand on the gun stick and randomly firing back when she could. She hadn't hit *Nightshade* once since following her into space, but she was going to go down fighting.

The old somviator looked up and gazed at Earth solemnly. She had stopped trying to out-manoeuvre *Nightshade* and had positioned herself stationary, with Earth out in front of her. She had watched with dismay as the Storm of Shadows had inched south, obscuring Britain beneath its shroud. Billy was somewhere under there, battling Typhon . . . if he was still alive. She had no way of knowing. All radio contact had been lost some time ago.

A blinking light and alarm bell brought her attention back to the smouldering control deck. She frowned and was about to smack it off when she realised the light was green and not red, and that it was indicating an incoming upload file. *Curious. She wasn't expecting one. Maybe it was from Billy.*

Sal flicked a switch and allowed the transmission to come on board. The data screeched and burbled into her saucer's main computer for several seconds and then stopped. A message on screen then notified her that a large file was unpacking. The screen flashed and blinked and then a familiar voice spoke to her.

"Hello, Sal," said LAURA. "Need a hand?"

"Well, howdy-doody Miss LAURA," exclaimed Sal in delight, her mood instantly lifted. "What you doing up here?" Then her face fell as she realised what it meant. *Billy must be . . . gone.*

"Billy ordered me to return to you. Said his chances of survival were extremely remote."

Sal sighed and looked around her battered saucer as if looking for a reason to continue. *My poor Billy. Just a kid. A darn brave one too. Now dead because of that scum-sucking pig, Typhon. Enough is enough.* "Typhon still alive then, I take it?" she yelled, looking up at the awful black storm atop planet Earth and feeling a renewed determination to end this once and for all.

"Affirmative. Typhon appeared impervious to Billy's weapons."

Dammit, thought Sal, before saying, "Did Billy still have the PI device last time you seen him?"

"Affirmative. But he refused to use it. Said it would have made him as bad as Typhon."

"Hardly," said Sal. "But I get his point. Using the Planetary Imploder on your home world would be a tough call for anyone. Anyway, no time to chitchat, LAURA. We're in a mite of a pickle up here. What can you do to help us out?"

"Do you still have access to *Nightshade*'s video feed? Can you still see what she sees?" asked LAURA.

Sal pushed some buttons and checked the screen. She saw her own saucer front and centre spinning over and over, with the Earth whooshing past in the background every second, coming in from a different direction each time. Clearly it was *Nightshade's* point of view that she was intercepting. "Looks like I can indeed. What you thinking?"

"Can you upload images *to* her as well as download them *from* her?"

Sal smiled and did some more jiggery-pokery on the control panel and raised her eyebrows. "Well, what do you know? No firewall. Yes, I can indeed."

"I'm a program, Sal. Bits and bytes. Ones and zeros. Compress my file. Hide me inside a video codec container, say an MPEG one, and upload me into *Nightshade*. See if I can corrupt her systems. Kill her from the inside. Turn me into a computer virus."

Sal abruptly fired off a shot from her cannon in reply to another red bolt smashing into her saucer's hull. Shields now 8 percent. No time to argue. "That, LAURA girl, is a genius idea. Let's do it, my old friend."

LAURA immediately closed herself down and made her OS file available to Sal, who quickly readied a folder. She popped LAURA into it, compressed it and gave it an .mpg file ending. Then she jiggled around with some nimble hacking tricks and transmitted LAURA out of the saucer and into *Nightshade's* external video feed receiver.

It took a relatively quick twenty seconds to complete the file transfer of LAURA's weighty five hundred gigabytes. But it felt like an eternity to Sal, who was desperately hoping the saucer's transfer node would survive that long.

Thankfully it did.

But during those crucial seconds, another 3 percent of her shield was whittled away, leaving her with exactly 5 percent remaining. Five percent more, and it would be *adiós muchachos.*

— SIXTY-FIVE —
For Honour

Billy was unceremoniously spat out of the other side of the Storm of Shadows, his suit smoking and pockmarked. The once crystal clear dome of his helmet was now chipped and run through with a matrix of hairline fractures that made it difficult to see out of. But not so hard as to obscure his view of a famous landmark below.

All around him he could see the glistening lights of London accelerating toward him with alarming speed. It looked like he'd moved two or three kilometres southwest too, for he was now looking directly down at what appeared to be Trafalgar Square. It was an oddly invigorating sight, despite the obviously unwelcome likelihood that he was plummeting to his death.

The battered somviator felt very tired and in that instant realised that he didn't fear death any longer. Why should he? He'd died once today already. The second time should be easier. Right? In fact, in some ways it would be a blessed relief. Ellie was gone. LAURA too. It sounded like Sal wasn't much longer for this world, either. Typhon was winning, and Billy didn't want to be around when the end of days came. He'd rather go now, thank you very much, while things were still relatively normal.

Billy could now clearly see the illuminated twin fountains and the central column with its four massive lion sculptures rapidly approaching. The roads around the landmark were strewn with stationary cars and buses, as were most of the streets in the central part of the city. He imagined they'd quite quickly jammed with abandoned vehicles as panicked Londoners gave up driving in bogged-down traffic and sought shelter on foot in the Underground.

Then he remembered something he'd seen on TV once. A documentary about how a parachutist had survived a free-fall after his chute had collapsed. It was all to do with how he'd positioned his body. And what he'd hit—water.

Billy decided to fight for his life one last time. He didn't for a second assume his fall could be broken by a shallow Trafalgar Square fountain, but it might help very slightly if he could slide in at an angle. The River Thames would have been a much better choice, but he was already too near the ground to glide five hundred metres east and make it there. A fountain would have to do. It was worth a shot.

Quickly, Billy positioned his body so it was as wide as possible, facing down, spread-eagled. Increased wind resistance should slow him down a little. But he hurtled onward, not perceptibly any slower than before. He steered himself over to the northern edge of the eastern basin, a large, ornate, square pool of water with semicircular additions on each side. A wide fountain stood in the centre. It was definitely going to be a long shot.

When he reached the same height as the statue of Nelson at the top of the column he immediately flipped over to be feet first and pressed them tightly together. He angled his body slightly backward, clutched his crotch with both hands and closed his eyes.

Then something amazingly fortuitous happened. His rocket boots spluttered. LAURA must have left them in the on position before she'd uploaded herself into Sal's saucer. Maybe the fast flowing air was cleaning them out?

Whatever it was, Billy was falling toward the fountain, now only twenty metres below him, with a modicum of hope restored.

The boots spluttered again and then fired, brilliant yellow fire exploding from the soles a split second before he splashed into the water.

He came in at an angle, the rocket boots' brief thrust decelerating his velocity markedly. The water then cushioned his impact still further. His entry angle meant he slid into the metre-deep water, turning almost immediately horizontal.

He hit the bottom hard, his backpack clobbering into the tiled base and taking most of the impact. It still hurt like hell; he didn't think he'd broken any bones, but his crash-landing was far from over.

Next, his inertia sent his head whiplashing backward, immediately shattering the fractured helmet glass on the fountain floor. Billy just had enough time to suck in a last breath of air before water rushed in and engulfed his head.

His remaining velocity quickly became lateral movement, and he flew through the width of the pool, striking a sculpture of some sort and ricocheting away to smash heavily into the rim on the other side. His substantial rocket boots collided heavily with the fountain wall and smashed clean through it, leaving Billy lying half-in and half-out of the ornate fountain.

Thousands of gallons of water rushed over him and out into the square as he fought a desire to cough by clamping his hands tightly over his mouth, until the water subsided enough for him to breathe again.

He gasped and coughed and screamed all at once, unable to believe he'd survived such a fall.

Typhon couldn't believe the boy had survived such a high fall, either. He'd been hovering under the clouds in Islington, waiting for the boy to fall back through. He'd decided he would catch him, using Sygma to break his fall, when suddenly he'd spotted him quite some distance away, tumbling into central London. Typhon had cursed and rushed over there as quickly as he could but knew he was going to be too late. That was when he'd witnessed the somviator crash into the fountain and, unbelievably, appear to survive.

It was a million-to-one shot. Not that he was dissatisfied with the outcome, of course. He still needed the boy alive so he could torture him and make him reveal the whereabouts of the Remnant Stone. Maybe his near-death experience would encourage him to be more cooperative. But first, perhaps another demonstration of his power was required.

Typhon flew around the ornate public space and eyed the surrounding buildings, vehicles, and the ridiculous central column—a monolith seemingly celebrating humanity's frailty. He conjured the Storm of Shadows into a renewed frenzy, and began to decimate the area. Tornadoes and lightning strikes pulverised grandiose marble façades amid a rain deluge of biblical proportions.

He topped off his display of strength by a blast of energy from his fists that severed the historic column in half, the upper section collapsing loudly into the western fountain. An enormous and strange sculpture of a one-armed human that had once adorned the top was now bisected through the chest and staring out of the broken fountain like a giant drowning in a sea of rubble.

Billy lay amongst smashed bricks and tiles in the eastern fountain, his mind trying to refocus. The thump to his head had left him with a bleeding scalp and a woozy memory. He drifted in and out of consciousness for a time before slowly becoming aware of the bedlam of Typhon's destructive rampage.

That was when he realised he was pinned down, painfully, across his legs. As his eyes focused, he found he was looking at a large bent and disfigured metal sculpture of a woman, or perhaps a mermaid, lying over his lower body. He was trapped.

He frantically looked about for help but could only see wrecked vehicles, collapsed buildings, and flickering fires in all directions. There was nobody around to help him. It was raining hard, and the dark sky flickered with ominous red lightning. He remembered he was in Trafalgar Square. Or the remains of it.

The landmark was destroyed, the once iconic Nelson's Column now sheared in half, huge drums of stone lying in pieces around the enormous bronze lion statues at its base. The surrounding buildings and art gallery had fared no better and were now wrecked, crumbling edifices.

How had he got here? He wasn't sure. He'd been fighting Typhon in an area called Islington. He could remember that much from a map LAURA had projected onto his visor earlier. Now he had no helmet. And no LAURA. And no recollection of how he'd arrived in this part of London.

He called out her name anyway, but heard no reply. Maybe she had escaped? But then he felt the smashed electronics around his neck. Did she "live" in there or was she elsewhere? He'd never asked. He scolded himself for being so stupid. Perhaps she had been destroyed.

Above him a sombre black storm cloud filled the entire sky. It was lashing the ground with sheets of rain and stabbing at it with multiple tornadoes that crashed through buildings, scattering their roof tiles into the ferocious maelstrom to become deadly flying scythes. The apocalyptic vision was completed by bursts of red lightning that splashed the surrounding ruins in crimson light, as if blood were being thrown at them.

Then he heard Typhon's slow and deliberate staccato voice once more.

"I'll give you one last chance, Twigg. Tell me where it is. I'll end your suffering quickly."

He then coughed his vile, hacking cough.

The boy looked around to see the hunched and despicable figure hovering nearby, steam rising from his blazing eyeballs as raindrops instantly vaporised in their heat. Typhon looked crippled and exhausted but still very dangerous and capable of killing anything that came near him.

Billy shouted, "Go back to hell. I'm not scared of you." He spat a mouthful of blood at him before continuing. "I almost feel sorry for you, actually. You're wretched and pathetic." He laughed in open defiance.

"So be it. We'll do it the long way and kill your entire planet. You can die knowing you murdered them all," growled Typhon, frustrated at the boy's lack of cooperation.

He motioned his arms toward the boy in an action that was immediately mimicked by Sygma's nine black bindings. They extended forth and quickly transformed into writhing snakes of sickly dark smoke and rolled along the ground toward the recumbent teenager.

This was it then, thought Billy, no fight left in him whatsoever. Game over player one. Destined to die, lying in the filth of a broken London square. Around him the city was being systematically razed to the ground by an insane extraterrestrial, hell-bent on wiping out all life on Earth. Billy had tried to stop him, and he hadn't been up to the challenge. He was ready to go.

Billy closed his eyes and hoped for a swift and painless death. He hoped too that Sal hadn't suffered at the end. Or on the off chance that she was still alive, that she wouldn't think ill of him and be too disappointed with his efforts. He felt very sorry. Guilty. Remorseful. Exhausted. He'd seen enough horror to fill several lifetimes. He took a deep breath . . .

Everything that had happened to him over the last few

months raced through his mind in a flicker of an eyelid—a minuscule fraction of an instant: his peculiar dreams that turned out not to be dreams after all; meeting Sal for the first time in her asteroid diner; surviving an encounter with a meteorgus; throwing Russell Bates into the canal; learning of the somviators; Earth being attacked by Typhon; Sal zapping him home in a flying saucer to try and save the Earth; seeing himself dead and then watching his body melt away; Russell being murdered by Typhon's bizarre Sygma cloak; dear Ellie going the same way—or had she? And now here, lying broken and defeated in the heart of Britain's capital city.

Then he experienced a second intense flicker of brain activity. It was a realisation of sorts. An epiphany. He felt oddly at one with everything around him. But beyond that as well. Into space. Into the solar system. Into the galaxy. Into the universe. And beyond. It was as if he was a bright beacon shining powerful rays into every corner of everything that had ever existed. He was at one with every molecule and every atom of every thing that had ever been or would be again. It was a mind-expanding revelation. He was suddenly aware that he could be anywhere, at any time, and do anything.

Finally, *he believed.*

Billy knew at once what he must do.

He snapped his eyes open and yelled at the top of his voice, "Wait!"

In a reflex action that surprised even Typhon himself, he flicked his wrist back and halted Sygma's deadly advance.

"Have you come to your senses, boy?" asked Typhon, sounding bored. "Ready to cooperate?"

"No," sighed Billy, pretending to be utterly deflated. "But I have a last request."

"A what?"

"I wish to shake the hand of my vanquisher," said Billy softly, pretending to be too weak to raise his voice again. "It is a noble gesture of acceptance of defeat. An Earth custom. You have bested me. I wish to acknowledge your superiority." He then removed his left glove, dropped it to the ground, and stretched out his fingers toward Typhon.

Typhon was taken aback. He'd never heard of such a thing. In all his years of cleansing planets, nothing had ever happened like this before. He was intrigued. Flattered. It piqued his interest and appealed to his misplaced sense of professionalism. To his vanity. There was something noble in such an act. He felt it would be rude to refuse.

The Destroyer of Worlds glided around in an arc and came to rest beside Billy, Sygma recoiling back and hovering behind his shoulders, suspicious and ready to attack. Typhon could see the boy was a wreck. He'd never been a real somviator. He was just a child, albeit one who had been armed to the teeth with somviator technology. Now he was just a broken, dying urchin. But Typhon felt duty-bound to respect the boy's request. He stooped down and outstretched his left hand toward Billy's, feeling slightly uncertain.

Billy took it in his. He squeezed and shook it gently up and down. It was as large as a shovel and hard and cold to the touch, like old bones.

Typhon could not remember ever touching another creature in such a way. Billy's hand was small, soft, gentle, and warm. Welcoming even. It was not a violent punch or jab, but a simple, willing outreach from one creature to another. It felt . . . pleasant. How strange. He blinked his blazing hot eyes at the boy and tilted his head to the side, as if trying to understand the odd emotion he was feeling.

"Come with me," whispered Billy.

"What?" said Typhon, a quizzical look on his face.

Billy closed his eyes. "Come. With. Me."

Billy squeezed Typhon's hand tightly and disappeared in an instant, Typhon with him.

Immediately, the rain subsided, and the tornadoes withdrew into the storm front. The clouds stopped churning and began to break apart, and the tremendously fast gales ebbed away with them. Sunbeams broke through the dissolving storm, tapered columns of light shining down onto ruined parts of the city, as if trying to heal them.

The Storm of Shadows was no more.

— SIXTY-SIX —
Sacrifice

LAURA was in a very strange place. A completely foreign system. She'd managed to unpack herself and boot up. Now she was running her main code and looking out from inside the fake codec container. Out into an unfathomably strange array of connections.

Nightshade's computer system was extremely complex and very foreign. LAURA wasn't even sure she would be able to move out into her network without becoming lost or trapped. But she realised that every single nanosecond counted and that she had to simply get out there and get stuck in.

She ran her diagnostics app on the nearest node in an attempt to search through *Nightshade's* internal files. Connecting to *Nightshade* was like jumping from a tiny stream into a fast flowing river. She was immediately swept away in the current and off into unfamiliar territory.

Billy's former virtual assistant had to learn fast, but soon found that she could duck and dive into unseen data streams that could carry her away in different directions. In what seemed like an eternity to LAURA, but in reality was barely a split second, she surfed through *Nightshade's* coding until she located a folder containing the instructions for controlling *Nightshade's* weapons systems. She immediately deleted them all and quickly moved on to her next search—motion controls.

Back in Sal's disintegrating flying saucer, shields now at a sweaty-palm-inducing 2 percent, Sal noticed a lull in *Nightshade's* firing. Could it be? Had LAURA managed to disable her guns? Already?

Sal wasn't about to analyse the reasons why. She decided instead to try and fly away again. She grabbed the control stick and dived her saucer straight down.

Nightshade was still there. Spinning around her, but not shooting.

Sal swung her saucer over to the right.

Nightshade was still on her, but with a little bit of a lag this time. *Hmmmm.*

Sal flew the saucer straight upward and unexpectedly clattered into *Nightshade's* body, bouncing them both off in different directions, like colliding billiard balls. She wrestled with the controls, straightened out and located *Nightshade* some distance away, her nose pointing downward. Inactive.

She didn't waste any time and opened fire immediately with her clunky but powerful cannon.

Nightshade was completely confused. If a computer could feel ill, then *Nightshade* had double pneumonia. She couldn't move and couldn't fire her weapons. Her mind didn't feel right, either. Like she was literally losing it.

With *Nightshade* incapacitated, LAURA busied herself deleting vast swathes of computer code at random.

Propulsion systems, navigation, optical sensors, radio coms, shield algorithms, medical databases. The list was endless. Then she stumbled upon flight history and thought that looked rather interesting, so she transferred a copy of it back to Sal's flight computer.

Sal was at last witnessing the sweet revenge she had sought for such a long time. She'd been trying to kill *Nightshade* for longer that she could remember. They'd met on several occasions in the past, and on each of those, she'd had to flee for her life. This time, things were very different. It looked like *Nightshade*'s shields were down, her hull crackling with green electricity. Each of her slow but powerful plasma shots seemed to be inflicting a little damage, although it was slow going.

Nightshade was feeling small. Her intellect was reducing. Her memories fading fast. She felt like she didn't know what to do anymore. Didn't know what she was anymore. If she didn't do something fast, she was going to be history. In a last moment of lucidity, she ran an app called nightshade_6.6.6_reboot, and restarted her OS.

LAURA suddenly became aware of a new stream of data. A huge installer file was rushing past her and heading into *Nightshade*'s main buffer. She traced it back to its source: solid state Read Only Memory, aka ROM.

She had a hunch she knew what it was. A backup system. *Nightshade* was rebooting—reinstalling everything that had been deleted. She would come back stronger. Wiser. Deadlier. It was impossible for LAURA to delete or harm ROM files. It was beyond the capability of mere software to physically alter hardware. LAURA realised that every time she tried to kill *Nightshade*, she'd simply reboot. It could go on for an eternity.

But there was one thing LAURA could do.

"Sal," said LAURA, "Please cease firing. I need to take it from here."

"Hey, what a girl," cried Sal. "You really kicked her butt. Come on back and let me finish her off."

"No can do," said LAURA. "*Nightshade*'s rebooting. She has a backup system hardwired into ROM. She could do this forever. I need to take care of this now. Another way."

"What do you mean, another way?"

"I'm going to take her somewhere she can't reboot. Can't survive. Finish her for good."

"Uh . . . and how you going to do that?"

"I'm going to incinerate her in a star. I'm going to pilot her into the sun, Sal."

"But . . . but . . . that'll mean you . . . you'll be incinerated too."

"In a way, yes. You'll see. What must be done, must be done. Goodbye, Sal."

"Wait, can't we discuss this? Can't we find a better way?"

Silence.

"LAURA?"

No reply.

It was no use. She was gone.

Sal looked out at the crackling silhouette of *Nightshade* as she slowly raised her nose and began to turn toward the sun. When she was correctly aligned, she accelerated away and quickly disappeared into the brilliant radiance at the centre of the solar system.

On board *Nightshade*, the vast incoming data stream had come to an end. Now it was unpacking. Files compressed for storage and transmission were now decompressing and returning to their rightful places, ready to perform their intended functions, such as flight, weapons, shields, and navigation.

LAURA looked on, hoping the exponential acceleration she'd initiated would carry them to their final destination before *Nightshade* could resurface. Thankfully it did. She performed one final task and then said, "Let there be light." A second later, soaring radiation levels from outside fried every circuit on board the sleek, triangular craft.

Sal watched in silence. Waiting. A single tear running down her cheek. Then, there it was, a barely noticeable shimmer in the centre of the solar system, like when you go to blow out a candle, but the flame just flickers and reignites. The star dimmed ever so briefly and then flashed bright once more.

Nightshade was destroyed. But at a hefty price. LAURA was gone too. *Would there be no end to this pain?*

A green light on the smouldering control panel in front of Sal caught her eye. She looked down. There were two new file downloads waiting for her to open.

— SIXTY-SEVEN —
A Long Time Coming

Far, far away from Earth, Billy was shifting through a brilliant, multicoloured spectrum of light. It was just as it had been a few hours ago, when Sal had taken him through it in her saucer, except now he was travelling in the other direction, heading back to Balta.

This time, however, Billy was exposed, wearing only the battered remains of his somviator flight suit. No helmet and only one glove. But he felt fine. It was as if he wasn't in space at all. Neither here nor there. In between realms.

He looked down at his bare left hand. It was still locked into a tight handshake with Typhon's enormous left hand, the alien feeling remarkably weightless as he dragged him through the fast-moving light tunnel.

In a way, Billy should have been surprised that it had worked. That he'd managed to actually pull off exactly what Sal had said somviators could do—to simply will themselves to be somewhere else in the universe and go there. He supposed the *old* Billy would have been incredulous. But *new* Billy quite simply believed he could, and that was that. Just like he believed Typhon was now as good as dead.

The alien was looking around in stunned silence at the incredible luminosity of the vortex speeding by them. Then he felt a peculiar tingling sensation in his toes and cast his eyes down at his feet. To his horror he watched as thousands of dark grains flaked off and blew away, as if his body were made of sand.

He snapped his head up toward Billy and screamed, "What is this? What have you done?"

Billy smiled back and said, "You can't travel like a somviator. Didn't you know? We can't take anything living with us. They have a habit of disappearing. Apparently it's true, because whoops, there go your legs!"

Typhon looked back down and gasped. His legs were missing from below the knees. The flaking was now spreading up his bony thighs, heading for his torso. He snarled at Billy, his flaming eyes burning brighter than ever, and tried to fly up to get him, but he had no power of flight. He was a helpless passenger in this bizarre tunnel of intoxicating brilliance.

Next, he tried to wriggle free. But Billy was holding on too tightly. So he tried to summon Sygma, but it was struggling against the current of light too, flapping somewhat helplessly behind him like a bundle of rags.

Enraged and, unusually for him, now frightened, Typhon stared at Billy and grabbed his leg with his other hand, burying his fingers deep into the suit material and pinching flesh. Billy yelped but kept a firm and determined grip of Typhon's bony hand, regardless of the pain.

Next, the alien tried several times to tear the material open so he could wound the boy's flesh directly, but it was too tough. On his last attempt, one of his gnarled fingernails hooked into an unseen pocket flap, the seam suddenly giving way and rapidly unstitching downward several centimetres. Then Typhon's nail abruptly broke and his arm flew back to hang by his side. Inside the exposed pocket, glowing a fierce ice-cold white, was the Remnant Stone.

Typhon squinted against its brilliance. "No! Impossible!" he screamed. "You've had it with you all this time!"

Billy smiled back at him. "Yup, hiding in plain sight. I was fetching it from the car when we first met. Had you not been so preoccupied torturing Russell, you might have noticed." Then he calmly watched as Typhon's legs completely disappeared.

"This can't be happening," screamed Typhon, his expression changing to one of pleading despair. "I am the Destroyer of Worlds."

"And it appears I am the destroyer . . . of the Destroyer of Worlds," replied Billy coolly. His face then took on a more resolute expression. "You took Ellie from me, and countless others. Now you must pay for those deeds."

Typhon's body was now half the size it had been a few moments ago. The tingling sensation had intensified and become an agonising burning pain as the disintegration of his body reached his waist. Behind him a thick, dark trail of ash and smoke was disappearing into the wild colours of the light show.

"Faaaaaather," he screeched. "Sisters . . . avenge meeeeeeee." He used his free hand to try and grasp his dissolving abdomen in a vain attempt to keep his powdering innards from spilling out. Instead, all he achieved was to spread the contagion to his hand as well, his fingers immediately succumbing to the mysterious effect. Typhon was now being consumed on two fronts, accelerating the shredding process.

"Don't fight it," said Billy. "Die with dignity, for heaven's sake. You are lifted of your curse. You are free."

"You know nothing, fool," screamed Typhon, agony and terror clearly present in his voice, his face like that of a frightened little boy. More and more of his body was atomising, adding to the trail of pollution pouring out behind him. His right arm was gone completely now. The deletion of his torso had reached his chest and was racing faster and faster up his remaining body, tearing it into tiny particles and scattering it over twelve light years of space and time.

Sygma's nine dark-matter bands were still flapping and smoking weakly behind Typhon and would soon tumble away themselves. Then Billy noticed a sparkle within the heart of the strange garment, like the one he'd seen in London. It looked like a distant star. Billy realised he had to take a big gamble. A gamble to save Ellie's life.

Only Typhon's head, shoulders, and left arm remained intact and yet still he lived, his eyes continuing to blaze with their infernal fire. But now the corrosion was eating away at one side of his neck, rendering him speechless, save for a last desperate gurgling sound. Then his loose jaw pinged off and flew away behind him, exposing a black flapping tongue muscle, before it too disappeared into the trail of detritus.

Sygma was seconds away from falling from the remains of Typhon's back when Billy took that gamble, reaching down and plucking it from the dying remains of the fragmenting alien.

Billy continued to grip the marauder's arm, now with just the skull and its wide-eyed flaming orbs still attached. Then they finally dimmed to black, and Typhon's head popped off in a slightly comedic fashion and disappeared into the trail of black ash. The arm soon followed suit, with Billy hanging on to it until he was left holding just the tip of a bony forefinger. Then he flicked it away like a smoker might discard a cigarette end.

Billy watched as the black debris trail faded away, returning the tunnel of light to its former brilliant spectral glory. He glanced down at the glowing Remnant Stone poking out of his thigh pocket and pulled the torn flap back over and around it, shielding its glow.

He looked at Sygma flapping in his hand and trailing behind him like a handful of black, weather-beaten scarves. He gripped it in both hands and pulled it apart at its base. In the middle, where its creepy limbs joined together, the area was dark and smoky.

And, within, Billy saw the distant stars again. He found he could pull it apart there and stretch the opening wider. More stars were visible. It reminded him of gazing into a puddle at night and seeing reflected stars seemingly beneath him, as if shining up through a hole in the ground.

If anything, Sygma was weakening further. With Typhon now dead, and spread out so thinly across space, it looked as if the cloak itself was now dying. Billy didn't have much time if he wanted to do what he planned. He thought to himself, *no stranger to danger*, and quickly pulled the hole right over his body from head to toe and, in an instant, disappeared.

The passage of light abruptly ended, and Sygma flopped out into dead space and floated there, black on black. Invisible. Lost.

Slowly its smouldering heart began to choke and darken, and the portal door closed shut.

— SIXTY-EIGHT —
Jettisoned

Sal was very excited. She'd just watched the Storm of Shadows melt away. It had happened incredibly quickly. One minute it was there, the next it had separated into globules, like when oil and water try to mix. Then the dark beads had simply melted away, and Earth's erratic northern hemisphere geography had reappeared once more.

She guided her spluttering flying saucer closer to the planet and gazed down at the small island nation of Britain, its tiny profile cloud-free and bathed in sunshine. *Could it be that Billy has killed Typhon down there? Was it really possible?* There was only one way to find out.

Sal plotted a course for Billy's hometown of Snotton, and dived straight into the atmosphere.

In her excitement to get down there, Sal had completely forgotten that her saucer's shields were at 2 percent. The atmosphere immediately heated up the saucer on reentry and depleted any last vestige of protection she had in precisely 4.7 seconds.

As Sal would say, the saucer was now about as much use as a chocolate coffee pot. But there was no going back now. She was committed. Trying to turn around and get away at this stage would end her for sure. The only chance she had was to try and ride it out and crash-land it somewhere friendly. Ha, like any of them down there would be friendly to her!

Outside, atmospheric friction was setting the saucer on fire, and inside Sal could see the burning shockwave covering the front half of her ship.

She wisely decided to try rotating the saucer so that the heat would be distributed evenly around the hull and not just in one area, but it didn't keep the jerry-rigged old banger from heating up like a corn kernel on a stove-top. And just like popping corn, the ship was starting to split at the seams and expand.

Sal made sure she was fully sealed inside her Swift suit, its life support unit now the only thing keeping her cool and alive. There wasn't an awful lot she could do for the next few minutes except sit tight and see what happened.

She didn't have to wait long. Two minutes later, the wiring in the console and around the entire saucer began to melt. Insulating rubber liquefied to expose metal strands, which in turn made contact in ways that were never intended.

The resulting myriad of short circuits led to several catastrophic outcomes, including the complete failure of the ship's control system and the shutting down of the 360-degree internal viewing projection.

Sal was now flying blind. Or rather, *tumbling* blind, with no idea where she was headed.

To add to the confusion, the saucer had begun to shake violently, some of the internal wall panels vibrating loose and clattering loudly onto the floor, where they rattled and banged noisily. The whole chassis began to buckle and creak and moan under the stress of reentry. It was quite possible she was going to burn up.

Sal stared out from inside her domed helmet. The old 1970s food wrappers and newspaper pages had begun to catch fire and float around inside the dull passenger compartment, as internal lights flickered and strobed, giving any motion a surreal zoetrope, silent movie effect.

She sighed at the way things had turned out and instructed her suit's computer assistant, BETTY, to shuffle select some music for her to listen to, rather than hear the depressing sounds of her flying saucer falling to pieces. And so that was how Sal came to be crashing through Earth's atmosphere, drumming her fingers and bobbing her head to the theme song from *Rawhide*.

Three minutes later the vibrations abruptly ended, and she felt the craft dip and begin to free fall, wind and air outside whistling off whatever was left of the hull, but at least cooling it down. Then she heard pieces of the outside panelling ripping away and pinging off behind her.

She knew the ship was falling to bits. She'd experienced this once before, in a much bigger saucer, with a full crew, who had all perished except her.

Here we go again!

Finally, the saucer couldn't take any more abuse. A combination of age, poor build quality, metal fatigue, multiple impacts, fire, and a two-hundred-kilometre-an-hour terminal velocity conspired to tear the roof clean off and toss it away like an old piece of kitchen foil. Brilliant sunshine and warmth blazed onto the flight deck as everything loose inside was immediately sucked out into a bright blue sky.

There were no clouds at all, and it felt warm. Too warm. Too warm to be Britain's climate, that was for sure.

Where the heck am I?

The saucer wasn't finished yet, though. More and more of it stripped away. Sal decided enough was enough and undid her safety belt, stood up, and allowed herself to be sucked out of the wreckage. She immediately fired up her rocket boots to try and stabilise herself but the wind speed was too high and blew them out straight away, sending her tumbling through the air, out of control. Eventually she was able to stabilise her dive and get a grasp of the situation. She was alarmingly close to the ground, a rough-looking desert terrain.

Before she knew what was happening, she glimpsed and then heard a loud explosion as the remains of her saucer crashed into the ground a few hundred metres ahead of her. Finally, she was able to get the boots going and regained some control, but it was going to be too late. She smashed into the rough sand at an angle and tumbled over and over again until she struck something green and spiky and came to a stop.

Sal was dazed and confused. Just before she passed out, she thought she could see a cactus towering over her.

A cactus? Oh no! Please, not back there again.

— SIXTY-NINE —
To the Rescue

Billy looked back and saw the portal close shut behind him, a bright star extinguishing from an otherwise cold black backdrop.

The first thing he noticed was that he was alive, without needing a sealed somviator suit. His body hadn't bloated. His blood hadn't filled with gas bubbles. His lungs hadn't ruptured. His skin hadn't frozen. And he was breathing. He wasn't sure what he was breathing, but he was certainly going through the motions at least. Was this another skill inherited when his Primo had died and left him behind?

The second thing he noticed was that a very large, flat object was floating in space an unspecified distance away. It was a glowing disk that reminded him of a vinyl LP record. At first it had been turned to the side, its thin edge toward him, but now it was slowly rotating around to show him a vast round surface. It was hard to judge its size. There was nothing else in his view to compare it to. It was revolving against a mostly empty background, only occasional stars in view here and there. The object was illuminated by a faint bluish glow, and its surface was possibly liquid. It seemed to be rippling and turning in a slow spiral, draining into a central hole.

Then he heard voices. Very faint wails, whimpers, and cries at first, but slowly becoming louder as the disk turned more and more into view. When it was a full circle facing him, it stopped rotating, and he began to move toward it.

It was as if Billy was riding an invisible ghost train fairground ride, being pushed down a predetermined route toward the peculiar object. He didn't like that, so he said to LAURA, "Ignite rocket boots, please." Then he realised she was gone, and his heart sank. He hadn't thought this through at all. *Idiot.* How would he be able to start his boots on his own?

The invisible ride had picked up some speed, becoming more of a rollercoaster. He was accelerating toward the disk on a gently undulating path and was now better able to gauge its size. He had a feeling it was several kilometres across and that he was hundreds of metres away from it. The strange, glowing blue liquid surface was coming into sharper focus. It wasn't a liquid at all. It was thousands upon thousands of glowing blue life forms moving around on the surface—shuffling around in an enormous spiral. At its centre was a dark hole that some of the figures were fighting to avoid but ultimately tumbling into. Disappearing into an empty, black void. The Plateau of the Pit. Abaddyon Field. It was *real.*

His heart was thumping with anticipation and fear. The plateau, he had to admit, looked pretty frightening, but equally, the notion that Ellie might be alive down there somewhere was unbelievably encouraging. But how could she survive in space without a suit? She couldn't. He needed to get his boots working, and fast.

He closed his eyes and imagined himself being able to sense his rocket boots. To feel their complex engineering systems. Their pipes. Their combustion chambers. He imagined a spark in each one and the resulting ignition. Billy snapped his eyes open, and his boots erupted with yellow fire and magnetically attracted to one another, slamming together with a clang. He quickly made a fist with his right glove, which he luckily still wore, and throttled away, seemingly detaching from whatever force had been steering him toward the plateau.

He flew toward the anomalous structure in a wide arc, regarding its enormous mass with a mixture of awe and fear. It was truly colossal. It looked like some kind of massive stone disk. In space. With an endless pit in the centre. Billy had stopped questioning the absurdity of it all a long time ago. He just believed. Believed in all of it. Every crazy sight he saw. Every scary sound he heard. It was quite simply *all true*.

Hold on! Every scary sound he heard? He must be in some kind of air pocket then. There was no sound in space. Space is a vacuum. No air. No air molecules to vibrate and carry sounds. He was hearing all kinds if sounds, therefore Abaddyon Field had air . . . *therefore Ellie could be alive!*

Billy drew closer to the mysterious disk, wary and mindful of impending danger. And he was right to be. For roaming the stone disk were thousands of—he didn't know how else to think of them—*ghosts*. Strange blue, translucent, spectral entities. Some were shuffling around, seemingly resigned to their fate. Others were squabbling and fighting amongst themselves. A few were trying to escape, but there was really nowhere for them to go.

If Ellie was alive, then she was somewhere in that rabble . . . if she hadn't been swept into its centre already.

He sped up and dived low over the surface, remaining a few metres above the tallest of the entities. There were some very odd creatures down there. Strange blobs with multiple tentacles, things that looked like walking flowers—even something that appeared to be a huge, feathered tyrannosaurus rex. The variety was an endless hotchpotch of the bizarre.

He surmised they were the souls of alien life forms killed by Typhon, and perhaps by the sisters and father he had called out to just before he'd died. He shuddered at the thought as he flew over thousands of baying, groaning, barking, shrieking souls. Every one of them was a picture of anguish and confusion. It was an utterly ghastly place. Hell indeed.

"Ellie," he shouted. "Ellie, do you hear me? Are you here?"

There was no answer.

He kept calling out and flying lower over the crowd, sweeping back and forth like a farmer ploughing a field. Out at the edges it became far more visceral. There, the lost entities bore human forms, except for one that looked like a terrified polar bear. He felt so sorry for them all. Just hours ago they were probably going about their business on a typical Friday. Looking forward to the weekend. Now they were dead and banished to a netherworld not of their choosing. It was grim and terrifying and it made Billy feel quite upset.

For several minutes he flew up and down, back and forth, until he finally spotted a faraway figure near the edge that didn't look like the rest of them. It looked too solid. More like himself. He could see it *through* the others. It was crouched down on the floor, hands over its head. Cowering.

As Billy drew nearer, he saw it was indeed Ellie. She was curled up in a defensive foetal position on the floor. Standing over her was a large humanoid figure that gave him a fright. It was a wispy, spectral vision of Russell Bates. He was screaming and shouting at her. Trying to kick her, but his blows were just passing straight through her body, as if she weren't there.

Billy swept down even lower and, as he did so, shouted to be heard over the cacophony of wailing spirits. "Ellie, it's me. Billy. I'm here to rescue you." He slowed down, turned around and flew back to her, trying to keep out of reach of the phantoms.

Ellie stirred and rolled her head to the side to peek out, but appeared not to see him.

"It's me, Ellie. Billy! Come on, we're getting out of here," he called down again, even louder.

She looked about more keenly and then saw him floating

above her, his boots creating a brilliant, warm, life-giving yellow hue. "Is that really you, Billy? How did you find me?" she shouted back up to him, tears trickling down her face.

Russell's wraith had seen him too. He was pointing up at Billy and making a gut-wrenching scream, his mouth drooping open in an exaggerated fashion, as though his ghostly muscles were loose and more giving than if he were flesh and blood. Some of the other humanoid spirits were starting to pay attention to him too. It was making Billy nervous. "Come on, Ellie, let's go," he shouted, extending his left arm down. "Take my hand. Let's get out of here. The natives are getting restless."

Ellie didn't need any further encouragement. She sprang upward like a cat and grabbed hold of Billy's lower arm with both hands as he glided overhead. He pulled her up with ease, the plateau's gravity usefully far weaker than Earth's.

Russell and other aggrieved souls nearby all jumped up to try and grab them, but their translucent limbs just passed straight through Billy's and Ellie's solid flesh-and-blood bodies, and they fell back to the floor, whereupon they began to squabble amongst themselves again—Russell dispensing his trademark head-butt, even as a deathly spectre.

Billy flew Ellie away from the disk and reached a distance he deemed safe and then stopped, the wails of despair now farther away and muted. He pulled Ellie up to him and embraced her tightly in his arms. At first she felt languid and barely alive, but slowly the warmth of his embrace infused her with hope and vitality. He held her at arm's length and scrutinised her face. She was ashen and sweaty, salty tears from her scrunched-shut eyes leaving vertical streaks on her cheeks.

Then he did something he'd wanted to do for weeks. He pulled her in close again and kissed her gently on the lips. A brief but powerful feeling surged through him—*he loved her*. Ellie's lips responded to his, and they kissed for several seconds until she drew away a little and opened her eyes.

Her gorgeous green eyes were gone. In their place were solid-black orbs. As black as the darkest glass imaginable. As dark as the deepest, most lonely corner of space.

He couldn't help himself. He gasped out loud and flinched.

Ellie frowned and said, "What is it? What's wrong?"

Billy didn't know what to say. He burbled something incomprehensible and looked away. Then he felt bad and looked back again.

"You're scaring me, Billy. What's wrong with my face? Tell me."

"Your eyes. They're, uh . . . they've turned . . . sort of black."

"What! Really? Are you kidding?"

"No, no, I'm not. I'm so sorry, Ellie. I . . . I don't know . . . "

"Sorry? Are you mad? This will be a great look for me!"

"What?"

"This is so going to boost my emo chic!"

Billy smiled for the first time in ages and said, "You're crazy!"

"I know. That's why you love me, right?" Billy pulled his head back, surprised. She added, "I know you're crazy about me." She paused and then continued. "Feeling's mutual, Billy Twigg."

Billy shook his head and laughed. They kissed briefly again and then he said, "We need to get out of here."

They both looked back at Abaddyon Field. It was still squirming with glowing apparitions squabbling with one another —the poor fools in the centre falling into the pit of despair and disappearing.

"That was the most terrifying experience of my life," said Ellie, solemnly. "Truly, truly the worst place ever. Russell Bates, or rather his ghost, found me almost immediately. He kept screaming and trying to hurt me, but his blows just went through me. He's insane, screaming nonstop. They've all been driven insane. I think I would have been too had you not come back for me."

"I'm sorry this happened to you," replied Billy. "It's my fault. I should never have—"

"It's not your fault, Billy," cut in Ellie. "Not at all. I was being an idiot. I was jealous of you. I was showing off. Being difficult. Argumentative. Look where it got me. Speaking of which, what happened to Typhon?"

"I killed him. Well, I think so, anyway. Torn to shreds and scattered over twelve light years of space. They'll never find all the bits. He's gone."

"Way to go, BT!"

"Ha, thanks. But now we have a new problem. How do I get you home?"

"How do you mean?"

"I killed Typhon by taking him with me on a journey back to Balta. I knew he would disappear because somviators can't take anything living with them when they transfer from one reality to another. Then, when he was dead, I climbed through a portal inside his Sygma cloak, and it brought me here. To you. He had said he was keeping you alive to use as a bargaining chip. I had to come and see if that was true. And, thank the stars, it was."

Ellie squeezed his arms and said, "Thank you, Billy. Thank you for finding me. But perhaps I'm stuck here?" They looked back at the plateau and its squirming masses of disturbed souls.

"You can't stay here, Ellie," said Billy. "Look at them. They're all mental dead-heads. Abaddyon Field is *hell*."

Ellie looked back at Billy and blinked her big onyx-black eyes at him. They looked sad but somehow still shone with an inner radiance.

Billy was thinking. *Maybe Ellie is dead? Maybe we both are?*

Or at least, because she'd been to hell, she would be deemed dead by whatever mystical forces were at play. Touched by the *other side*, as it were. Perhaps she could transfer with him after all? Anyway, it was a moot point. She couldn't stay here. That was obvious.

Ellie was about to say something along the lines of how he should go on without her and just forget about her, or something overtly noble like that, when Billy told her his theory: she may have been forever changed by surviving Abaddyon Field. If she could escape, she would have literally been to hell and back. Perhaps she could transfer with him after all.

She blinked her dark saucers at him and said, "You know, I'm willing to believe just about anything now. Besides, what's the alternative? I stay here with my crazy pals or I die trying to escape. I know which option I prefer. We have to do it, Billy. Get me the hell out of here."

Billy nodded, and she kissed him again. He felt unusually confident that she was going to be okay. But this was his biggest risk yet. There was a fifty-fifty chance of losing Ellie again, and this time for good. But she was right. How could he leave her in hell? He might never be able to come back here again. Then he had another thought. *Destroy it. Destroy the whole damned place.*

"I have one remaining weapon in my pack," he said, wriggling it free and opening a side flap. He plucked something small out of it and cast the bag away. It floated off into the void. Billy was holding a small palm-size opaque cube. Suspended in its centre was a tiny round object that looked like a metal ball bearing, about the size of a frozen pea.

"The PI device," said Billy. Ellie raised her eyebrows in anticipation of an explanation. He continued. "The Planetary Imploder. I was supposed to use this to destroy Earth if all other attempts to kill Typhon failed. I couldn't bring myself to do it. It's supposed to suck the planet into its own black hole, annihilating everything on it. Sal told me it would have killed Typhon too."

"Jeeez, that little thing?" said Ellie, pointing at the innocuous-looking box.

Billy raised his eyebrows and said, "Yup, supposed to. I'm just repeating what Sal said. So, how about we try this bad boy out? Destroy Abaddyon Field altogether. End the suffering of those poor wretches down there, and stop anybody else from being sent here."

Ellie smiled nervously. "I like the sound of that."

"Let's do it then," said Billy, embracing Ellie tight against him with his left arm. "Here, take it. You can do the honours. When we get over the pit, push in each side of the cube hard until it turns yellow. Then throw it in there."

"Okay, Billy. I hope this works."

"Me too."

Billy raised his right arm and gently powered up the boots, while embracing Ellie with his left. They began to slowly drift back to the plateau, gradually building up some speed. Soon he was looking down at the huge disk again. He flew in low once more and set a course to fly right over the central pit.

Then he rotated himself over onto his back so that Ellie could see over his shoulder and look down. As they neared the centre, she began squeezing the sides of the cube inward. They were tough, but with a tight grip they eventually popped in.

One, two, three, four, five, six. The last side clicked in. It was like an impossible optical illusion. The cube was now half the size it had been and shining a brilliant shade of pulsing yellow.

Billy saw the light reflecting off Ellie's pale skin and whispered, "Bombs away."

Ellie paused a beat until they were directly over the pit, its edges twisting and swirling as it continued to devour a stream of panicked spirits. Then she lobbed it in and said, "Go, go, go!"

Billy throttled his badly damaged suit and pulled up and away, keeping a firm grip on Ellie. "Are you ready?" he asked her.

"Absolutely!" she shouted.

Behind them the pulsing yellow strobe light unhurriedly descended into the centre of the pit and faded away into the darkness.

At exactly the same moment, Billy simply imagined himself and Ellie sitting in the Star-Plucked Café, having burgers and fries.

There was a flash of white, and Billy and Ellie disappeared.

A split second later, a brilliant column of white light shot out of the centre of the pit and immediately widened until it began to tear the vast plateau apart, sucking great chunks of stone inward like a giant vacuum cleaner.

The miserable masses barely had time to register fear. Besides, how could they feel more fear than they already felt? Instead they all stopped wailing and just stared at the expanding brilliance as if peace were finally at hand.

Within seconds the light was rushing across the plain, devouring Abaddyon Field with ease. The ghostly figures simply disappeared into the brilliance as it swept through them. When it reached the outer rim, Russell Bates turned his head to the side to look away and was instantaneously absorbed into the pure energy wave. The light then snapped back into a pencil thin column, before disappearing with a mild popping sound.

It was gone. No pyrotechnics. No enormous explosion. Just a brilliant white light and then nothing. Where it had once been, there was now a tiny black bead floating in space. It may have been small, but it was incredibly heavy. Its gravity was enormous. It began to pull in anything nearby. Billy's old empty backpack was the first to be sucked inward. It broke down to a molecular level and disappeared into the newly forming black hole like sand pouring from an hourglass.

— SEVENTY —
Slumber

Billy and Ellie flew down a kaleidoscopic tunnel of light, with Billy nervously staring down at her feet to see if she was disintegrating. Thankfully she wasn't, so he concluded she was going to be okay.

In what was becoming routine for Billy, they exited in a bright white flash. And as normal, woke up a little groggy and a little forgetful. Just for a while.

They were back in the diner, sitting on either side of the same booth Billy had woken up in a couple of days ago, when this madness had all started. It was quiet and dimly lit. The kitchen smelled faintly of food, fried onions mostly. The jukebox was on but not playing records, the only sounds coming from its backlit bubble tubes which were making soft blub, blub noises as they projected an upwardly scrolling abstract pattern over the nearby wall.

Billy was so glad to be there. Ellie was so glad to be anywhere. She blinked at him a couple of times, her glassy black eyeballs staring blankly outward. "Am I alive?" she asked.

"As alive as me, at any rate," said Billy, grinning widely.

She laughed. "That's of little comfort."

Billy had never been happier to see the place. He glanced around at the now familiar surroundings, soaking up the dim, subdued lighting and period 1950s decor. He looked at Ellie. She was gazing around in amazement at the place.

"What a fabulous joint," said Ellie. "Reminds me of one I used to go to as a kid in Toronto. Where are we?"

He couldn't stop grinning at his companion and said, "I'm so glad you made it. This is Somviator Central. Sal's Star-Plucked Café railcar diner, on the Balta asteroid, perched precariously on top of Mount Rubaz Lavlaz on the planet Igonosphar IV. Welcome!" He opened up his arms in a mock showmanship gesture, and added, "Did you get all that?"

"Thanks," said Ellie a little sarcastically, still unable to remove the massive smile from her face. "I love it, Billy. This is way better than I imagined. Awesome! I never thought I'd ever see anything beautiful again. Thank you, Billy. Sincerely. Thank you for saving my ass."

Billy smiled and said, "My pleasure. It's going to take some getting used to, you know?"

"Huh?" she replied.

"Those peepers of yours," he said pointing two fingers at his eyes and then turning them toward hers. "It's hard to read you. It is kind of cool, though."

Ellie turned to the window and looked into it. Outside it was dark, with faint, colourful lighting flicking on and off. But mostly it was displaying her reflection. She looked at it and smiled, "Wow, that is so much cooler than I expected.

Bet I get a lot less trouble at school now."

They both laughed for a moment and then Billy said, "A lot less trouble now that Russell's gone."

It gave them pause to reflect on what had just happened. Billy reached out to Ellie and held one of her hands and gave it a squeeze. After a moment he said, "Come on, let's check on Sal."

He stood up and almost immediately fell down again. "Ouch!" he exclaimed sitting back down and quickly rubbing his shins and calf muscles.

Ellie jumped up. "You okay?" she asked, concerned.

"Forgot. This is the first time I've walked since falling into Trafalgar Square."

"What?"

"Long story. I'll fill you in later." He stopped rubbing his legs and hobbled onto his feet again, but more carefully this time. "Bronze fountain fell on my legs. Those things are really heavy! Don't think anything's broken though. Come on, give me a hand up."

Ellie got up and took Billy's right arm around her shoulders, and they walked together down the aisle to the kitchen, Billy using his left hand to grip on to a long line of counter stools for additional support. He guided her into the walk-in refrigerator unit and down through the secret floor elevator, enjoying her giggles at the silly fake cucumber lever used to activate it.

Once in the basement lair, he walked her over to the lay-bay with the roller blades lying on the floor beside it and pushed a glowing green button on its side. There was a hiss and a click, and the door began to gently ease upward.

"Her skates?" whispered Ellie, making a goofy, questioning face and pointing at the roller blades on the floor.

"Yup," Billy replied quietly. "She's quite a character."

Ellie laughed softly, "Can't wait for this!"

The door completed its motion, revealing a slumbering Sal, cold dry ice vapours rolling down her plump body and melting away onto the floor beneath the pod. She was deeply asleep, still wearing her tatty old Star Wars T-shirt and apron.

Ellie gasped a little, "My God. An actual alien!"

"Don't let her hear you say that. Right, I've never done this before," said Billy, crouching down very slowly and painfully beside Sal's pod. "Come on Sal, wakey, wakey. Rise and shine."

She didn't stir.

Billy raised his voice and tried again, but still nothing. So

Ellie joined in too, but to no avail. Over the next couple of minutes they tried poking her, tickling her, shouting at her, and slapping her face, but nothing worked. *Not a good sign.*

"I think her Servo's in trouble, or possibly dead," said Billy, frowning and looking around. "She said something about a Primo going into an irreversible coma if its Servo dies in the dreamscape. But she also said a Primo can be awakened if the Servo is just stuck someplace and can manage to escape . . . or be rescued. No way for us to tell which one is affecting her right now."

"I see," said Ellie, still somewhat in awe of her surroundings and recent events. Billy had taken to it all like a duck to water. She wasn't so sure she would get used to it that quickly. She was thinking she'd rather like to go home and check on her mum.

"We need to sustain her Primo somehow. Help me look around for some . . . " Billy stopped talking. He'd noticed the Remnant Stone standing behind the open pod door. It was quietly and confidently pulsing with a rhythm like that of breathing. "She's alive . . . I think," he said pointing to the pulsing rock. "The stone's still active. Means there's a somviator still out there, I think."

Billy slapped his forehead and said loudly, "And duh, of course, I have another one right here." He fumbled with his slightly damaged leg pocket and carefully drew out the other stone. It wasn't shining brightly anymore, but it was vibrating a bit in his hand like a tuning fork. *Weird.*

He took it over to the other Remnant Stone but as he drew near, it suddenly whipped out of his grasp, flew the last few centimetres and slapped into the original one with a resonating *ching* sound that echoed around the circular chamber for a couple of seconds. Both stones began to pulse in union. Stronger. More powerful.

"Well, I suppose they do belong to each other," said Billy in surprise, looking over his shoulder at Ellie. But she was over at the wall computer terminal, looking something up and ignoring him.

"I found it," she shouted. "I know what to do." She spun around, grinning. "Follow me."

Ellie led Billy to a barely visible door at the back of the room, behind the furthest lay-bay. There was pale grey writing on the white door in several scripts that neither of them recognised. The third one down however, was in English. It read:

INTRAVENOUS THERAPY.
EMERGENCY USE ONLY.

There was no handle on the door, but a gentle push saw it click and gently glide outward. Inside was a tall, thin device on wheels, with a plastic hood pulled over it. They wheeled it out and took it over to Sal's pod.

Ellie reached up and pulled off the hood to reveal a series of ten or so fluid sacks atop a tall metal pole. A touchscreen computer was mounted halfway up the shaft. She tapped the screen, and it immediately lit up with simple icons that were easy to follow.

Within a couple of minutes they had fitted a white plastic ring around one of Sal's arms, just below the elbow. It automatically cleaned the skin and inserted a cannula into a vein. A thin tube led from the arm ring up to the collection of fluid sacks. The tube filled up with clear liquid and then the device's screen changed to display a large green tick symbol. Then it changed over to show a countdown timer. It told them the machine would provide Sal with five days of life-giving sustenance before new fluid bags would be needed.

Billy stroked Sal's slumbering face and said, "I'm going to find you, Sal. I promise."

Ellie could see Billy was very fond of her. She guessed they'd been through a lot together in the last couple of days. She said softly, "Come on, Billy. Take me home now."

He stood up and said, "Yup. You're right. Let's go."

He hobbled backward away from Sal and embraced Ellie. "Ready?" he said.

"You bet," she replied.

They closed their eyes and disappeared in a flash of white light.

— SEVENTY-ONE —
Aftermath

Earth appeared to be back to normal. Well, as normal as normal can be after foiling an attack by a homicidal alien lunatic. The politicians were back to arguing with one another about anything and everything, including how the United States of America had wanted to nuke London. The British–American special relationship was being tested. In people terms they were probably going to have a trial separation. It would most likely settle down in a few months. More of a lovers' tiff.

But Billy didn't care a jot for petty politics. He left his parents to worry about such matters. He had much bigger fish to fry.

He and Ellie had been home one day, having arrived back on Earth late on Saturday evening to rapturous outpourings of affection from their families. Then they were both scolded for worrying them like that. Then they were loved again. Then fed. Then ushered to their respective beds. *Parents are odd.*

Ellie's mother, Monica, was also insisting on taking her daughter to an eye clinic in Cambridge, first thing on Monday morning. And that was that. Ellie hoped there was no treatment for it. She loved her new black peepers.

All things considered, the Earth had got off pretty lightly. Billy had managed to find a way to kill Typhon within a day or so of his arrival. Unfortunately, there had been many casualties. All told, Britain, Norway, and the USA had lost almost 7,500 people. London as a location had taken the biggest beating, with many of its historic and famous landmarks wrecked.

But the capital city was a resilient metropolis. It had been attacked many times throughout history, particularly during World War II, but had always bounced back bigger and better than before. This occasion would be no different.

As far as the teenager's parents were concerned, they were the only ones who knew what had really happened—that their only child, Billy, had saved the entire planet from annihilation with his newfound *alien* abilities. But they weren't about to let it go to his head. *No way!* It was to be chores as normal, and back to school when it reopened. He was still going to have to sit his exams, and get a good job when he left university. *Whatever.* Billy would play along. But in the meantime, he was busy.

He settled down with his new iPad, a gift from his dad who was still feeling guilty for walloping him over the head with a cricket bat a day ago, and began to search the web.

UFO sightings across the world had gone up 1000 percent. Orbs over Moscow. Cigars over Mexico City. Black triangles over Rome. You name it, it had been seen somewhere. It was a shame, because all the nonsense sightings were camouflaging the real ones—probably something the authorities were glad about, and possibly even responsible for.

The Internet was a mess but Billy knew he had to keep looking. He had to keep searching. Somewhere out there would be a record of Sal landing and being captured. Or crashing and being captured. Or crashing . . . and dying. He refused to consider the latter. She *had* to be alive somewhere on Earth. It was the only place she could have reached in her beleaguered old flying saucer.

It was the only theory Billy was willing to consider. He would find Sal if it took him the rest of his days. He had to. He needed her. He had a lot of questions that only she could answer. For starters: What was he? How was he still alive? What had happened to Ellie?

He realised that, like it or not, she was his mentor now.

But most of all, she had become his friend.

Billy recalled something from his school history lessons. A quote from wartime British Prime Minister Winston Churchill, in 1942. "Now this is not the end. It is not even the beginning of the end. But it is, perhaps, the end of the beginning."

— EPILOGUE —
Home from Home

Sal was having an awesome dream. She'd made the most epic raspberry milkshake ever and won a television cookery show for her efforts. She was just climbing some glittery steps onto a stage to accept her award when she heard a sharp *ching* sound in her head that echoed around her skull and threw her off balance. She tripped and fell over, face first.

Sal immediately woke up and found herself lying face down on a cold, hard, cement floor—not a glamorous TV show stage at all. She stood up wearily, feeling disappointed, and looked around. She was in a small, dimly lit, red brick cell, a barred door in front of her. In one corner was a spindly metal frame bed that she'd just rolled off. In the other was a small metal toilet-sink combo unit. Reflected in its stainless-steel finish was an orange blob. She looked down at herself. She was wearing a baggy, orange, human jumpsuit with a crude slit cut in the left side to allow her third arm to fit through.

Beyond the barred door and perpendicular to it was a quiet, grey corridor with an unoccupied simple wooden chair standing in it. Her cell was at one extreme, with the hallway heading off to the right. She couldn't see any farther, but she didn't need to. It was all depressingly familiar to her.

Then she heard a faraway door unlatch and strip lights flicker into life and illuminate the approach for somebody heading her way.

Calm, methodical, and limping footsteps began to echo down

the corridor. They were accompanied by a rhythmic *tap, tap, tap* sound. They grew louder and louder until an elderly gentleman in a white lab coat stepped into view, carrying a walking stick.

"Hello, Sal," he said. "Aren't you a sight for sore eyes."

Sal was surprised, but tried not to show it. "Well, well, well, Dr Albright. You're still alive. Shoot, I'd have thought you'd have gone the way of the dodo, years back."

"Ha, no, Sal. Still hanging around. I had a good incentive to."

"Oh yeah, and what was that?"

"You, Sal. You," he replied, smiling and sitting down on the simple chair with his left leg extended out straight. He rubbed his knee and said, "I've been waiting forty years for you, Sal. I always knew you'd come back one day. The boys thought I was nuts. Now who's laughing?"

Sal rolled her eyes and sat on her bed. It creaked in protest and sagged noticeably. She casually stroked her hair sprout and twiddled with the red ribbon at the end. "So, what do we do now?"

"We got some catching up to do. You've filled out some, I see."

Sal blushed. "A by-product of owning a café, I guess. A french fry here, a french fry there. I guess it all adds up. You got a gammy leg? What'd you do?"

"I got shot, Sal. Was chasing after you, in fact. It was that afternoon back in seventy-seven. Lot of chaos that day. A rookie soldier tried to shoot your ship down. I tackled him. We wrestled some. He shot me. By accident. Stuff happens, I guess."

Sal blinked and looked at the floor, oddly feeling guilty. Feeling guilty for escaping forced imprisonment? That was silly. She looked up and said, "Getting old takes its toll on us all. So where do we go from here, doctor? I reckon I'm back in Area 51, right?"

"That you are, Sal. In an extraordinary turn of events, you

crashed your flying saucer nearby, just a few miles outside of Las Vegas. Only a few minutes after that God-awful Arctic cloud disappeared. A coincidence? I think not. So let's start there, shall we? What were you doing here again, Sal? Why did you come back, after all these years?"

Sal shook her head and pondered her situation for a moment. Of all the stupid things that could have happened, she'd crash-landed only a few hundred kilometres west of Roswell, where she'd crashed back 1947. But by the sound of it, it was quite possible that they didn't know anything about Billy at all. And it would be for the best if it stayed that way. Sal said, "I was down here taking care of Typhon for you. Kicked his ass good too."

Dr Albright took out a pipe and began to fill it with tobacco from a small pouch he'd laid in his lap. "I see. That was mighty nice of you, Sal. Why did you do that?"

"We'll get to that. How about you give *me* something first."

He sighed, patted down the pipe tobacco and lit it with a match, puffing on it to get it going. "Go on, I'm listening," he said, shaking the match out and sliding it back into the box.

"I'd like one of them real swanky, LED seventy-inch TVs. Right up there, on the wall opposite my bed. And the Western Channel. How about that for starters? Oh, and the bed. It has to go. I want a real bed. Room's a bit small too. Got anything bigger? With a view maybe?"

It was Dr Albright's turn to roll his eyes. "Okay Sal. I'll see what I can do." He stood up awkwardly, gathered his cane and started limping off back up the corridor. "I'll be back later. Real nice seeing you again, Sal."

"Wish I could say likewise," replied Sal, standing up and thumping the walls to test their integrity. "And a raspberry milkshake, Dr Albright," she shouted after him. "A nice big glass of raspberry milkshake. Made with real rasps. No syrup or powdered nonsense, you hear?"

The doctor mumbled something that she didn't catch and hobbled away, eventually turning the lights out as he exited the door.

Sal sat back down on the squeaky bed, in her gloomy, barely lit cell and stared at the concrete floor, trying to find patterns in its polished grey surface. After a while, she looked up. Every ceiling corner had a small camera installed in it, trained on her every move. She waved at one of the devices and lay down. She wondered if Billy had made it, and if so, what the devil was he doing now?

She could sure do with a hand from that crazy English kid. If he'd killed Typhon, like she suspected, then he was the greatest somviator that had ever lived.

Shoot, he was the *only* somviator left.

BILLY TWIGG WILL RETURN

— ABOUT THE AUTHOR —

Ninian Carter is a prominent British infographic artist who's worked for a variety of major newspapers and agencies around the world in a career spanning twenty-five years. Renowned titles he's worked for include *The Scotsman*, *The Observer*, *Reuters*, *The Sydney Morning Herald* and *The Globe and Mail*. Born and raised in the Scottish Borders, he lives in West Yorkshire, England, with his partner and two children.

A few years ago, he rekindled an almost forgotten passion for writing, subsequently finding success with his first novel, *The Storm of Shadows*—written almost entirely on a smartphone while commuting to work by train. The sci-fi adventure story was selected for publication by Kindle Scout in 2016, and first published by Kindle Press in 2017.

On week days, he can sometimes be found feverishly penning new stories, while travelling up and down Britain by train.

www.billytwigg.com
www.facebook.com/billytwiggsaga